Case and Phoenix rose to the surface of the pool hand in hand, their heads breaking through the water at the same moment. In those few seconds, a faint blue light had gone on automatically, illuminating the pool area with artificial moonlight. It softened Case's features, but revealed the lopsided grin a man wore when desire played havoc with his reasoning powers.

"I meant what I said. You are beautiful," he said.

She expected him to kiss her, but instead he brushed aside the hair streaming over her forehead and ran his fingers lightly over her closed lids. She sighed, wondering if he knew how disarming tenderness was in a man. He touched her lips with his, not kissing, only savoring the gentle tickle of skin against skin. He must have known what he was doing to her.

She couldn't stand it! She dove and touched the bottom again, putting distance between them in a mad scramble not to let him past her defenses. She'd chosen a poor place to evade him. He was the stronger swimmer. After catching her in his arms and pulling her to the surface this time, he backed her against the edge of the pool and kept her captive between his arms.

Other *Love Spell* Books by Pam Rock:
**A WORLD AWAY
LOVE'S CHANGING MOON
MOON OF DESIRE**

PAM ROCK

STAR Searcher

LOVE SPELL **NEW YORK CITY**

To Chris Andrews, with love.

LOVE SPELL®

April 1996

Published by

Dorchester Publishing Co., Inc.
276 Fifth Avenue
New York, NY 10001

If you purchased this book without a cover you should be aware that this book is stolen property. It was reported as "unsold and destroyed" to the publisher and neither the author nor the publisher has received any payment for this "stripped book."

Copyright © 1996 by Pamela S. Hanson & Barbara Andrews

All rights reserved. No part of this book may be reproduced or transmitted in any form or by any electronic or mechanical means, including photocopying, recording or by any information storage and retrieval system, without the written permission of the Publisher, except where permitted by law.

The name "Love Spell" and its logo are trademarks of Dorchester Publishing Co., Inc.

Printed in the United States of America.

STAR Searcher

Chapter One

Case knew he was being stalked. Twice he whirled around and tried to catch a glimpse of his would-be assailant, but the dense, ever-present fog obscured his vision like a gauze curtain.

Like all visitors on Bast, he was wearing a green-tinted face mask as protection against the particles of dust in constant suspension in the planet's atmosphere. The mist was so thick here in the lowlands by the Sea of Oyl, he could see little beyond the length of his own arm. Luminous stakes had been driven into the thick dust every ten paces to mark the footpath, and he had to pay attention or risk missing one and getting lost.

His vision was sorely impaired, but his hearing seemed abnormally keen in the eerie silence of the Bast dusk. He heard another soft swishing sound, and cursed the bureaucratic regulations that had forced him to leave all weapons behind in his ship before he was permitted to leave the space dock. He patted his vest pocket to be sure the packets of tribute were still there. He could only hope the info-banks on his vessel had given him accurate data on the natives of this remote outlaw planet.

Ahead he saw a glowing tube of light shaped like the Bast symbol for cantina. He started to sprint toward the relative safety of the public gathering place, but the stalker was too quick. A whip-like tentacle grabbed his arm, tightening around his bicep until Case gasped in pain.

"I have a gift for you," he said, forcing himself not to resist. If the info-bank warning was right, the worst thing he could do was make a hostile move.

The Bastian loosened its grip but didn't release him. The feline-faced creature, a large male, stood upright on two legs, its thick furred body almost as long as Case's. The feral odor of the beast was almost as overpowering as the grip of its long, powerful tail on his arm.

"Release me so I can remove the tribute from my pocket and give it to you."

The Bastian responded with a spate of grunts unintelligible to all but its own species. Although most of the planet's native inhabitants could understand Instell, the interstellar language, they couldn't speak it. They didn't have the vocal chords necessary to produce the words, but Case didn't think he was imagining the threat in the Bastian's outpouring of sounds.

"I can't get it unless you let me use both hands," he insisted, speaking politely but firmly, his own common sense telling him not to let any alien detect weakness.

Star Searcher

The thick hairless tail slid away but hovered inches from his head. Case knew the dangerous appendage could snap his neck like a brittle twig. It was the only weapon the Bastians used, and the only one they needed. The worst punishment inflicted on Bastians who broke their own lax criminal code was tail amputation. Deprived of the powerful tentacle-like tail, an offender was practically helpless. Although the Bastians had arms, they were disproportionately short, ending in four stiff digits made even clumsier by thick fur on all but the tips.

Case unfastened the security closure on his vest pocket and drew out one of the small packets of dried leaves. Taking his time so he didn't appear to be intimidated, he offered it to the Bastian on his extended palm. The creature made a cooing noise and delicately snatched up the offering with its tail.

"Nepetac," Case said. "The best grown on my home world, the planet Athera. I gave the same grade as tribute to your Entry Master."

And to a dozen other addicted Bastians, he thought sourly.

Case wasn't alone in not understanding the reason for their reliance on nepetac. Elsewhere in the galaxy, the minty leaves were distilled into an oil and used as a mild flavoring agent, but on Bast the inhabitants lived to ingest it, enjoying narcotic properties that were known to affect only their own species.

Decades ago an infestation of moon weevils had permanently wiped out the nepetac crop on Bast. Since then the creatures' need for it had made their planet a haven for the dregs of the Phara galaxy: outlaws, mercenaries looking for employment, deposed dictators, unethical traders, and the most unsavory exiles in the known universe. As a backward planet in the Qeb system, Bast had nothing to attract legitimate enterprise: no natural resources of commercial value except deposits of iron in areas so remote it was too expensive to mine; no food exports because the root crops grown there barely fed the native population. To get the substance they desperately craved, the Bastians offered sanctuary—hiding places, new identities, secret meeting places—to anyone who paid them in nepetac.

The Bastian immediately began chewing the leaves and the paper packet, since removing the wrapping with his clumsy digits was too difficult. He grunted in satisfaction and lumbered away, quickly lost from sight in the dense green-tinted fog.

Case shook his head. He'd paid his official tribute, but he knew that was only the beginning of the demands for nepetac. How many more times would he be held up for a packet? He could only hope his supply would be adequate. His official status meant nothing on this miserable world. No one here cared that he was Diplomatic Officer Remo of the Galactic Coalition Star Service. More than one Coalition representative had disappeared on the mist-shrouded planet, perhaps because their stay outlasted their supply of the addictive nepetac. Coalition Special Police who came here to track runaway felons received extra hazard pay, and by all accounts, earned it.

He hurried toward the cantina, hoping he wouldn't be stopped again. Assaulting strangers was against Bast law, but the local law enforcers made little or no effort to curtail crimes against visitors. It was far too easy for offenders to disappear under cover of fog. The planet's leaders exercised what control they had over

Star Searcher

the native inhabitants through a monopoly on the nepetac trade. When supplies were scarce, as they often were, almost no Bastian would pass up a chance to steal from a visitor and escape into the fog.

It wasn't sanctuary Case was seeking in the public gathering place. He had to get on with his mission, even though he was travel-weary, famished, and out of patience after dealing with the addicted Bastians at the docking station. He didn't have time to dwell on annoyances, and he put the stalker out of his mind. A peculiar mix of dread and anticipation was making him edgy and anxious, and he wanted to put this assignment behind him as quickly as possible.

He was here to find Phoenix Landau. Given a choice, he would rather hunt down a pack of poison-spitting, rampaging razor-beasts. He didn't have that option, not if he placed any value on his own future.

What he did have were questions, lots of questions and no answers, about the elusive female. Why had she dropped out of sight, severing all obvious contacts with her home planet of Athera? Why did the Coalition want her so badly? She had a reputation as the best antiquities tracker in the galaxy, but he found it hard to believe there was anything for her to find on Bast. What could she be doing on this forsaken planet?

The question that made him most anxious was personal: What would Phoenix say when she learned he'd been sent to find her? His superiors believed she'd be more responsive to a familiar face from her past than to a stranger. Case couldn't agree less. He'd come close to mutiny trying to persuade Star Service Commander Barkus to assign someone else to track her down. Without the influence of his father, Commander-in-

Pam Rock

Chief Oaker Remo, Retired with Honor from the Galactic Coalition Star Service, Case might be serving a disciplinary sentence on the moon of Tarrack. Instead he was reluctantly searching for a woman who had every reason to hate him.

He pushed open the solid, snug-fitting door of the cantina, and his face mask immediately fogged over. Buildings where outsiders were permitted had water-filtered air, and Case pulled off his mask, letting it hang from a strap around his neck. He sucked in a lungful of damp, musty air, heavy with the pungent odors of many alien bodies, and was tempted to replace the mask. Only the prospect of a brawl if he offended someone by wearing it inside made him steel himself and take shallow gulps of air that smelled like swamp rot.

His well-paid informant had to be wrong: He couldn't imagine finding Phoenix Landau in a place like this. She was an outdoor girl, feminine, almost delicate, as sweet-smelling as wild flowers on the plains of Athera. The young woman he'd known couldn't stand a place like this.

His throat ached at the thought of her as a dark-haired, vivacious student. He vividly remembered a time when he'd surprised her at the task of manicuring her shapely oval nails in her quarters at the Star Service Academy. It was a free-day on Athera, and he'd deserted his grueling studies to sneak into the female dormitory, an area forbidden to male students. Young and so much in love he couldn't look at his study screen without imagining her face there, he'd been naive enough to believe holding her in his arms was worth any penalty the Academy Master might inflict on him.

Star Searcher

He'd found her alone, buffing her nails at a small study table, trying to concentrate on her task and, at the same time, memorize an assignment in microbiology illuminated on her screen. She was petite, her head barely coming to his shoulder, but even then her breasts had been full, womanly and luscious under the drab tunic of a uniform designed to conceal them. For the first time in nearly three years of friendship-bonding, he saw her clad only in a short chemise. He wasn't naive enough to believe it was regulation underwear for a female cadet.

Also for the first time, he'd been tempted to defy the stringent rules governing his existence and do the forbidden act. Phoenix had held him in thrall that day; he'd been ready to sacrifice anything, even his own hide, to make her completely his. Then she'd looked up and smiled as only she could, and he'd admitted to himself the risk was too great. He loved her more than he lusted for her. He had to control his own urges so he wouldn't jeopardize her career and her future.

He grinned ruefully and scanned the crowded cantina, not wanting to dredge up old pain. Thinking about their last happy moments together made him feel sick with regret.

She'd let him touch her on that long-ago enchanted day. He would still swear on his life she'd been totally innocent, yet she'd guided his hand until he was cupping one warm, bare breast, making him dizzy with longing and mesmerized by the low cooing moans that escaped from her throat.

In the crowded cantina, he could feel perspiration beading his forehead and staining the coarse white fabric of the shirt he was wearing to make him less conspicuous. He'd left his military garb on the vessel, exchanging it for wrinkled tan trousers and a loose-fitting vest, but he still felt out of place. His dark blond hair was brushed back military style, and his rigid posture reflected service training as surely as if he'd been branded. His two-day growth of beard wasn't enough to make him blend in, but on Bast no one asked questions. He could be a deserter searching for work as a mercenary or a newly arrived refugee from a politically unstable planet. If anyone did become curious, he had a plausible story ready.

The cantina was one huge room divided by posts, screens, high-backed booths, and curtained niches. He went to the long bar where customers were lined up two and three deep waiting for service and focused his eyes on the age-stained mud-colored wall ahead of him. He was rubbing elbows on one side with a scary creature making belch-like sounds to a companion and on the other with a dark-robed space hobo whose face was concealed by a hood. Wherever interstellar travelers gathered, it was rude and offensive to look directly at a stranger. Staring was an intolerable insult in some cultures, and the last thing Case wanted was involvement in a brawl. He kept his eyes carefully averted until he'd handed over two golbriks, the universal currency of the galaxy, for a wet mug of bitter drink brewed from gingess tubers. He loathed the Bast concoction, but he forced himself to gulp a few swallows to keep the yellow-brown liquid from foaming over the edge of the heavy earthen vessel.

Searching the room was going to be tricky. He wandered between haphazardly placed tables, pretending to scan for an empty seat. The cantina was so crowded he had to duck and weave to avoid physical contact, which could be even more offensive than staring.

Star Searcher

Some aliens, like the Marshusites from Star System 749, tended to bleed copious quantities of watery blue fluid at the slightest touch.

The atmospheric pressure here was very similar to that of Athera, as were many other conditions on Bast, but Case's info-banks had been inadequate in trying to explain why the highest life form to evolve on the planet had humanoid intelligence trapped in an inefficient bestial body. He hoped he wouldn't be there long enough to learn more.

There were no Bastians in the crowded cantina. Once their need for a fix of nepetac was satisfied, the natives wanted nothing more to do with visitors. When travelers had a compelling reason to stay permanently on the planet, some, like the cantina's barkeep, ended up as semi-respectable small-business owners catering to other outsiders.

Case circled the room seeing very few females. No doubt some were out of sight in the curtained niches, but he couldn't believe Phoenix would be in one of the mating cribs rented to patrons of the cantina for sexual encounters. She had spunk, style, class. . . .

And he needed a hard boot in the backside to jump-start his brain! The woman he was searching for wasn't the sweet, beguiling student cadet he'd last seen more than nine years ago. She hadn't made her reputation as a top-notch antiquities tracker without sacrificing the vulnerability and innocence that had made him love her. He wasn't looking for the same person, and if he wanted to succeed on this crucial mission, he'd better be on guard. If he didn't treat her as a wily fugitive, she might evade him.

His mug was empty, and he had to get it refilled as an excuse to keep wandering through the cantina. He went back to the bar, not maneuvering his way forward in a hurry as some impatient customers did. He wasn't in a hurry to tackle another serving of the bitter brew. He needed food, but all the cantina had to offer was a paper cone of the grease-fried yellow roots called chrits. He'd brought his own food and stowed it in the tiny room he'd rented for the night. With luck, he might be able to return to his small ship before his supply ran out.

A commotion broke out at the far end of the bar where a few stools were provided for patrons who got there early enough to grab a perch. He gave up his place in the milling throng and wandered in the direction of the ruckus.

Case saw a Lug, a short, squat alien with yellowish scales covering an unclothed, repellently humanoid body. The creature was gesturing with wide sweeps of its long, unjointed arms, punctuating the conversation with unintelligible outbursts, not unlike the cursing of a frustrated freightloader Case had once heard on Athera. He edged closer, more curious when he heard a woman's voice speaking in the familiar singsong accent of his own planet.

This was neither the time nor the place to rescue a fellow Atheran, but the Lug was arguing with a female of Case's species. His conscience compelled him to see whether she was in serious trouble. He sidestepped around a pair of immensely tall, stick-like men in bark loincloths, their skin glistening red in the humid atmosphere of the cantina. Wishing for the hundredth time his mission was something less challenging, like confronting a tribe of hostile warriors, he stopped and stared slack-jawed at the person arguing with the Lug: the woman he'd been sent to find.

Star Searcher

The disagreement reached an angry conclusion, and the Lug stalked away, coiling his arms together and muttering in low, hissing syllables. He was a bad alien to cross; a Lug would sell his own parent for a purse of golbriks. In fact, the name of the species, Lug, had become part of the Atheran language. It meant a devious, dangerous person not to be trusted under any circumstances.

Case wouldn't be rescuing anyone today. Phoenix seemed to have bested the Lug in this round of their argument and sent him packing. Case watched her turn back to the bar, drink the dregs of her brew, and set the mug down with an emphatic thump.

Her nondescript khaki trousers and belted shirt didn't disguise the voluptuous curves of her body, and black hair was tumbling out from under a soiled sun hat, her curly strands escaping confinement as though they had a life of their own. Even though nothing in her attire was worn to enhance her charms, she was achingly beautiful. It hurt to watch her, knowing as Case did that she could have been his. The intelligence and self-confidence of an adult woman made her even more attractive than she'd been when her youthful innocence had first drawn him to her at the Academy.

He bit his lower lip, trying to push aside feelings that could only be nostalgic longing for his less complicated life as a cadet. Any male of their species would find her shapely body desirable, but she meant nothing to him now. Her fascinating face and physical vitality suggested a passionate, captivating nature, but he dreaded what he would see in her eyes when they met his.

Normally he wasn't a man who tormented himself with sexual fantasies. He took his pleasure when he could and disciplined his mind to endure his many celibate forays into space. Yet, he reluctantly admitted to himself, seeing her did stimulate his imagination. She had an intangible appeal that brought heat to his groin. She was forbidden fruit, made more alluring by the fact that he would never, ever give her the opportunity to refuse his attentions. What more suitable revenge could she extract from him than to lead him on, then reject his sexual advances? It would never happen. He wouldn't let it.

Turning to leave, she looked in his direction without any sign of recognition, her indifferent glance cooling his lecherous thoughts. Her dark eyes were focused beyond him, but a peculiar tingling sensation raced along his spine, as though he'd been stripped naked and examined under a bright light by tiny, questing hands. He shook his head to drive away the intensity of his reaction to her.

Without any awareness of his presence, she still was making him hellishly uncomfortable. He rejected the possibility that he still felt anything like love for her—perhaps he'd never loved her. But he had desired her and had been denied satisfaction by the stringent rules of the Academy and all that followed. He'd been obsessed, and had cloaked his passion for her in the more respectable guise of love. That was all he'd ever felt for her. It couldn't have been more.

She couldn't mean anything to him now. After all, would he have deserted her if he'd really loved her?

She turned to leave, and even in the dimly lit cantina Case imagined he could see sparks radiating from her mercurial eyes. Anger had always brought out green glints in those warm brown orbs, and the altercation with the Lug had made them sparkle like highly polished gemstones.

She was fighting mad, and his timing was terrible. She looked ready to cuff anyone who crossed her path, and he suspected she'd rather vent her anger on him—the man who'd let her down when she most needed him—than on the Lug.

She hadn't noticed him. It wasn't too late to pretend he couldn't find her, but duty had dictated the course of his life for too many years to shirk it when the stakes were so high. He stepped forward with the trepidation of a man stepping into the path of a roaring funnel cloud, and spoke just loud enough to get her attention.

"Het shaynon, Phoenix," he said, using his planet's traditional way of wishing her good health and long life.

He braced himself for anger or bitterness, but she looked at him with the cool indifference of a stranger.

"You do remember me, don't you?" He shifted his weight from one foot to the other, afraid she was going to deny knowing him.

"You haven't changed that much," she said, walking past him as though she had no intention of talking to him.

"How have you been?" He fell in step by her side.

"How have I been?" She stopped and faced him, her eyes sparkling with suppressed fury. "Do you really want to know?"

"Yes."

She stopped and laughed. Scorn for him didn't dull the melodic bell-like quality of her voice.

"I need to talk to you," he said. He squared his shoulders as though his greater height could, in some mysterious way, help him gain the moral high ground.

"We don't see many Star Service Officers on Bast. Do they have you chasing felons?" she asked in the same disinterested voice.

"No, I'm in the diplomatic service. Is there some place we can speak privately, Phoenix?"

"I think not."

She still hadn't called him by name.

"I'm here on behalf of the Galactic Coalition's Commander-in-Chief."

"Is that supposed to impress me?"

"No, but I've been authorized to contract for your services. You would be very well paid."

"I'm not interested." She stalked toward the exit, forcing him to block her way in order to stop her.

"Please don't make me follow you through the smog. I've already been held up for a packet of nepetac. I don't have enough to satisfy every greedy Bastian on the planet."

"If the Bastians were greedy, they wouldn't be satisfied with a single packet when they stop you. They'd take your whole supply and let you worry about the consequences."

"You're right, of course," he said stiffly, wondering what he could say to make her more receptive to his offer.

"Do you mind?" she said, trying to reach around him to push open the door.

"Phoenix, it's urgent that you hear me out."

"I'm not interested in your proposal—in the Coalition's proposal. I can't imagine why they sent you, of all people, as a messenger boy."

His face was hot, and he knew the rush of blood to his cheeks betrayed his anger. His tendency to become

Star Searcher

flushed was his worst career liability. Diplomats were supposed to be impassive, never betraying emotion or giving clues to their mental state. After all these years she could still make him angrier than anyone he'd ever known. Why had he forgotten that when he was reminiscing?

"You haven't heard it yet," he said, taking hold of her arm.

"Nothing coming from you could do me any good," she said flippantly. "Kindly remove your hand."

"Must you make everything difficult?" he said, not letting go.

He was beginning to sympathize with the Lug. Phoenix was the only woman he'd ever felt so frustrated by, and the only female who could make the vein in his forehead throb.

"It's not my choice to be here," he said. "The commander gave me two options: look for you or work in the mine on the moon of Tarrack. I thought seriously of choosing slave labor. I knew you wouldn't have enough sense to hear me out. I don't know why anyone thought you might be interested in earning a fortune."

Case released her and stepped outside, gambling that her presence on Bast meant she was struggling with lean times.

"You probably have your own vessel and are ready to leave on a treasure-hunting expedition," he said when she followed him out of the cantina. "I'll have to find someone more interested in the Coalition's golbriks."

"Do that," she said, but she didn't seem in quite such a hurry to get away from him.

Was she weakening? He was tempted to let her dangle for a few days until her curiosity made her more amenable, but time was working against the success of his mission. Catastrophic war could erupt at any time.

"What do you have to say? You haven't told me very much," she said, her voice muffled by the face mask she'd donned.

"Nor will I, not until we can speak alone."

Neither the green tint of his mask nor the noxious fog swirling around it made her seem less vital, less attractive to his space-weary eyes.

"We're alone now," she said impatiently.

"Are we? Your eyes are better than mine if you can see through this damnable mist."

"Actually the dampness is rather good for my hair," she said, flippant again, as though she regretted showing any interest in his proposal.

"I don't have time to play games. I need an answer soon," he warned.

"All right. I'll take a meal with you. There's a place just beyond the market square that caters to visitors. Follow the red stakes until you see a symbol that looks like an inverted two-handled cup—that's the best I can describe it."

"I know the Bast symbol for restaurant," he said.

"Of course. Star Service prepares its officers to look out for their own needs in any situation," she said with such venom that guilt gnawed at him like a sharp-toothed rodent.

"We can talk about what happened between us. . . ."

"No, Officer Remo, we can't." She moved away with the quick step of someone used to walking the foot-paths in dense fog.

"Wait! What time shall I meet you?"

Star Searcher

"When I get there—if I don't change my mind," she called back over her shoulder, disappearing before her last words were out.

He followed and called her name, but she'd vanished like an apparition, swallowed up by the thick wall of moisture-laden air.

Her heart was hammering so furiously she was afraid he'd be able to track her by listening to its loud beat. Her legs were trembling from the exertion of running in the dense atmosphere, and her shirt was sticking to her back like a clammy second skin.

Thankfully she made it back to the miserable little room where she was staying without being accosted by a Bastian. Her supply of nepetac was desperately short, one more complication in the hopeless tangle of affairs that kept her on this detestable planet. What she wouldn't give to bask in the warmth of Athera's sun! She longed to strip off all her clothes and let the blessed rays restore her pale body to its former honey-gold hue.

She'd stayed too long in the Bastian lowlands where the infernal fog never completely dissipated. She hated the cold, damp feeling that never left her; she loathed the never-ending game of hide-and-seek with the addicted creatures who stalked every species but their own. Most of all, she hated not being in control of her destiny.

These were familiar woes; the fog had nothing to do with the pounding of her heart or the ache in her throat. Where did Case Remo get the gall to track her down?

She used her metal card to gain entrance to the dreary corridor of her rooming compound, then opened her door by jamming it into the slit between the door and the jamb. Security measures were primitive in this poor section of Gocellus, the Bastian capital and site of the only space-docking facility on the planet. Still, she felt relatively safe. Bastians never stole anything but nepetac, and she carried her supply in a waist pouch next to her skin. Nor were the scruffy assortment of exiles who lodged in the same building any threat to her. Only males of her own species coveted the use of her loins, and Case was the first she'd seen in a long time.

She couldn't believe the all-mighty Coalition had a use for her services. Their star commander had thousands of well-armed space vessels at his disposal if he wanted to search the galaxy; what interest could they possibly have in her? She was justly proud of her instinctive ability to find antiquities where no one else could, but what could they possibly want her to find?

She threw herself down on the sleep-shelf, wrinkling her nose at the musty odor of the bedcovers. Moisture seeped through the thick stucco walls and brought with it the swampy odor carried by the fog. These quarters for impoverished aliens were windowless, but even if she'd had a view-hole in her wall, there was nothing to see outside but fog.

Water-filtered air flowed sluggishly through a vent near the floor, making her feet constantly cold, but at least she had a water closet for private use. She got up to splash water on her face, desperately needing to sharpen her mind and figure out what the Coalition was up to. Her facilities didn't have a shower or tub for bathing, and she'd give anything to sit in warm scented water instead of dipping a ragged cloth into icy water that dripped with maddening slowness into

Star Searcher

a metal basin. On her home planet, felons were confined in better cells than this! If her luck didn't change soon . . .

Phoenix paced the tiny concrete floor, sidestepping the only furniture besides the sleep shelf, a bench that held her gear. Thinking of the past made tears well up in her eyes. How could Case waltz back into her life after breaking her heart and shattering her hopes so many years ago?

At the Academy he'd been her first love, her best friend, her confidant and companion. They'd defied the strict rules about cadets of the opposite sex fraternizing, and had spent three years building a relationship she'd expected to last for life.

She could still remember him in his dark green parade uniform, tall and straight-backed, so handsome he made her throat ache. But unlike many future Coalition officers, he'd never lost his uniqueness, never become regimented. He'd excelled in the rigid training without sacrificing his individuality. He'd been her rock, her support when things got tough, and she'd come to depend on his loyalty, devotion—and love.

That was what had made it so terrible when he failed her. Given a choice between standing up for her and buckling under to pressure, he'd abandoned her.

She'd needed him once, and he'd betrayed her. She didn't need him or the Coalition now, and she would never give him another opportunity to hurt her.

For the first few years after her dark night of despair, she'd fantasized about the day when he would re-enter her life. She'd wanted vengeance, but she'd also wanted him back. She'd lived to see him on his knees begging her forgiveness. More than that, she'd wanted to understand why he wasn't willing to sacrifice his career for a love as great as theirs. Even after his cruel betrayal, she'd been willing to wait for his repentance because, for her, love was stronger than the pull of family or honor or duty.

Her hope of being reunited with him had died the day she read a notice of his engagement to the daughter of a high-ranking Coalition officer. Now she realized the folly of her girlish longings. If she hadn't been blinded by love, she would have known from the beginning that the son of Commander-in-Chief Remo had to marry a woman who was an asset, not a liability, to his career.

Phoenix was still lost in thought when a loud knock on the door startled her. Had Case managed to follow her? She wasn't ready to face him again. Not yet. Maybe not ever.

"Are you there, Phoenix Landau?" a loud voice thundered, rapping hard enough to take the skin off ordinary humanoid knuckles.

It was Mol'ar Fap, the last person on the planet she wanted to see. She thought of not opening the door, but she knew from past experience he would force it open if he suspected she was there. Reluctantly she answered his summons.

"Well, did you do it?" he asked without preamble, pushing past her into the room that seemed too small to contain him.

Phoenix didn't know Mol'ar Fap's history; his origin was a mystery, and the name of his home planet was a well-kept secret. Her sources told her he'd been a permanent fixture on Bast for decades, disappearing at intervals but reappearing after short absences.

As always she felt dwarfed by the sheer bulk of the creature, even though he loomed no more than a hand's measurement above the top of her head. Everything about him was massive. The fat digits that served him as fingers reminded her of bulging sausages, and his forearms were as thick as her waist. With legs like tree trunks and a neck like the columns on public buildings on Athera, he would have made a formidable opponent in the manual combat arenas on her planet in his youth, but she doubted he'd made the beginning of his fortune there. The source of his considerable wealth was as mysterious as the rest of his life.

She looked into his face, knowing he respected her only because she never allowed him to intimidate her. Rumor had it he'd altered his appearance so many times, even he'd forgotten how his original face looked. His last transformation had been seriously botched, leaving him with a swollen, lumpish nose that stood out like the highest peak in a time-worn range of mountains. The haphazard arrangement of angry red bumps and scaly depressions might have been comical, but his mean, hard eyes weren't. The wicked silvery slashes set into the folds under sparse, whitish brows discouraged any comparison with a clown's deliberately grotesque face. Looking into them, Phoenix shivered in spite of her determination not to cower.

"Have you found a pilot yet?" he asked in a voice loud enough to crack a plaster wall.

"I had a long talk with the Lug. He isn't interested. The Coalition has been cracking down on illegal flights to Horus."

"A Lug will do anything if the price is right. Did you tell him my top offer?"

"Of course. He got nasty. Said he wouldn't risk his hide for a pittance."

"A pittance!" Fap roared his displeasure. "That slime monster won't see a thousand golbriks in his whole lifespan."

"Horus has a spooky reputation, Mol'ar. The Lugs think the planet is haunted by inhabitants wiped out by the solar flare."

"Superstitious nonsense! That happened a millennium ago. I'm not asking much—only a trip in this solar system. The Lugs know the Qeb system like their own scaly bellies."

"Still, it is a dead planet. . . ."

"Bah! That didn't stop Coalition archaeologists from discovering the last ruler's state documents. If we don't hurry, Horus will be swarming with treasure hunters. I tell you, Phoenix, we can't waste time. This will be the ultimate find I've been waiting a lifetime to uncover. I have a client. . . ."

He broke off, telling her without words that he'd never reveal the extent of his confidential dealings with the power brokers of the galaxy. Fap was a procurer, willing to go to any lengths to find elusive artifacts and treasures for those who hired him. He'd contracted for Phoenix's help and paid her passage to Bast because of her reputation as a tracker. She was the antiquities hunter who'd found the elusive tomb treasure of Elanza, a priceless trove concealed in the bowels of the planet's largest city. No archeologist had even suspected its location until her uncanny instinct had led her to dig there for her sponsors. Unfortunately the planet's corrupt government had seized the find, and she hadn't been paid.

Fap's business was legitimate, if only marginally so.

Star Searcher

Since coming to Bast she'd heard whispers that he held out on those who paid for his services, sometimes keeping choice items for himself. The more she learned about Fap, the more she wanted to be released from her agreement with him.

"I want to know when you're going to do the job I hired you to do," he said.

The threat in his words was frightening, but she tilted her chin at a jaunty angle and answered pertly, knowing the worst thing she could do was show fear.

"You led me to believe unauthorized flights to Horus were easy to arrange. I'm an antiquities tracker, not a travel agent. With your connections on Bast, you should be able to find a pilot yourself."

"I don't want my name to come into it."

"Fine, but don't expect me to kidnap a pilot and make him take us there."

"The people who recommended you said you were resourceful," he complained, every word sounding like a threat.

"If there's something to find on Horus, I'll find it, but I'm not a miracle worker when it comes to arranging expeditions."

"You'd better be. When my clients put pressure on me, I pass it along to those who disappoint me."

"The Lug turned me down—emphatically. I don't know what else I can do."

"Can you pay me back for your passage here?"

"You can't expect me to! I've done everything you told me to do."

"Except find a pilot."

His cold malice made her want to squirm, but she held herself rigid, playing the childish staring game, refusing to blink until he took his icy gaze from her.

Pam Rock

"You're encountering a few difficulties. Nothing a charming young lady like you can't handle, I'm sure," he said in a conciliatory tone, focusing his eyes on the blank wall behind her, releasing her from the stare-down. "By the way, my dear, have you heard from your step-sister lately? I understand her older daughter is quite bright—ready to begin guided instruction a year earlier than her age-peers."

Phoenix felt as though she were standing on sinking sand. Her blood ran cold at the sinister implications in his seemingly innocent question. Her small family mattered to her more than anything else in her life. Her widowed father, Judson Landau, had found happiness in later years with a widow who had a daughter a few years younger than Phoenix, his only child. Phoenix had great affection for her step-sister, Dena Atwel, although their lives couldn't be more different. Dena, a clerk in the Coalition Hall of Records, had married another bright but unadventurous civil employee, and neither of them had ever left the surface of their own planet.

Phoenix adored their children, her two young step-nieces, Ina and Celline, showering on them all the love stored up in her heart. She treasured every childish scrawl they sent her, especially since she hadn't been able to afford the costly passage back to Athera to visit them in a long time. She'd accepted Fap's offer and come to Bast mainly because she desperately wanted to see them again.

Legitimate treasure hunting had brought her fame, but barely enough income to exist. It was getting more and more difficult to keep even a paltry share of her finds, as the planets in the Phara galaxy increasingly confiscated antiquities for state museums.

Star Searcher

"I have a friend on Athera who can look in on those two lovely children, should the need arise," Fap said, contorting his ill-shapen mouth into what he probably thought was a smile. "I suggest you call in all the favors owed you and find me a pilot—before I get impatient."

He left quietly, easing the door shut, no doubt satisfied with the effect he'd had on her.

Phoenix stood trembling in the center of the musty cubicle, badly shaken by the unexpected threat to her family. A crisis usually called forth her reserves of strength and ingenuity, but she felt totally helpless, a hateful and horrifying state for her.

She'd been trying for what seemed like ages to satisfy Fap's demands. She wasn't well connected on Bast, and she didn't have the foggiest idea what to try next.

Her stomach rumbled, reminding her that one mug of bitter drink was a woefully poor substitute for the food she couldn't afford to buy. Fap had paid her passage there and her rent, but had withheld the promised salary, indicating she wouldn't receive the funds stipulated in their contract until all arrangements for their expedition to Horus had been finalized. She was reduced to living on cheap native root foods, a diet no humanoid digestive system could tolerate for long.

Not tonight! Intolerable as it was to meet Case again, she was too upset by Fap's visit to pass up even a remote chance of an offer that might change her run of bad luck. If nothing else came of her meeting with him, at least she could eat her fill and carry away enough for the next day. Technically she was in Fap's employ, but she had nothing to lose by listening to the Coalition's offer. She detested the self-satisfied overseers of the Galaxy, the politicians who had ruined her father's career and her life, but they did have what she most needed: a space vessel. They had fleets of sleek ships, powerful star searchers, so many that the commander-in-chief couldn't possibly know where they all were or what each one was doing.

Her bubble of hope burst after only an instant of optimism. Any help from the Coalition came with a high price tag. She would become their lackey—a fate even worse than working for Fap. The evil procurer liked his facade of legality; he would release her after she upheld her part of the contract. Involvement with the Coalition was risky in ways she could only begin to imagine. In her worst nightmares she saw endless lines of people in Star Service uniforms, all of them marching in parade formation, each one following some invisible line she couldn't see. She was always the cadet who got out of step or lost her regulation helmet, the misfit who got into trouble because she couldn't be exactly like the others.

She whistled through her teeth to bolster her spirits, and found the hairbrush in her stack of gear. Yanking it through her tangled curls until they floated around her face like fluffy clouds, she thought of all the reasons why an alliance with the Coalition was impossible. There was one absolutely insurmountable obstacle: Case Remo. She had to find a way out of her dilemma without teaming up with the man she most despised.

Chapter Two

Almost as an afterthought, Phoenix changed into the only truly feminine garment she owned, a form-fitting, ankle-sweeping scarlet dress, slit up one side nearly to her waist to expose an expanse of creamy white thigh and hip. With hands still shaking from the impact of Fap's threat against her family, she piled long, unruly black curls on top of her head and secured them with an ornately carved comb, an heirloom from a mother she didn't remember. She pushed her feet into thin-strapped, thick-soled sandals, and added blood-red carnelia ear bobs to dangle from her lobes.

It would take more than clinging fabric and simulated jewels to lift her sagging spirits, but she knew the males of her species were flattered when women displayed their charms to good advantage. She'd resisted the impulse to sell her comb and ear bobs in anticipation of just this kind of situation, rare as it was. Even grizzled old warriors had been known to speak softly to her and show great courtesy when she wore a gown and ornaments. Phoenix had landed more than one lucrative assignment dressed as she was now in this female finery.

She caught the underground transport, then hurried along a footpath so thickly shrouded by fog and darkness only the luminous marker stakes kept her from getting lost. By holding her skirt above her knees, she managed to reach the restaurant without soiling the hem on the damp ground.

She paused outside the entrance to give her heart a chance to slow down. It was ludicrous to think she could beguile Case into agreeing to a deal advantageous to her. More likely, he'd tired of waiting for her and had left.

She'd been in emotional turmoil for hours: first her anger at the Lug, then the dread inspired by Fap's threat. Her pulse was racing, her mouth was cottony, and her face felt feverish under her mask. She breathed deeply, let her fringed black shawl drape nonchalantly over one bare shoulder, and steeled herself to parlay with the man who'd broken her heart.

The interior of the eating establishment was dark except for recessed yellow-orange lights along the top of walls covered by zania, deep red vines with midnight-black foliage that reminded Phoenix of vipers' tongues. Diners ate in secluded bowers with wooden lattices straining under the weight of the same sensuous black-leafed vines that covered the walls. She'd suggested this place in spite of the creepy decor; it was the only restaurant in the capital city that catered to wealthy aliens. Fap had taken her there before she'd signed their contract, and she couldn't wait to fill her hollow stomach with imported delicacies that wouldn't give her Bast-belly, the excruciating cramps caused by a diet of native-grown tubers. Unless her luck improved soon, she was going to have to choose between pain and hunger.

The waiter who approached her was grotesque by Atheran standards, with thick rubbery lips and pitted skin emphasized by a yellowish-green tint, but he spoke Instell in a cultured voice, informing her that a male of her species had been waiting for her arrival for some time. She followed his hunched shoulders to a bower in a rear room.

Case was sitting at a small table, reading the thick leaves of a menu, flipping the pages so rapidly she suspected he'd gone through the cosmopolitan list of entrees enough times to memorize it. He was older and even more impossibly handsome than he'd been the last night she saw him at the Galactic Coalition Star Service Academy. The memory of their last meeting on Athera clouded her vision, anger rising like steam hissing from a boiling pot, and she dug her nails into her palms to keep from crying out in long-suppressed pain and anger.

Dredging up old memories was a terrible mistake. She stood, frozen on the spot, fighting for composure.

He looked up, his face shadowy in the eerie bower formed by leaves like serpents' tongues, and she tried to pretend she was meeting him for the first time.

"I thought you'd changed your mind about coming," he said.

She tossed her shawl over the back of the chair across from him, not missing his surprised expression when he saw her choice of a dress. She crossed her arms, spreading her fingers over bare shoulders as though she were cold, although, in truth, she felt hot and flushed.

"I told you I'd probably be here," she said.

"It's a strange place," he said, but his eyes were making more intimate observations.

"The whole planet is strange," she said.

"You seem at home here."

"I neither have nor want a home anymore."

She turned slightly and pretended to adjust her comb so he couldn't read anything on her face. The first part was certainly true; she sometimes felt like fluff borne by the winds of fortune. At first tracking antiquities on her own had been an endless adventure, but lately she was getting weary of exotic places and hazardous expeditions hampered by bureaucratic obstacles. She was ready for a permanent base, one where she could recoup between jobs and take a hot bath whenever she pleased.

She sat across from him, wiggling to arrange her skirt so there was cloth between the rough woven reeds of the seat and her bare thigh and bottom. He was watching her intently, and his eyes had a strange glint, appreciative but curious.

Secretly pleased with the admiration she saw on his face, she remembered the way his pupils changed color according to his moods. When he was angry or upset, his eyes appeared to be gray with only a hint of blue; when he was happy, they took on bright blue tint. In the dim orange light she couldn't tell what color they were now, but she hated herself for remembering how those cool, appraising eyes used to make her tingle with excitement.

The waiter returned, and Case ordered her favorite drink, berrywine, for both of them.

Star Searcher

"Unless you'd rather have something else," he offered.

"My taste in beverages hasn't changed," she said, forcing herself to look directly into his eyes. They looked almost green in the weird lighting.

"How is your father?" He took a deep breath as though dreading her answer.

"He died a year and a half ago."

"I'm sorry."

"Please, no platitudes. He died with his honor restored."

"Phoenix, I never wanted things to end the way they did. . . ."

"I'm not going to talk about the past!"

"You can't just bury it!"

"I can—I have."

She struggled to control her temper, knowing she couldn't storm out—not with Fap's terrible threat hanging over her head. Case was her one chance to get to Horus. Even if Fap found a vessel she was able to pilot herself, she didn't have the special skills of a Lug: the ability to evade Star Service sensors and make an illegal landing without being detected. She needed a legitimate way of getting to the forbidden planet.

"Have you been here long?" he asked conversationally.

"Not too long." She wasn't going to tell him she'd counted the days: 32 unpleasant, frustrating Bast days.

"What brought you here?"

"Just business—my business."

The waiter returned with the mildly intoxicating drinks in transparent beakers, and she sipped hers eagerly, welcoming the distraction.

Case ordered their meal, looking at her for approval after each item. She felt peculiar, surprised he'd remembered all her favorite foods.

They shared a dish of thin egg noodles with hot, bubbly cheese and tiny broiled sea creatures raised in special tanks in the restaurant's kitchen. She hadn't tasted anything like it in ages, but being with Case took the edge off her pleasure. She couldn't help remembering life at the Academy and the time they'd spent together; recalling the past left a bitter aftertaste in her mouth.

Case had been the best-looking, smartest cadet there, and she'd adored him with the wild, unbridled passion of a young girl in love for the first time. All that was over. If any residue of feeling remained, it was hatred, not love.

He ate little and instructed the waiter to wrap most of his portion to be carried away.

"Take this with you," he said, handing over the packet of food.

She saw the knowing look in his eyes and wondered if he suspected how desperate she was.

"No, thank you."

"Take it, Phoenix. I know you're starving here."

"Bast food doesn't agree with me."

"Your ribs are showing. That dress is hanging on you."

"You're wrong!" She sprang to her feet, but he caught her wrist. His touch alone was enough to make her knees buckle; he didn't need force to persuade her to collapse back on the chair.

"I came here with a proposition for you. Are you ready to hear it?" he asked.

Star Searcher

"All I promise to do is listen. I can't imagine working for the Star Service!"

"Let me explain. You know the planets of Thal and Zazar have been bitter enemies for decades."

"Of course, every schoolchild knows about their feud—something to do with the first-ever Zazar expedition to Thal. Didn't the Thals kill them all for no reason?"

"The Thals were a xenophobic race at that phase of their evolution, but they've made some progress in relating to other peoples. The Coalition has brought their leaders together with the Zazars to discuss peace."

"Why does the Coalition care what two minor planets do?"

He leaned forward and spoke in a whisper. "The rumors about a wormhole are true."

"I don't believe it!"

She'd learned about the wormhole theory from her father long before she went to the Academy to study. If an entrance to one of these mysterious passageways could be found, it would open up the possibility of travel to another galaxy.

"The best scientists in the galaxy have confirmed it," he said. "It's not just an intriguing theory anymore."

"Then why isn't everyone talking about it? I haven't heard or read a word about it. Have they sent exploratory probes?"

"The entrance is dead-center in the disputed area between Thal and Zazar. Neither side will give permission for anyone to enter the territory, and their continual skirmishes make it impossible to mount an expedition without starting a war."

"But it could mean so much to both planets—a

route to another galaxy!" She was breathless with excitement, hardly daring to guess what it would mean to travel to the infinite reaches of space.

"There's been progress in ending the feud. The Thals have wanted to join the Coalition for a long time, but constant fighting kept them from forming a single planetary government. Without it, they weren't eligible. Now they've finally achieved a single political voice to speak for the planet."

"I can imagine the Thals wanting to join the Coalition, but the Zazars are so ruthless. . . ."

"They're also fearless interstellar traders. A gateway to a new galaxy could make their rulers rich beyond imagining."

"All this has nothing to do with me." She pulled her shawl over her shoulders to signal her unwillingness to hear more.

"Hear me out." He was whispering even though the bower seemed to muffle all sound from the rest of the restaurant. "Peace negotiations were going well until recently. Then a mysterious illness struck the Coalition's chief negotiator, Orde Ngate. Most of the Thal and Zazar representatives—including the two ambassadors—were stricken too. Ngate lapsed into a coma, and everyone affected had severe nausea and dangerous fevers."

"Was it a disease? Or are you suggesting food poisoning?" She was openly curious now, forgetting her reluctance to hear how her fate could possibly be linked to an ancient feud.

"If the physicians know the cause, they've been ordered to keep silent. The whole peace accord is in jeopardy. Each side suspects the other, even though everyone survived. But there's something worse."

Star Searcher

"I'm waiting to hear what all this has to do with me."

"Please, hear me out. The negotiations are near collapse, but not just because of the sickness. As a supreme goodwill gesture, the Thals were going to present one half of the famous Star Stone to the Zazars. It disappeared during the epidemic."

"The Star Stone!"

Phoenix didn't need to ask what the famous treasure was. According to the Thal legend, a meteor fell to the planet over 1000 years ago and cracked open, revealing two blood-red jewels, redder than any carnelia known. When set side by side, the precious stones formed a perfect six-point star. They were the most unique gems in the galaxy, and one of the two halves would be the ultimate peace offering from one warring planet to another.

She looked up to see his eyes searching her face, and a sensation like tiny feet on the march crept down her spine.

"Someone stole half of the Thals' Star Stone," she said in wonderment. "Where's the other half?"

"Still safe on Thal, but the people there would dismember any leader who even suggested parting with the second half too. It's sacred to their religion as well as being a symbol of the government. It was a very risky political move to bring even one half of it to the negotiations, and now it's missing."

"No museum in the galaxy will buy the Thal Star Stone. It's too well known."

"It wasn't stolen for that purpose. Whoever took it wanted to scuttle the peace talks. It had to be someone who had inside connections to bring it off. The Coalition has authorized me to offer you the job of retrieving it."

Pam Rock

She'd seen it coming, but was still stunned.

"You have the best reputation of any antiquities hunter in the galaxy. It was a major news story on Athera when you found the Statue of Axioprothisis. You have a special gift, Phoenix. If anyone can find the Star Stone, you can."

"You don't know what you're asking. Some obsessed collectors would pay anything to possess it, even if ownership has to be a secret. But tracing private sales isn't like tracking pieces offered on the underground market. It could take years to get a hint of where it's gone," she said.

"It wasn't stolen to go into a collection."

"Now you're an expert on stolen relics?"

"No, but this is political, Phoenix. Someone wants to stop the peace accord."

"That doesn't mean the Star Stone won't be sold. There are collectors rich enough to buy a planet!"

He shook his head. "The Coalition is sure the theft was politically motivated. Profit wasn't the objective."

"Objective or not, the thief must have had enormous expenses. Why not sell the Star Stone to recoup them?"

"Too risky. What if the buyer betrayed the seller? No amount of money would induce a political fanatic to risk failure."

"You seem to have it all figured out. Let the Coalition Special Police track it down."

She was furious! He was never willing to consider anything that didn't fit his political views of the universe.

"They're looking, of course, but so far they haven't come up with a lead."

"A shame they're so ineffectual," she said sarcasti-

Star Searcher

cally. "What am I supposed to do that they can't accomplish with fleets of ships. . . ."

"You have contacts the police don't," he told her. "Sources who would rather face a Taranian tar beast than talk to Coalition forces. I want you to work with me on finding the Star Stone, Phoenix. You won't regret it. You can almost write your own contract on this quest. And I'll help you in every possible way."

Against her will she remembered tutoring him in ancient Atheran history in exchange for his help in quantum physics. Learning about relics of the past had bored him, and he was the last person she would choose to help track down a stolen treasure.

"I don't think it's a job for me."

"I have this for you," he said.

He loosened the white shirt neatly tucked into his trousers and reached into the pouch strapped around his waist. She was distracted by the sight of his lean, taut, golden-haired torso, but when he laid an official-looking green paper in front of her, she gave it her full attention.

"Five million golbriks!" She picked up the rectangular slip and read the small print authorizing deposit in her name at any Instell Financial Center. "It's signed by the commander-in-chief."

"Of course."

"Are you trying to buy my services or my soul?" She couldn't believe what she was reading on the flimsy bit of paper.

"Only your expertise in tracking artifacts. The Coalition has the resources; they don't have anyone with your instincts. People say you can land on a planet and sense whether there's a treasure trove there."

"I have a gift," she admitted, "but I can't turn it on

and off at will. It just comes."

"Even if your instinct doesn't kick in, you know more about the underground market than anyone in the Coalition. Take the money and give it a try."

"I can't." She forced the words through her constricted throat, realizing that once again a fortune was within reach but that the chance of earning it was nil.

"Isn't it enough?" There was scorn in his voice.

She knew it was many times more than he would be paid for a lifetime career in the Star Service.

"It's too much."

"Not for the return of the Star Stone."

"The chance of finding it is one in a billion. I could spend the rest of my life searching and not succeed. It's cruel to dangle this in front of me when there's no chance I'll earn it."

"This is yours, Phoenix, whether you find the Star Stone or not."

"That's crazy! Unreal! Trackers only get paid expenses until they make the find."

"Not in this case. The Coalition wants your help. You can deposit the authorization electronically from my ship and draw on it at any time."

"How many years do you expect me to work for the Coalition?" The serpent-like vines of the bower seemed to be closing in on her.

"We don't have years. Relations between Thal and Zazar are too volatile. Ngate wants diplomatic talks to resume immediately, but each side suspects the other of stealing the Star Stone to sabotage the negotiations. Finding the thief is just as important as returning the gem."

"The Coalition has police to do that."

"They're working on it, but Ngate believes you have

Star Searcher

a better chance of picking up the trail. He thinks the thief will cut up the Star Stone once the peace talks completely break down."

"That would be tragic! The two halves are the rarest gemstones in the galaxy, so unique they haven't even been classified and named."

"That's why the thief won't risk selling it—in its original form. Imagine what a collection of small stones cut from the half-star would sell for."

"Enough to make this look like pocket money," she admitted, staring at the impressive payment on the authorization. "But the stone wouldn't be easy to divide. One wrong cut, and it could crumble into valueless slivers."

She looked up at him, realizing why the Coalition was willing to pay her so generously.

"No legitimate gem cutter will touch it," she said.

"No."

"And you think I have connections in the criminal undermarket?"

"You've made some amazing finds," he said dryly.

"You still believe my father was diverting stolen artifacts to the illegal market!"

She read the truth of her accusation in his eyes, and a sharp-clawed hand seemed to be twisting her intestines into knots. Case hadn't believed in her father's innocence those long years ago, and not even a Star Chamber acquittal was enough to make him accept the fact that Judson Landau hadn't been guilty of any crime. Case still thought her father was a criminal. He still believed Judson Landau's daughter had criminal connections. No wonder he thought she was unfit for the son of a retired Star Service commander-in-chief, his father.

"If I help you find the Star Stone, it will be a tremendous boost to your career, won't it?" she asked bitterly. "At last I may be of some use to you!"

"That's not why I'm here," he said angrily. "I did everything I could short of mutiny to avoid this assignment."

"And you think that makes everything all right!" She flung the paper at him, but it sailed downward and landed on the table between them.

Grabbing her shawl, she ran, so blinded by tears she forgot to put on her mask until noxious particles of dust got into her lungs and made her double over coughing.

She fervently wished she'd never met Case! She should have realized from the beginning the Star Service was his whole life. His father, his grandfather, and several generations of his ancestors had lived and died for the Coalition. His forebears were among the original founders of the Galactic Coalition, and his love for her had meant nothing compared to family pride and honor.

Moving quickly through the night fog, she lost her way twice and had to search for familiar markers. She was short of breath inside her mask, so furious that air seemed to hiss from her nostrils.

She couldn't believe she'd trusted Case enough to hear him out. He was only there because he still believed the allegations of wrongdoing against her father. He thought her father had been guilty, even though proven innocent, and in Case's eyes that meant she must be in league with criminals, tainted by association with her own parent. It didn't matter that Judson Landau had been cleared of all charges. It mattered even less that she'd earned her reputation as an antiquities tracker with grueling hard work and total dedication to her career. Before Mol'ar Fap came into her life, she'd worked for museums and private treasure seekers, legitimate employers who used legal means to get what they wanted. She wasn't a criminal!

Her sandals made muffled slaps on the dusty footpath, and she tried to hold back her tears of rage. Case wasn't worth crying over. He wasn't worth the dirt under her feet. He was space slime! Flotsam ejected from that great, self-satisfied slug, the Coalition!

She stopped suddenly, sure she'd heard a telltale scuffling noise in the fog behind her. Her lodgings were still too far away for comfort, and she'd dashed out without her meager stock of nepetac. Bastians could be dangerous, but she couldn't remember hearing of any homicides perpetrated by one of the addicted natives. Maybe she could convince the stalker to come to her room for one of her few remaining packets. She'd heard of severe beatings from drug-starved Bastians who used their tails like whips.

Propelled forward by fear, she ran as fast as she could in sandals, even though she knew it was impossible to outrun any but the oldest, most feeble Bastian.

At the restaurant Case hastily paid the exorbitant bill, wondering what he'd really consumed under the guise of imported Atheran delicacies. His stomach was sour, and his mouth burned.

The artificial food wasn't the worst thing about the evening. He tucked away the slip of paper that could make Phoenix a wealthy woman and hurried after her, wondering if he'd ever be done with regrets about their breakup.

He remembered the terrible interview he'd had with

his father, who'd traveled to the Academy on the fastest available planet-liner after the news broke about Judson Landau. Commander-in-Chief Oaker Remo had ordered his son to sever all ties with the daughter of a suspected criminal; his father had asked, then begged him not to sully the family honor by continuing to see Phoenix.

Case had resisted, argued, then pleaded with his father to reconsider. The clash of wills went on throughout a long night that seemed to last an eternity. Commander Remo lost his temper, even striking his son with an open-handed slap that bruised Case's cheek and made his ear ring. Eventually Case forgave the blow, the first his father had struck since his son had grown too big to lay across his knees, but Case would never forget his parent's decisive tactic. The senior Remo had chosen that emotion-charged night to tell Case that his mother's recent bout of ill health was the beginning of what could be a terminal illness if she had to endure the shock of a scandal linking her only son to a criminal's daughter. If Case persisted in his loyalty to Phoenix, it could hasten his mother's death.

Phoenix would never believe how deeply he regretted turning his back on her; she couldn't guess the pain that was still there, nibbling away at every success that came his way. He'd been relieved when his brief engagement to another woman had floundered because there was no real love on either side. He had what his father wanted for him: a career with boundless possibilities. But now Case was too busy to wonder if it fulfilled his own expectations for himself.

He followed her, difficult as it was with her head start, but he made a lucky guess and managed to come within hearing distance of the rhythmic slap of her sandals.

The footpath swerved abruptly to the left, and he nearly walked into a high, featureless wall. He grunted in surprise, and heard a muffled outburst. Dashing along the trail of pale, luminous stakes, he overtook Phoenix and grabbed her shoulder, not prepared for her terrified shriek.

"It's only me!" He released her shoulder, but fumbled for her hand.

"Are you trying to scare me to death? I thought I was being stalked by a Bastian."

"They'll settle for a packet of nepetac. You told me they're not greedy."

"I forgot mine—not that it's any concern of yours." She sounded angry at him for not being an addicted stalker.

"In that case, I'll see you to your room."

"No, thank you. I don't need an escort. There's a terminal for a transport just ahead that goes directly to my district."

"Happens I need to ride the transport too. I'm staying in the visitors' section."

"Then take the next transport. I don't want your company."

"You have it anyway," he said impatiently, tired of being treated like a villain.

She walked ahead of him, the square set of her shoulders and the exaggerated sway of her hips conveying her contempt. More familiar with the invisible twists and turns of the path than he was, she moved quickly enough to make him take an occasional running step to keep up. In truth, he might have bypassed the poorly marked entrance to the underground transport system if she hadn't led the way.

He felt rather than saw the slippery stone steps under his feet as he walked down them side by side with her. Inside the tunnel, widely spaced light globes illuminated the track, and the air was filtered enough to breathe without a mask. The pungent odor of urine and decay made him wrinkle his nose, but he kept the mask off and hoped they wouldn't have long to wait.

She didn't speak to him, didn't look at him, but he stayed close, determined not to let her disappear in the maze of foot tunnels branching off from the central waiting area. A small alien with an almost featureless face was standing a few paces away, clutching a dark cape around its shoulders. The cool, damp air on Bast seeped into Case's bones, making him feel old and stiff, and he could imagine how punishing it must be for visitors from hotter planets than Athera. The characteristic that best qualified him for diplomatic service was his ability to imagine himself in the place of almost any alien. His empathy made him a valued aide on Orde Ngate's staff, which made his current assignment all the more puzzling. Did Commander Barkus and Ngate really think he had special influence with Phoenix? He'd tried every way he could to convince his superiors that she hated him and would resist any suggestion he made.

"The transport's coming," she said, breaking the awkward silence between them.

"I don't have a transport pass. I'll have to bribe the overseer with nepetac."

"I don't have one either. There's not supposed to be a fee for riding. The overseer won't dare accost you on a public transport."

He took a packet of the dried leaves from his vest

pocket anyway, preferring to spread goodwill at the Coalition's expense. His supply of nepetac was practically valueless everywhere but on Bast, and he hoped to leave this accursed swamp-planet soon. How could outsiders spend months, even years, surrounded by thick air that reeked of rotting vegetation?

"You seem to know your way around pretty well," he said. "You must have spent quite a bit of time here."

He didn't need an accounting of her time there; his info-banks had given him a good rundown on her activities almost since birth. He just wanted to lessen the silent tension between them.

"Long enough to be ready to leave."

"Then why don't you?"

"My business isn't done."

"I could expedite it for you."

It was a long shot; he hadn't given up on his mission. He had to take her with him when he left, even if it meant stuffing her in a bag and carrying her aboard slung over his shoulder. It wasn't a pleasant prospect. He'd rather try to bag a wild four-horned dragobeest.

"I doubt it."

"We should talk about the Coalition offer some more."

"Felons aren't hard to find. You'll find some other criminal to do your dirty work."

The transport rumbled up to the waiting area, and Case ducked though the open doorway of the cylindrical-shaped conveyance. He wasn't claustrophobic, but the roof was so low he had to sit hugging his knees to keep from bumping his head. He sat on a hard metal bench that faced the opposite side of the tube, so close to Phoenix their thighs melded together.

A dark, long-haired Bastian crept down the narrow

aisle, pointing at the restraining belt Case hadn't bothered to fasten. Instead of securing it, he dropped a packet of Nepetac into the furry palm. The tube was shaped for aerodynamic speed, but the only fast thing about Bast transport was the speed with which the overseer made the nepetac disappear.

The transport lumbered off through a tunnel so black Case wondered if this was how it felt to be a fetus in the womb. He reached over and touched Phoenix's hand, expecting to be slapped or pushed away. Instead she gripped his fingers, telling him this jaunt through the dark tunnels of Bast scared her more than she would ever admit in words.

"I prefer to walk," she whispered, a good sign her anger had cooled because there was no one close by but him to hear her innocuous comment.

"Why ride tonight?"

She didn't answer; maybe he didn't deserve an answer. She'd been making her own decisions for too many years to feel accountable to him.

They entered another murky waiting area after a ride that seemed a lot longer than it was. He donned his mask, feeling as though his clothes and hair must reek of the damp, fetid air in the tube. The little alien he'd noticed earlier looked furtively in all directions, pulled the cape closer, and scurried up the dark steps to the surface. Even strangers with completely innocent reasons for being on Bast seemed furtive and harried. The fog seemed to conceal unimaginable evil and intangible threats. Case responded to the eerie atmosphere, even though he knew it was irrational.

"I'll see you to your dwelling," he said curtly.

Star Searcher

"It's not necessary."

He stayed by her side, and she didn't argue against it. Bast was the kind of place that made even enemies willing to huddle together.

Chapter Three

"I'll walk the rest of the way by myself."

"No, I'll see you to your dwelling."

"You're wasting your time, Case. I'm not up for sale to the highest bidder. The Coalition can buy itself another alleged criminal."

He continued walking with her as though he hadn't heard. "This reminds me of sneaking in after hours at the Academy," he said. "I'm surprised we never got caught."

"I did."

"You never told me."

"You were so honorable, you would have confessed to being with me. There was no reason for both of us to do penalty marches."

"You were close to graduating with honor when you disappeared."

She blinked back tears under the mask, still bitterly

regretting her hasty departure only days before her final round of examinations.

"I was called to stand before a fitness court," she finally said. "They wanted to question me about my father's involvement in the antiquities trade. They warned me anything I said could be used against him at his trial."

"How could they do that?" he asked angrily, talking to the back of her head as he followed her through a narrow alley between two buildings.

"They had orders from higher up." She suspected his father, then the commander-in-chief. "If I told the truth and tried to clear my father, the fitness court planned to accuse me of lying and dismiss me for dishonorable conduct. The cadet representative on the court was a close friend of mine. She warned me. I left before they could throw me out."

"After all those years of studying and training...."

"It's over. I don't want to rehash it."

"That's why you don't want to work for the Coalition. You're still angry...."

"No, Case, it's not anger." She whirled around to face him and lifted her mask to be sure he heard her. "I hate the Star Service. I hate its code: guilty until proven innocent. I hate self-serving politicians who think they can use people."

She coughed breathlessly and slapped the mask back over her face.

"Here's my entrance. Good-bye, Officer Remo." She pulled out her comb and let curls spill over her shoulders, retrieving the keyplate she'd secured in her upswept hair. She felt naked without her waist pack to hide things, but it was too bulky to wear under a form-fitting dress.

Case was standing so close she could feel heat from his body. She shivered and pulled her shawl tighter around her shoulders. She would rather freeze than wrap herself around him like a Bast female in heat.

"Before you go, I want to ask you something. Has there been another man in your life?" he said, surprising her with his intimate question.

"Are you asking if I'm still a virgin?" she countered, hoping to unsettle him with bluntness.

"It was a rude question. I withdraw it," he said stiffly.

"I'll answer anyway. I didn't run to a celibate retreat on Abbess II. I've had a lover—two actually, but the males of our species have an unfortunate tendency: they try to dominate their females. I'm happier making my own decisions." She opened the door a few inches, speaking without looking at him. "I read about your engagement on my newspad some years ago. No doubt you've fathered another generation of Star Service officers by now."

He hesitated a moment, as though he didn't like her question, then flatly denied her allegation. "I've never been wed, and there are no little Remos."

"Your engagement . . ."

"A mistake remedied in time." His flat tone discouraged further discussion.

"Fortunate woman to escape being a space widow." She shoved open the door, intending to send him out into the night fog, then cried out in disbelief. "My room!"

She couldn't believe the sparse furnishings in the room could be reduced to such a colossal mess. The bench was smashed to splinters, the bedcovers shredded into useless rags and scattered everywhere. Even her heavy canvas luggage had been cut to ribbons, and the remnants of clothing she could still identify were tangled and filthy.

"Who would do this?" Case demanded to know, bending to pick up two small packets of nepetac, seemingly the only undamaged objects in the room. "Not Bastians. They wouldn't overlook two fixes. The intruder left them deliberately so you wouldn't blame the natives."

She spotted something lying on the bare wood of the sleeping shelf, and gingerly picked her way through the litter on the floor. Quickly palming it to avoid explanations, she trembled with dread at the impact of Fap's message. His henchmen had done this and left intact a picture of her step-sister's family. It was his way of emphasizing the threat he'd made against them.

"I have to get to Horus," she said without looking at Case.

"It's a dead planet. No one goes there without authorization."

"Get me there, and I'll accept the Coalition's offer."

"Why this sudden change? What happened here tonight? Phoenix, tell me what's going on! This doesn't look like purposeless vandalism. Someone wanted to hurt you."

"You don't need to know my personal business. I accept your offer—if you can find a way for me to go to Horus."

"There are scientific expeditions. . . ." He put his hands on her shoulders and looked into her face. "First you have to track down all the leads on the Star Stone."

"I might be able to do that first," she said, talking

more to herself than him. "But you have to swear I can go to Horus. I want a legal document agreeing to my terms."

"I should be able to arrange it, but I have to know more. You have to tell me the truth."

"Do you want me to track the Star Stone?" She was so upset her temper was boiling up like lava ready to erupt from a volcano.

"Yes, but . . ."

"Then I'll do it on my own terms."

"We'll talk about it in the morning." He put his arm around her shoulders and pulled her against him. "You can't stay here alone."

"I can take care of myself."

"I'm not leaving you here. Whoever did this could be waiting for your return. Maybe destroying your possessions wasn't enough."

"I had a few coins left." She pulled away and kicked at the rubble, hoping Fap had left her enough money to rent a cheap sleeping stall for the night. Case was right about one thing: There was a good chance the vandals would return and take her to Fap. It would be his style to intimidate her again before she could recover from the shock of seeing all her possessions destroyed.

"They were in my bag. The vandals must have taken them."

"Let's go." Case pulled harder than necessary on her arm, demonstrating how easily he could overpower her if she resisted. He propelled her down the corridor and out into the fog before she objected.

"Where are you taking me?"

"To my room."

"No."

Star Searcher

"No time to argue. I want you away from here. Lead the way back to the transport tunnel. I know the footpath to my lodging from there."

As they rushed through the fog, she thought of a dozen reasons why she shouldn't spend the night in Case's room, but the only alternative was to return to her trashed room. She was alone and friendless on an alien planet without a single golbrik in her possession. Last year she'd gambled everything she had to mount an expedition to Glomis Xeres, hoping to find a rich treasure trove that would allow her to retire from her hazardous profession. Someone, perhaps centuries earlier, had stripped the ancient, long-lost temple of its relics, leaving behind only pottery shards and scattered bones.

Had the desolate temple on Glomis Xeres been an omen? Was there nothing in her future but ruins and refuse?

It was a relief of sorts when they reached the entrance to the transport tunnel. From that point, Case led her. She was so weary and heartsick only pride kept her from collapsing on the murky footpath.

Case knew she was reeling from shock and fatigue. He resisted an urge to pick her up and carry her to safety, afraid she might resent it and change her mind about accepting the Coalition's offer. When the shock of being vandalized wore off, would she still be willing to sell her services? He frowned at the thought of trying to get her to Horus, but the important thing was to enroll her in the search for the Star Stone immediately.

The footpath here was wider and firmer, with thick, closely placed stakes. They were still in the district reserved for aliens, but rented rooms here were larger and cleaner. A Bast doorguard checked Case's keyplate and allowed him to enter the Clarion, one of the planet's best guest lodgings. Case remembered to offer the guard a gratuity: a small packet of the coveted leaves. The native grunted his thanks and went back to indolently swatting gnats with his black furless tail.

Case's room wasn't plush by Atheran standards, but it did contain a large, free-standing bed, an overstuffed chair, a drawered chest, and a somewhat rickety bedside table.

"I'm not sleeping with you," she said in a weary voice, speaking for the first time since they'd entered the transport.

"I'll sleep in the chair and use the table as a footstool."

He'd never seen her looking so tired and defeated. He wanted to offer some kind of comfort but knew she'd resent his sympathy.

"First we need to talk about our agreement." She yawned and shook her head impatiently as though trying to stay awake. "I'll find the Star Stone if it can be found in a reasonable length of time. Then I get immediate access to Horus." She sank down on the edge of the bed.

"Agreed. We'll work out the details in the morning. Can I get you anything?"

"Water, please. I'm thirsty."

He went into the water closet and waited for water to drip slowly out of the faucet, then returned with a beaker of the filtered liquid. Phoenix was already asleep, curled up on top of the bed covers with her cheek cradled on her arm. She looked small and vulnerable, and at the same time wantonly enticing. Her

Star Searcher

dark hair was in wild disarray, and the slinky red skirt had parted to expose her lush thigh and hip. He wondered what would happen if he stretched out beside her and cradled her against him. Much as he wanted to deny it, he knew there was still chemistry between them. He wanted to cup her breasts in his hands as he had long years ago. She was the only treasure trove he'd ever coveted: mysterious, unattainable, and infinitely fascinating.

He shook his head impatiently, and whispered her name several times to be sure she was sleeping soundly.

As quietly as possible on the glazed tile floor, he walked to the water closet and secured the door behind him. The fixtures were primitive, operated by rusty chains that released water, but the overhead tank was perfect for concealing his compact hyperwave communicator. He pulled himself up to stand on the rim of the metal washbasin, hoping it wouldn't break loose from the wall, and reached into the water tank. The waterproof communicator was floating on the surface in an inflatable airbag just as he'd left it, dry and ready to use.

There was no law on Bast against communicators. The natives had no interest in them, even though they were costly; it wasn't fear of thieves that prompted Case to conceal his. He didn't for a single instant believe one person working alone had been able to steal and hide the Star Stone. The Coalition was up against a ruthless, powerful group, and the messages he had to send could target him for assassination.

He set up the black rectangular communicator with practiced ease and activated the energy cells. Communiques between solar systems were relayed through hyperwaves, but because Bast was so far from the Coalition Central Command Center, he'd have to send his message and wait hours for a response. There was only one drawback: The communicator would beep softly at regular intervals when the response came, and he had too much to do to sit waiting for it.

He didn't like the idea of letting it beep in the water closet tank, but this was less conspicuous than carrying it on his person. With luck, he'd be nearby when he received the answer he needed.

He pressed the automatic coder and dictated his message, keeping it as short as possible: "Affirmative response dependent access Horus. Motivation unknown."

He entered the code to classify his message, adding an urgency warning: Permission to accept her terms was crucial to his assignment. After signing off, he quickly concealed the communicator.

How long had it been since he'd slept more than a few hours at a stretch? He was bone-weary, but his clothes, his hair, even his skin seemed to stink of Bast mustiness. He stripped and stood under the anemic trickle of water that passed as a shower. Bastians didn't bathe, and even in a lodging like this designed by and for aliens, they begrudged wasting water to wash bodies. As damp as the planet was, it still was plagued by a shortage of fresh water. Every drop used by non-natives had to be extensively filtered.

Case cupped the tepid trickle in both hands, then scrubbed hard, too exhausted to fret over the absence of soap and warm water. At least the management provided a large, thin length of cloth for drying. He wrapped it around his waist and let the air dry the rest of his torso.

Star Searcher

He wanted to stretch out on the bed and sleep for a dozen hours, but he couldn't risk offending Phoenix. She might regret her change of heart in the morning—or she might present a new list of demands. He didn't want to negotiate with a woman who was seething with righteous indignation.

He stretched out in the chair, propping his feet on the small table, so tired he hardly noticed the scratchy upholstery on his bare back. He dozed, but instead of being soothed by the dreamless sleep he craved, his mind was bombarded by erotic images, fantasies so disturbing they became a nightmare. He awoke suddenly and sprang to his feet, tremendously aroused. The ache of it was unlike anything he'd ever experienced, and he couldn't seem to separate the dream from reality. His sudden, sharp need for the woman on the bed shocked him, and it took tremendous willpower not to lie beside her and wake her with fierce, demanding kisses. He wanted to taste the sweetness of her mouth and make hard, searing love to her, and the effort of denying himself made him feel ill.

He sank down on the chair again, surprised to find the flimsy cloth still clinging damply to his stomach and groin. Fully awake now, he couldn't believe a passionate but brief dream could affect him so powerfully. He was unusually anxious about completing his mission; it was the only possible explanation for his agitation.

Too unsettled to sleep again, he started to dress. Even the clothing left in his travel bag smelled musty; the atmosphere on Bast permeated everything, seeping through the yellow stucco walls in spite of the filtering system. He put on a pair of once-crisp trousers and pulled on a loose-fitting black tunic, less con-

63

spicuous than his usual starched and pressed off-duty clothes.

Dressed but still barefooted, he extinguished an incandescent bulb screwed into the socket of a floor lamp, the metal of the pole and base green with corrosion from the dampness. He covered Phoenix with the bed covering and took the lumpy pillow she wasn't using, hoping to avoid a crick in his neck by stuffing it behind his head in the chair. His feet hung over the makeshift footstool, the hard edge pressing uncomfortably into his calves. The metal springs in the chair seat had long ago ceased providing comfort, instead poking his backside in a threatening way. He closed his eyes, but was too uncomfortable to relax, nor could he turn off his disturbing thoughts.

If Phoenix agreed to search for the Star Stone, they'd be together through countless nights. His orders were clear: never let down his guard; trust her no more than he would a renegade Lug; monitor every move she made until the stone was found or he was recalled; above all, spend every minute close to her.

He groaned at the prospect, squirmed on the lumpy seat cushion, and wished Judson Landau had had a son instead of a daughter.

Phoenix woke up with a dull ache in her head and a knot of apprehension in the pit of her stomach. She vaguely remembered her dream: Some horrible creature had pursued her until she fell into a pit of suffocating muck.

She could handle nightmares; it was reality that made her reluctant to open her eyes. Everything she owned was ruined. Fap and Case both wanted her to perform miracles. Fap was a menace to her family and

Star Searcher

her person; Case was threatening in a different but no less dangerous way.

She sat up and massaged the pressure points beside her eyes, trying to dull the pain in her forehead so she could think clearly. Her headache gradually subsided, but her worries didn't. All she had was the clothing on her back and her own resourcefulness. In this predicament it might not be enough!

She fingered the ear bob still clinging to her right lobe, found the mate missing, and searched the bed until she found it. She couldn't be sentimental about this gift from her first lover. For a brief time she'd hoped to forge a relationship with him, but it hadn't worked out. He'd taught her the mechanics of lovemaking without touching the wellspring of her passion. It had been a relief to leave him when he demanded more than she was willing to give.

The blood-red stones would bring enough at the trader's mart to replace a few of her belongings. She pushed aside the coverlet, wondering if Case had covered her out of kindness or because her naked hip and thigh made him uncomfortable.

Where was he? The room was empty; the entrance to the water closet was open, showing it to be deserted. She ran to the door leading to the lobby, shivering as her bare feet padded across cold tiles. There was no sign of him in the corridor. Her first impulse was to run to the mart and sell her gemstones, but she needed to bathe and work the snarls from her hair.

Too tense to enjoy her first real shower since coming to Bast over a month ago, she hurriedly got ready to leave, borrowing a white shirt from Case's gear. She was buttoning the purloined garment, not sorry that it hung nearly to her knees, when an odd beeping sound caught her attention.

A communicator!

The beeps stopped, but she waited silently, almost sure the signals being sent would keep repeating.

Minutes dragged by, but at last she heard another beep, a soft summons not likely to be heard as far away as the corridor.

It was definitely hidden somewhere in the water closet, but she checked the obvious places without success. In fact, there was only one possibility: the water tank far above her head. It was open on top, but her problem was reaching it.

She hauled the rickety table into the water closet and used it to climb onto the rim of the washbasin. The metal was cold and slippery under her feet, and it was going to be a real stretch to reach into the tank. She stood on tiptoes, balanced herself with one hand pressed against the wall, and reached as high as she could.

"Looking for something?"

She shrieked and lost her balance before her brain registered his identity. By then she'd tumbled into Case's arms.

"I don't mind you wearing my shirt, but you're pushing hospitality too far when you search my room," he said angrily, letting her slide down his torso until her toes touched the floor.

"You weren't here when I woke up." She didn't have a glib excuse handy, and he looked ready to throttle her.

The beeper sounded again, distracting him for the minute she needed to back away.

"So you heard it," he said sternly. "I brought you some clothes. Get dressed on the far side of the bed

Star Searcher

while I check it. Try sneaking over to listen at the door, and I guarantee you won't sit down for the rest of the day."

"You can't threaten me like that...."

He didn't say anything, just pointed at the far side of the room, his lips tight and menacing. The smoky gray hue of his eyes reminded her of an overcast sky on Athera just before a violent storm.

She backed up until she bumped into the bed, then scurried around it. He had all the advantages now, but she wouldn't forget the way he'd threatened her.

The door between them slammed shut, and she realized her chance of hearing anything was practically nil. She wasn't going to risk her tender hide to hear anything a Coalition voice-box jockey had to say. She had her own agenda!

If she hadn't been so angry, she would've been pleased with the bundle Case had brought for her: two pairs of serviceable tan trousers, a short-sleeved white shirt, and a lightweight jacket with dozens of pockets. He'd even bought two pairs of skimpy panties, making her wonder if he'd been embarrassed to buy them. He apparently saw no need for an undergarment above her waist, but he did well on footwear: thick-soled ankle boots with six pairs of heavy stockings. Amazingly, everything fit, and he'd brought some toiletries and a small carrying case for the spare garments. Procuring all of it in a short time couldn't have been easy. Shopping for clothing on Bast was like looking for icicles in a desert. Visitors to the planet came in so many sizes and shapes, with such varying clothing needs, that no one merchant could supply them all.

If she had any complaint, it was that Case had tried to outfit her as his twin. Everything he wore looked like a uniform on his lean, powerful body. Even his physical characteristics shouted Star Service: his short honey-blond hair combed back military style; his patrician nose and the smooth lines of his clean-shaven jaw; the way he walked with his muscular shoulders thrown back and his tight round buttocks tucked in. She could see his parade-ground training in every step he took, and when she allowed herself to think about it, her spine tingled.

She couldn't understand what was taking him so long, and was greatly tempted to snatch a quick listen at the door, but fate was on her side for once. Case came out before she could get herself in trouble.

"Everything is set. We can leave for the space dock right away. I have a shuttle in readiness to take us up to the ship to negotiate."

"All you've left out is everything I need to know. Am I approved to go to Horus?"

"Yes, but only after you've satisfied your obligation to the Coalition. We'll sign a formal contract when we get to my shuttle. The Head of Archaeology is sputtering, but wormholes take precedence over planetary junk piles."

"It's just like you to belittle anything ancient or beautiful!"

"I'm not belittling your profession, Phoenix."

He rubbed his forehead above his nose as though it ached, making her wonder if he'd been able to sleep on his makeshift bed. She didn't ask.

"You'll be allowed to join a contingent going to Horus after the Coalition is through with your services. The situation is critical. The Thal and Zazar ambassadors are still on the Coalition Command Vessel, but they're both pressing to return to their home planets.

Star Searcher

The Thals have peculiar dietary requirements, and food supplies for them are running low. The Zazars aren't noted for their patience in the best of situations. The Coalition is walking a fine line. The ambassadors can't be treated as prisoners, but they can't be allowed to go home before signing a peace treaty."

He shrugged his shoulders as though he'd like to shake off the heavy responsibilities heaped on him. She almost sympathized with him; then she remembered his threat to chastise her if she tried to listen to his precious message. Someday he'd pay for that indignity!

"The deal still includes five million golbriks paid to my account when I sign?"

"I'm authorized to pay you that," he said impatiently, as though giving her a fortune in galactic currency was a minor annoyance to him.

"I need to eat before we leave." She couldn't go anywhere until she told Fap she'd soon have access to Horus. If it wasn't enough for him . . . if he didn't believe her . . .

"We can eat at the space dock. Get your things."

"No! I mean, I don't want space-dock food—nothing but freeze-dried chemicals."

"Don't tell me you've developed a taste for Bast cuisine. Have you seen the muck fields where they raise their tubers?"

"I just want something closer. Trust me." She was pleading for more than a plate of fried roots.

She led the way to the herb shop where Fap could be found most of the time, but before she could risk seeing him she had to locate an eating place nearby. The fog was at its thinnest, but she still couldn't see more than two storefronts ahead. Fortune smiled on her one more time; she spotted a grimy little place run by exiles from some planet she'd never heard of. Their style of cooking couldn't possibly be as horrible as Bast dishes.

Phoenix and Case sat on a bench along the wall until a round, plump waiter with features almost lost in his roly-poly face came to ask what they'd like. He spoke Instell with a harsh guttural accent, but brought them a basket of buns made from imported grains and little cups of steaming hot blue-green liquid. Case paid enough to feed a family of four for a month on Athera, but only grumbled when he bit into a small hard pellet in his bun. She told him it was probably a stone, not a rodent dropping, and generously offered to share hers.

Getting away from him was tricky. She decided on the oldest ploy of all, a trip to the water closet, but instead ran through the kitchen trying not to see the bugs crawling on the floor and counters. The alley behind the eating place reeked of refuse and stronger-than-usual Bast decay, and she had to run past more than a dozen back entries before she could circle around to the front of Fap's herb shop.

She'd been there several times before, and still didn't know whether it was fear or the overpowering herbal aroma that made her feel lightheaded. The walls on all sides were one huge cabinet with glass-fronted drawers and open compartments, each housing some wondrous herb gathered from the far reaches of the galaxy. Fap's customers were other aliens; the Basts valued only one narcotic herb: nepetac. But the proprietor boasted he could cure impotence in 2,481 different species and, if he choose to, make a Lug's scales curl.

Star Searcher

"My dear Phoenix," Fap said, rising to meet her when she poked her head around the edge of the curtain that separated the shop from an office cluttered with the relics and antiquities that fed his obsession for more.

He actually stood and walked toward her, the rolls of fat on his torso jiggling as he reached out with his sausage fingers to pat her arm. "Good to see you, child."

"You wrecked my room! You ruined everything I own!" She hadn't intended to say anything, but she was too angry to play games.

"What are you suggesting? Never mind, tell me why you've honored my humble establishment with your luminous presence."

"I have legal authorization to go to Horus."

"Splendid. Have I given you any of my trophylac elixir? You'll love it—a few drops a day can soothe the inner beast in all of us."

"Mol'ar! I said I have access to Horus. But I have to do another job first."

"No problem, my little tracker. The treasure will wait, and so will I. All that matters is your enthusiasm for our project."

She frowned, totally perplexed by his congenial attitude. She'd expected to argue, plead for time, beg him not to harm her family while she did the other job she had to do.

"You won't hurt. . . ."

"Your loved ones? I'll watch over them like a guardian angle. I know you'll fulfill your part of our bargain as soon as possible."

"Yes, I will," she agreed weakly, wondering if Fap had dual personalities. She hardly knew this kinder, gentler version of the thug. "I won't back out of our agreement. It's only a temporary postponement, and everything is set."

He waved her off, and she felt like a babbling child trying to explain more than he cared to know.

"Fine, fine, fine . . ." Fap clamped his lumpy lips together and looked beyond her, backing up a few steps in surprise.

"Here you are!" Case flung aside the curtain and stepped into the office.

"I wanted to say good-bye to a friend," she alibied weakly.

"Have you finished?" He gripped her upper arm with hard, punishing fingers and started backing toward the shop.

"We're quite finished for now," Fap said, "I won't detain you."

Case rushed her out of the shop, not releasing her arm until she dug in her heels and refused to walk another step.

"You had no right to follow me!"

"Have you lost your senses? Mol'ar Fap is notorious on more planets than I can name. I thought you were scraping the bottom of the barrel being seen in public with a Lug, but that scaly alien is an honor cadet compared to Fap!"

"Officer Remo," she said, pulling herself up to her full height, "you gave up all rights to meddle in my business when you didn't believe in my father's innocence. Don't ever interfere in my personal business or, contract or no contract, you'll never see me again."

He recoiled like a man who'd been slapped. "I'm adding one more condition to your contract. You're to have no dealings with Mol'ar Fap while on assignment for the Coalition. If you can't live with that, tell me now or forget about tracking the Star Stone—and going to Horus."

She'd never been more tempted to throw words back in his face, but losing access to Horus was not only suicidal, it was a death sentence for her family.

"I'll do the Coalition's dirty work, but I'll be longing for the day when I'm free of you!"

Chapter Four

"Why are you so hostile toward the Coalition?" Case asked as they were riding through the underground labyrinth to the docking station. "The incident with your father was unfortunate, but he was cleared. The Galactic Coalition system of justice worked."

"Easy for you to say!" She resented his attitude almost as much as the Coalition's. "They think I'm in cahoots with criminals just because my father was accused of breaking the law."

"Are you?"

"Believe whatever you like."

"Doing business with Mol'ar Fap won't enhance your reputation."

She'd expected him to ask more questions about the sinister procurer, but she wasn't sure he'd buy the excuse she'd concocted for his benefit.

Star Searcher

"I went to him because I needed a remedy—for a female complaint,"

He could believe that or not; she didn't need his good opinion.

"Why sneak out the back way of the restaurant to elude me? No, don't make up another story." He reached over and touched her lips with the backs of his fingers. "The fewer lies you tell, the less complicated our relationship will be."

His touch was light and playful, but she loathed his patronizing tone.

"We have no relationship! Once I've signed the contract and been briefed, I'll do much better working alone."

"Maybe, but I'm your official shadow. Wherever you go, I'll be right behind you."

"Forget it! I can't get a lead on the Star Stone if I travel with a police escort."

"I'm in the diplomatic service."

"In my profession, one Coalition lackey is the same as any other! People won't talk to me when you're around."

"Why not—if your acquaintances aren't criminals?"

"The Coalition is getting rich on antiquities hunting without taking any of the risks. They demand a large part of every treasure trove discovered in the galaxy. Their license fees and permits cost a small fortune, and if an expedition is successful, they take an exorbitant share under the guise of taxation. And that doesn't even count the bribes!"

"Bribery is a serious charge," he said.

"You wanted to know why antiquities hunters hate the Coalition. No one in the profession will give me the time of day if I'm with one of their flunkies."

"I don't intend to wear my uniform."

"You won't need to! The Academy molded you! I'd recognize your stance anywhere: an iron rod for a spine; buttocks like stones; square shoulders. And then there's the arrogant way you carry your head!"

"You've made your point! I'm a walking statue. I'll slouch...."

"You don't get it! It's all of you—your hair, your walk, your way of speaking. Worst of all, you're an Atheran; the Coalition is riddled with people from your planet."

"It's your home planet too! I'm proud to be an Atheran. Our people were instrumental in founding the Coalition."

"That was hundreds of years ago, Case. I try to make the people I work with forget my origin. I can't travel with you."

The transport was chugging up an incline, emerging from the tunnel for the first time on its route. They were approaching the docking station.

"You don't have a choice," he said. "Nor do I. I'm not going to throw away my career and disgrace my family...."

"It all comes back to your family, doesn't it? You're just a little branch on the big Remo tree! Have you ever made a decision that didn't please your illustrious father?"

"I'm proud of what my father has accomplished," he said, anger making his eyes as gray as the murky rivers of Bast.

"Fine. Be his shadow. I can't possibly find the Star Stone with you hanging around."

"You'll have to," he said grimly, looking away from

Star Searcher

her and staring out at the dense fog.

She knew arguing with him was futile; he'd do what he was ordered to do. Nothing she could say would sway him, but she knew more than one way to evade unwanted surveillance. Secrecy was her game. Successful antiquities trackers had to operate covertly, and she was one of the best. Above all, she couldn't let him suspect she was in Fap's employ. If a Lug couldn't be bribed to go to Horus, no one could. She needed legal access to the planet and a ship to take her there, or her loved ones would suffer the consequences. Case might back out of the deal if he knew she was connected to the unsavory procurer. For now she had to pacify him, even though she'd rather eat ground glass.

Except for a nondescript hooded alien, they were the only ones who got off the transport. Traffic was never heavy at the Bast space station, particularly not in the damp season when even the highlands were shrouded in noxious mist.

Case handed over three packets of nepetac to a crew lethargically replacing a board in the railing along steep steps leading up to the docking area. The original builders had used the porous wood grown locally with predictable results. A large number of Bastians were continually employed replacing rotted planks, using their jobs to threaten travelers with iron hammers held in their tails.

She loathed this planet! Not just because of the continual extortion by the natives, but because there were no treasures, no antiquities to discover. The natives had never produced beautiful objects. Even if they weren't lacking in the necessary skills, there were no durable raw materials. Everything, even furniture kept inside the stucco buildings, rotted in a generation or so.

"I can't wait to get away from here," she whispered when they were past the work crew.

"Then we agree on one thing."

They had to put in an appearance at a series of sheds, each one manned by an addicted Bastian who demanded nepetac in exchange for examining their permits and passing them on to the next. By the time they reached the exit master, Case was exasperated and she was appalled. She'd arrived in a public vessel and had had no idea it took so many packets to be cleared to leave. Without the Coalition's offer, she might have been stranded a long time. Mol'ar Fap could've kept her there by bribing the Basts to block any financial help her sister or friends might send. Her two remaining packets wouldn't have gotten her past the work crew, and she was relieved to be getting away finally. But it still amazed her that Fap had put off his own project without strenuous objections.

She couldn't feel any gratitude toward Case, not even for facilitating her escape from Bast. His methods of control were no better than Fap's. With the procurer, all she had to deal with was his greed, but Officer Remo was a betrayer. Case had a rigid code of honor where the Coalition was concerned, but in her present circumstances, that made him even more detrimental to her need to satisfy Mo'lar Fap.

After Case handed over the last of his nepetac, she added her two packets to the pile. The exit master grunted in satisfaction, inked their permits with a flourish of his hairless black tail, and led them out to the launch pad where Case's shuttle was docked.

"The *Galactic Coalition Ship Seker*," Case said, wiping away the oily condensation that obscured the name on the silvery surface of the craft.

"*GCS Seker*. It's one of the newest, isn't it?" she asked.

"Fairly new." He watched the officious Bastian saunter away to wait for his next victim.

"How about telling me where we're going?"

For discretion's sake, she hadn't wanted to ask until she was sure they were alone.

"To the *GCS Isis*." He opened the hatch, and retractable steps slid down to the ground. "Get on board before some Bast underling tries to hold us up for another fix."

She didn't need urging. Scurrying up, she practically dove into the small but welcoming interior of a shuttlecraft designed for Atherans' comfort. On her right was the oval cockpit crowded with automated navigational equipment. She turned left into the main compartment, the small but cozy quarters she'd be sharing with Case. There were two benches and a table that could be pulled down from the wall after takeoff, and a minuscule galley with a flash cooker to heat frozen meals. At the rear was a water closet and the engine access room. Two sets of narrow bunk beds were tucked into the midsection of a vessel less than five meters long. They had everything they needed for survival and reasonable comfort—except space to get away from each other.

"Where is the *Isis*?"

"Orbiting Thal in the Bes System."

"I guess it could be worse," she muttered, knowing the distance between the Qeb, where they were, and the Bes wasn't great by galactic standards. "How long will it take?"

"Not long. This craft is small, but it has the latest hyperdrive."

"Nothing but the best for Officer Remo."

She was using sarcasm to keep a distance between them. It didn't make her proud of herself, but even with the best hyperdrive, far exceeding the speed of light, this trip would last too long for her peace of mind. She dreaded being confined in a small space with Case. He was a threat to everything she had to do.

"We can make it in a little over five days," he said. "Look at the bright side: I'm not a Lug. I hear they have some pretty disgusting personal habits. Why were you so mad at the one in the cantina?"

He'd seen her arguing with the Lug. It wouldn't do any good to deny it, but she couldn't tell him the reason for her disagreement with the alien. How could she stand traveling with Case when everything he asked was a potential pitfall? The past was a taboo subject, and talking about her work was like being on the edge of an abyss. She might slip at any moment through no fault of her own. She hated this trip already, and they weren't even off the pad.

"That Lug was just a stranger. Apparently I offended him without meaning to," she said as coolly as possible. "Which bunk is mine?"

"Take your choice," he said. "I'm going to program the auto-pilot so we can get started."

Case welcomed the routine duties of casting off. When the auto-program was set, he opted to operate the lift-off engines manually. Time would drag once the ship went into hyperdrive and there was nothing to do but try to extract information from Phoenix. He dreaded crossing verbal swords on this short hop, and the prospect of a long space mission with her was awful.

She hadn't forgiven him for letting her down when her father was in trouble, and the worst of it was, he hadn't forgiven himself. It was the one truly dishonorable thing he'd ever done, but hating himself couldn't erase the past. Now he had to look forward to countless days of resentment, recriminations, bitterness, wrangling, and manipulation on both their parts. He'd rather go to a penal lockup and choose the roughest felon under confinement to be his co-worker than deal with Phoenix's prickly temperament and caustic remarks.

In all fairness, she didn't want to be on this mission anymore than he did. She hadn't been swayed by the ridiculously generous payment or any other appeals he'd made. There was more behind her capitulation than having her possessions destroyed. She had to have friends, a whole network of people in the antiquities business, who would've helped her out of a tight squeeze on Bast. When she saw the vandalism, she'd been terrified—literally scared into accepting the Coalition's offer. That meant she must know who trashed her room. Her possessions had been destroyed to send her a message.

Where did Mol'ar Fap fit in? He had a sinister reputation but no criminal record. He was well known to the Coalition, but his schemes were as mysterious as his vast collection of plants and herbs.

Case leaned back in the pilot's seat and stretched his legs after they left Bast's atmosphere, letting the auto-pilot assume control of the vessel. He still had work to do, but all of it involved his passenger. This must be how a zookeeper felt when he had to groom a ferocious veld devil, but an animal handler could protect himself with a face guard and leather shields. Case didn't have any defenses against Phoenix's anger and indignation. He'd been pressured into this assignment, and he resented the Coalition's high-handed tactics almost as much as she did.

"I could fix a meal," she suggested, coming up behind him in the doorless cubicle.

"That would be nice, thank you."

"Well? What do you want?"

"The *Seker* only carries deep-space rations. Fix whatever you like."

"I'm only doing it because you're busy now."

He wasn't, but some primitive instinct in his genetic makeup liked the idea of a female slaving over a cookstove. Of course, it would only take seconds to heat the frozen food in the flash cooker, but he sat back in satisfaction and waited until she had the steaming trays on the table.

"It's ready," she called out.

He ate slowly, rolling bites of the slightly salty protein patty over his tongue as though savoring a gourmet delicacy. He liked watching her eat, breaking apart the grayish entree with the cutting end of a ute, then deftly flipping it around to use the prongs on the other end. She made eating with the utilitarian space utensil look like an art form, switching ends so quickly he had trouble following the motion of her fingers.

"You're handy with a ute," he remarked.

"I spend a lot of time in space." She flicked it again and pointed the prongs at him. "I can do more than eat with it."

Was she threatening to spear him with the metal

tines? He saw the mischief in her eyes, and remembered how she liked to tease. Had she been teasing when she bared her breasts for him on that long-ago day when they were still young and naive? It didn't matter now, but he wished the memory of those creamy, brown-tipped globes wasn't quite so vivid.

"Most successful space tramps know how to utilize whatever's at hand," he said.

"Is that what you think I am? A space tramp?"

She sounded more amused than offended. He almost relaxed his guard.

"Am I?" she persisted.

He felt a sudden pricking. Looking down, he saw the prongs of the ute spearing the cloth of his breast pocket, penetrating the paper notepad inside it and breaking through to scratch his skin.

"I didn't see it leave your hand." He was too surprised to feign indifference.

"I could have buried it to the hilt."

"You've made your point," he said dryly, pulling the utensil away, but not without leaving two tiny tears in the cloth pocket. "You won't need to defend yourself against me."

"No, I won't."

They finished the meal in silence. Even the sweet, juicy serving of fruit compote tasted bitter and dry to him as he thought of the complications of going on a mission with Phoenix.

Neither rose to clear away the trays and drinking cups. Case pushed his aside. The sooner he carried out his orders about briefing her, the sooner he could drop into one of the bunks and sleep.

"You already know the treaty-signing ceremony between the Thals and Zazars had to be postponed because of the sickness," he began.

"Yes, you think it was done deliberately to sabotage the negotiations."

She sounded impatient, as though she didn't want to hear the same thing twice, but he had orders to be concise. He had to be sure she understood the gravity of the situation.

"I don't understand everything about the Thals' dietary requirements," he went on. "They have religious taboos about food, but their biochemistry is touchy too."

"They have to maintain exceptionally strong bodies to survive on their heavy-gravity planet. You're not lecturing a green cadet, Officer Remo. I've been around."

"So I understand," he said, trying to hide his irritation at her attitude, "but it's my responsibility to give you an initial briefing."

"By all means, don't let my boredom hinder you. Assume I know absolutely nothing."

"The Thals are flesh-eaters," he went on, trying to ignore her obvious pouting. "They brought their own galley staff to be sure their meat was properly prepared—although we'd call what they eat raw. They brought their own animals aboard the *Isis* too."

"They have to be penned separately from other animals and slaughtered under ritual circumstances a short time before they're consumed," she said, interrupting him. "Sorry, just speeding up your story."

He clenched his fists under the table. Someday he'd have the last word in a conversation with Phoenix Landau, even if he had to gag her to accomplish it.

"Someone went to a lot of trouble to be sure almost everyone was affected to some degree," he continued.

"Naturally the culprit made sure he—"

"Or she." It was his turn to interrupt.

"He or she ingested enough of the poison to avoid suspicion."

"That's one possible theory. May I tell you about the security arrangements for the Star Stone?"

"At last the important stuff." She wiggled sideways, putting her feet on the bench and resting her chin on pulled-up knees, not looking at him as he went on.

"The Star Stone was stolen from high-security storage in the diplomatic offices on deck three of the *Isis*."

"Ah, your department!" She looked at him with her first show of interest. "No wonder the powers-that-be have your balls in a vise."

"It won't work, Phoenix."

"What won't work?" She swiveled and put her feet under the table with a thump.

"Using crude language to get a rise out of someone—in this case me. You got into trouble more than once at the Academy for mouthing off when listening would have been the smart thing to do."

"If you're going to analyze everything I say, I quit. Find someone else to chase after the Star Stone."

"I'd like to, but someone in authority thinks you can do the job. Are you ready to hear me out?"

"Yes, sir, Officer Remo." She sat up straight and executed a mocking salute. "Tell me how your precious Star Stone was protected."

"It was in a high-security safe. . . ."

"Not so high-security the thief couldn't walk off with it."

"Phoenix . . ." He caught a hint of a grin and realized she was baiting him, trying to make him suffer in small ways for all the pain he'd caused her in the past.

"You're right. There were access codes, but no retinal scans. Given the importance of the Star Stone, the Service should have installed a new system based on eye patterns. Usually the safe held only diplomatic papers and golbriks to finance the mission, nothing irreplaceable."

"How often were the codes changed?"

"At the beginning of every mission."

"That means the thief had to have inside help, someone in the diplomatic service assigned to the *Isis*."

"Not necessarily. Anyway, I can't believe anyone with security clearance would jeopardize the peace talks. The wormhole is important to the whole galaxy. Every diplomatic officer on the *Isis* has a personal stake in the success of the mission. Promotions will be handed out across the board when the accord is signed."

"And everyone knows how important careers are," she said sarcastically. "There's only one alternative. Someone else on board must have breached the security system."

"I hate to admit it, but yes. Anyone with access to the Coalition's information banks on Athera might have been able to dredge out the components and run them through a computational scanner. The information could have been passed on to anyone on the *Isis*."

"How many people have access?"

"Thousands."

"Thousands!"

"The diplomatic service is large, but the culprit had to be a genius at manipulating the info-banks."

"Great!" She stood and paced the few short steps to

the rear and back. "A thousand leads to check. Add in all their friends, relatives, and acquaintances.... You're talking millions, Case."

"The Galactic police are handling that part. All you need to do is find the Star Stone."

"I haven't signed a contract yet."

"You have a green paper for five million golbriks. Do you want to give it back?"

"I'm tempted."

"What about access to Horus?"

She didn't have a glib answer for that, so he pressed his advantage. "I'll get my auto-printer, and we'll finalize the agreement."

A short while later, he had her sign the signature box. He printed out a copy for her and locked the contract into the data-save.

"I can process your payment," he offered. "Where do you want it sent?"

"The Instell Financial Center on Athera. I'll give you my access number."

"I thought you weren't a citizen of Athera anymore."

"My step-sister lives there. It's convenient to keep my funds there."

"It's also the safest banking system in the Galaxy," he reminded her. "Being an Atheran isn't all bad."

Phoenix felt drained by all the verbal sparring with Case. How could she possibly stand being with him for five days, let alone the time required for a lengthy assignment?

It might be easier if he didn't have a body like a professional competitor in the endurance games on Athera and a face that made women's hearts beat faster, a traitorous voice inside her skull reminded her.

"I need sleep," she said curtly, walking back toward the two tiers of narrow bunks.

"There's enough water for a short shower if you'd like to wash away the stink of Bast. You can go first."

His offer was too appealing to turn down, even if it meant being indebted to him for a small kindness.

"Thank you. I'll do that."

The water closet was tiny with undersized steel fixtures. She stripped off her clothing and stepped into a shower stall so small her elbows bumped the walls as she first scrubbed with a pleasantly scented antiseptic gel, then pulled down the knob for her water ration. The trickle was soothingly warm and adequate to rinse her hair and body. As was the case on most space vehicles, the spray was automatically saved in the basin-like floor of the shower. The ankle-high mix of water and cleaning gel could still be used to launder garments, and she dumped every scrap of cloth contaminated by the sulfurous odors of Bast into it.

When she'd wrung out the towel and her clothing, hanging them to dry on racks set into one wall, she felt clean and fresh for the first time since landing on the noxious planet. She was also stark naked, a state that wouldn't have mattered if she hadn't been traveling with a male of her own species.

She couldn't walk out to her bunk without giving Case an entirely misleading impression. Mating was an acceptable form of recreation on long space journeys, so much so that Coalition ships were stocked with protective devices to prevent impregnation of female eggs. But casual, playful sex would never be possible with Case. There was too much anger, resentment, and disappointment between them. Just thinking about lying with him made her angry at herself. She was ready to struggle into wet trousers and shirt when he knocked loudly on the metal door.

"Have you fallen asleep in there?"

"No, I'm waiting for my clothes to dry."

"Great! Have you ever heard of sharing facilities? I need a shower too."

"If you must know," she shouted through the closed door, "I can't come out because all my clothes are wet."

There was a long silence, then the door opened and his hand slid through the crack.

"Wear this." He handed over a bunched white garment.

"Thank you."

"I'm only loaning you a shirt so you'll come out of there."

"That's understood," she said sharply, thrusting her arms into a shirt with small metallic closures down the front.

The soft cloth clung to her torso and upper thighs, ending just above her knees. It was a standard-issue dress shirt for Coalition officers, and Case had worn it at least briefly, leaving creases at the inner elbows and a slight but enticing male scent. Fortunately she was too tired to be stimulated by the pleasant musk.

"Do you want the top bunk or the bottom?" he asked when she came out, obviously checking out the way his shirt fit.

"I thought you were in a rush to use the shower."

"As captain of the *Seker*, I'm obliged to see the passengers settled in."

"You only have one—and I'm more hostage than passenger. Maybe you should delete my contract from the storage banks before we both regret the arrangement."

"I already do, but it's too late. I completed phase one of my mission and sent your contract ahead to the *Isis*."

"Then I guess we're both stuck." She yanked on the lever to bring down the mattress and bedding for a bottom bunk, but nothing happened.

"New safeguard against a gravitational malfunction. Everything has to be firmly secured. You need a key to bring down the mattress and bedding." He dangled a metallic rod near her face.

"Give it to me."

"You may address me as Captain Remo or sir."

"Oh, don't be silly. I'm too tired to play games."

"No game, Landau. You'll have input on the ground, but in space, I'm in charge."

"In charge of what? This little tin can flies itself."

"In charge of you!"

"There was nothing like that in the contract I signed!"

"I'm your transport officer. In an emergency, there has to be a chain of command."

"There's going to be an emergency if I don't get some sleep! Are you going to release some bedding, or do I have to sleep on the metal frame?"

"Just so long as we understand each other." He reached around her, brushing her shoulder with his arm, and inserted the rod, releasing a bundle stored under the upper bunk. "Sweet dreams."

He left so quickly, she found herself sputtering at the air.

Chapter Five

Case switched off the Grodacian language tape, but kept his earphones on so Phoenix would think he was still listening to it. He had speaking ability in 31 different languages and dialects, thanks to the learning programs he used to fill idle time on space flights, but he couldn't remember a word he'd heard in the last hour. In five days Phoenix had annihilated his concentration and ruined his composure. And this was only the beginning of his unwanted assignment: monitoring every move she made.

Some of her moves were pleasurable to watch: the seductive sway of her hips; the way she nibbled her lower lip when she was agitated; the way she curled in her bunk like a little girl and sighed just before going to sleep, as though reluctantly giving up her hold on consciousness. What made his duty so difficult was the wall of anger and resentment she'd erected between them.

He deeply regretted letting her down when her father was accused of criminal activities, but he couldn't have done otherwise. His mother had been deathly ill. Scandal and disgrace would surely have hastened the end of her days. After her death, he didn't even know where Phoenix was, much as he wanted to make amends.

"Caught you!" Phoenix said, pulling the earphones away from his head. "I saw you switch off the tape. You're pretending to listen so you won't have to answer my questions."

"I've told you all I can," he said warily. "Save your questions for Orde Ngate. You'll be meeting with him in a few hours."

"One thing I forgot to ask you," she said, standing over him with folded arms. "Were you sick when the Star Stone was stolen?"

"No."

"Peculiar. How did you happen to avoid it?"

"I had a cold meal sent to my quarters instead of attending the banquet. Ngate was unhappy with some of the language in the agreement to give the Thals access to Coalition technology. I had to work on the rewrite."

"Convenient."

"Coincidence."

"I don't believe in them." She stalked away and lapsed into a moody silence.

Phoenix watched listlessly through a tiny porthole while the *GCS Isis* came into sight, first as a distant speck, then as a massive hulk 500 meters long. She

Star Searcher

was suffering from a strange malady: self-doubt. How could she possibly locate a treasure no larger than her own hand in the infinite reaches of the galaxy?

The closer they came to the flagship, the more trepidation she felt, as though that space monstrosity would swallow her up, imprisoning her body and her spirit in the labyrinth of intrigue and politics that lived within it. She had no way of telling friend from enemy: no reason to trust anyone connected with the Coalition, not even Case.

She shuddered and hoped she was overdramatizing the situation. The only way she could protect her family from Mol'ar Fap's long and sinister reach was to do whatever Orde Ngate asked of her.

"Think of it as a floating office building," Case said, startling her by coming up behind her and putting his hands on her shoulders. "From the outside it's all battleship, but inside life is pretty ordinary."

"Except for poisoned meals and the theft of a priceless relic," she said, shrugging off his hands, determined not to let him know how intimidated she was by the aura of power surrounding the *Isis*. "I wonder how the thief got the Star Stone off the ship—or is it still on board?"

"Impossible. Every square inch of the ship was searched. Every person on board—even the Thal and Zazar ambassadors—submitted to a body search."

"Are you saying a shuttle craft locked onto the *Isis* and left with the Star Stone without attracting attention?"

"Someone smuggled it off—there's no way to be sure how or when. Several smaller vehicles locked onto the *Isis* over a period of days."

"Surely every arrival has to log in."

"Believe me, Phoenix, the theft has been thoroughly investigated by the Coalition Special Police. You don't need to waste time doing their job."

"I can't track it unless I find leads. That means going over the circumstances of the theft—no matter who objects."

"I'm not objecting," he said crossly. "I'm just trying to warn you not to stir up a political hornets' nest. Your job will be to garner information from . . ."

"My criminal connections."

"I didn't say that."

"No, but you've made it plain enough. I'm the outlaw connection. My father was accused of a crime, so I must consort with lawbreakers."

"Must we quarrel about the same thing over and over?" he asked angrily, dropping all pretense of geniality.

"No, because I have nothing more to say to you," she said stiffly.

"That's a relief." He went back to the pilot's seat, and didn't speak to her again until they were inside the *Isis*.

Phoenix was impressed with the huge ship in spite of her resolve not to be. The *Seker* locked onto the hangar deck, and she saw more shuttles and fighter craft than she could count as Case hurriedly led her to the lift. Inside the fast-moving box, the floor was covered with deep turquoise carpeting and the walls were lined with marbleized fiberglass in matching shades. The recessed lights gave off an other-worldly blue-green glow, and the doors parted soundlessly at their destination: Deck Three.

Diplomatic business on the *Isis* was conducted away from the bustle of the docking facilities below and the command bridge and armaments on top. Phoenix didn't need to be told she was being taken directly to the ranking diplomat, Orde Ngate.

Three young men, their apparent leader a thin man with beautiful, dark eyes and sleek black hair hanging to his shoulders, met them in the red-carpeted corridor outside the lift.

"Welcome, Citizen Landau, Officer Remo."

"This is Secretary Ban," Case said, curtly introducing the spokesman.

"Nevin Ban, personal recorder to Chief Negotiator Orde Ngate." He reached out and grasped Phoenix's hand, holding it exactly the proper amount of time. "It's a profound pleasure to welcome you to the *GCS Isis.*"

"Thank you."

She smiled, conscious of Case's glum expression.

Either he was still angry at her, or he disliked Nevin Ban. For her part, she'd never seen such finely honed features or long lashes on a man. Ban's face was beautiful except for the sallowness of his complexion, a hint of yellowness showing on the sides of his patrician nose and full-lipped mouth. She wondered if he could be trusted, then accepted the truth of her situation: She couldn't rely on anyone but herself.

The other two young men were dressed much the same as Ban in official Coalition uniforms: black and silver jump suits with thigh-high boots that gleamed like polished onyx. Apparently they were not important enough to merit introductions.

"I deeply apologize for rushing you to an interview without time to refresh yourself," Ban said, "but Chief Ngate is most eager to confer with you."

"That's fine." Phoenix glanced over at Case, wondering again if his thunderous expression was solely her fault. He looked like a man about to lose his temper, and she was having a hard time reconciling Officer Remo with her memories of the amusing, outgoing youth she'd once loved.

"This way," Ban said, offering his arm in a courtly way she couldn't refuse.

He used his identity card to open a door, a means of entry that confirmed Case's assessment of the ship's security system. It was adequate on a vessel designed for the gracious hospitality that went with diplomatic missions, but wholly inadequate against a clever thief.

The room dazzled her. Faux windows had painted scenes of lush vegetation behind the glass panes, and the ceiling and wall motif was one continuous mural of sky and garden. The furnishings belonged in a country gazebo: ornate white reed benches and tables with flowered cushions on the seats.

"Sir, may I present Citizen Phoenix Landau," Ban said, formally introducing her to a handsome man with a sweeping mane of silver hair and steely-gray eyes. He wore a blue and silver version of the Coalition uniform, but it was exquisitely tailored to enhance his robust physique.

"I'm deeply pleased to meet you," he said, stepping forward and grasping both her hands in his, a gesture of cordiality seldom used at a first meeting.

He dismissed the two young officers and his recorder with an impatient flick of his hand, and greeted Case with a few cordial comments before turning the full intensity of his charm back on Phoenix.

"Please sit and let me serve you," he said, indicating a low table laden with glass trays of delicacies and a frosty pitcher of pale pink liquid.

Star Searcher

He made a ritual of passing a selection of exotic tidbits, many of which Phoenix couldn't identify. They were served on crisp, salty cracker rounds, and after eating one she gladly accepted a glass of the bubbly fruit drink to quench her thirst. Ngate radiated confidence and vitality, making it hard to remember this was no social get-together. She had to remind herself to keep her guard up.

"My dear Phoenix—if I may call you that . . ."

She couldn't imagine refusing him anything; even Case had lost his scowl in the pleasant surroundings.

"I was acquainted with your father, although not intimately, and I hope you'll accept my sincere condolences. I was saddened to hear of his passing."

She searched his face and measured his words, searching for signs of insincerity but detecting none.

Ngate sat, sipped fruit drink, and popped a small cheesy morsel into his mouth, making her wonder if he was acting as a taster to demonstrate they weren't poisonous. She put a partially consumed cracker with a dark minced substance on the glass plate he'd provided, realizing she was eating only to please him. It wasn't a good beginning to the session she hoped would clear up her misgivings about the mission.

"This room is wonderful—so soothing," she said.

"We try to simulate settings from many planets," he said. "It puts our guests at ease and facilitates the business at hand. I regret there's no time for me to show you the other wonders on our starship. It would be a great pleasure to have you as my guest for an extended period, Phoenix, but I'm sure you understand the urgency of your mission."

"Yes, but I'd like to hear about it from you." She didn't look at Case.

Pam Rock

The chief negotiator told her about the missing Star Stone, adding nothing new to what Case had already told her. In fact, their accounts were so similar, they seemed to be verbatim recitations from an officially approved version of the theft.

"I regret to say the Thal and Zazar delegations have returned to their home planets," Ngate said.

"Why wasn't I told?" Case's voice was guarded, but Phoenix knew him well enough to sense the anger behind his question.

"It's a recent development," Ngate said sharply, dropping for an instant his genial tone. "The Thal dietary needs are impossible, and the gravity adjusters in their staterooms didn't seem to satisfy them either. When they left, the Zazars saw no reason to stay. The whole accord is going to fall apart if war between them breaks out before we can account for the missing half of the Star Stone. I'm counting a great deal on your expertise, my dear." Ngate reached over and patted the back of her hand.

At least he hadn't given her a speech on how vital the treaty was to Coalition interests. She didn't give a rodent's behind about their concerns, and he was wise enough to realize it. Apparently his reputation as a master negotiator was deserved.

"The wormhole will mean a great deal to antiquities trackers like yourself," he said. "Imagine the potential of a pathway to a new galaxy."

The idea of going to a new galaxy did excite her, but she was resolved to retire instead, using her payment for this job to go into a safer, saner line of work. She never again wanted to be at the disposal of a man like Mol'ar Fap—or Orde Ngate.

"Sir, may I speak to you alone?" Phoenix asked.

Star Searcher

She heard Case's sharp intake of air, but this might be her only chance to get rid of him.

"Of course." Ngate repeated the gesture that had sent Nevin Ban scurrying from the room. Case's exit was less hurried, but he did leave, the door shutting automatically behind him.

"Chief Ngate, I beg you to reconsider sending Officer Remo with me. Antiquities trackers and relics dealers will shun me if I bring a Coalition representative with me. He can only hinder my search."

"You don't know what you're up against," he said sternly. "We strongly suspect a xenophobic group on Thal, the Neosouls, of engineering the theft."

"I've heard of them. They slaughtered the first group of Zazars and started all the hostilities between the two planets."

"More than that, they opposed the formation of one central government, effectively keeping Thal out of the Coalition for many years."

"I thought they'd been defeated, all their leaders executed."

"True, but their isolationist ideas didn't die with the leaders. They're growing strong again, supported by fanatics who think the wormhole is a pathway to the place where dead souls live in eternal torment."

"I'd still rather do this on my own. I can call on friends for information and help. I don't need or want Officer Remo with me."

"Perhaps you have the wrong idea about your mission."

Without raising his voice, he spoke in a stern tone that sent shivers down her spine. She'd never been in the presence of such absolute power before.

"Remo will accompany you to serve as my liaison," he said.

"I work alone, Chief Ngate." Her knees were trembling, but she couldn't blindly follow orders the way this Coalition leader expected. "If you want me to go on this mission, I have to be wholly in charge."

He took a sip from his glass, then slowly returned it to the table.

"You have a contract, Citizen Landau. Failure to fulfill it will be considered an act of treason against the Galactic Coalition, punishable by up to fifty years of penal servitude."

She looked into his eyes, frightened by the single-minded intensity of his gaze. He wasn't making idle threats. He meant to prosecute if she tried to break the contract.

"You leave me no choice," she said.

"Splendid." His voice was soft and pleasant again, but his polished mannerisms no longer seemed charming. "I've had a copy of the case file made to take with you. The *Seker* will be serviced and ready to leave for Thal in the morning. You have forty days to complete your mission."

"Forty days! The Star Stone could be anywhere in the galaxy."

"We believe it's still in the Qeb or Bes systems. The *GCS Seker* has the latest hyperdrive, so travel time will be minimal."

"Contract or no contract, you're asking the impossible."

"I'm not an unreasonable man." He smiled without real warmth. "I'll allow an extra twenty days, but when the sixty-day period is over, you must tell me the whereabouts of the Star Stone or forfeit your passage to Horus. Your fee, of course, has already been paid to your account and will be yours to keep for your time."

She knew it was futile to argue with him, but the money meant nothing if she couldn't get access to Horus. Mol'ar Fap was too rich to be bought off; her stepsister and nieces would die—perhaps horribly—if she failed to find the blood-red relic.

"You will dine at my table this evening," he said, once again the urbane host. "I think suitable garments have been made available in your quarters. An orderly will confer with you on additional personal items for the mission. May I say what a great pleasure it's been to meet a famous antiquities tracker."

Her face was stiff from the shock of his threat: penal servitude if she didn't live up to the terms of the contract, and that included taking Case with her. The years of the sentence hardly mattered: No one ever survived long enough to be released from one of the grueling labor camps for political prisoners. She tried to return his smile, if only to show she wasn't terrified by the scope of his power, but all she managed was a weak grimace.

In the luxurious stateroom assigned to her, she bathed, then stretched out on the bed, trying to prepare her mind for the ordeal to come. She wanted to fling Ngate's dinner invitation in his face, but there was nothing to gain by antagonizing him.

Relaxing was impossible; she paced the carpeted room and tried to put herself in the place of a thief who'd stolen a relic so precious and famous it would be virtually impossible to sell it. For once her imagination failed her. For all she knew, some political or religious fanatic might have jettisoned it into space, never to be retrieved.

She was tempted to tell Ngate that her step-sister's life depended on her reaching Horus, but in her heart she knew it wouldn't change anything. The chief negotiator didn't care about her personal concerns. All he wanted was the return of the Star Stone.

An orderly came to her quarters, as Ngate had promised, and conferred at length about supplies for the mission. Then it was time to get ready for dinner. She dressed in the garments provided, her uneasiness increasing when she realized everything was a perfect fit. The ship's data banks must have searched Star Service Academy records, prying into her life to the point of dredging up her old uniform sizes.

She didn't know what to expect at a command ship dinner as she pulled on a teeny pair of black thong panties, the only undergarment provided to wear under a filmy gown that swirled around her ankles and dipped so low in front her nipples just missed being exposed. Silky black feathers from some exotic bird banded the cuffs of the full but transparent sleeves and the hem of the equally transparent skirt. She brushed her shiny dark hair, letting it flow wild and free as a gesture of defiance, however unlikely it was anyone would see protest in her hairstyle, then slipped her feet into exquisitely embroidered black slippers that fit perfectly.

What possible reason did Ngate have for expecting her to dress like a professional pleasure-giver? She was tempted to appear in the serviceable tunic and trousers Case had secured for her, but she wouldn't gain anything if the chief negotiator was offended by the switch. For now, she had to play the game by his rules.

She had no idea where to go for dinner, so when Nevin Ban presented himself at her door, she was more than pleased to let him escort her. Ngate's personal recorder was dressed in a black jacket with wide satin lapels, a silky blue shirt with a ruffled front, black satin trousers, and pumps so shiny they dazzled. His coal-black hair hung over his forehead and cheeks in artful ringlets, and he'd obviously taken great pains to dress for dinner.

Ban was a handsome young man and an amusing conversationalist, but she had a hard time concentrating on his comments as they boarded the lift, then walked down a long gold-carpeted corridor to the diplomatic dining room. She wondered if Case would be there; she wasn't looking forward to his questions about her private conference with Ngate.

There were a few other women among the 50 or so diners, all the females wearing floor-length gowns but none so seductive as Phoenix's. Was Ngate trying to present her as a flamboyant adventuress, or did he really believe she'd be pleased with a transparent dress?

Ban escorted her to one of the small round tables intimately set for four, seating her but standing ramrod straight behind his chair until Chief Negotiator Ngate arrived with a striking blond woman many years his junior.

"My companion, Juleese. My dear, this is the famous antiquities tracker, Phoenix Landau. My sources say she has an extraordinary gift for locating lost treasures—a virtual pyschic connection to ancient valuables."

Juleese nodded with regal indifference, and Phoenix

knew it was going to be a long evening. She glanced around as others were seating themselves and caught Case's eyes. He was sitting on the opposite side of the room wearing an ordinary black and silver uniform, as were the three other officers at his table. The bored indifference on all their faces showed that Ngate's formal dinners were more duty than pleasure.

Phoenix had never expected to see a room like this on a space vessel: thick golden draperies artfully arranged to set off some of the finest paintings she'd ever seen outside a museum, mostly scenes of the historical quest in space and dramatic portraits of the early heroes. Three heavy cut-glass chandeliers hung above the lace-draped tables, although certainly they would be taken down and put into storage on long space runs where there was danger from meteor storms.

The meal was sublime: plump poulets stuffed with nutmeats and spices served on a bed of vegetables in a creamy sauce. Every time she sipped the bubbly clear wine, her goblet was refilled. It was hard to believe such dining existed in the same galaxy with Bast root foods.

Ngate was a riveting host, regaling them with humorous anecdotes and encouraging Phoenix to tell about some of her famous finds. Ban hung on every word she said, so attentive he made her feel like a queen. Juleese glared and pouted, so obviously envious of the attention heaped on Phoenix that her attitude became another source of amusement.

It was a perfect meal and an enchanting evening, but Phoenix couldn't wait for it to end. She felt like an unwilling player in a satirical stage performance. Ngate had arranged this spectacle to impress her, perhaps to soften the impact of the threats he'd used to

Star Searcher

hold her to the contract. He seemed to want her approval and admiration, although they both knew he was only using her. If this was life in the diplomatic service, she didn't know how Case endured being part of it.

When the evening finally concluded, Ban tucked her hand in the crook of his arm to escort her back to her room.

"It's been my great privilege to meet you," he said with a ring of genuine sincerity in his voice. "I hope we'll meet again."

"Perhaps we will," she said, then thanked him for escorting her.

Case watched from the doorway of his own room down the corridor until he saw Ban enter the lift. Ngate had given Phoenix the kind of dinner usually reserved for visitors with high diplomatic status, and that in itself was puzzling. Also, why had he provided her with a gown that made her seductively irresistible? Why allow Ban to fawn over her, flatter her, and do everything but walk on his hands to impress her?

Case didn't like any of it, but he had a more pressing concern: Why did Phoenix have him expelled from the meeting with Ngate?

She opened the door as soon as he buzzed, stepping back with a startled expression.

"I didn't expect to see you until morning," she said.

"Are you expecting other company?"

"No, of course not. Whom could I possibly be expecting? I'm going to bed."

"Secretary Ban seemed smitten," he said sarcastically, stepping into the room without being asked.

"You sound as if it matters to you. Should I be flattered because you're jealous?"

"Part of my job is to watch your back. Nevin Ban can't be trusted."

"Would you consider him more trustworthy if he had the face of a wartdog and the body of a porkus?"

"Save your clever barbs for someone who appreciates them. Ban is dangerous. Only a fool ignores a well-intentioned warning."

"It's your intentions I doubt."

She crossed her arms in a defiant stance, concealing the creamy swell of her breasts under the filmy black fabric, but making it easier to see the black triangle under the skirt. He tried not to look at that skimpy bit of cloth covering her, but one quick glance was enough to stamp the image indelibly on his mind. Why the devil had Ngate paraded her in front of the diplomatic corps dressed like a pleasure girl? He liked his own whores to look like respectable women.

"Doubt if you like," Case said, "but do you remember that rash of petty thefts our third year at the Academy?"

"Vaguely—yes. Didn't the thief's classmates find him out and punish him themselves?"

"One of the cadets was badly beaten for the crimes, but you of all people should know an accusation isn't proof of guilt."

"What are you trying to tell me?"

Her eyes clouded with anger, but he was tired of letting her have the moral high ground. He was tempted to tell her the circumstances of his betrayal, but it was more urgent that she understand what she was up against working for the intrigue-ridden Coalition.

"The cadet who was thrashed lost partial use of his

hand—it was crushed with a rock by his chief accuser, Nevin Ban."

"Ban—how awful! That's a harsh punishment, even for a thief."

"The boy wasn't guilty. He was never arrested by the police. We never found enough proof to denounce Ban, but some of us were sure he was the thief."

"Are you sure this isn't another case of 'guilty until proven innocent'?"

"Decide for yourself. I'm going to my quarters now."

"I'm not surprised you chose the diplomatic service."

"Why?" he asked, but he didn't really want to hear her answer.

"Because whenever you're faced with a confrontation, you excuse yourself. Why did you really come here tonight?"

"To find out why you had me sent away from your meeting with Ngate."

"I asked him to let me go on the mission without you."

"Nothing would please me more!" he said fervently. "But since my orders haven't been changed, you couldn't have persuaded him."

"No, but don't get in my way on this mission, Case. I can't operate with you dogging my every step."

"Can't you?" He raised one eyebrow and stared at her, wondering what unpleasant surprises were in store for him.

"If you interfere, you'll ruin my chance of success," she insisted.

"I'm not coming along to get in your way—only to keep you on track and out of trouble."

"I call the shots on land."

"Yes," he reluctantly agreed, still not wanting to promise something he couldn't guarantee. "Unless you're endangering yourself or the mission."

"And you, of course, will decide that?"

"Don't let your bitterness get in the way of finding the Star Stone," he warned.

"I'm not bitter. Neither of us can change the past. I just don't want you interfering in my business."

"You've made that clear enough." He wanted to help her, but if she persisted in treating him as an enemy, there was nothing more he could say. "We'll be leaving at the sixth hour. Don't be late, or I'll have to repeat the descent sequence. That means a wait of at least two hours to get new departure coordinates cleared."

"Yes, sir, Commander Remo." She stepped around him to open the door. "Just see that you're ready to leave when I get there."

He stalked out, letting her have the last word—for now. When she learned the full extent of his orders from Chief Ngate, he was going to have the battle of his life on his hands.

Much as he needed sleep, he lay wide-eyed for hours, trying to forget the way a slender thong disappeared between her firm, lush buttocks and the front of her dress dipped down and tempted him to caress nipples as dark and sweet as honey from the flowery meadows of Athera.

Chapter Six

Phoenix had never been on Thal. There were no culturally rich ruins to lure an antiquities tracker to the planet, no treasures to make it worthwhile enduring the adverse conditions of a heavy-gravity planet. In the three thousand years since Thals had lived in hive-shaped shelters made of sticks and mud, they'd single-mindedly mastered the mathematics of astronomy and space technology, but joy in the fine arts eluded them. Their architecture was utilitarian: thick-walled square and rectangular buildings that all looked much the same. Decorative arts were neglected as the Thals concentrated on creating everything around them to be massive and strong. She wasn't looking forward to going there now, but Orde Ngate wouldn't be satisfied unless she made an effort to check for leads with the officials involved in the failed negotiations.

She still couldn't believe he'd threatened her with

penal servitude if she didn't fulfill her contract. Whatever happened to asking nicely?

She got to the hangar on time in the morning.

The *GCS Isis* was orbiting just above the planet's atmosphere, so the trip to the surface of Thal was a quick one. Case used manual controls to dock the *Seker*, then waited inside while a crew rolled a long portable tunnel to his ship's hatch.

"Is this the Thal version of red-carpet treatment?" Phoenix asked, staring out at the rubbery gray walkway.

"Hardly. They have a morbid fear of alien germs. We'll have to be decontaminated."

"There hasn't been a space-born plague in centuries!"

"Try to explain that to a Thal health monitor. No—don't! I don't want to be stuck here while you sit out a ten-day quarantine. Whatever you do, cooperate!"

"I know how to deal with officious entry clerks. Will they expect bribes?"

"Absolutely not! They literally won't touch them."

He laughed at some secret joke, but she refused to play into his hands and ask what was so funny.

"Just remember you're supposed to be watching my back," she said dryly.

"Oh, I will. Your back, your front, and your sides."

The tunnel attached itself to the *Seker* with a loud, sucking noise, reminding her of a parasitic worm latching onto its prey; then a recorded voice, harsh and guttural, boomed out: "Proceed through the decontamination walkway."

"Leave everything here but your identity card," Case warned.

"What if we have to stay awhile?"

Star Searcher

He shrugged. "This is a communal society. If we need something, all we have to do is ask."

He opened the hatch and stepped out into an eerie gray tunnel that swayed under his weight.

"Will it hold both of us?"

"Hopefully. Take my hand. It's hard to balance."

"I'll manage." She stepped onto the rubbery floor of the tunnel, bounced once, and fell on her face.

"Are you all right?" He sounded more amused than concerned.

"Oh . . ." She was winded from landing on her stomach but uninjured; it was like falling on a trampoline.

He offered his hand, and she reluctantly let him help her stand.

"Don't worry. The best is yet to come," he said with a grin.

The tunnel led into the drab interior of a concrete building where they were met by a figure in a rubbery yellow suit, heavy boots, and a plastic-fronted helmet that seemed to magnify large, wide-spread eyes.

Apparently the creature's deep guttural command meant something to Case.

"Step up to the red line," he translated. "Remember, if you give them any trouble, they'll slap you in quarantine for ten days of tests."

"I know how to respect the customs of alien planets," she said with irritation. "You don't need to treat me like a rookie."

"Okay, but don't say I didn't warn you."

She couldn't tell whether the helmeted Thal was male or female, but the alien was a head taller than Case and at least twice Phoenix's weight. He or she walked over to the wall, picked up a long pole with a net hanging on the end, and waved it in front of them with another angry-sounding command.

"Put all your clothes and your identity card in there," Case said.

"You're making that up!"

"No, take off everything and drop it all into the net. You'll get it back when it's been sterilized." He was already taking off the black and silver Coalition jacket he was wearing over his flight tunic.

"Don't they believe in separate dressing rooms?" She deposited her jacket, slipped her tunic over her head, and started to take off her chemise. "Don't look."

He laughed and pulled off his boots, gracefully balancing on one foot, then the other.

She could sense the heat of his body, and her nostrils tingled from the scent of soap and toiletries clinging to his skin. It was easy to tell him not to look, but hard to keep her own eyes from straying. She wiggled one foot out of a flight boot and caught a glimpse of his lean, smooth, naked thigh.

The second boot caught on her heel, and she jumped around on one bare foot, trying to wiggle it off. It was wholly unintentional when she saw him step out of his briefs with his back toward her. She couldn't help but see his delightfully rounded backside. She must be lightheaded from the descent to the planet; it was the only explanation for a sudden urge to run her hands over those sleek, muscular buttocks.

She quickly turned her back to him, a little shaken by her unexpected interest in Remo's rear. Any attraction she'd felt for his admittedly exceptional body had died long ago. Inside that manly chest was the heart of a craven betrayer, and she wasn't about to forget it.

Case knew what was coming, but it was some compensation that Phoenix didn't. For once he'd like to

Star Searcher

hear her drop the tough-girl role and squeal like a babe.

"Follow the yellow-clad Thal," he said when they were both naked and shivering in the dank air of the shed.

They had to walk barefooted on damp, slippery cement for what seemed like a kilometer following the monitor through a tunnel where their clothes were dropped through an opening in the wall. At last they came to the decontamination room.

"Keep your eyes and mouth shut," he quickly warned her when the Thal motioned them through a doorway.

It was all he had time to say. A whole squad of yellow-suited giants surrounded them. The first spray of disinfectant hit him squarely in the face. He cringed as icy jets came at him from all directions, stinging like nettles on his bare flesh. Gloved hands lifted his arms to bombard his armpits, and picked up his feet one at a time to shoot blasts at the soles of his feet. They made him stretch, bend, and spread. He lost track of Phoenix and did some squealing himself.

When it was over, the crew stomped off. He was shivering, breathless, and humiliated, and this was his third trip to Thal.

"Damn you!" Phoenix sputtered. "You could have warned me." She was squeezing the pungent-smelling disinfectant out of her long, thoroughly soaked hair.

"Why make you dread it before it happened? They won't even let the chief ambassador visit without going through decontamination."

"I'm afraid to ask what happens next."

"We wait here and air-dry until our clothes are ready."

Pam Rock

"I hate the way I smell!"

"It will fade. In a few days you'll hardly notice it."

"Before we do anything else, I want to find lodgings and take a shower."

"That's not how it's done here." She wasn't going to like this either.

"Thals don't bathe?" She was stomping around, waving her arms to dry faster. He watched with considerable amusement, then felt guilty and turned away. Then looked again.

"Yes—in community baths. Big pools of hot water with the whole neighborhood joining in."

"No private tubs or showers?"

"Privacy is a concept they don't seem to understand."

"Oh . . . Oh . . ."

"That says it all," he said, being careful not to smile.

When Case said he'd watch her back, she hadn't expected to show him quite so much of it. It was pointless to tell him not to look at her. They were both naked, shivering, and pink-skinned from the caustic spray. She wandered to the far side of the room, but couldn't bring herself to sit on a cold concrete bench. When he followed and put his arm around her shoulders, she allowed him to comfort her, trying not to notice the effect her nudity was having on him.

"Ugga bosta zas-zas foosta fis-fis," one of the yellow-suited Thals said—or something close to that, she thought.

"This is supposed to be a civilized planet. Doesn't anyone speak Instell?" she asked Case.

"Only public officials and a handful of the better educated. Most feel it's beneath them to learn it. He said our clothes are ready."

They followed the Thal to another room where an unsuited, heavy-boned female in a pale green dress handed them two neat piles reeking of something that smelled like ammonia. She had coarse features and a prominent brow, but her widely spaced, large, violet-blue eyes were oddly beautiful.

"Dress," she ordered, and Phoenix managed a weak smile to acknowledge the trouble she'd taken to learn the command in Instell.

"Now we need a travel pass," he said wearily as they walked away from the cluster of dockside buildings.

"Any more rituals?" she asked suspiciously.

"No, applying for a pass is a simple formality. The Thals are big on formalities. We can walk to the visitors' building from here."

"I bet there's no line waiting to get passes," she said.

"This isn't exactly a tourists' paradise."

There were two kinds of surfaces between them and the squat, gray block buildings of the capitol city of Duonn: muddy flagstones and muddy mud. They walked on the stones, but couldn't avoid the insidious mud that stuck to the soles of their boots.

"They cleaned us up to send us out in the mud," she complained.

"Everything on Thal is sacred, even dirt. It's our alien microorganisms they don't want polluting their planet. Whatever you do, try not to sneeze or cough. I wasn't kidding about the ten-day quarantine."

As they followed the flagstone path toward the visitors' building, Phoenix heard a scuffing sound. She started to turn, not comfortable having any Thal behind her, but she was caught off guard for the second time that day.

She shrieked once as something thick and dark was thrust over her head. Frantically tugging at the coarse fabric of what seemed to be a bag, she heard sounds of a struggle, then an ominous "oof." Case had been subdued too, but not without a fight.

Big hard hands grabbed her arms and forced them behind her back, tying her wrists together with quick, punishing jerks.

"You people have strange ways of welcoming visitors," she cried out through the muffling thickness of the hood. "I'm not going to recommend this place to my friends."

If her captors understood, they definitely didn't have a sense of humor. She was half-pushed, half-dragged a short distance, then lifted and deposited on a narrow seat with no regard for her hands tied behind her back.

"Case?"

"Here." He sounded groggy.

"Are you all right?" It was a silly question; of course, he wasn't!

"Socked me on the jaw. Not broken. I'm just a little dizzy."

She heard guttural spurts of conversation coming from in front of them, then felt the bumpy movement of a land vehicle.

"Where are you taking us? We represent Chief Negotiator Orde Ngate of the Galactic Coalition," she called out through the stifling sack, feeling silly as well as scared. What were the odds these guys would tremble in their boots at the mention of anyone from the Coalition?

"To close please mouth," a deep-throated voice said, hesitating over the Instell words but definitely getting his message across.

Whatever the vehicle was, it didn't seem to have springs. At first it stopped at short intervals, probably traveling through the city near the docking facility, grinding gears every time it moved forward. The seat was smooth, possibly covered with some kind of hide, but no softer than concrete. Underfoot the floor seemed to be metal with no rubber matting or carpeting. The soles of her boots grated on mud that had dried into gritty deposits. Without hands or eyes, there wasn't much else she could learn, but at least the interior was warm, dehumidified to be more comfortable than the cold, damp atmosphere outside.

The Thals were big-boned and ponderous, chunky giants by Atheran standards, because of the heavy gravity on the planet. She assumed their vehicles had to have big wheels, heavy axles, and sturdy frames to support their weight, but they certainly weren't designed for comfort. She squirmed and wiggled, battered by the unrelenting bounce of the vehicle, and her arms ached from being tied behind her.

"Are you all right?" she risked whispering to Case when they began moving faster, hoping the noisy motor would drown out her words.

They hit a rut, and she was thrown against his shoulder. He grunted, but she didn't move away. Much as she hated to admit it, there was some comfort in having him trussed up beside her.

He didn't answer, but she could feel what he was doing: edging around so his back was toward her. She did the same until she felt his fingers groping for her wrists. He urgently picked at the knot, but the slippery, ropey material that bound her wrists was tied into an knot that was impossible to loosen without seeing it. She tried to use her sharper nails to loosen his bindings, but only succeeded in painfully breaking one off. Working blindly, they had zero chance of getting loose.

"When we stop . . ." she started to say, but the gruff voice interrupted her.

"Talk no!"

A second Thal said something, but she couldn't make out the words. An especially nasty bump threw her against the door, and all she could do was silently catalog her aches and pains. Her hands hurt so much she wanted to cry, and her imagination raced out of control envisioning horrible tortures that might lie ahead.

What did these bestial thugs hope to accomplish by kidnapping them?

The effort of sitting erect seemed more than she could manage, and she let her head rest against Case.

Case was greatly tempted to fall asleep after Phoenix's soft, rhythmic breathing told him she had, but he forced himself to stay alert, wanting some sense of how far they were being taken. Her head was heavy on his upper arm, but he understood why she was sleeping. The gravity on Thal made Atherans tire quickly, and his eyes kept drooping shut under the stifling hood.

"Why are you abducting us?" he asked the Thals in their language.

He didn't quite understand the harsh answer, but thought it had something to do with an anatomical impossibility.

Star Searcher

Even through the air inside the vehicle was heated, he felt chilled to the bone. He'd never warmed up after the icy dousing, and tied as he was, he couldn't move enough to increase his circulation. At last he succumbed to his own overwhelming weariness and fell asleep.

When he awoke, he was immediately reminded of his captive state. Excruciating pain flowed from his fingertips to his shoulders, nearly making him moan aloud, but he wasn't eager to let the Thals know he was awake. His hood was gone, and so was Phoenix's. Possibly they'd been afraid their prisoners would suffocate in their sleep. Or perhaps it no longer mattered if they saw where they were going.

He closed his eyes and tried not to move, although it was difficult to resist trying to get into a less painful position. While he slept, Phoenix had curled up on her side with her head on his lap, an intimacy he was in no position to appreciate at the moment.

Except for a short, lush growing season, Thal enjoyed very little sun, and today was no exception. They'd arrived under a gray sky that was much darker now, and he suspected it would soon be night. Outside the square, thick-glassed window, he saw forests of squat trees with massive trunks, most of them not much higher than his head since the heavy gravity seemed to stunt everything but the people.

They were traveling in a sort of convoy; he could see two boxy drab-green vehicles ahead of theirs. He tried to observe as much as he could without moving; he didn't want one of the two shaggy-haired brutes in front to toss a sack over his head again.

The driver had the stark-white hands and hair of an albino, not rare on this planet, and the other had pale yellow hair, more like animal than Atheran hair. He guessed both were male, although it was hard to tell unless a female's breasts were swollen from nursing an infant.

It was pitch black outside when Phoenix finally stirred, awaking with a tortured groan. Case made a shushing noise, but the Thal in the passenger seat heard. He turned and grunted something unintelligible, but apparently he thought it was too dark to bother with the hoods.

"My arms . . ." she whimpered as she struggled to sit.

"I know."

"Next time you watch my back, Remo, I hope you do it with your eyes open."

It wasn't much of a wisecrack, but at least it showed she still had some fight in her. She might need it.

Thal's single moon broke through the cloud cover, illuminating the sky enough to show more forest, thicker than before. Their driver was closely following the vehicle ahead, neither using lights on the rutted dirt road.

According to everything Case had learned, law enforcement on Thal was efficient and sometimes brutal, but almost never secretive. It was highly unlikely they were in the hands of some clandestine branch of the domestic police or the military.

"Who are these Thals?" Phoenix whispered, as though she'd read his thoughts.

"Not government officials."

"They don't want to be seen." Her breath was warm and ticklish in his ear.

"Our story is: We're here to buy direnium plutonis for export to our home planet, Tagawa II," he said, angry at himself because they hadn't worked out a plausible cover for an emergency like this.

"Direnium plutonis," she repeated in his ear, her ticklish breath making his ear itch unbearably. "What is it?"

"I made it up!" he hissed in her ear. "Scratch my lobe."

"What?"

Agony made him squirm on the seat. "Your whisper tickles my ear."

He tried to tip his head sideways and scratch it on his shoulder, but it only made a spasm of pain shoot through his back.

"Oh, for goodness sake!" she said aloud, causing one of the Thals to turn his head and grunt again. "Lean closer," she whispered more cautiously.

She tried scratching with her nose, but it was too smooth and delicate.

"Doesn't help," he complained hoarsely

"When do you start taking care of me?"

Her whispered taunt tickled the most of all, but she surprised him by literally taking his ear into her mouth and bedeviling it with her tongue and teeth. She nipped and licked until his whole ear was damp and tingly—but the itching had stopped.

"Thank you—I think," he mumbled, feeling the little tingles all the way to his groin.

"Are you the head buyer or am I?"

He was still so dazed he only managed a strangled "What?"

"The direnium plutonis. Who's in charge of making the decision? You or me?"

She was whispering in his ear again, and he definitely wasn't up to another session of tickle tortures.

Pam Rock

"You're the boss-lady. Try to figure out some logical use for it!"

The caravan was slowing, and their driver yanked the wheel hard to the right, coming to a stop within sight of a long, squat building with a bluish light in one window.

The two Thals got out, each coming to one of the back doors. Case expected to get out; he didn't expect to be bodily lifted, picked up by the shoulders, and slammed down on his feet with ankle-wrenching force.

Apparently Phoenix had suffered in silence as long as she could.

"You moron!" she said to the Thal who removed her from the vehicle in the same way. "What are you trying to accomplish by shattering my knees? I want to see your leader. Take me to the person in charge! Right now!"

Case was afraid she was going to get what she wanted.

They were shoved more roughly than necessary toward a small shed beside the larger building, then pushed inside. One of their guards followed, and Case heard a string of little cries coming from Phoenix. Then the door banged shut ominously.

"Are you all right?"

"That—that zombie took the ropes off. Oh, Case, it hurts—my arms . . . Are you still tied?"

"Yes, but give yourself time to get circulation back before you try to free me."

"No, I'll be all right. Damn!" She banged into a wall as she groped to find him. "What do these people have, a darkness fetish? It smells awful in here. Yuck, even that vile disinfectant wasn't this bad!"

"I think this is a barn or a holding pen. That's an animal smell."

"Wild or domestic?" She bumped into him and started worrying the ropes on his wrist.

"Probably the ones they raise for food. Everyone who went near the pen they set up on the *Isis* complained about the stink."

"Darn! I hope you appreciate this. That's the second nail I've broken trying to untie you."

He didn't let the sarcasm in her voice bother him. Neither of them was having a great time.

The ropes fell away from his wrists, and he tried slowly flexing his fingers. "Thanks, you did well."

The door opened again, letting damp, chill night air flow into the small enclosure.

"Come, please." The speaker had a small light that he used to gesture toward the large building. He also had a virtual mob of Thals behind him, dark, lumbering hulks who surrounded the two of them as they walked. Apparently their kidnappers had recruited all this help to be sure they couldn't get away on the trip to the main building. Or maybe the gang was curious about the prisoners. Thal discouraged aliens from leaving the capital city and visiting the countryside. They claimed small bands of isolationists were still dangerous.

Case and Phoenix were left alone again, this time in a large, dimly lit room with thick dusty-rose carpeting and huge overstuffed chairs in solid greens, blues, and purples.

In spite of the chairs designed for heavy Thal bodies, there was little comfort for them in the room. It was cold and dank, but they did hear a low, anemic hum. Hopefully it was a furnace; there seemed to be some warmer, dryer air coming though a floor register.

"This feels like a place that hasn't been used lately," Phoenix said, reaching the same conclusion he had. "I'm frozen to my marrow."

"Do you want my..." He stopped, realizing his jacket and tunic had the Coalition insignia. "Jacket? And forget the cover story. They'll never buy it. I'll tell them you're just my pilot—that you have nothing to do with the Coalition. Maybe they'll let you go."

"I'll do without your jacket, thanks, and you're assuming it's you they want."

"The Thals have a lot of rituals and traditions, but kidnapping visitors isn't one of them. This has something to do with opposition to the Coalition."

The door opened and a lone Thal entered carrying a heavy metal tray. Case thought of rushing him; it might be their only chance. Then he caught the glint of a stunner and realized the heavy belt around the Thal's waist was a holster. The weapon could be set to stun—or kill. He was willing to risk his own life to escape, but he was responsible for Phoenix, like it or not.

Phoenix followed Case's glance and saw the stunner. She flexed her arms and prepared to help him if he decided to make a fight of it. She was both disappointed and relieved when Case backed up and let the Thal set several dishes on a stout table between two chairs. The Thal left, backing out through the doorway and inclining his head slightly on his thick, short neck.

"Dinner?" She looked at two clear glasses full of a watery white liquid and a shallow dish of blue stalks. "I don't think I can eat any of this."

Star Searcher

"Don't try. It could be drugged."

"I feel drugged already." She listlessly opened a door that proved to be an empty closet.

"It's the heavy gravity. I've trained for it in a simulator, but I still feel like I've been on a three-day binge."

She wandered around the room, pulling out drawers in the tables, patting chair backs, and opening several doors leading off the main room.

"Here's a water closet," she called from the back of the room. "Do you think the water's safe to drink?"

He agreed they should risk it, then took the precaution of disposing of their meal to avoid offending the Thals unnecessarily.

"There's no way out, is there?" she asked.

"No."

"This isn't a bad room until you realize there are no windows."

"The thick glass they have to use is expensive."

"Do you really believe that's why there aren't any windows at all?"

He shook his head. "It might be a comfortable room by Thal standards, but it's as escape-proof as a prison cell."

The door crashed inward, or so it seemed, and a gang of Thals dressed in long, formless gray robes hovered outside it. She had a bad feeling: The hospitality was over. They were going to learn what was in store for them.

Case reached for her hand. This was time for a little human comfort.

They were escorted outside, then inside again, as though the rooms in the building weren't connected in any way. Most of their guards stayed outside, but the two who had driven them led the way down a silent, thickly carpeted corridor to another hospitable room with massive upholstered chairs. Three were occupied.

Their escorts left and closed the door.

"Please sit."

The speaker was elderly, his massive face a map of wrinkles surrounded by a thick white mane. The other two, one possibly female, were younger, with typical pasty-white coloring and manes like straw. All three wore floor-length gray robes, but the elderly Thal's had mystical symbols embroidered with gold thread.

Case sat in one of two chairs facing them, and Phoenix took the other, temporarily silenced by the strangeness of their situation.

"I am Hesmanar, Honorable Guide of the Sacred Order of Neosouls. I humbly thank you for accepting our rude hospitality."

"As if we had . . ."

Case squeezed her hand so hard her eyes watered, but she got the message: Don't talk

"We're most grateful for the opportunity to sit in your presence, Honorable Hesmanar," he said.

"It has come to my attention that our order has been mentioned in the high councils of the Galactic Coalition," the old Thal said.

"It is possible. I'm but a humble courier."

This was a new Case; she wanted to laugh, but visions of sadistic rituals stifled her sense of humor.

"I'm old enough to number my remaining days on one knotted life-thread," Hesmanar said. "This leaves me little time or patience for dissembling. You're here in search of the Star Stone. Neosouls do not glory in material symbols. We do not have it."

Star Searcher

"Can you speak for all in your order, Honorable Guide?" Case asked with grave courtesy, and she was momentarily proud of him.

"We want no part of the Coalition! We would never steal that evil relic and call attention to ourselves," said one of the other Thals.

"Silence!" The old man's voice seemed to echo from a great distance, and the speaker visibly trembled, his great bulk shaking the heavy chair that held him.

"I, and only I, speak for the Neosouls," Hesmanar said. "I am prepared to swear a blood oath that no member of our order has forfeited his eternal soul by purloining that vile relic."

"What about her soul? A woman could have done it?" Phoenix felt she had to ask.

"Our sisters live to please their brothers and their Honorable Guide."

Phoenix didn't think much of his answer, but a withering glance from Case made her decide to fight that battle another day.

"We deeply respect your belief," Case said. "A blood oath will satisfy my superiors."

"Do you agree to drink the sacred elixir that opens the heart to the truth?"

"I do."

"And the woman?"

"I'm not so sure," Phoenix protested.

"She does."

"Let it be done then. Follow me."

"Not a word!" Case warned, falling into step beside her as they followed the old Thal. "If you try to thwart their purpose for bringing us here, you'll become dispensable."

"Give me credit for some sense!"

127

She didn't like anything about this blood-oath business, especially not the sacred-elixir part. She was the one who decided what went into her mouth, and so far on Thal even water from a tap tasted like something concocted as a joke.

She didn't care much for the dark, cavernous room either. She and Case were told to drop to their knees in front of a huge, flat block of stone with the center hollowed out for a fire pit. It was pitch black all around them except for the coals glowing in the pit, and the old man had to be helped up onto the knee-high slab of rock.

All three Thals shed their robes and knelt around the fire pit wearing only thick loincloths and heavy chains with amulets. One was female, with four black nipples but little breast tissue. She held her hand over the fire pit, chanting softly, her pale skin orange where the glowing coals reflected on it.

Phoenix was braced for something bad to happen, but she still gasped when Hesmanar raised a long dagger and cut into the fleshy pad below the female Thal's thumb. Her blood hissed on the hot coals, and Case took Phoenix's hand again, this time gently caressing it.

The dagger came down a second time, and the younger male gave his blood in the same way for the ritual oath. Neither cried out, but only continued the eerie chant.

She was prepared for the third stab—if squeezing her eyes shut could be called that. Just when she thought it was safe to look again, Hesmanar stepped into the fire pit, blood running down his massive leg from a stab wound on his thigh and sizzling on the hot coals.

Star Searcher

The room was suddenly filled with sound, a harsh guttural chanting, and she realized the dark recesses were crowded with followers of the Neosoul leader.

Someone stepped up behind her, roughly grabbing her head so she couldn't twist around to see, and pressed metal to her lips. She tried to keep them together, but a spout was rammed into her mouth and nasty, sour liquid filled it. She gagged on the foreign object, and another rough hand pinched her cheeks together, forcing her to swallow the foul concoction.

Beside her Case made a tortured, gurgling sound. Then both of them were bodily carried from the room and tossed into the back seat of what was probably the kidnap vehicle.

Case didn't know if Phoenix had passed out or fallen asleep as the vehicle retraced the route to a public roadway, but he envied her. She still didn't understand what they'd participated in. When she did, her dreams would be nightmares for a long time to come.

Chapter Seven

"What was that awful stuff they made us swallow?"

It was Phoenix's first question when she woke up on his shoulder in the back seat of the vehicle. Case wasn't eager to speculate about it, but she wasn't an easy person to put off.

"We'll probably never know for sure," he said.

"It was horrible, nasty, vile! My mouth tastes like the inside of a trash compressor."

"We're nearly back to Duonn," he said, trying to change the subject. "I recognized a Technological Center we passed a while back."

"What was that ritual about?" she asked insistently.

"I can explain." The Thal in the passenger seat turned enough for Case to realize this was a new face; under a massively protruding brow, his eyes were hooded slits a hand-span apart.

"You speak Instell!" Phoenix said.

Star Searcher

"Of course. Most of the Neosoul leaders do. You were given uneducated drivers on your trip to meet our Honorable Guide so they could in no way, however inadvertently, reveal the location of our sacred retreat. Perhaps they overstepped their authority and made the trip unnecessarily unpleasant."

"They succeeded in keeping the route a secret," Case said, "and I think you're trying to confuse us by taking a different route back."

"You're very observant," the Thal said with a soft laugh. "I apologize, both for your earlier discomfort and the extra length of this trip, but few outsiders have ever passed through a sacred portal. It's a matter of greatest urgency that you carry back the message: We did not steal the Star Stone."

"We still only have your word," Phoenix said.

"No," Case said, trying to find words to convince her the Neosouls were innocent. "We know they're not guilty of the theft."

"Case, I'm sick! Make them stop!"

She turned ghastly pale in front of his eyes and doubled over on the seat. The driver pulled to the edge of the roadway, but left it to Case to open the unlocked rear door, help her out, and hold her head while she was violently ill.

When she was able, they got back into the vehicle and continued to the capital city. Once there, the driver stopped in front of a public accommodation known to Case.

"A room has been secured for you, Officer Remo. You'll find all that you need. The Brotherhood of the Neosoul has touched your soul: Go in peace."

"And live in eternal light," Case said, shaken because he didn't know why he responded that way.

Pam Rock

Somehow Case got Phoenix to the room without actually carrying her. She was so weak she swayed on her feet, toppling over on a large sleeping pad on the floor as soon as he closed the door behind them.

When Phoenix awoke, Case was sitting on a window seat, staring at the slate gray building across from their lodging place.

"We've already lost two days," he said morosely. "And now we have to present ourselves to Minister Qaart at our earliest convenience."

"Two days? How long did I sleep?"

"Around the clock. There's your presentation robe."

He was wearing a dark green coat that shimmered with a peculiar iridescence and trousers of the same material. A broad black belt of plaited hair held the coat shut. She saw a garment spread out beside her on the pad that served as a bed, but didn't quite believe her eyes. It was made of brown quilted material nearly an inch thick and at least a foot too long for her.

"I can't wear that. What made me so sick?"

"Your doubts."

"My what?"

"You doubted the validity of a blood oath. The Neosoul essence deep within you meted out punishment."

"Case, be straight with me! I've had enough weirdness for one trip." She sniffed, and realized a strange odor was coming from her. "And I still smell like disinfectant!"

"The Neosouls believe it's impossible to doubt the truth after witnessing a blood oath and swallowing the sacred elixir. If you allow an evil doubt to surface, your altered soul punishes you. I can't explain it any better than that. You'll smell better if you take your clothes off. Hurry and change, but put your own clothes in the pockets of the robe."

"Do you really buy all that?" She frowned and fingered the garment beside her. "I can't wear this tent!"

"Minister Qaart's staff sent it over, and this is no time to offend the second most powerful Thal in the government. We have to explain where we've been since the *Seker* docked. I'll wait outside the door while you change."

"Never mind. I'll put the blasted thing on over my clothes. I'll still cold anyway. Can I wash? Clean my teeth?"

He gestured at a curtained alcove. "Use the water closet, but hurry."

She reluctantly joined him in a few minutes.

"Where did you sleep?" she asked, trying to hold up the hem of the robe and keep up with him without tripping.

"You don't want to know."

"You didn't!"

"I was in no position to ask for another room. The Thals don't understand what the big deal is about males and females sharing things like beds. And they treat all aliens as guests. There's never a charge for lodging, which makes it awkward to ask for double accommodations."

"What happens next on our free tour of Drearyville?"

"I hope we'll get to see the other half of the Star Stone. Let me handle it."

"Of course. You're the diplomat. I'm only the person who knows darn well we're wasting precious time here."

"Then you do believe the Neosouls are innocent?"

Her heart hammered in her chest, and she nearly sank to her knees under the weight of the preposterously heavy robe, but the frightening truth was: She did believe it.

"Were we hypnotized? Drugged? Enchanted? Programmed? Case, tell me the truth!"

"We've become believers," he said.

"I don't want to be one!"

"Then do your doubting when I'm not around. Holding your head while you're sick isn't on my duty roster."

"Oh, wow!" She felt hot for the first time since landing on the wretched planet. "Is there anything else I can't doubt without having my stomach turned inside out?"

"No, only that the Neosouls stole the Star Stone."

A black vehicle less clunky than most in the capital city of Duonn pulled up to the walkway outside their lodgings and came to a stop beside them.

"Have you ever been to Zazar?" she asked.

"No."

She smiled but didn't bother to mention there might be a few surprises for him on that very different world.

"Any chance of some edible food?" she whispered as the driver got out and walked over to them.

"Possibly."

The Thal driver was dressed in a rusty-brown uniform, and his pale blond mane was pulled away from his head and secured in back with a leather thong. He didn't seem offended when Case asked to see his identity card.

"Get in the back," Case told her, slipping in beside the driver when she was seated.

He was going to love Zazar where women walked a

Star Searcher

shadow's length behind their mates! And she'd do her best to make sure it was as pleasurable for him there as it was for her on Thal.

Minister Qaart was gigantic, towering over his aides who were tall enough to be intimidating on their own. A great bony ridge protruded over his eyes, and Phoenix could've spread her fingers between his eyes without any danger of obscuring his vision. With virtually no neck and skin as pale as a sea slug's, he was practically a caricature of his own species, but when he spoke, he radiated charm.

"If I can in any way make your stay on Thal more pleasant, you have only to ask," he said in crystal-clear Instell.

She had a list of requests beginning with real food, but Case glared at her with the sternness of a schoolmaster preparing to administer well-deserved pain. She inclined her head and stepped back in her best imitation of a humble female. This was his show; her turn would come on Zazar.

"We're deeply indebted to you for inviting us into your presence," Case said.

She hardly heard the rest of the flowery speeches required by protocol; her stomach was rumbling so loudly, she was almost grateful to the heavy pyramid of padded cloth that muffled the noise. When Case finally got down to business, the minister seemed genuinely surprised that they'd witnessed a blood oath.

"It's unheard of—with outsiders—I'm astonished." He pulled on his rubbery lower lip and was silent for an awkwardly long time. "Of course, the oath is valid only if the head of the order was involved. I've heard the Honorable Guide is elderly and unwell. Maybe some of his followers tried to dupe you."

"Hesmanar cut his thigh and walked across the coals," Case said.

Minister Qaart's face seemed even whiter than before, blanched to an unhealthy dead-white hue by the shock of their news.

"Then it seems your mission here is completed, and I'm spared the potentially explosive task of searching for the missing half of the Star Stone in the Neosoul enclaves."

"You don't seem happy about it," Phoenix said.

"I'm stunned," Qaart admitted. "The Neosouls are vehemently opposed to any contact with outsiders. The Council of Ministers was sure they engineered the theft to scuttle the accord with Zazar. We've been combing the planet, searching for proof, but this is a very large world. It seems we were wrong. . . ."

"You believe in the validity of the blood oath?" Case asked urgently.

"Absolutely. Swearing a false blood oath would condemn all the Neosouls who participated or witnessed it to an eternity of horrendous deaths and torturous rebirths. Or so I've been told," he added quickly. "But I'm remiss in not seeing to your welfare after that harrowing experience. Please, join me for a small repast."

The small repast was a banquet for a few hundred upper-echelon Thals. Phoenix sat on a chair so large her feet didn't touch the floor, the bulky sleeves of the robe folded over to uncover her hands. Case had a seat of honor, it appeared, sharing a head table alone with Qaart.

To Case the banquet was like any other official dinner: overly long and uncomfortably formal. It was awkward trying to explain why they'd made the other guests wait a full day before they'd put in an appearance, especially since Minister Qaart had sternly forbidden him to mention the kidnapping or the blood oath in his obligatory speech of thanks for other Thals in attendance. Case's head ached from the strain of trying to remain politically neutral in what was obviously a hotbed of dissension. Orde Ngate was right about one thing: If they didn't discover who was to blame—and soon—all chance of an accord would be lost. The war party on Thal was gaining strength, and all hell could break out at any time.

At least Phoenix seemed to be enjoying the banquet. Qaart had thoughtfully provided bottled distilled water and imported prepackaged meals like those carried on Coalition vessels. Instead of warming them in a flash cooker, the Thals heated them over pans of hot coals carried to the table. The food on the bottom burnt, leaving a brown layer that stuck to the tray, and the top part was barely thawed, but Phoenix was finishing her third one.

Watching the Thal across from him suck up long, thin strips of raw meat and swallow them without chewing dulled Case's appetite. He barely managed to finish two servings, in spite of his long fast.

Phoenix played the humble female because it gave her an excuse to keep her eyes averted and not see what the Thals were eating. She used two fingers as a scoop, glancing at Case to see how it was done, dipping them in a water bowl beside her plate and wiping them on a small square of linen whenever they got too sticky. It was messy, but she'd never been so hungry.

After the banquet, Case had to greet an interminable line of Thals for what seemed like hours. She stood behind him, so weary the only thing holding her up was the stiff robe. Could an Atheran ever get used to the gravity here?

"Can we leave this bizarre planet now?" she asked when the last Thal had left.

"Quiet!" He put his fingers on her lips, then yanked her along a corridor as drab and utilitarian as the decontamination shed.

She bunched up the robe and ran to keep up, following him down a flight of awkwardly high concrete steps into a labyrinth of basement tunnels.

"Will you tell me where we're going?" She hated this planet even more than Bast. It siphoned off her vitality and left her feeling like a marionette with broken strings.

"To meet Qaart."

"We just left him!"

"Trust me."

"Oh, sure, now there's an idea. All we're doing here is wasting time!"

"We've eliminated the Neosouls, but that's only half of our assignment here."

"Our assignment? I thought I was the one hired to find the Star Stone. You don't need me to play mind games with the Thals."

"You certainly haven't contributed anything so far—but it wasn't my idea to bring you into this."

"Well, Mr. Ambassador, eliminating the Neosouls doesn't put us one step closer to finding the real thief. There's nothing I can do on this wretched planet."

The corridor ended at a heavy plank door, unpainted but dingy from age and dampness. Case opened it with some effort and motioned her into a dimly lit room, the cement block walls discolored with mold.

"Yuck!"

"Take off the robe." He was stripping off his fancy jacket and trousers, revealing his uniform underneath. "Roll it up and follow me."

"This is an initiation, right? Pretty soon a whole bunch of Coalition types are going to jump out and yell, 'Surprise, you're a member of the club now.'"

"Don't be silly. Qaart is taking a big risk smuggling us into the museum. There's a strict policy about never admitting aliens to the national treasure trove."

"This is the way to the museum?"

"Wouldn't you like to see what you're looking for: the identical other half of the gem they still keep here?"

"Of course, but I didn't think you could arrange it." She felt breathless with excitement.

"It's a payoff for not saying anything about the blood oath. For now, Qaart wants it to be his secret."

"Why?" She was trying to make a neat bundle of the ridiculously thick robe.

"Without the Neosouls to blame, the internal fighting will heat up, I guess. Here, down this way."

"How do you know where to go?" The next corridor was even darker and more forbidding."

"Qaart said to follow the blue line."

She looked down and barely managed to make out a narrow strip of well-worn paint, faintly visible under the widely placed light globes.

"When did the two of you do all this arranging?"

"In bits and snatches at the banquet. Very few Thals have mastered Instell as well as Qaart, so we were able to talk without danger of being overheard. These tunnels go under all the government buildings. See, there's a yellow line merging from the left. We stick with the blue."

"If we come to a red one, I'm out of here," she warned, shivering at the thought of another icy dousing with disinfectant. "I can still smell. . . ."

He wheeled around and pushed her against a wall, bending his head and covering her mouth with his. It didn't start out as a kiss; he locked his lips on hers, pressing so hard she couldn't squawk in protest. She tried to push him away, but the robe was an awkward bundle between them, occupying both her hands.

His lips moved against hers, and she tried to say something—a bad mistake. He was kissing her now—hard. His tongue pressed against her teeth until she gasped for breath and let it slip down, down, down.

"Oh!" For one heady moment she was mad at him for stopping—then she was just plain mad.

"What was that about?"

"I head something. It was the quickest way to shut you up. Maybe it was only a subterranean rodent."

"Oh!" Later she'd have a lot to say to this low-life, good-for-nothing, conniving . . . "How big do they get here?"

"I'm a diplomat, not a zoologist. Come on!" He took her arm and hustled her along.

For now she was too agitated to notice whether they were still following the blue line.

"Here they are!" Case's triumphant chortle brought her back to full alertness.

"They're sacks."

She fingered a coarse fabric bag with a drawstring, a vivid reminder of the hood the kidnappers had used. These had a few objects inside: a pair of cloth dolls fashioned to look like Thals in yellow coveralls, a necklace of polished stones, a booklet written in the peculiar block letters that she recognized as the Thal language.

"What on earth..."

"Souvenirs. We're tourists. Naturally we want to visit a few shops. Apparently I'm taking home a globe of Thal and these."

He pulled out a pair of beautifully stitched slippers made of soft-looking, creamy leather. Each was large enough for both his feet with room to spare.

"So we've been shopping...."

"Not making a clandestine visit to the State Museum."

"Okay. My nieces might like the dolls, but how did Qaart know about them?"

"All Thals are xenophobic at heart. The Coalition had to send complete dossiers to get permission for us to come here."

They left the Thal clothing in the same room and followed the blue line through more tunnels until she was ready to drop. At long last, Case rapped on another plank door. Qaart himself opened it.

"There isn't much time before a cleaning crew comes," the giant said. "Fortunately, theft is a rarity here. Guards are posted outside, but there's never been a need to patrol the interior."

Phoenix followed Case and Qaart through the dimly lit museum, not surprised by the absence of guards. There was little worth protecting. The paintings were mostly dark dabs with more historical than artistic value. Heavy undecorated pottery, drab faded wall hangings, and massive carved stones from the prehistoric period were displayed along the wall without any obvious grouping by period or type. No self-respecting antiquities hunter would bother coming to Thal to haul off the lot.

They came to a cordoned-off area, and she could sense the tension in their guide. This was it. He stepped around the ropes and walked up to a hand-activated security lock. Qaart placed his left hand on the scanner and waited until a blue light showed above the entrance.

"Stay close to me," he said.

Phoenix was impressed by the hand scanner and astonished by the security precautions. A simple display case sat in the middle of a stark, windowless, solid concrete room. An extremely fine-wired, hive-shaped barrier protected the case on all sides.

"Don't get too close," Qaart warned. "Touch any of those wires, and you'll die instantly. It takes three sets of coded instructions to deactivate the power—which, by the way, runs under the case too. I know one set; the museum director guards the second with his life; the First Minister is the only one who has the third. If he leaves office, his successor has to reprogram that part of the code."

Case whistled through his teeth, but Phoenix was too mesmerized by the brightly lit object in the case to react. There, resting on white velvet, was half of the fabulous six-pointed Star Stone. The blood-red jewel was more dazzling than any Phoenix had ever seen, its brilliance undimmed by the thick glass of the case and the mesh of protective wiring. The sparkling red depths were so beautiful her chest ached and her eyes filled with tears. Seeing it made everything worthwhile: the kidnapping, the blood oath, Case. . . .

"The fragments behind it are pieces of the original

meteor that transported it to Thal," Qaart said.

"What a sacrifice to give up half of it," she said, awestruck and hardly aware of Case's hand on her shoulder, a reminder not to lean too close.

"Some of us believe," Qaart whispered, as though fearing he might be overheard, "that the meteor came through the wormhole—that the Star Stone didn't originate in our galaxy." He laughed softly as though embarrassed by the idea. "Of course, it's only a theory—the stuff of legends and fantasy. We Thals are a pragmatic race, but some of us are very eager to ensure peace in the region of the wormhole so that exploration is possible. Now that you've seen it . . ."

"Yes, we'll leave now," Case said.

"Just a minute more," Phoenix pleaded. She couldn't take her eyes off the mysterious red depths of the stone.

"I'll show you the way to reach the street without seeming to come from the museum," Qaart said uneasily, clearly eager to see the last of them.

"This is dangerous for Minister Qaart," Case said. "I'm sorry, Phoenix. We have to leave."

"Yes, I understand," She started to leave, but twice she turned around for another glimpse of the beautiful jewel.

Case hurried her back the way they'd come, turning onto a green line that took them to a staircase, then to the street. The sky was a dismal gray, and a cold drizzle blew into their faces, but Phoenix felt like herself for the first time on this planet. Just seeing the Star Stone had renewed her vigor. If she could find the other half and actually hold it in her hand, it would be a miracle. It would mean everything would be all right. She was ready to do anything and everything to find the missing half of the mystical gem.

"So beautiful," she murmured, following Case over gritty flagstones to the docking area.

"You are," Case said so softly she might have imagined hearing it.

Leaving Thal was much less troublesome than entering it. Soon they were on their way to Zazar, both of them lost in their own thoughts.

Chapter Eight

In space, there was no sense of time passing. Phoenix was able to push aside the nagging worry that she'd never be able to learn where the Star Stone was in 60 days.

When they landed on Zazar, she was forced to tally up the wasted days. True, they'd eliminated the Neo-souls as suspects; she still felt queasy when she thought about the blood oath. Also, she'd had an opportunity to see the other half of the fabulous gem, but nothing that had happened on Thal would get her to Horus. After five days on Thal and in space, her family was in as much jeopardy as ever.

She wanted to catapult Mol'ar Fap into space without a ship, but Case was the only handy target for her frustration.

"Are you sure you have enough golbriks?" she asked after he handed over a hefty bribe to an officious but smiling docking clerk passing judgment on the validity of their entry permit.

"Unless you want to dip into your ill-gotten gains, you'll have to trust me," he said dryly.

"I'm earning every golbrik the Coalition paid me just by putting up with you! So far you've kept me from tracking down any real leads."

"We did everything that had to be done on Thal."

"You did."

She tried to think through her strategy while they went through a tedious series of checkpoints, the only object of which was to extract more fees from them. If Case knew how eager she was to check out her private source of information here on Zazar, he'd be even harder to ditch.

The Zazars were small-boned, olive-skinned aliens, most of the males a head shorter than Phoenix. Their smiling faces and gregarious behavior was calculated to lure strangers into underestimating their shrewd minds and voracious lust for commerce. They were warlike when Zazar's commercial interests were threatened, but their rapacious greed was well masked by outwardly sunny dispositions.

Phoenix liked dealing with the wealthy merchants willing to sponsor expeditions—they frequently speculated in antiquities—but she was worldly enough to count her fingers after shaking hands with any of them.

The Star Stone was supposed to be added to the immense storehouse of galactic treasures gathered by the central government on Zazar, but there were fabulously rich merchants who wouldn't have any scruples about adding it to their personal treasure troves in ordinary circumstances. But would any Zazar jeopardize the peace accord with Thal when it might put off exploration of the wormhole indefinitely? She didn't think so, nor did she believe the government wanted to waste resources on warfare when they could be building space vessels capable of exploring another galaxy—with Coalition help.

Every trader on Zazar had a tremendous stake in peaceful exploitation of the wormhole. She was counting on them to be better at ferreting out the thief who was jeopardizing it than the Coalition was. If anyone in the government knew who was responsible, word would leak out. All secrets were for sale on the fiercely competitive planet.

"At least we weren't disinfected," Case said when they finally passed through a maze of iron-pipe fencing into the blazing hot sunlight.

"You can bring all the bacteria you like to Zazar—if you pay entry fees for it," she said, in no mood to be reminded of the humiliating process on Thal.

People were passing them on all sides, including many Zazars in long flowing robes for sun protection but without the goggles or dark lenses essential for most aliens visiting there. The native inhabitants had large supraorbital ridges, built-in sun shields over their eyes, their most distinctive characteristic. A small alien walked past Phoenix when she stopped to adjust her backpack more comfortably. He seemed vaguely familiar, but his face was too pale and flat-browed to belong to a Zazar.

"Do you know him?" she asked Case.

"No. Do you have your oxygen inhaler?"

"I'm fully equipped for Zazar. I know about the low gravity, thin air, and hot pepper plants that raise blisters on tongues like ours. So you're really superfluous."

"I need to check in with the Minister of Alien Affairs," he said, ignoring her barb but taking time to look at the milling crowd. "I may like this planet. Look at the way that woman is walking behind her man: head bowed, face covered. Women know their place here."

Phoenix snorted her disgust. "If you're not too busy reveling in that poor woman's humiliation, can we find rooms? That's plural: rooms," she said.

"We're on our own this time. The lodgings listed in our info-banks were all booked solid."

"Great! Our toes will hang over the ends on Zazar-sized beds."

She'd slept on rocky ground, rope hammocks, and in a hollowed-out log. It was Case, not the prospect of a bed designed for little people, that was making her grumpy.

They hopped onto a darzing, a uniquely Zazaran form of urban rail transport. It was a fast-moving flatbed with widely spaced poles holding up a bright yellow awning. Zazars stood without holding on, somehow swaying and keeping their balance in spite of the rough, bumpy ride. Phoenix managed to grab a pole on the crowded conveyance, hanging on for her life as the darzing sped toward the heart of Abaz, the capital city and commercial hub of the small planet.

The ride was harrowing but short. With firm ground under her feet again, she began to enjoy the teeming, noisy city. They entered the main thoroughfare, nearly blocked by pedestrian traffic. Signs indicated that all motorized vehicles but two-wheeled motoscoots were banned from the center of the city.

Star Searcher

No one could possibly know all the narrow, twisting streets in the ancient quarters of the city, but walking in the commercial district was a sensory adventure with new sights, sounds, and smells everywhere. Zazar had a sophisticated society a millennium before Athera, but the people enjoyed clinging to the old lifestyle even as they expanded their technologically based interstellar trade.

Case took her arm, and she didn't shake it off. She wanted to lose him, but not on a crowded street in the old city—and definitely not before he'd used Coalition golbriks to secure rooms. She might be a rich woman on Athera, but she'd only been able to withdraw a small amount of money on the *Isis*. She suspected Ngate of limiting her funds to make her more dependent on Case.

She knew the city, but it didn't do them any good in searching for a place to stay.

They were trying what seemed like the tenth place when one of the lodging masters explained.

"'Tis Festival of Eham-rah," he said in his own version of Instell. "No beds, sorry, please."

"Do you know where we can get lodging?" Case asked in passable Zazar, which Phoenix had learned when she'd supervised a treasure hunt for a group of Zazaran merchants.

"No lodging. Fine riz-rings," the little man said, taking a tray of nose rings from under the counter. No self-respecting Zazar passed up an opportunity to sell something. "Lady-so must wear riz-ring."

"Many thanks, but I don't require lady-so to wear a riz-ring," Case said, glancing at her with a grin.

"Bad, bad, lady-so." Not discouraged, the Zazar brought out another tray and pushed it at Case. "Lady-so needs whipping, yes?" He picked up a short, wide leather strap and slapped the counter vigorously with it. "Very good for lady-so."

"If she were my lady-so, I would buy," Case said, nodding his head solemnly as he backed toward the curtained exit. "He's an astute judge of character," he teased Phoenix. "What is this Festival of Eham-rah?"

"A big three-day excuse to sell decorations and boham," she said disgustedly.

"What's boham?"

"A drink so potent it makes my eyes water just smelling it."

"Is this a religious festival?"

"Some of the village grammas, the elderly women, still worship nature spirits, but most Zazars are confirmed members of the golbrik cult. Don't tell me Eham-rah isn't in your info-banks?"

"It probably is. I specialized in learning all I could about Thal."

"Figures."

"Be snide if you like, but the Thals were the holdouts on the accord. It was tough getting them to the bargaining table; it will be nearly impossible to get them to talk peace a second time if the Star Stone doesn't show up."

The lodging situation went from grim to hopeless, but at least they weren't going to starve on Zazar. Case bought huge fried cakes filled with a sweet, crunchy filling from a street vendor who pushed a cart with a glass oven that baked them fresh while they waited. They washed them down with bottles of pale pink fruit juice, and Phoenix licked her fingers with gusto, enjoying food for the first time in ages.

"You always did have a yen for sweets," Case reminded her. "You used to smuggle sugared nut bars into your room at the Academy. I expected you to have a fat bottom some day."

"As you can see, you worried for nothing," she said indignantly.

"I wasn't worried. More for me to squeeze."

He was trying to rile her, and he was succeeding. She pressed her lips together, holding her temper by thinking of ways to get rid of him. If she could make him feel like a total idiot in the process, so much the better! Fat bottom, indeed! She'd nearly starved on Thal, and the space rations on the *Seker* were about as appetizing as dust.

On their tramp around the city in search of lodgings, they learned that the festival started at sundown and lasted for three days. No official business could be conducted until after the last big feast was over and all the celebrants had drained a long glass horn of boham. Of course, some of the merrymakers might take a few days to recover from the festivities, one particularly jovial lodging master told them.

"Everybody comes here from the countryside," Phoenix said dejectedly. "Maybe we'd better get on with our business and plan on sleeping on the shuttle, even if it does mean paying all the entry fees and bribes again."

"I thought you were worried about my golbrik supply?" He took off his sun shades in the shadow of a towering stucco building and brushed back his dark blond hair, a gesture she remembered only too well. It angered her to feel a little shiver of longing after all he'd done to betray her trust—and destroy her love.

"I'm all turned around," she said, hating to admit the maze of narrow streets crowded with people, animals, motoscoots, and vendors had confused her sense of direction. "I'll ask a vendor how to get back to the main thoroughfare."

"You're right about getting on with our business," he admitted. "Let's try to find Minister Yasimen's residence."

"Can't you stop playing boy-diplomat? We're not going to find the Star Stone by talking to politicians."

"Maybe not, but he's sure to learn there's a Coalition officer on the planet. If we don't make a courtesy visit, he'll have spies swarming around us."

"I must have missed the course on foot-licking at the Academy," she said, still trying to come up with a plan to dodge him that didn't depend on securing rooms.

"I've had it with tramping the streets," he said.

He stepped in front of a motoscoot, a small motorized cycle with a precarious perch behind the driver for a paying customer. Golbriks passed hands, and Case motioned her to hop on the back.

"He'll take you to the minister's. I'll be along as soon as I can get another motoscoot."

She rode off behind her demonic driver, more worried about life and limb than where she was going. She had to keep her feet from dragging and her rear from sliding off the seat, and the Zazar in front of her seemed committed to hitting every pothole in the ancient brick paving.

There were no traffic lights or stop signs; every intersection was a contest, and her driver seemed determined never to yield the right-of-way. Her only consolation was that Case would be even more uncomfortable than she was on an undersized scooter.

Robes billowing and long hair whipping out from

under his white turban, the driver allowed nothing to slow him. He drove around pedestrians and vendors, hawking everything from pooi punch to icons of revered beasts, and took detours on the planked walkway flanking the road whenever it suited him. Finally he came to a schreeching halt in front of a nondescript wall, well away from the commotion of the busier streets.

She stood and backed away from the bright yellow scooter, wondering why on earth the money-hungry Zazars hadn't come up with more comfortable public transportation. It wasn't because aliens were a novelty on the planet. Visitors from all over the galaxy were drawn to this commercial hub, although she'd yet to see a Thal. No wonder, considering how miserable the pale giants would be baking in the sun on a world designed for bustling little Zazars.

Not surprisingly, Case was right behind her. When a bright yellow commercial motoscoot wasn't available, drivers on private vehicles would usually take a passenger for a price. Everything and everyone was for sale on Zazar; she couldn't allow herself to forget that.

Case tipped her driver more than was necessary considering her horrendous ride, but she didn't care how freely he spent Coalition money. She had the satisfaction of seeing him rub his battered backside, confirming that the undersized motoscoot had given him a miserable trip. He wouldn't be so quick to opt for native transportation next time.

"Can you comb your hair?" he asked, looking at her critically.

She pushed dark, windblown strands away from her face, but refused to dig into her backpack for a comb.

Pam Rock

The Zazars had one of the most repressive societies in the galaxy when it came to women; she'd been able to work with them only because the gender of aliens was considered secondary to their profit-yielding potential. She wasn't going to look pretty to enhance Case's prestige. She wasn't his woman, no matter what any Zazar thought!

An ancient brass knocker was mounted on a door stout enough for a fortress. Case lifted it, visibly startled when it triggered an electronic buzzer.

"The Zazars are masters at combining tradition and technology," she said with a smirk. "Chances are, there's a peephole concealed in the design of the knocker."

"Thank you for sharing your expertise," he said sarcastically. "Let me do the talking with Yasimen."

The door creaked inward before she could answer, and a slight man in ballooning trousers and a tight-fitting white jacket greeted them with the Zazaran equivalent of: "Please state your business."

Case gave a wordy explanation about wanting to present his credentials to the honorable minister, while Phoenix studied the little man. His beard was shaped into a precise point a few inches below his chin, and a thin mustache was barely visible over his upper lip.

Once she'd gotten used to their supraorbital ridges, she'd found a great deal to admire in the physical appearance of the Zazar men. They were invariably slender and fit; their genetic makeup apparently included safeguards against accumulating unnecessary weight. They moved quickly and were light on their feet, and they were trained from birth to keep a pleasant, or at least a bland, expression on their faces.

While Case exchanged pleasantries, she looked beyond him into a spacious entryway with shiny cobalt blue floor tiles and walls hung with silk tapestries. She'd never been in a private Zazar home, nor had she ever seen an unveiled female. Zazars would do business with aliens, but they didn't invite them into their personal dwelling places to chat with their mates.

At last the man, who'd identified himself as the Minister's First Servant, Zahed, stepped aside and let them enter. They followed him through a series of cool, high-ceilinged rooms so lavishly decorated she barely had time to glance at all the tastefully assembled treasures: carpets handwoven in vibrant reds, purples, and blues, ceramic jars as high as her waist, and brass shields from a savage planet in the Gogal system, each one worth a small fortune since the original owners would rather die than part with one. She could spend a year admiring and studying all the trade-war trophies accumulated in this dwelling.

They walked through a courtyard resplendent with brilliant yellow, orange, and red flowers growing in great clay tubs, the effect so stunning it took her breath away.

"The garden is watered by an underground system that monitors the needs of each individual plant," the little man explained, answering the question she hadn't asked.

"You've read my mind," she said. "I can't believe how perfect each bloom is."

If he was surprised that a female was allowed to speak, he covered it well. "I'm an empath, lady-so, sensitive to the moods of others but not privy to thoughts."

She wasn't sure how to react to a real empath. She'd

heard of them existing among the Zazars, but no trader would give away a bargaining advantage by revealing this about himself.

They entered a huge room with white plaster walls that served as a backdrop for as fine a collection of statues as any she'd ever seen in a museum: heroic male nudes carved from dark granite, sprightly females from the mythology of a dozen planets, and graceful representations of the sacred beasts of Zazaran legends. Her senses were reeling, and Yasimen was only marginally wealthy by the standards of this planet.

"Wait, please," the guide said, disappearing before she could see where he'd gone.

"Nice," Case said.

"That's like calling the sun a little bit shiny. How powerful is this minister?"

"He's on the committee that rules Zazar, but he's only fourth or fifth behind the First Minister."

"I know the royal figurehead is virtually powerless."

"He's a twelve-year-old boy, and our info-banks show the legitimate royal family died out centuries ago. The Zazars like the tradition of having a royal family, but they don't let them interfere with their trading empire."

"I thought Thal was your specialty, not Zazar."

She didn't need to be an empath to read his face. Before she could quiz him about his alleged ignorance about Zazar, a gray-bearded, blue-turbaned male walked into the room pushing a wheeled cart of refreshments.

He served them frosty glasses of a pale green fruit drink, and invited them to partake from a huge tray of sweet cakes and tarts elaborately embellished with sugary white flowers and leaves. Phoenix ate a tart filled with caramelized nutmeats, and took another when the man left the room.

"I've never tasted anything this good," she said, deciding she might as well enjoy some treats as compensation for being stuck with the Coalition's wretched mission.

"They're *your* hips," Case said. "I'd rather have your mouth full of sweets than words. Don't volunteer any information to Yasimen. He has data banks, and by now he knows all about your mother's cousin's husband's business."

"My mother never had a cousin!"

"Whatever there is to know, he'll know. Don't help him out by telling him anything about why we're here."

"I've dealt with Zazars before!" She was so irritated she wanted to squash a creamy cake in his smug face. Her turn was coming!

"My sincere apologies for the delay in greeting you! Welcome to my humble abode, Officer Remo and Lady-so Phoenix Landau," the minister said as he entered the room.

Case said all the correct but dull things; she smiled and nodded demurely.

Yasimen was unusually tall for a Zazar; his dark gray eyes were almost level with hers, and Phoenix had the odd sensation he was probing her mind. She didn't need Case's warning to be cautious with any Zazar.

"Our glorious festival of Eham-rah is troubling to you," Yasimen said. "No, no, I'm not an empath like faithful Zahed, but I deeply regret that your mission on Zazar must be delayed. Not even I, appointed to see to the needs of honored visitors, can conduct official business past the twelfth hour on this day, the beginning of the festival." He spoke in flawless Instell.

"It's never the intention of the Coalition to interfere with sacred tradition," Case said.

Phoenix had to keep careful track of her hands and feet; overblown rhetoric always made her fidget.

"Still, I regret that a representative of Orde Ngate must face delays," Yasimen said. "Such is not the intention of our government or this humble servant. I trust your accommodations are satisfactory?"

Phoenix pursed her lips but didn't say what she was thinking: His data banks must have shown they hadn't found lodging.

"Unfortunately, we didn't make arrangements far enough ahead of time," Case said. "We'll return to our ship until the festival is over."

Minister Yasimen couldn't have sounded more distressed if his lady-so had run off with a Lug.

"This can't be!" He pulled on his beard until Phoenix expected him to yank it off. "An officer of the Coalition is an honored guest. It's unthinkable that you languish in your ship! You must stay and enjoy the festivities. Afterward, you must come back here and tell me all you know about the accord with Thal. We're eager to see this matter to a successful conclusion."

Phoenix moved to Case's side and nudged him with her elbow. He couldn't possibly agree to another delay; the last thing they needed was an invitation to a three-day bash.

"The Coalition is steadfast in its determination to bring it about," Case answered him.

"Alas!" The minister was actually wringing his small, slender hands. "The Palace of Welcome is full of representatives from far-flung reaches of our galaxy. I cannot offer you the accommodations an officer of the Coalition deserves. However, there is a place...."

"We really can't trouble you," Phoenix said.

The minister couldn't have looked more startled if one of his statues had spoken.

Case looked embarrassed; he actually blushed as he stammered an apology for the female's brash interruption.

"No matter!" Yasimen wasn't the official greeter of aliens for nothing; he smoothly repeated his offer. "It's a humble place, not convenient to the city, but I will gladly loan you a motoscoot from my own fleet so you can go there."

Case was smiling like a boy about to get a new toy when they were ushered out a different door, this one leading outside to a long low utility building where the First Servant had a sleek white motoscoot waiting for them. He gave Case elaborate directions on how to drive it, and allowed him to practice by taking it around a circular brick path several times.

Unlike the commercial vehicles, this one had a seat with a back rest for the driver and a larger passenger seat with room for their backpacks and a spillproof metal container of spare fuel.

"I thought this was a high-tech society," she grumbled, reluctantly perching behind Case when the Zazar went to open the exit in the back wall of Yasimen's estate.

"Liquid fuel is cost-effective for these little scooters. A single tank will take us a long way. Yasimen only sent a reserve supply as a courtesy."

"You were pretty chummy with him."

"He was on the diplomatic team sent to the *Isis*. He's one of the strongest supporters of the peace accord—not that any of the Zazars seriously oppose it."

Phoenix held the hand-drawn map and shouted directions to Case over the din of the motor. They left the crowded city and followed a hardened dirt road into the countryside.

Zazar had little surface water; even the oceans were small by galactic standards. But it did have deep aqua reserves underground. Wherever a well brought water above the ground, the planet was astonishingly fertile, growing ample food to meet the needs of a large population. But there was little rainfall, and the irrigated fields were green patches surrounded by bleak yellow sand and rocky formations. There were no true mountains near the capital city of Abaz, but they were gradually riding to higher ground, their weight straining the small motoscoot. Case stopped several times to cool the motor and give them relief from sitting on the undersized vehicle.

"According to the map, this is the way," Phoenix said skeptically, wondering if Minister Yasimen was playing games with them, sending them to a barren area for some sinister purpose of his own.

Case took the map from her, and didn't find any fault with the directions she'd been shouting at him.

"Revelers in the city won't keep us awake out here, that's for sure," he said.

"Do you think Yasimen has some ulterior motive for wanting us far from the capital?"

"That's my guess. I think it's business as usual for anyone who spreads around enough golbriks."

"Does Yasimen expect payment?"

"Not from us. He's above petty payoffs. When he

collects a bribe, it probably makes your pay from the Coalition look like pocket money."

"He must have some reason for sending us out here," she insisted.

Dealing with politicians made her feel like a bug caught in a big sticky web. But she was carefully noting the way back to Abaz; the remote location Yasimen recommended could work in her favor.

When they finally pulled up in front of a nondescript wall with the correct identity number, she carefully watched to see where Case put the motoscoot key.

Visitors announced themselves by pulling on a cord, but no sound carried out to them where they stood beside a thick stone wall once painted bright pink but now peeling and faded.

When the door finally swung open, they were greeted by a clone of Yasimen's First Servant, but this man was silent, motioning them to follow him but not looking into their eyes. On Athera she would have called him spooky.

Once inside the wall, they walked through lush gardens with shady nooks and woven reed loungers for guests to enjoy the outdoor setting. The building itself was opulent, a gleaming white stucco palace with shuttered windows, balconies, turrets, and patios. Pastel awnings provided sun shelter over silk hammocks and reclining chairs.

They looked at each other but didn't say anything. Something about the place made their utilitarian trousers and shirts seem much more alien than in Abaz.

The silent servant led them into the large center section of the building, and they both stopped to gape. A huge indoor pool dominated the lobby, with roof-high trees providing shade from the sun that poured in from a skylight high above. Elaborate mosaics were set into the floor around the pool, and it took Phoenix a moment to realize what she was seeing: a panorama of sexual encounters between slender-hipped but highly endowed Zazar males and lush, round-bellied females.

"Oh." It was all she could say, but now she knew the reason for this secret hideaway.

A tiny female in voluminous pink trousers and a transparent jacket rushed up to them like a small bird diving for pollen. Her tiny feet were bare, every toenail polished with a vivid shade of purple, and her hands fluttered like hummingbird wings. She doubled over in a low bow that made Phoenix feel as thick-boned and clunky as a Thal.

"Honorable him-sir, it is my pleasure and delight to welcome you to the house of Kami." She bowed again in front of Case, but gave Phoenix a look that should have been reserved for a seven-headed serpent trailing swamp muck on the spotlessly white tile floor. Apparently women of any species were not welcome guests.

"Minister Yasimen told you we were coming?" Case asked needlessly, knowing he'd sent a message on their behalf.

"Yes, honorable him-sir. All preparations have been made; no delights will be denied you. We can offer you our very best during Eham-rah. It is a time for families, not a time for great pleasure. Honorable Proprietor Kami wishes to greet you now."

A male with long black curls stepped forward and shooed away the female with a sharp clap of his hands, then nodded and led them to a small side room. Phoenix scarcely listened while Case bargained

Star Searcher

with him over the price of their lodgings, a heated exchange in the Zazaran language. This was how all business was done on the planet. There were no set prices; bargaining was the heart of the system.

Case held his own better than she'd expected. He passed up offers to be bathed, shaved, oiled, steamed, massaged, manicured, whipped, purged, and serviced by a trio, a pair, and a single pleasure giver. Honorable Proprietor Kami wasn't pleased; obviously he wasn't used to renting rooms for the sake of a good night's sleep.

Lodging didn't come cheap. Case handed over a ridiculously thick wad of golbriks, while Phoenix idly wondered why the proprietor reminded her of Nevin Ban. Ngate's personal recorder was thin and had eyes nearly as black as the Zazar's, but his sleek black hair and sallow good looks, not to mention his height, made him totally different. Kami motioned them down a dimly lit corridor carpeted in pale blue, and she and Case followed. He opened a carved and gilded door with an identity card, then handed it to Case.

Phoenix was so awestruck by the great circular bed covered with mounds of multicolored silk pillows and the mirror above it, she let the Zazar get away without showing her to her room.

"We have our own fountain," Case said, sounding as impressed as she was. "And wardrobe."

He opened a sliding door to reveal a long rack of garments and, hanging on the wall behind it, an array of pain- and pleasure-giving equipment worthy of the best brothel anywhere in the galaxy—or so Phoenix thought, not wanting to look too closely.

"Where's my room?" she asked with a startled gasp, sliding the door shut with a thud.

"Be reasonable," Case began.

"Then where's your room?"

"Phoenix, you saw how much this costs!"

"One room?"

"The bed is big enough for a dozen Zazars to hold an orgy."

"That makes me really eager to try it out—alone," she said angrily. "Did you know where Yasimen was sending us?"

"I suspected—this is the only place anywhere near Abaz where there are no family feasts planned for the next three days."

She had two choices: ride back to the *Seker* in a huff—with Case still monitoring every move she made—or turn this into an opportunity to get away from him for a while.

The round bed reminded her of Mol'ar Fap's great belly. It also forced her to remember there were probably a hundred poisons that could inflict horrible death in the jars and drawers of his herb shop.

She forced herself to smile.

"We'll just have to make the best of it, won't we, Officer Remo?"

Chapter Nine

There was much more to their den of pleasure than met the eye.

"Be careful what you touch," Case warned, propped up by pillows on a divan beside the fountain as he finished a cup of bittersweet chikow.

Phoenix touched one of the many buttons on a control panel by the door, and the room was illuminated by a soft blue light. Diaphanous curtains at the open windows fluttered gently in the breeze, looking like angels' wings in the muted light.

Encouraged by the pleasing effect, she touched another, and the fragrance of an exotic perfume wafted through the air. A third try brought soft, lilting music into the room.

"Don't say I didn't warn you." Case's voice was a lazy drawl, mellowed by the succulent dinner they'd eaten on trays brought to the room.

This was her first and probably her last stay in a brothel. She was too curious to resist trying again.

The ceiling was suddenly illuminated. What she'd thought was a mirror became a huge screen filled with the images of a male and female writhing in the throes of passion. She'd been right about male Zazars: There was much to admire. Cheeks flushed, she pushed a red button, and everything stopped except Case's mocking laughter.

"This may be old stuff to you," she sputtered.

"It's not, and I'm as curious as you are. Let's see what other delights Kami has provided for the small fortune I paid him."

He stood, barefooted and wearing only a pair of balloon trousers from the closet, and padded over to a doorway hung with strands of brightly colored glass beads. He parted them and let her go ahead of him, still grinning as she circled a sunken tub with jeweled fixtures. Four Thals could bathe together in it, but it was too shallow to be called a pool.

"Out here," Case called from a small balcony entered by way of a frosted-glass door etched with silhouettes of naked water nymphs. Below them, accessible by white metal steps spiraling downward, was a pristine blue pool enclosed on all sides by flowering bushes. The sun was low in a golden-orange sky, and as if they needed more to lure them down to the picture-perfect pool, a huge basket of fruit and bottled beverages sat beside a cushioned divan designed for two occupants with room to spare.

"Do you suppose the costumes for this party include swimsuits?" she asked.

"Check if you feel a need for one," he said. "I'll be by the pool."

Star Searcher

She watched him descend, the trousers designed for a Zazar covering only half of his muscular calves, and for a moment she was paralyzed by regrets for what could have been. When he wasn't playing pompous word games with politicians or trying to whittle away her self-esteem, he was all the man any woman could want—and more.

Shaking her head to break the spell, she forced herself to remember he was also a nuisance, a hindrance on her quest for the Star Stone. She'd never get a lead if she didn't tap into her own sources of information—without a Coalition officer to intimidate them.

A hazy, half-formed plan came into focus, and she hurried to explore the rest of the pleasure den. A lacquered cabinet with scenes of erotic lovemaking painted on two door panels remained to be investigated. She opened one door gingerly, leery of what she might find. The shelves were covered with rubber and metal objects, the uses of which she preferred not to know. The second door revealed exactly what she'd hoped to find: bottles and vials of pharmaceuticals.

"I have you, Remo!" she said, quickly scanning labels.

Some were printed in the crablike Zazaran symbols; others gave careful directions for use in the interstellar language of Instell. She read them quickly in the fading light and found exactly what she wanted: a sedative that would give Case a long night of deep, untroubled sleep—totally oblivious to her departure.

She read the directions carefully: Two of the small yellow tablets would guarantee a full night's sleep. Larger doses were strongly discouraged. She shook out two and stared at them, wondering how to get Case to swallow them. Obviously she had to put him off guard first. She wrapped the tablets in a piece of tissue and went to work.

Her khaki trousers and shirt were about as seductive as a freighter mechanic's coveralls. She quickly stripped down to her panties and plunged into the row of filmy garments in the closet, trying not to imagine what former wearers had done in them.

She couldn't hope to wear anything designed for a diminutive Zazar female, but there was little gender distinction in the clothes provided in this pleasure den. She put on a pair of nearly transparent white trousers that ballooned out along her legs and were elasticized at the waist and ankles. Her arms were too long for the largest jacket, but she found a jeweled vest that buttoned across her midriff, covering her nipples but leaving enough of her breasts exposed to make an impression—one she hoped Case couldn't resist.

This wasn't going to be easy. She'd rather walk across hot coals in a Thal firepit than let Case think he was irresistible, but Fap and Ngate had taken away all her options. She had to do this job—and Case was holding her back.

She tucked the two pills under the elastic at her ankle and located two delicately etched goblets. No doubt one of the bottles in the hospitality basket would serve her purpose.

Case was stretched out in regal comfort, his eyes closed, the sun's last light softening his finely chiseled features and giving the skin on his bare chest a golden glow.

"Are you asleep?" She almost wished he was, but natural slumber wasn't enough to guarantee he wouldn't catch her leaving.

Star Searcher

"I'm not sure," he said sleepily. "Do you want me to be?"

"I couldn't find swimsuits, but I've brought glasses."

"The fruit juice in those bottles is fermented—potent stuff, I'd guess." He glanced at her under hooded lids. "You've gone native."

"There wasn't much that would fit me—and not because I'm hippy!" She bit her tongue, mad at herself for letting her antagonism show.

"I'm sorry for the cracks." He smiled sheepishly. "I just don't like admitting to myself that I let the most beautiful woman I've ever seen get away from me."

"I'm here now." She didn't need to fake a husky whisper; she could hardly get the words out.

"You certainly are. Do you still want to swim? It should be dark soon now that the sun's gone down."

"I thought we'd have a drink."

He stood, slipping out of the trousers and tossing them onto the divan. He wasn't wearing anything under them.

"Swimming nude . . ." She hadn't planned on that.

"We've been decontaminated together—what more do we have to reveal?"

"Go ahead. I'll be right behind you."

She watched him walk to the pool's edge and pause for a moment, giving her time to admire his broad, muscular shoulders and slender waist sloping down to lean hips and the provocative pads of his buttocks. His unabashed nudity did what none of the erotic trappings of the pleasure den could do: It eroded her self-control and made the secret recesses of her body tingle. She felt a stirring, a tightening as unwelcome as it was unsettling. Pretending to seduce him was hard enough without wanting to reach out to him and press her body against his, without wanting to feel his lips moving on hers again after so many years.

Was she strong enough to let him fondle her, stroke her breasts, touch her between her legs? Would she then be able carry out her plan to drug him?

She unbuttoned the vest, so agitated she fumbled with the closures, and dropped it beside his trousers. She couldn't be careless and lose the pills. Stooping, she took out the pills and dropped them into one of the goblets she'd set beside the basket. They only had to swim a short while, and then the sky would be mercifully dark.

When her clothes were off, she stepped to the side of the pool, bending to test the sun-warmed water with her hand. She was surprised by the faint, flowery scent of the droplets that fell from her fingers.

The pool was small; Case had already swum its length several times. Expecting it to be shallow, she sat and slid into the water, surprised when she sank and sank, down unexpected depths to the smoothly tiled bottom where Case was waiting for her.

They rose to the surface hand in hand, their heads breaking though the water at the same moment. In those few seconds, a faint blue light had gone on automatically, illuminating the pool area with artificial moonlight. It softened his features, but revealed the lopsided grin a man wore when desire played havoc with his reasoning powers.

"I meant what I said. You are beautiful," he said.

She expected him to kiss her, but instead he brushed aside the hair streaming over her forehead and ran his fingers lightly over her closed lids.

Star Searcher

"Beautiful." He touched her lips with the tips of his fingers.

She sighed, wondering if he knew how disarming tenderness was in a man.

"I've wanted to do this since I first saw you on Bast."

He touched her lips with his, not kissing, only savoring the gentle tickle of skin against skin.

"Oh . . ."

He had to know what he was doing to her! This had to be more of his cruelty, devastating because he was pretending to be the kindest of lovers.

She couldn't stand it! She dove and touched the bottom again, putting distance between them in a mad scramble not to let him past her defenses. She'd chosen a poor place to evade him. He was the stronger swimmer. After catching her in his arms and pulling her to the surface this time, he backed her against the edge of the pool and kept her captive between his arms.

"Let me go!"

"What did I do to make you scoot away?"

"Nothing!"

"Ah, I offended you by doing nothing! Did you expect me to ravish you?"

"Of course not! Don't be silly!"

"I only want to know if you're trying to seduce me—or torture me."

"You're being melodramatic!"

"Maybe, but a gorgeous naked woman in a tiny perfumed pool would give any man ideas."

"You suggested swimming!"

"When did you start docilely going along with everything I suggest?"

"I was—warm."

"Are you now?" He put his hands on her waist, letting his fingers spread out over her hips.

She was aware of smooth tiles against her back, water lapping at her chin, and his leg sliding between hers. He was holding her up, treading water for both of them, his face so close she could feel the warmth of his breath.

"Tell me the truth," he said.

He cupped his hands on her bottom, squeezing hard enough to make her squirm.

"Let me out of the water!"

"I'll take that as an answer. Whatever game you're playing, you don't like the way it's going now."

He released her and swam away, his arms slicing through the water as though he could put a thousand meters of water between them.

She pulled herself onto the tiled apron, feeling breathless and shaky in a way that had nothing to do with swimming. He'd bested her, and she wasn't even sure how he'd done it.

The spiral stairs tempted her, but she couldn't allow herself the luxury of running away. She had to play out this deception until Case was too sedated to stop her from leaving—on the motoscoot he'd borrowed from Minister Yasimen.

Too wet to dress in the filmy, clinging trousers and silky brocade vest, she went over to the table holding the basket. Working quickly, she pulled out a bottle sealed with a cork and desperately yanked at it to remove it. The cork broke off in her hand, and she felt around in the basket until she located a corkscrew opener. She tried a second bottle, this time opening it easily.

Crumbling the two pills as best she could, she

poured a pale amber liquid over them, and was relieved when they seemed to be dissolving. She held up the goblet and didn't see any trace of the drug. As an afterthought, she filled the second goblet for herself.

She thought Case would never come out, but at last he did, dripping water on the apron as he stared in her direction.

"I'm sorry." Her best chance was to be apologetic. The words sounded sincere in her own ears, mainly because she really did regret the necessity of tricking Case.

He stared, but didn't move closer.

"I didn't intend to be a tease." She tugged on a strand of hair, as though it were long enough to bring forward and cover her erect nipples. "I poured some of that. It smells fruity," she said, gesturing at the table.

Say something! she wanted to shout.

"I'm not angry." He strolled casually to the divan and sat. "Come here."

It was a command. She wanted to resist it, but her feet carried her closer without a conscious decision to obey him.

He reached out, and she put her hand in his, allowing him to pull her down beside him.

"Do you want a drink?" She had to remember why she was doing this.

"Later."

He pushed her backward, then lifted her legs until she was stretched out on her back, close to panicking because she felt the years of anger and bitterness slipping away.

He leaned over until his lips were grazing one nipple, teasing it with his tongue as a genuine moan welled up in her throat.

She was being betrayed by her own body. Her lips parted, and she gasped aloud as he took the weight of her breasts in his hands and gently fondled them until she trembled with pleasure.

She was barely coherent when he straddled her hips and leaned down to cover her face with hot, urgent kisses.

"Do you want this, Phoenix?"

She didn't know how to answer. If she said yes, there was no turning back. Saying no would be lying.

"And this, do you want this?"

He parted her thighs, firmly but gently. She braced herself, but all he did was rest his hand against the moist, hot opening he found there.

"You'll have to say the word. It's your decision, Phoenix."

She didn't want that choice, she couldn't make a decision with his mouth trailing kisses over her face and his hand making her throb in pained ecstasy. She burned to be impaled; she wanted to claw and shriek and forget who they were and why they were together. Before this, her lust had always been an itch to be scratched—or eradicated—as quickly as possible. Now it was possessing her, clouding her mind and inflaming her senses.

She was shaking, quivering, reaching out for his hardness but sick at heart because all she was bringing to this union was deceit and years of angry longing. She wanted to be loved, but part of her still wanted to savage him for the way he'd hurt her.

He covered her mouth with his, penetrating with his tongue and sending shock waves through her when he intruded between her thighs. He was touching himself and her, and she didn't know how she could endure another moment of anticipation.

He rose above her, his breath ragged, but his words still controlled.

"Don't let this happen unless you're ready to forgive me."

"I . . ." He couldn't have said anything more devastating. "I need to think." Her throat was so constricted she could barely speak. "I'm so thirsty . . . need a drink."

"Do you?" he asked dryly, pulling his hand away and rising from the divan.

Her insides were quivering like jelly; she didn't think she'd ever lose the aching need to have him fill her.

"Just dry . . ." She pretended to cough. "A sip . . ."

He let her walk past him to the table where she'd left the two filled goblets. She took a deep gulp from the safe one, coughing in earnest as the surprisingly fiery liquid burned her throat.

"Is it thirst-quenching?" he asked.

"Oh, yes, delicious." Compared to what she'd nearly done, this was a small deception.

"Are you going to give me some?"

"If you like."

Was he suspicious? She used every ounce of self-control she had not to seem eager to give him the other goblet.

"You poured one for me, didn't you?" he asked.

"I thought—after your swim."

"Not after sex?"

"I didn't plan. . . ."

"Didn't you?"

He sounded angry in the worst possible way: internalizing it, storing up the pain to bring it out when it could do the most damage. She knew; she'd done just that for years. It was a sure formula for misery, but she couldn't summon up any elation. Revenge wasn't supposed to hurt this much.

"Oh, let's do it, if you want to," she said, realizing how badly she wanted to feel him inside her.

"Let's do it? It? I'm not one of the services provided with the room."

"I never suggested you were!"

She picked up his goblet, torn between throwing it in his face and letting him drain it to the last drugged drop.

"Here." She thrust it into his hand.

"No toast? Not even a half-hearted 'cheers' as we prepare to go to our separate beds?"

"There's only one bed."

"I'll sleep here." He lifted the goblet and brought it to his lips.

She closed her eyes and drained hers, a punishment for pretending it was delicious. She couldn't hold back an agonized cough as the fiery liquid burned its way down her gullet.

"Here, take my glass," he ordered, sitting down on the divan as though confused about something.

It was empty.

"You'll need a cover if you sleep out here. The air may get chilly during the night."

"Your concern is touching."

His words were slurred; she'd never dreamed the sleeping drug would work so quickly.

"I'll get a blanket."

She ran up the spiral stairs, forgetting her own shivering nakedness in her haste to see him bedded down for the night. The bed covering was too huge to drag down the steps, but she found a plush robe on a shelf in the closet and raced back with it.

Case was curled on his side on the divan, so quiet she wasn't sure he was still breathing. Her conscience forced her to feel for a sign of life; she could feel a strong pulse beating in his neck, but she still regretted the desperate means she'd taken to get away from him.

"I had to do it," she whispered to his immobile form as she arranged the robe over his bare back and limbs. He seemed almost childlike, lying naked and vulnerable with his hands curled under his chin.

Impulsively, she bent over him one more time, brushing aside the still-damp hair clinging to his forehead. She kissed him softly on the brow, wishing things didn't have to be this way between them.

After gathering the garments she'd worn, she hurried back to the pleasure den and quickly made her preparations. Borrowed clothes would be less conspicuous than her own. She put on the trousers and vest, then added a man's flowing robe and coiled her hair, covering it with a makeshift turban ripped from one of the pillows. A pair of silk embroidered slippers completed her disguise, although it wouldn't fool anyone in bright daylight.

After all she'd done, it seemed only a minor crime to appropriate some golbriks and the key to the motoscoot. It wasn't as if she didn't intend to return when she'd learned all she could from her source on Zazar. Case would be livid—furious. She couldn't imagine what he'd do, but there wasn't time to worry about it now.

She drove back toward Abaz as recklessly as any

native, not sparing the motoscoot or herself. All she had was a name, and a notorious one at that. She had to find Alo, a dealer in slightly "unmarketable" goods. She'd heard of him from a friend, an antiquities dealer from the planet Delamara in the Ka system, who told her Alo would buy anything if there was enough profit involved.

If the Zazars had sabotaged the peace talks by stealing the Star Stone, Alo would know. He'd also know if an alien had brought it to Zazar. Alo was rich enough and powerful enough to buy the information and handle the transaction.

Getting him to tell her about it was the biggest problem. She'd thought long and hard about ways to make him admit the truth. If necessary, she'd pretend to be there on Mol'ar Fap's behalf. He seemed to inspire terror in the far-flung reaches of the galaxy. If only she'd known that before she accepted passage to Bast to talk a deal with him! Until she met Fap, she really hadn't had any underworld dealings, no matter what Case thought.

The festivities were in full force in the city. She could see a brightly colored display of pyrotechnics flashing across the sky long before she reached the outskirts.

The inner city was packed when she got there, and the motoscoot became a nuisance. She had to push it through throngs of merrymakers, so when she found a lock-lot, she took advantage of it. After chaining it to one of the long bars, she slipped the claim-key into the small pocket she'd discovered in the vest. Her life was complicated enough without losing a minister's vehicle, and she'd need it to return.

She didn't dare hope she could do her business and

be back before Case woke up, but he should still be oblivious to her flight. It would be easier to face his fury than lose her ride off Zazar. She was banking on his sense of duty, hoping not to be abandoned there. He wouldn't like reporting he'd botched his assignment to watch her.

The few females she saw were alien visitors or fallen women, poor creatures who would have been publicly chastised if they'd appeared on the streets at any other time.

Apparently all the rules were relaxed during Ehamrah. She hoped her male disguise would hold up, but if it didn't, this was still a good time to be involved in clandestine business.

Alo wasn't a person who would let his location be shown in a public data bank, but she tried anyway, depositing a golbrik for the privilege of making a search on one of the machines in front of a foreign currency exchange.

As she suspected, Alo lived an anonymous life, but she did have one good clue to his whereabouts. Her friend had told her he owned a legitimate business in Abaz as a front for his other activities. It was an establishment in the Bolar quarter, a sort of red-light district where anything and everything was for sale. She had the impression it was a cantina or public house, outwardly respectable and named after one of the revered Zazaran beasts whose statues she'd seen at Minister Yasimen's.

To her dismay, she found no less than seven establishments in the Bolar quarter that could be his. She pressed her forehead against the cold metal casing of the data bank and tried to think back to a casual conversation several years ago that was now crucial to the safety of her family.

"Beest, beest, beest," she repeated, trying to probe her own subconscious for a name stored there.

"Something beest!" she said aloud, elated because she'd mentally narrowed the search down to two establishments: Harbeest Place or the Sign of the Hobeest.

She made a mental note of the numerals beside each name. There were no named streets on Zazar, but every building had a seven-digit number, a code for the location. She called up the city grid on the screen and decided to strike off for the closer place, the Sign of the Hobeest. The two possibilities were widely separated, but both were in the Bolar quarter. The only way to reach either was to fight her way though streets packed solid with Zazars celebrating the festival.

Her height and smooth brow marked her as an alien, but even drunken Zazars were courteous to visitors, not wanting to jeopardize a lucrative transaction in the future. She treaded the streets carefully but not fearfully. She had more to fear from Case than from casual passersby, and he was slumbering like a babe, still unaware of her defection. She didn't waste time looking over her shoulder.

The Bolar quarter was less crowded, but also unsavory. Shabby stucco buildings crowded a street so narrow she had to turn sideways to let a slender Zazar pass. She didn't like the dark alleys that led off from the street, but the dim illumination from widely scattered lamps showed the people lurking in them were either copulating or sleeping.

The Sign of the Hobeest had legible lettering on the

front and a welcoming light over the entrance. She took a deep breath and pushed open the door.

The celebration was in full swing here too. The smoky interior reeked of potent spirits and too much flesh crowded into a small space, but it wasn't quite as seedy as the district around it suggested.

She approached a barkeep behind an ornate, polished bar, noting that the unchipped glassware behind him gleamed like fine crystal. In spite of the setting, some effort had been put forth to make it a classy place.

"Your desire, him-sir?" he asked with the usual Zazaran courtesy but a suspicious gleam in his eyes.

"I've come a great distance," she said with as much self-importance as she could put into her voice.

"This humble establishment welcomes you," he said.

It was a conventional response, but there was something unusual about this Zazar. He wasn't wearing a head covering, and thick coils of blue-black hair hung to his shoulders, but it was his expression that made her uneasy. There was keen intelligence behind his scrutiny, and he looked more like a peacekeeper or guardian of an estate than a dispenser of beverages.

"It's urgent that I speak to the great trader Alo," she said.

"You'll find only less exalted personages here."

She hadn't expected it to be easy, but she had some bait prepared.

"What a shame. I have a rarity that might interest a person of rare good taste and discretion. It would be unfortunate to let my treasure fall into the hands of a crass and unworthy merchant."

"What rarity is that, lady-so?" His eyes narrowed

shrewdly. "You are a female, are you not? My ears are pleasured by your melodious voice."

Now he had an expression she could read. He was examining her chest, looking for the swell of her bosom that Zazars seemed to enjoy as much as men of her own species.

"I have an ancient sword so sharp it will slice through a silk cloth floating down on the blade."

If Alo had one weakness, it was a passion for ancient weapons. If this didn't persuade the barkeep to arrange a meeting, he probably wasn't Alo's employee.

To her surprise, the lithe Zazar leaped over the counter and put his hands on her shoulders, pulling her so close she felt menaced. Forcing herself not to jerk away from the pungent stench of his body, she felt as silly as she did endangered. The man scarcely came to her chin, and he was accosting her within sight of dozens of patrons.

"Do you want to be paid to take me to Alo?" she asked, dumbfounded by his agitated state.

He squeezed her upper arm so hard tears came to her eyes, and she still didn't know whether to scream, fight, or protest verbally.

"Do you have golbriks on your person?" he asked.

She seemed to have said the magic word, but he still didn't release her.

"I have access to many golbriks."

"If you want to see Alo, you must follow me. Not a sound, mind you."

"How much . . ."

"We'll speak of that later."

"Is Alo in this building?"

"Silence!" He dug his fingers into her arm again, making her cry out in pain.

"Take your hands off me," she said. "I'm deeply offended by your touch."

It seemed to be the right thing to say. He dropped his hands to his sides but didn't offer an apology.

"Follow me, lady-so. I will show you the way."

She looked around, wondering if any of the occupants of the room were sober enough to remember this mistreatment if things didn't work out as she hoped.

The loathsome little Zazar made an impatient hissing noise. "Come now or leave this establishment," he said. "I must tend to the needs of the patrons."

She was tempted to swat him when he took her wrist and pulled her toward a narrow staircase to one side of the serving bar.

The building was much larger than she would have guessed from the exterior, and she followed him down twisty hallways and up another flight of steps, this one much more rickety than the first. She didn't like it, but she remembered why she was doing it and tried to push aside the fear slowing her feet. She could take care of herself—she hoped. Her little nieces couldn't, not if Mol'ar Fap made good on his threats. Belatedly she wondered if she should have mentioned Fap to the barkeep to establish the kind of clout she was pretending to have.

They entered a corridor so dark she couldn't see two steps ahead. He stepped up to a door and opened it.

"Wait here, please, lady-so."

She balked at walking into the dark interior of the room, but he shoved her from behind, nearly knocking her off her feet.

She was fighting for balance when she heard a heavy thump: He'd barred the door behind her.

Chapter Ten

Phoenix pounded on the door even though she knew it was probably futile. The barkeep wouldn't be swayed by anything she did, and he'd lured her to a deserted part of the building where no one else was likely to hear her.

"'Tis no use," a voice called out to her from the darkness. "You only hurt your hands and my ears."

The voice belonged to a female Zazar, but it was too dark to see her.

"What's happening here? Why is the door locked?" Phoenix asked.

"To keep the merchandise from being diverted." Her laugh was cynical.

"Aliens aren't treated this way on Zazar!"

"Ah, no doubt your data banks tell you that."

"You're locked in too, and you don't sound worried."

"My master sold me, and I'm glad to see no more of

him. He was too quick with the whip, that one."

"There's no slavery on Zazar!" She didn't know whether to feel horrified or foolish for being naive.

The female chortled. In Phoenix's estimation, she had a weird sense of humor, but maybe that was better than self-pity.

"How long have you been here?" Phoenix asked.

"Not long. Don't worry. You'll go out with the next shipment."

"Shipment of what?"

"Pleasure givers! What else?" She sounded highly amused by Phoenix's ignorance.

"I'm an alien! Zazar males aren't interested in me."

"There's no accounting for tastes. Also, many aliens come here. In the flesh trade, you need only youth and beauty."

"And when that goes?"

"Foolish alien! Ask me no more questions!"

The room had narrow slits for windows, and the negligible amount of light coming through them did nothing to reassure Phoenix. Her eyes became accustomed to the darkness, but there was nothing to see, only a boxy room with no exits except the barred door. The female Zazar stayed in the shadows, and hissed when Phoenix came too close.

Every minute seemed like an hour; Phoenix alternately paced and pounded on the door, much to the annoyance of her fellow captive, who roundly cursed her in colorful language of the sort not recorded on the tapes Phoenix had used to learn the language.

By the time Case woke up and found her missing, she could be hidden away in a retreat like the house of Kami or someplace far worse.

She stopped pacing when she heard muffled sounds

through the door. The female Zazar squealed, either from fear or excitement, but over the commotion Phoenix heard a familiar voice. Impossible as it seemed, Case was here.

The bar scraped as it was lifted, and for a moment she thought of cowering in the corner and playing on Case's sympathies. She thought of telling him she'd been abducted, but her saner self knew he wouldn't buy it.

"Phoenix?"

She braced herself to face his wrath. "I'm here."

He ducked his head and entered the room with the barkeep literally groveling at his feet.

"Please, him-sir! Had I but known she belonged to an honorable officer of the Coalition . . . Be merciful, honorable him-sir. I will pay restitution for your trouble. You have only to ask."

Case was wearing his silver and black uniform; he'd come prepared to use his authority as a Coalition officer.

"Ask him if Alo really owns this establishment," she said to Case.

"You heard the question. Answer!" Case lifted the whining barkeep off his feet by the front of his vest and shook him until he whimpered.

"Is so—yes, yes! But this is my own enterprise, to secure pleasure for the weary traveler."

"I don't know whether I should inform the government about your flesh-trading," Case said sternly to barkeep.

"I beg you, honorable him-sir! I have golbriks to pay for your silence. Please, for the sake of my seven babes who will starve if I lose my employment . . ."

"I can forget," Case said sternly, "but you owe me a

debt that can't be paid by golbriks."

The female Zazar laughed, and Case released his hold on the barkeep.

"You're free to go, lady-so," Case said to the other captive.

"Him-sir, I paid a great price for that pleasure giver." The barkeep was so indignant he forgot to play the humble penitent.

"I know slavery is illegal here," Case said.

"Foolish alien!" the little female sputtered at him. "Go and take your woman with you. Do you think I want to ply my trade without a protector? If I must inhabit the streets, I'll be whipped until I'm desirable to no Zazar. Do not meddle in what you don't understand!"

"I'll take my property now," Case said, not trying to conceal his anger.

He grabbed Phoenix's arm, half-dragging and half-carrying her out of the room.

"I have to see Alo, the owner," she protested, shaking free of his grip.

"We've got to get out of here," he said angrily, swatting her rear when she refused to move.

"You're out of line, Remo! I was hired by the Coalition, and I decide what to do in this investigation." She was smarting in more ways than one.

"Out of here!" He grabbed her arm and left her no choice unless she wanted a scene that would reverberate all the way back to the *Isis*.

He was angry enough to throttle her, but he was also reeling from the scare of his life. Her dealings with the wily Zazars were going to get her into a mess he couldn't straighten out by intimidating a barkeep. They were a long way from home on a planet neither of them understood very well, no matter what information they'd absorbed from info-banks or what she'd learned from previous dealings.

Outside he pulled her none too gently down the street to a deserted alley, keeping a hard grip on her wrist while he demanded to know whether she knew the way back to the motoscoot.

"Yes, and I have the claim-key. I'm not incompetent, no matter what you think! You have no right to manhandle me!"

"I have the right to put you under military arrest and subject you to any discipline I deem necessary for the furtherance of Coalition interests. You'd better get legal assistance the next time you sign a contract, ladyso!"

"Don't call me that!"

"I shouldn't! You're no lady!"

He checked the street, then hurriedly walked back the way he'd come when he followed her.

"Why are you here?" she asked angrily.

"Don't you mean, why am I here instead of sleeping off the drug you slipped into my drink?"

"If you saw me . . ."

"I didn't, but I knew you were playing games. The drink you gave me was so nasty-tasting, one sip puckered my mouth. Anyway, your little scheme was doomed to failure if you raided the painted cupboard. All the drugs in it have directions geared to the weight of a Zazar. It would take a double or triple dose to knock me out the way you planned."

"I'll remember that next time," she said bitterly. "But I have to go back and make the barkeep take me to Alo."

"Not now."

Star Searcher

"I can't waste any more time!"

"You don't have any choice." He tightened his grip on her wrist and tried not to think of the way she'd looked beside the pool with droplets of perfumed water trickling off her nipples and a wet silky thatch clinging damply to her groin.

None of the erotic stimulants in Kami's pleasure den could stimulate him the way the mere sight of her naked shoulder or gently rounded thigh did. He didn't know how much longer he could stand living in a state of constant arousal, tortured by his own conscience and the complicated situation that made him her guardian. She wouldn't play seductive games if she knew how close he'd come to calling her bluff and ravishing her until neither of them had the strength left to rise from the divan.

"How did you follow the motoscoot?" she asked.

"Kami, the whoremaster, brought me here in his own vehicle. I'm not going to like explaining that expenditure to a finance officer."

"I never heard—never saw . . ."

"You don't suppose a wealthy man relies on one of those infernal motoscoots, do you? As for seeing us, Kami knows the way to Abaz without the need to use lights."

"This was all for nothing!"

"No, you confirmed what I only suspected: I should keep you chained to me."

"Then why pretend you were sleeping?"

"I needed to know what you'd do on your own." He didn't tell her how his heart had pounded with fear whenever he lost sight of her for an instant.

* * *

The double moons of Zazar were high above them as he drove back to the house of Kami at a breakneck speed that forced Phoenix to cling to him or risk being hurled off her perch. Any other time he might have enjoyed her fingers digging into his shoulders, but he hated losing control of a situation. He was used to the devious maneuvering of politicians, but he was losing his professional objectivity with her. He'd never wanted to be her watchdog, and things were going even worse than he'd expected.

He didn't want to return to the brothel room; all the tasteless erotica cheapened what he felt for Phoenix, but at the same time made it impossible to forget the woes of his recent celibate lifestyle. Unfortunately, the Coalition didn't have a bottomless purse when it came to financing missions, and it was only practical to use the expensive lodgings he'd paid for. Zazars didn't even have a word for refund. The only alternative was returning to the *Seker*, and he didn't want to go back to the ship until he knew what Phoenix was up to.

He breathed a sigh of relief when he closed the door of their room behind them; at least here he wouldn't have to chase after her on one of those hellish motoscoots. He ached from his tailbone to his ankles from the rough ride on the undersized vehicle, and his shoulders were tender where she'd clung to him.

"Sit," he said, indicating a small gilt chair beside a little writing table.

Her face fascinated him. He could read defiance in the tilt of her chin and anger in the depths of her pupils, but she had her emotions under control. She'd pick and choose her battles wisely; she wouldn't squander her wrath when there was nothing to win. This made her either a formidable ally or a dangerous enemy. He still wasn't sure which.

"I apologize for getting rough with you," he began, calling on all his diplomatic skills to dampen the enmity between them. In truth, he thought she deserved the lodging master's strap on her backside for all the trouble she'd put him to.

"I shouldn't have drugged you—or tried to," she said in a sullen tone that told him she regretted her failure, not the attempt.

Her lack of contrition almost made him smile. He was a fool if he thought she could be tamed across his knees—or in his arms.

"I want answers, Phoenix. Like it or not, we're in this together. I don't have the patience to play detective and follow whenever you get a crazy notion to go off on your own."

"Do you want thanks for getting me out of that room? The barkeep wasn't going to sell me to a flesh-peddler—not when I told him . . ."

"Told him what?"

"It doesn't matter. You had your chance to play hero, but I didn't get the information I need. I'd say you came out ahead."

"I came out with you. Right now that's not reward enough for tearing into Abaz with our maniacal host and riding back on that damn motoscoot."

"If you want to learn anything from me, you could try being nice."

"Nice? The way you pretended to be nice to me?"

She had the grace to look uncomfortable, but didn't say anything.

"Was seducing me an essential part of your plan?" he asked angrily, forgetting diplomacy.

He was playing a dangerous game, but couldn't stop

himself. She'd nearly driven him crazy with desire, and he needed to know whether she'd paid a price for her deceit. Beneath the surface contempt, was there a woman who hungered for him, who wanted to be in his arms? It would lessen his pain if he knew she felt genuine physical attraction. He'd long ago given up hope of touching her heart again.

"Trying to seduce you was a bad idea," she admitted.

"One more thing we agree on."

He stared at her, sensing her growing unease, and was determined to take advantage of it.

She was afraid of something. It hit him suddenly and hard, giving him more questions than answers: afraid of what or whom? Did it have anything to do with the way he'd reentered her life, or was that only wishful thinking on his part, unfounded hope that he still had the power to draw an emotional response from her, however negative?

He was on shaky ground, trying to guess her feelings.

"Why did you run off without me?" He breathed easier; he could handle an interrogation about her actions.

"I had a lead to follow. I don't have time to waste sitting around this—this disgusting sex house."

"I don't see where we have much choice. The festival . . ."

"It's only an excuse to stay drunk for three days. You're staying here and doing nothing because you don't want to offend Yasimen or those like him. Working for the Coalition is the perfect job for you. Just follow orders, don't take unnecessary risks . . . You always were good at going along with your superiors."

"If you're through trying to distract me, let's get

back to the question. Why evade me? Aren't we looking for the same thing?"

"Are we? If the Star Stone isn't on Zazar, we've already wasted too much time for nothing."

"Do you think it is? Do you know something you're keeping from me?"

"I know the person to ask."

"Alo?"

"Yes."

"What makes you think he'll tell you anything?"

"I'm sure he won't, if I drag along a Coalition officer."

"So we're back to that."

"You don't really expect to learn anything through a self-serving politician like Yasimen, do you?"

"Tell me about Alo."

He was at the end of his patience, and she seemed to know it.

"He can sell anything—and does. A friend in the antiquities trade—never mind who—told me about him when I was trying to sell some temple treasures."

"From where?"

"That's not important. I found a legal buyer, so the Coalition got a full share of the profits."

"But you were tempted to move it through an illegal channel—and Alo is the biggest crook on Zazar?"

"If you want to put it that way, I don't care!" She stood and paced, as though she had to let off pent-up energy.

"So you were going to march in and find out if he's involved in selling the hottest artifact in the galaxy. Naturally he'd confess if you wiggled your butt and gave him a big happy smile."

"The Coalition hired me for this job. They wasted

their money if you won't let me do it my way."

"I'll let you," he said, too furious to pull his punches, "but you have two choices: Give me your solemn oath not to go off without me again, or I'll have to tie you to me."

"You wouldn't!"

"No?" He banged open the closet door and pushed aside the clothes hanging on the rod. "How about a silk cord? Or maybe a leather thong?" He threw them out on the floor. "There must be twenty things here to keep you in bondage. I like these wrist cuffs."

"You've made your point. I swear I won't try to get away from you again."

"Fine. Give me your visitor's card."

"You can't be serious! Zazaran law says I have to carry it with me. I could be arrested."

"And you wouldn't like a Zazaran prison. According to our info-banks, their zoos are more humane. But why worry? I'll always be right by your side to slip it to you if necessary."

Her eyes promised to get even, but she reached into a vest pocket and handed over her identity card.

"You can have the bed, master," she said.

"Fine." If she expected him to be gallant and refuse, she was trying to manipulate the wrong person.

The huge round bed was almost worth the price of the room. It molded to his form and soothed muscles cramped from riding on undersized vehicles. Any other time he would have slept like a babe, but he could hear Phoenix shifting restlessly on the divan by the indoor fountain. Try as he would, he couldn't erase her image from his mind.

He loved her grace and quickness, the way she

moved without obvious artifice. Her sensual qualities were so much a part of her nature, she didn't need to flaunt them. She'd played seductress with a childlike naivete, as though she really didn't understand what she was doing to him. She thought it was her nudity that put him off guard, but he was affected by dozens of unconscious gestures: the way she ran her tongue over her lower lip when she was agitated; her habit of tucking her hair behind her ears when she was trying to concentrate; her trick of rising up on her toes when she was confronting him, as though sheer willpower could equalize their heights.

If you knew what power you wield, darling Phoenix, he said to himself, you'd be too dangerous for one Coalition officer to handle.

Abaz was a different city under the glare of the early morning sun: peaceful, quiet, and cluttered with debris from the unrestrained merrymaking. Phoenix stepped gingerly over an unconscious Zazaran male, one of many they'd seen sleeping off a night of revelry on the streets. The Sign of the Hobeest was no more welcoming than it had been at night, however, and she pushed open the door with trepidation.

"Let me do the talking," she told Case, ignoring the look on his face that reminded her of the previous night's fiasco.

She'd tried to convince him they'd be less conspicious dressed as Zazars. She was beginning to like the balloon trousers and flowing coat, but Case refused to appear in public in clothes that didn't fit. He looked every inch a Coalition officer in khaki pants and white tunic.

The establishment seemed to be empty except for a

figure curled up on top of the bar like a pile of dirty laundry. Stepping close, Phoenix saw the sleeper had blue-black curls and a distressingly familiar face. It was the barkeep who'd tried to peddle her to flesh traders. In spite of her bravado, she was glad to have Case behind her.

"Barkeep!" She spoke loudly, hoping she wouldn't have to touch him to wake him. She didn't like to handle reptiles, not even the two-legged variety.

"Ah, ah . . ." He rolled off and landed on his feet behind the counter. "How may I serve. . . . Oh, honorable him-sir, I beg your forgiveness yet again. My dreams were troubled by the terrible outrage I perpetrated against you. If only I'd known the female belonged to you . . ."

"I don't think she belongs to anyone," a commanding voice said, its owner making himself visible by stepping out from behind a curtained recess.

Phoenix recognized him as the empath they'd met in Minister Yasimen's home.

Case greeted him by name: "Honorable Zahed."

"Captain Remo, lady-so, what a pleasure to see you again. I didn't expect you to leave the delights of the Kami. I trust you're not trying to conduct any official business. Minister Yasimen would be most disturbed if honored guests did not understand how sacred the Eham-rah is."

"We honor your customs," Case said.

Phoenix agreed in monosyllables, wondering if she could fool a Zazar capable of reading emotions.

"The truth is," she said, "I have a marvelous sword, and I would like to show it to someone with expertise in ancient weapons. It's a small matter of no great importance. I didn't think of it as business, only sharing my pleasure in a treasure."

"Of course, that's perfectly acceptable," Zahed said. "Perhaps the son of my father's brother, the man you know as Alo, would like to feast his eyes on this wonderful relic, but you don't appear to have it with you."

"We left it on the shuttle for security reasons," Case said, unexpectedly helping her.

"If you would like to make the acquaintance of my relative, I would be happy to escort you," Zahed offered.

"We would be most grateful," Phoenix said.

She was nervous following Zahed up familiar stairs and through hallways that were almost as dark by day as by night, but this could be a real break. Case was at her back, a comfort, even though she still thought mentioning Mol'ar Fap's name would give her an edge if she got in trouble again.

She was sure they passed the room where she'd been imprisoned, but Zahed didn't stop. The thought of the female Zazar locked behind the door made her want to help, but she knew a hopeless cause when she saw one.

Yasimen's man led them down a long curving stairwell into a courtyard bright with sunshine, then down an alley to another street.

"My cousin is breaking his fast at that eating establishment," Zahed said, gesturing at a nondescript doorway between a tailor shop and a store selling foodstuffs. "Tell the host that Zahed has sent you to see the honorable Alo, and give my regards to my kinsman. Unfortunately, I have a small errand to perform for Minister Yasimen—one unrelated to official business, of course."

"Of course," Phoenix said dryly, pretty sure he didn't want to be seen with them.

Case thanked the empath profusely enough for both of them, hardly getting the words out of his mouth before Zahed retreated the way he'd come.

Turning and stepping into the street to cross, Case was caught unawares. A motoscoot barreled down the narrow roadway toward him. He dove across to the other side, saved from being hit by his quick reflexes.

Phoenix raced after him, heart pounding in her throat.

"I'm okay," he said, but he looked as pale and shaken as she felt.

"It wasn't an accident," she whispered urgently.

She could tell from the look on his face he was thinking the same thing, but he shook his head, giving her a message he didn't need to verbalize: They couldn't talk here.

"Let's meet this crook Alo," he whispered.

All the tables in the small stucco-walled establishment were occupied, and a bustling little Zazar with a ridge so prominent it nearly hid his eyes tried to turn them away.

"Very sorry, him-sir. No room. Full today."

"Zahed, friend of Minister Yasimen, directed us to ask after his blood kin, Alo," Case said.

She stared at him, wondering where he'd learned to master the stilted, formal phrasing of the upper-class Zazars. If he used it for the purpose of intimidating, it worked. The little Zazar led them through a maze of tables, back to a secluded room where only one patron was seated. A Zazar with a close resemblance to Zahed was dipping pieces of fruit into a cut-glass bowl of raw egg yolk, wiping his fingers on a wet towel after every bite.

He didn't seem in the least surprised to see them.

"Maybe you should guard the door," Phoenix suggested to Case in a low whisper.

Case glared at her; she might as well suggest that a mountain wander across a roadway.

"Please join me, Phoenix Landau," Alo said. "I'm most pleased to meet such an illustrious antiquities tracker. I'm in awe of your great gift for divining the location of treasure troves." He nodded coolly at Case; men like Alo could sniff out a Coalition officer in a dark room.

"I'm surprised you recognized me." She wasn't. He'd probably had her file and a likeness pilfered from the Coalition info-banks before they finished handing out golbriks to docking bureaucrats. It was that kind of planet.

"Your reputation precedes you," Alo told her. "Please sit."

There was only one chair; it was a calculated insult, but Case didn't react to it. He pulled out the chair for her, then took a parade-stance position slightly to her right.

"I apologize for the unfortunate incident with my barkeep. I allow him to run his own small venture on my premises provided it doesn't interfere with my business. He couldn't resist a female as beautiful as you, lady-so, but this in no way excuses him. He will pay a hefty penalty. If you feel that parting with golbriks will not cause him sufficient distress, I will be happy to have him whipped for you."

"That won't be necessary, thank you." She loathed the barkeep, but the offer still made her a little queasy.

She didn't want anyone to bleed on her account.

"I will apprise him of your mercy." Alo smiled, but it didn't bring any warmth to his pinched face. "No doubt you will have his eternal gratitude. May I offer you a repast?"

"Thank you, no. I will presume on your generous nature to ask one question," she said, wondering if she was starting to talk like Case.

"Let there be no deception between us, Phoenix Landau," Alo said, "The sword was, I believe, an invention to pique my interest."

"It was, and I'm humbly sorry for my ruse."

"I suspect it was done with the best of intentions." He glared up at Case. "Is this something for my ears only?"

She wished!

"I can speak in front of my escort," she replied.

Alo frowned, but didn't object. He pushed his food away, her signal to state her business, and leaned back in his chair, looking regal in a tight-fitting purple jacket with silver braid and trousers and turban of a silvery fabric.

"I learned your name from one in my trade. He spoke of you as the greatest of merchant princes," Phoenix said. She racked her brain for flattering things to say about the nasty little Zazar. "I honor your great reputation."

The lie left a bad taste in her mouth, but Alo wasn't giving her any encouragement.

"If anyone can unravel the greatest puzzle in the galaxy, it's you, honorable Alo." Now she was afraid she'd overdone it. He looked as disgusted as she felt.

"I'm privy to all that happens on Zazar," Alo stated. "As you've noted, my blood kin serves a great minister, nor is he my only source of information. But what makes you believe I'll share my knowledge with you?"

She was pretty sure he wouldn't—not unless she played rough. With an uneasy glance at Case, she plunged ahead.

"Your kindness would not escape the attention of the great merchant Mol'ar Fap."

Alo fixed his dark eyes on hers, staring so hard she didn't dare blink. It was a childish game, seeing who would look away first. Her eyes ached from the strain, but at last he looked at Case, then back at her.

"Ask," he said curtly.

"Is the Star Stone on Zazar?"

"You certainly can't believe it was stolen by Zazars," he said angrily. "We have too much to lose if the accord fails."

"Yes, but Zazar also has a host of enemies."

"True, the moronic Thals aren't the only ones who'd like to see us brought low. The Star Stone could have been stolen by an enemy."

"What enemy?" Case asked.

Phoenix glared at him. This was no time to probe for political rumors.

"Another trading race perhaps." Alo's answer was cryptic, but not grudgingly given. "It's possible the thief wants to damage our commerce, and scuttling the peace accord is a sure way to do that. In which case, it might. . . ."

"Be for sale?" Phoenix asked when it seemed he wouldn't say more.

"It hasn't been brought to my attention—and I'm the only one on Zazar who could market such a rarity."

She was amused by the miffed tone of his voice. He

was personally affronted because it hadn't been offered to him.

"If it is on Zazar?" She hardly dared hope for more from him.

"Zazaran gem cutters are inferior to none in the galaxy. If the thief wishes to market it without detection..."

"The only way is to cut it."

"Unfortunately, yes."

Alo seemed genuinely moved by the thought of a great rarity being destroyed—or maybe he was regretting lost profit. Even a clandestine sale of the Star Stone would bring him enough wealth to make up a hundred fortunes.

"It could be cut and scattered to the far reaches of the galaxy by now." She deliberately played on his—and her own—worst fear.

"No, I think not," he said slowly. "I would have heard. If it is on Zazar, one of the great gem cutters is still studying it. One false cut, and it could crumble into worthless fragments. Imagine the fear of failure, the terror of disappointing a ruthless thief. No gem cutter will risk it without exhaustive study."

"So may I tell Mol'ar Fap there's still hope?" she asked.

She heard a furious mutter from Case, but she'd have to worry about his anger later.

"Mol'ar Fap's reach is long, but he'll need a connection on Zazar to expedite the sale if it is here," Alo suggested.

She swallowed and played the staring game again. "Most assuredly, selling the Star Stone demands expertise beyond the powers of ordinary merchants," she said.

"And him?" Alo almost spat in Case's direction.

"Everyone has a price." She hoped Case wouldn't get noble on her and deny it.

"It's not forbidden to travel during the festival of Eham-rah," Alo said.

"It would be pleasant to see more of your wondrous planet," she said.

"Particularly the region to the north of the Wasteral Range where the finest gems on Zazar are found."

"Naturally such a site would attract the finest gem cutters," she said. "I am indebted, Honorable Alo."

"I have a thousand eyes, Phoenix Landau. Should a great rarity be discovered . . ."

"I understand."

Her blood ran cold. Just what she needed: another greedy, barbaric merchant threatening her. At least he hadn't thought of using her family as hostages yet.

Back on the street, she took in great gulps of air, trying to expel the vile atmosphere that surrounded Alo. She had her answer, but it didn't bring her any peace of mind.

"You're playing with fire, mentioning Fap's name," Case said disgustedly.

She agreed, but wouldn't admit it to him.

They reclaimed the motoscoot and drove outside the city, not speaking until they were well away from eavesdroppers. He pulled up in the shadow of a rocky overhang and shared a bottle of water he'd brought from the Kami.

"If you believe Alo, you do need a keeper," he said with disgust.

"He's telling the truth. If the Star Stone is here, he doesn't know where it is."

"Why send you to the gem cutters? Couldn't his

spies do a lot better job of searching for it?"

"Ordinarily, yes, but they've probably come up empty already. I'm his last shot at finding it, if it's here. He thinks I can find it by instinct, the way I find buried artifacts."

"I don't believe anything he said."

"Maybe we should ask him to take a blood oath! Something really conclusive!" She felt a sudden flash of nausea, and decided to drop that subject. "You don't like it because you're not in control of the situation here. I just may have more influence than you do. Alo treated you like a bug he'd like to squash under his heel."

"I doubt he'd want to get his pretty little slippers dirty."

"He has plenty of people to do it for him," she reminded him.

"You found that out last night, didn't you?"

"You had a pretty close call yourself with the motoscoot."

"I don't think getting hit by one of those things would kill me," he said thoughtfully, "but a broken leg or two would put me out of the game and leave you on your own. That's exactly what I don't want to happen."

She didn't either, but she was in no mood to say so.

"I'm afraid to ask what's next on your bizarre agenda," he said.

"Some sightseeing—north of the Wasteral Range."

"The gem cutters?" He made it sound like an excursion to the center of a black hole.

Chapter Eleven

"You can't travel like that!"

Phoenix looked him over so critically he felt an unwarranted flash of guilt.

"You make it sound like I'm parading around naked," he said. He looked down at his tunic and drab khaki trousers, so ordinary he thought they'd be inconspicuous anywhere.

"If I can wear this bizarre outfit, you can too," she replied. "We don't want to be more conspicuous than necessary when we get to the gem cutters' region."

"Easy for you to say. The men's clothes fit you. I feel ridiculous in fancy pants that only go halfway down my leg."

"We'll have to improvise. The way you're dressed, you might as well have COALITION stamped on your forehead."

"A lot of aliens respect the Coalition. It might be an advantage...."

"No, Case." She sounded like a mother correcting an obstinate child. "Believe me, the Coalition isn't a beloved big brother anywhere but in the political bubble where you live."

"The Coalition has helped raise the standard of living and promote political freedom across the galaxy."

"Yes, but wherever the Coalition exerts influence, there's change, something that's always unpopular. If we're going to learn anything, we have to blend in."

"You have a point, but I'm a giant here. What can I do about my height?"

"Not much." She was standing on tiptoes again. "Give me some golbriks."

"You're not going anywhere without me."

"No—you have my card and the key to the motoscoot. I just want to see if Kami has any larger sizes in stock. We can't be the first aliens to be entertained here."

"All right." He reluctantly handed over some of the remaining currency. "But Phoenix, if you try sneaking off, I won't follow. I'll go directly to the ship and leave you stranded here."

"With no visitor's card." Her face paled; she knew how dangerous that would be.

He knew he'd never abandon her; it was enough if she believed he might.

She left the room, and he was so sure she'd return, he ran water into the opulent tub and enjoyed what could be his last hot bath for a long time.

When she finally got back, he was stretched out on the divan, wrapped in a towel from his armpits to his knees, fascinated by the play of sunlight on water cascading over a naked water nymph in their little fountain.

"Try these on," she ordered breathlessly, dropping a bundle of suspiciously transparent cloth into his arms. "I'm going to take a quick bath, then we'll be off."

He watched her rummage in the closet and disappear with an armload of fluff.

"I had to pay a hefty sum," she said from behind strands of beads still tinkling in the doorway to the bath. "But apparently Kami does cater to the occasional alien."

Case felt ridiculous looking over the clothes and called out to tell her so several times, rewarded by bursts of mischievous laughter. Maybe it was worth looking silly to have her amused instead of angry.

She'd managed to procure a pair of the sheer white, balloon-legged trousers in a length that went to his ankles. The long gold and scarlet sash was pretty theatrical, even for Zazar, but he went along with it. A vest trimmed with gold braiding was too tight to consider, but he could wear the open-front white silk coat with symbols embroidered in gold thread. It billowed out behind him with full sleeves to his wrists and a hood he could pull over his head for protection from the sun. Even the flimsy slippers fit, although beaded red velvet wouldn't have been his first choice.

"You look like an ancient pirate—no, a nomad chieftain!" She peeked out between the strands of beads. "When I retire, I'm going to tell my nieces the story of how I rode across the desert of Zazar with a dangerous bandit in fancy footwear. Have you studied the map?"

He picked up a folded square of paper he'd tossed

on the divan with the clothing. "Did you buy this from Kami?" He didn't like the idea of the brothel proprietor knowing where they were going.

"No, I stole it from a rack in his office while he was out getting your duds. With any luck, he won't notice it's gone. Most of his literature is—you know—brothel stuff. I'll dress while you study it."

He caught a glimpse of bare leg through the swaying beads, but forced himself to look at the map. It was annotated in Zazaran, but he could read most of it. By the time he figured out the route, she was ready.

Her trousers were as transparent as his; he could see the outline of her skimpy pink panties, but at least she'd found a less revealing top, one that left her midriff bare but covered her cleavage. When she pulled on a hooded coat similar to the one he was wearing, she was less conspicuous than he'd expected.

Taking their backpacks with them, they quickly departed by way of the spiral stairs to the pool, keeping bushes between them and the pleasure palace as much as possible until they reached the gate. Case suspected they were under constant observation, and this ploy would hardly buy them any lead time if someone wanted to follow. But Phoenix was throwing herself wholeheartedly into this clandestine trip to the gem cutters' region, and there was no reason to dampen her enthusiasm or alarm her unnecessarily.

Outside the wall, she climbed behind him on the wretched motoscoot and wrapped her arms around his middle, her fingers resting on his bare midsection. He tensed under her touch, then roared off, hoping the miserable, jostling ride would help him forget the subtle fragrance of her still-damp hair.

The air was hot, and the landscape arid. The sketchy

map guided them through largely unpopulated areas toward a region called Summa where the gem cutters worked in a village of the same name. The settlement was an oasis in a vast desert surrounded by mountain ranges where the great gemstones of Zazar were found. All Case knew of the place came from the infobanks, but he did remember reports indicating it was an easy place to enter but difficult to leave. Security for the lucrative gem cutting and polishing activities was the tightest on the planet. In fact, the craftsmen probably worked close to the source because it was easy to secure the desolate, sparsely populated region.

If, by some miracle, they did locate the Star Stone, getting it away from Summa would require a large army or incredible cunning. Fortunately for their mission, all they had to do was locate it, report to Ngate, and wait for Coalition forces to provide backup.

The few villages they passed were nearly deserted; a few elders dozed on benches in the shade of sand-colored buildings, but most inhabitants seemed to be away celebrating Eham-rah in the capital city or some other congenial place. The leap to technology had only lightly touched the rural areas, and the road they were following was a wide track of sun-hardened earth.

When they came to the last village shown on the map before Summa, they stopped for an evening meal at a sorry-looking cantina. He didn't bother to look for a lock-bar for the motoscoot. They hadn't seen a soul as they rode down the village's only street.

"Welcome, honorable him-sir," a withered little Zazar said when they walked into his establishment. He averted his eyes so he wouldn't look directly at Phoenix; conservative Zazars were prohibited from speaking to females unrelated to them.

Pam Rock

Phoenix let Case do the talking; she was taking the planet's traditions seriously today, much to his relief.

The best—safest—meal available was a platter of dried fruit with individual bowls of slightly fermented curds, the pungent mainstay of the villagers' diet. They both ate sparingly, but drained two bottles of refreshing pooi punch, one of the best liquids in the galaxy to prevent dehydration. They talked desolately about the curious blend of tradition and technology, but it was mostly tourist talk for the benefit of the proprietor who hovered over them.

It didn't look like a promising place for lodgings, and neither of them were eager to stop yet.

"Your village is very quiet today," Case said.

"Oh, yes, honorable him-sir. All have left for the second feast of Eham-rah. I too will soon depart to join my father's sister's blood kin."

"We won't keep you then," Case said, glad for an excuse to push away the uneaten portion of his curds. He had a diplomat's stomach, unfazed by the most bizarre foods, but sometimes his taste buds rebelled. Phoenix had barely tasted the unappetizing yellowish curds in her bowl.

He did take the precaution of filling the fuel tank to the top and replenishing the reserve supply. If they ran out, they couldn't rely on finding a solar-powered vehicle like the one Kami had used to take him into Abaz.

"Maybe we should've stayed in that village," Phoenix said after they had ridden directly into the blazing orange sun low on the horizon for nearly half an hour. "My eyes burn, and you're the one who's been watching the road."

"We could go back. It looks like quite a distance to

the next oasis. I can't see well enough to make good time."

He stopped so they could stretch their legs and recheck the map, then turned back the way they'd come, irritable because sitting on the motoscoot so long had given him cramped calves and a sore seat.

"I hope this trip isn't a waste of time," he grumbled.

They had to weave their way back around a high hill scoured clean of vegetation by the hot desert winds. Much as he disliked wearing the hood, it was as necessary as the tinted lenses they both wore.

"We probably won't get a room back there now," he complained, ruefully aware it wasn't just the prospect of sleeping out in the desert that soured his disposition. "The proprietor has probably left for his feast."

"Remind me never to take you on a dig," she said. "The Coalition has spoiled you: nothing but soft beds and hot meals."

"I've never been chained to a console. That's why I've liked my job—until recently."

"Blame me if . . ."

She stopped abruptly, shocked by what she saw. Directly ahead a column of black smoke was billowing up.

"The village!" she cried out.

"It looks like the whole place is burning!"

He drove forward, stopping when they were close enough to the gigantic fire to feel the heat. Flames were engulfing every structure in the small village, crackling, hissing, and licking the sky with brilliant orange tongues. His eyes watered, and the stench of the incineration forced them to retreat.

"That poor little proprietor!"

"Maybe he got away," Case said. "He seemed eager

to leave as soon as he could."

"If we'd decided to get a room there . . ."

"Don't even think about it!"

"Could a fire like that start by accident?" She'd asked the question foremost in his own thoughts.

"It could—if a fuel supply exploded."

"All I saw was the one little pump where you refilled our tank."

"An underground tank wouldn't explode by itself."

"Lightning—heat lightning—a cook stove overheating . . ."

He could hear the terror in her voice; she knew the truth as well as he did. Someone had deliberately, maliciously torched every structure in the small desert village.

They stood side by side, watching the flames make blackened shells of the little stucco hovels.

"It doesn't make sense. Could it be a warning to us?" she asked.

"Maybe. Or a warning to anyone who even thinks of giving us information."

He put his arm around her shoulders. She didn't pull away; he wasn't even sure she noticed.

"There's nothing we can do here," he said softly, uneasily surveying the hills that formed a backdrop for the devastated village. The arsonists couldn't be far away. He was almost sure one man couldn't have ignited so many widely spread buildings so quickly.

They hastily mounted the motoscoot.

"Let's get as far away from here as we can," she said.

"I agree." He revved the motor and threw up sand in his haste to reverse their direction.

"Maybe someone doesn't want us going to the gem cutters' region," Phoenix suggested thoughtfully.

Star Searcher

"The next oasis is the first place anyone would look for us," he said. "See if the map shows any watering spots close enough for a detour."

Sharp-eyed and quick, she spotted the symbol of a water source some distance out of their way.

"This is the closest, unless we risk going to the traditional stopping spot."

He looked in all directions, but knew there were many hills and valleys where assailants could hide. He resigned himself to more hard riding.

After a long, tense ride, they spotted a distinctive flat-topped peak where they had to turn off to find the spot marked on the map. They'd lost sight of the last wisps of smoke spiraling upward into the gray twilight sky, but Case wouldn't feel safe until they were well into the trackless foothills.

He drove through a stretch of desert made menacing by the dark shadows of night, not sorry when Phoenix finally slumped forward on his backrest and rested her head on his shoulder. Even though it was his job to protect her, he felt reassured by her arms locked around his torso.

He almost missed the watering spot; they were nearly past it when he saw a glint of moonlight on the high, spiky leaves of a slender desert tree. Slowly approaching, he saw a group of the top-heavy trees clustered around the shimmering surface of a pool.

"We're here," he whispered softly, waking her gently before getting off the motoscoot.

The desert sand was soft and loose around the deserted oasis, and it was hard work pushing the vehicle to the far side where some frilly bushes would hide it from casual scrutiny. So far, he hadn't seen or heard any indication they'd been followed, but he was cautious by nature and deeply concerned for Phoenix's safety. They were virtually defenseless on an alien planet, and he was certain the burning of the village was an ominous message connected to their mission.

When he was satisfied with the way he'd concealed the motoscoot, he went back for Phoenix. She seemed frozen to the spot where they'd stopped.

"We'll try to sleep on the far side of the pool," he whispered.

"It must be horrible to burn to death. The pain—flaming clothes . . ."

"There's a good chance the proprietor got away. His curd was terrible, but he didn't deserve to be cooked. . . ." He tried to reassure her with humor, but it fell flat, as it deserved.

"In the other villages, old people stayed behind."

He put his arm around her, feeling her tremble and knowing how she must hate showing weakness in front of him.

"The village seemed deserted," he insisted so emphatically he almost believed it himself.

"Who could be so ruthless?"

"Phoenix, I have to ask you." He held her tighter, hoping just this one time she'd accept the help he wanted to give. "Why did you mention Mol'ar Fap to Alo?"

"He's a trader and the nastiest alien I know. I thought I had a better chance of getting answers if I pretended to come from him."

Her shoulders still sagged listlessly, but defending her ruse with Alo put some spunk back into her voice.

He led her to the spot he'd chosen on the far side of the midnight-blue pool, carrying both their backpacks in one hand.

"I didn't pack for desert survival," he said, trying to pull her thoughts away from the blazing village and onto practical considerations. "I do have an insulated ground cloth, if you don't mind sharing."

She shivered, and he pulled her closer so they were walking around the pool with their hips and upper bodies touching. It was the only genuine intimacy they'd shared in many years, and it made his heart ache for what could have been.

He picked a spot in the cluster of stately trees. As long as it was dark, they couldn't be seen from the other side of the pool. He wasn't totally satisfied, but it was the safest refuge they were likely to find until they returned to the *Seker*.

He spread the thin silvery ground cloth and used the two backpacks to keep it from blowing away in the soft desert breeze.

"Can you build a fire?" Her voice seemed to come from far away.

"I'd pluck a star from the sky and give it to you on a crystal platter, if it were within my power to do so," he said softly, taking her cold hands in his. "But a fire is too risky if we're being tracked."

"I shouldn't have asked—not thinking clearly—I'm sorry."

"You're cold."

"Yes."

"Lie down. I'll put this ridiculous coat over you." He slipped out of it, welcoming the cool air on his bare arms and back.

Her legs buckled, and she sank down, but she seemed to regain some of her spirit after a minute of silence, sitting and pulling her knees up as an arm rest.

"I suppose we should try to sort the bad guys from the good guys," she said.

"Put all the Zazars on the bad guys list. Most would sell their old grandmas for a shot at the Star Stone."

"But their trading interests . . ."

"Make the accord valuable to all of them. But we can't discount private agendas."

"It's not as if we're working against their trade."

He sat beside her, not sure whether the moment for holding her in his arms had passed. He wanted—longed—to offer what comfort he could! She'd shown him a sweet, vulnerable side of herself that didn't surface often.

"Let's sleep on it. Our minds will be clearer in the morning when the shock wears off," he suggested.

"I'm afraid to go to sleep."

"We should be safe here."

"Yes, but how can I keep nightmares away? Those little hovels turned into ovens. Imagine being roasted alive. . . ."

"Darling . . ." He used the endearment without thinking. "If people were left behind, which I doubt, they died quickly from smoke inhalation, not the way you're imagining."

"But Case, why burn a whole village?" She sat up straighter, but didn't shy away from his arm. "It's cruel and pointless—all because of us."

"I don't think it was directed at us. Someone wants to terrorize all the villages in the region—possibly so no one will talk to us. But that brings us back to why."

"Why make the gem cutters too scared to talk to us?"

"It doesn't make sense unless someone wants to be sure we don't get a lead on the Star Stone."

He pulled her closer, realizing he wanted to hold her for his own comfort.

"This mission is turning into a living nightmare," she said.

"If you don't find the Star Stone, it's not a great catastrophe."

"Isn't it?"

She sounded so miserable he wanted her to cry and release some of the despair he heard in her voice. A usually dormant instinct warned him not to push her for explanations. This wasn't a time for exchanging confidences. He was grateful they could speak without bitterness or anger.

"Thank you, Case." She sounded less shaky and more like herself.

"For what?" He reached out and covered one of her hands with his.

"For not being condescending. For taking my fears seriously."

"For not asking questions you don't want to answer, mystery lady?"

"That too." There was a smile in her voice. "But mostly for believing the fire was no accident. For acknowledging we're in real danger."

"I've believed that since your room on Bast was destroyed."

He had dozens of questions, but he didn't want to destroy the fragile accord between them. He didn't fully understand his own mission; at this moment he didn't want to know about her secret agenda.

"I'm all right now," she said.

"I believe you are."

"You can have your coat back." She couldn't drop it

from her shoulders unless he moved his arm. He didn't.

"I don't care much for Zazar apparel," he said.

"You should. It makes you look dashing and romantic like a hero in the old myths: Cotitus battling the seven demons, or the wind spirit dueling with the keeper of the heavenly peak."

"This is a side of you I haven't seen before."

"I love heroic legends. When I was young . . ."

"Go on." He bent his head, loving the way her words caressed his spirit.

"When I was young, I used to dream Cotitus would gather the treasures of the universe and spread them at my feet."

"You'd be wealthy beyond belief."

"Oh, no, I'd insist he give them to the worthy poor and leave me with only a kiss to remember him."

"You were a noble little child."

"Not so little!" She laughed at herself.

"I'm glad there are things about Athera you remember with fondness." He didn't think about what he was saying; it only seemed important to use a soothing tone. He felt blessed, having heard her adolescent fantasies, and knew he'd cherish her confidences.

"I think I can sleep now—if you'll hold me," she said.

Surprisingly, he felt nothing but an aching tenderness when she snuggled into his arms, his filmy coat covering both of them. Her hair was silky on his shoulder and arm, making him feel protective but not lustful.

At first she trembled slightly, cradled against him and absorbing his warmth in silence.

"I'm asking too much of you," she whispered after a while.

Star Searcher

"No, I'm content."

It was true. Holding her aroused him, but it also made him feel protective. He was hard against her backside, but the peace between them was more precious than a shattering climax. He hadn't felt such inner contentment in years.

"Case . . ."

"What?"

"Oh, nothing. Is my head heavy?"

"Not heavy, no."

She stirred and moved even closer. He experienced a sensual shiver that reverberated like a high note in an echo chamber.

She turned toward him, revealing parted closures on her bodice. He felt the lush warmth of her breasts against his chest, her nipples as hard as little stones against his skin.

"In the pool—it wasn't just . . ." he started to ask.

"A trick? A game? No."

He let go of his pain and met her lips, nibbling at the corners of her mouth while she purred with a contentment of her own.

"I hated myself for deceiving you," she whispered, parting her lips and catching his lower lips between the smooth ivory of her teeth. Gently suckling, she was intent on her own pleasure until he responded with kisses that ravished her mouth and made her giddy with joy. She cried out, burying both hands in his hair and responding with a fervor that took his breath away.

"Darling." Freed at last to call her this, he repeated it over and over between frantic, devouring kisses.

His love had been dammed up so many years, he was like a man swept down a rushing river with nothing to cling to. He wanted all of her and more, but he couldn't tear himself away from the frantic urgency of their kisses.

Like a man in a trance, he laid her on her back and lavished the same attention on her breasts, kissing and suckling the luscious peaks, urged on by her nails rippling down his back.

He worked her vest and open coat over her arms, tossing them aside and raining kisses on her satiny throat and breasts. Blood was pounding in his ears as he peeled off her billowing trousers, leaving her clad only in the skimpy V of her panties. His hands trembled as he rolled these slowly down her thighs.

Spread out before him with the pale glow of starlight illuminating her skin, she was so beautiful he mourned for all the wasted minutes and hours and years they'd been apart. Everything but his love for her diminished in importance, and he began anticipating the fulfillment he'd longed for since she'd first come into his life. He loved her so much his heart ached; he was weak with longing.

Stunned by this sudden chance at happiness, he hovered over her, paralyzed by a momentary fear of being less than she deserved.

"Case."

Her whisper dissolved his hesitation, and he reached out for her.

She clung to Case, and it helped ease the horrors replaying themselves in her mind.

She'd been in harrowing situations before; she could live with near misses: What if they'd found lodging in one of the incinerated hovels? What if they'd still been eating when the village was torched?

Star Searcher

What shattered her was the possibility an inoffensive Zazar might have died a terrible death because she had to find the Star Stone.

Surrendering to Case's kisses, she found balm for her troubled spirit.

Overhead the stars were bright reminders of cosmic fireworks more ancient than her mind could grasp. The sky was a twinkling canopy dwarfing the small concerns of living creatures even as it made her feel at one with the universe.

Case towered over her, casting aside his remaining garments, and with them the conventions that compelled a man of their species to cover the hallmark of his gender. Phoenix had never envied males, preferring the secretive passageway of her own sex, but she was touched by his naked beauty. His erection completed him, a visible symbol of his power and energy and purpose. She was awestruck, reaching out to him even before he closed the distance between them.

What she felt was so far removed from her shameful playacting, she seemed to be a new and better woman, desirable because Case desired her. She was beyond choice, beyond resistance. She wanted to belong to him, to feel him moving inside her.

He dropped to his knees and touched her face lightly with the tips of his fingers. She stroked his wrist, his knee, the clean, hard line of his jaw, excited because he was a wonder to be explored, a man who deserved to be loved.

"Phoenix." He bent over her and whispered close to her ear, his breath a warm tickle that made her tingle with excitement. He could have taken her then. She spread her thighs without conscious decision, braced for the violence of his entry, but he caressed her gently, reading her body with his hands, letting them linger on her throat, her wrists, the creases between her torso and thighs.

The flame he ignited was white-hot, as dazzling as a distant sun, and she didn't know how much longer she could bear the pain of this ecstasy. Her only defense was to reach out to him, letting her fingers raise the silky hairs on his torso and comb the brush that framed, but didn't conceal, the object of her burning need.

She'd taken men to her bed, but curiosity was a poor substitute for passion, no more than the scratching of an itch when her heart wasn't involved. She began to be afraid; anticipation this great could only lead to disappointment. This was the man who'd hurt her, deserted her. She tensed against his touch, shut her eyes, tried to withdraw within herself.

Don't do this to me! she wanted to cry out at one moment, but the next he was caressing her with his lips, covering her eyelids with impassioned kisses and making her throat hum when he found the vulnerable spot beneath her ear.

She covered her breasts with her own hands, sure they were too sensitive to endure another assault. But he spread her fingers and moistened the nipples with his tongue until she lifted one breast and eased it into his mouth, electrified by his passionate tenderness.

"I want you to melt for me." His voice was so husky it seemed to come from some great depth.

He rolled her on her stomach, as though she were a cloth doll with no will to resist, and lifted the heavy mane of hair from her neck. Her brain stem scattered sparks from the top of her head to the tips of her toes, making her writhe under his demanding lips.

Star Searcher

She tried to wiggle away, not to avoid a love bite but because she was crazed by the intensity of her feelings. She wanted to impale herself and exorcise the demons of desire coursing through her body, but she might as well have struggled to move a mountain from her neck.

He held her between his knees and massaged her shoulders and back until her skin moved like a pool of mercury under his hands. Her spine was a newly sprouted reed, so flexible and yielding she moaned with pleasure.

"No, no," she cried out when he spread his fingers over her buttocks and kneaded with the same sure touch, his fingers bedeviling her until she twisted and struggled to roll to her back.

Her victory was an easy one. She was staring up at him again, hearing his rapid breathing. Her own breath ragged, she pulled him toward her, arching her back as his mouth locked on hers.

They kissed frantically, gasping for air, and she dug her fingers into his back.

"Soon, soon," he murmured, making slow circles on her thighs, coming closer and closer to her hidden moisture.

She was beyond expectations, reaching out to him with hunger and need. She abandoned herself, relinquished control, plunged joyfully into a whirling vortex of emotions.

She received him.

Slowly at first—sparing her—quickening—thrusting harder and deeper, he called out her name like a chant. Her spasms began, shocking at first, but building with a natural rhythm that matched his.

Cries in the night, then she was his and he was hers,

and she surrendered to the one perfect moment.

She pulled him down on top of her, clinging to him with her arms and legs while he kissed away tears of sheer joy trickling from her eyes.

Later, much later because they were like explorers who had to press on to greater wonders, he slept, holding her in his arms with her face pressed against his cheek. She raised her head and gazed at his countenance, handsome and serene as the first gray streaks of dawn pushed away the night.

Did he realize the enormity of what she'd done? Had he felt the love pouring out of her like water through a shattered dam? How was she going to face him in the grim reality of daybreak?

It didn't matter that she'd given him her body: Someday they'd both be dust, their coupling less memorable in the cosmic scheme of things than the sudden impact of the tiniest meteor. But giving love was something separate, touching the indestructible wellsprings of their souls.

He couldn't know; if he even suspected, she had to dissuade him. It was difficult enough admitting to herself she still loved him. She couldn't put her happiness, her life, in his hands again. Trust meant little when they both were consumed by desire, but she couldn't risk another betrayal.

They didn't have a future together: any attempt was doomed to failure. She couldn't even bring herself to reveal the awful threat hanging over her head: the danger to her family. She didn't know why she was embroiled in this frenetic quest or why Case, of all the officers in the Coalition, was her appointed guardian.

Star Searcher

Nothing added up, and she couldn't trust anyone but herself.

Drowsy at last, she turned away from him and surrendered to a restless, troubled sleep.

Chapter Twelve

Were they friends or enemies? Case wondered as he stood waist-deep in the azure pool and scrubbed himself with his hands.

All of it seemed like a dream: black smoke billowing up in the sky; the two of them racing across the desert to the secluded oasis; the culmination in each other's arms. But his tender parts told him differently, and he knew they'd made love in the fullest sense of the word.

He wanted to go to her now and rouse her with lovemaking. She was sleeping soundly, curled on her side, and he thought of kissing her shoulder first, warming his lips on her silky skin. Maybe, if she were willing, he'd take her as she lay on her tummy, softly kneading those pert globes, or more challenging, make love to her standing in the pool, thrusting into her until the placid water made waves around them.

He changed his mind. Nothing could be more satisfying than holding her in his arms, seeing her face softened by passion, and slowly joining their bodies.

He walked out of the pool, slightly embarrassed to be so obviously aroused in broad daylight, but eager to be by her side. Phoenix was the first woman he'd ever loved; now he was sure she was the only one he would ever love. His besotted thoughts ignored a warning from the rational part of his brain: It was one thing to taste the sweetest of fruits; quite another to own the garden.

He tried to ignore the painful memories: years of bitterness on her part; guilt and yearning on his. He wasn't a fool; he knew a single night of lovemaking, however exquisite, couldn't erase the past. He could and did hope it could be a new beginning.

Even without the slightest hint of a breeze, the hot desert air dried him quickly. They'd slept later than was prudent, but there was no sign of life in any direction. He hoped the arsonists who'd torched the village had fled to some distant place, but he was too well trained to rely on it. Soon they'd have to be on their way, but not immediately—not before . . .

"Why didn't you wake me?" She sat up abruptly and covered her breasts with her arms when he came near.

Dropping to his knees, he nuzzled her ear and kissed her throat. "I wanted you to get more rest," he murmured.

"We should leave. What if someone is following us?"

She stood with her back toward him, an oddly hurtful stance even though he admired her from every conceivable angle.

He stepped behind her and put his arms around her, his hands lightly cupping her breasts.

"This isn't—this isn't why we're here." She pulled

away and scooped up her discarded clothing, tied in a bundle with her slippers so nothing would blow away during the night. "I'll just be a minute. I have to wash off the sand."

She hurried toward the pool without looking at him, dropping her garments on the edge and plunging in, swimming underwater long enough to alarm him. He hurried after her, but by the time he caught up, she'd surfaced, standing waist-deep on the far side, wringing water from her dark hair.

"You're all right!" he called out in relief.

"Of course."

"About last night . . ."

"There's nothing to talk about, Case. Let me dress, and we'll be on our way."

"There's a lot I need to say . . ."

"Not now, please."

"What if something comes of this?"

"It won't."

He had a sudden mental image of a babe with a head of dark curls, driven to howl indignantly by a temper like his mother's. Surprisingly, the thought pleased him.

"I took no precautions."

"I've been implanted with the latest in reproductive control devices," she said, keeping her gaze averted as she walked around the pool to her clothes.

"Very sensible." He felt like a wounded man who was too much in shock to know how serious the injury was. "I'm relieved."

"No doubt you are."

She sounded callous, which made him want to shake her, but she was on the far shore, struggling to pull on her panties over wet skin.

If unusual awkwardness was any sign, she wasn't as unaffected as she pretended. She hopped on one foot, trying to get into the ridiculous balloon-legged trousers, roundly cursing when she slipped and sat down hard in the sand.

He laughed to cover his pain. He felt betrayed because she'd promised something with her body but now denied it with her words. How could she surrender to love so completely, then renew the stale old antagonism as if she'd never welcomed him into her arms?

Woman were maddening, warm and sensual one moment, cold and rejecting the next. Worse, they might grant temporary forgiveness, but they hoarded up offenses like a miser piling up coins. And of all the women he'd met, she had the longest memory and the most unforgiving nature. He tried to console himself by believing this.

"Forget what happened," she told him.

She plunged into the water again, still wearing sand-covered panties, and scrubbed away the grit clinging to her legs and bottom.

"I shouldn't have let the fire affect me that way," she said without looking at him after she finished dressing.

"The flames in the village made you burn for me? I'm having trouble understanding that," he lied, not wanting to accept the truth: She'd only turned to him because she was emotionally distraught.

"That's no surprise. It probably doesn't fit into your concept of duty, honor, and all the other pretty words that give you an excuse to walk away when the going gets rough."

They faced each other over a shimmering expanse

of water, the only living beings in the desert oasis, but they could have been a galaxy apart.

"You're like an info-bank that can't be reprogrammed," he said angrily. "You've locked in all your anger and resentment, and you don't want to let go of it, not even to make yourself happy. I think we'd better get on with this mission."

"I've never considered doing anything else. I hope this will be the last delay."

"Count on it." He tried to ignore the shield of ice encasing his heart.

Phoenix fought against an irrational urge to cry; bawling wasn't her style, and she wasn't going to turn weepy now, not when her family's safety was in her hands. But she couldn't help brooding over life's unfairness. She couldn't love any man but Case, but she didn't trust him not to fail her again. She could only avoid total devastation by keeping him at arm's length from now on.

They ate dry biscuits from his backpack and drank water from the pool that was purified by tablets he carried. She had to force herself to swallow, but not because of the chemical taste; it was regret for what could have been that closed her throat.

Case rode hard, and the motoscoot shook and rattled from the continuous impact of ruts and potholes. If this was his way of punishing her, Phoenix didn't object. If he kept up the grueling pace, they might reach the gem cutters' region before dusk. She'd made a terrible mistake, letting her heart rule instead of her head, but now she was totally focused on completing her mission.

She was glad for every kilometer they put behind

them, but she didn't protest when he came to a sudden stop, scattering sand and stones as he dug his heels into the unpaved track. She was stiff and sore from her tailbone to her toes from balancing on the narrow seat over the rear wheel, and was grateful for a short break.

"We need to talk," he said, dismounting and stretching.

"Not here—not now."

"Not about us." He scowled down at her. "I know there isn't any us. We need to assess the situation."

His words had more sting than the fine sand that blew in her face when they were riding.

"That's a Coalition phrase if I've ever heard one."

"I don't have time for word games," he said angrily. "Someone tried to knock me down with a motoscoot in Abaz. Yesterday a village burned right after we stopped there. We're not on one of your treasure hunts where all that matters is the value of the loot. More is at stake than you can possibly imagine."

"I know more about the stakes than you do," she said, furious at his arrogant attitude and stung by the implication that she only cared about personal gain.

"Can you put aside what you think you know and look at the situation logically for a minute?"

"Is this what they taught you in the diplomatic corps: how to be offensive and insulting?"

He ignored her barbs, which only made her angrier, and held up one hand with fingers spread wide.

"We know the Thals aren't involved," he said. He tucked his thumb out of sight. "That leaves Alo, a government faction on Zazar—possibly represented by Yasimen or Zahed, a rival trading planet, or . . ." He paused for effect. "A shadowy unknown." He ticked them off on his fingers as he spoke, making his point but annoying her beyond reason. She wasn't a schoolchild who had to memorize a teacher's words of wisdom.

"You don't know for sure the Thals aren't involved," she said petulantly, punished by a sudden spasm of nausea. "Why are you wasting time telling me what I already know?"

"Sometimes it's helpful to summarize. We need to formulate a plan."

"You mean a battle plan—with you as the commander-in-chief."

"Were you always so unreasonable? It's only logical to—"

"There's nothing logical about this mission! Why were you assigned to keep watch on me? Was it because you were the most likely to seduce me—and make me waste valuable time?"

"*Me* seduce *you?* You're the one who insisted on wearing see-through trousers you picked up at a brothel!"

"You wanted to parade around the planet looking like a blasted Coalition cop!"

"If you weren't so busy treating me like the enemy, you might be able to focus on the problem at hand!"

"You are the problem at hand! You have no right to—"

"Make love to you? That's what this is all about, isn't it? I broke through your steely reserve, and you can't forgive yourself for acting like a real woman for a change!"

"Your idea of a real woman is someone you can tumble. . . ."

"I made love to you. It was a colossal mistake, but

that's what it was! You can bet it won't happen again."

He covered the distance to the motoscoot in three angry strides, revving the motor before she had a chance to react.

"Where are you going?" she cried out, realizing his intention when it was too late to stop him.

"We're almost there. The walk will do you good!" he called back, throwing up dirt as he sped away.

"Come back, you miserable son of a hobeest!" she cried, running after him and choking on the sand and exhaust he'd thrown into the air.

She was so mad she stamped her feet, roundly berating him as he left her behind. She watched the motoscoot chew up the desert trail until it disappeared over one of the rolling hills.

If he thought she couldn't get along without him, he was grossly mistaken. Not only would she walk to the gem cutters' region, she'd see that he never interfered with her mission again. She didn't need him, his ship, or that blasted motoscoot. All three were a big pain in the behind.

At least she couldn't get lost. There was only a single track, and they hadn't passed a cutoff since the burned village. Still trembling with rage, she started walking toward her destination.

She could feel the burning heat of the sand through the soles of the flimsy slippers, and her voluminous costume hung around her like sails without a wind. Every step she took made her seethe with anger, but colorful images of vengeance kept her going. She wanted to stake him out naked in the desert and let sand bugs nibble at him. He deserved to do a penalty march around a planet the size of Thal.

Absorbed in her fantasies of revenge, she didn't notice the low hum of a motor until it was nearly upon her. For a second she thought Case had come back, but the sound was behind her. She turned to see a sleek black vehicle bearing down on her, a sort of desert buggy with four large wheels sending a cloud of sand in its wake.

Before she could get out of the way, the vehicle stopped beside her and two black-clad figures bounded out, taking her arms and thrusting her into the vehicle with a wiry strength she never would've expected from such little people.

Case brought the miserable little machine to a screeching halt and looked back over his shoulder, shielding his eyes against the glare of the sun. Phoenix was out of sight, as he'd expected, and he tried to guess the distance between them.

He had every intention of going back for her; that had been his plan even as he'd roared off like an idiot. He wanted to teach her a lesson, but he was probably more anxious than she was. None of his diplomatic training had prepared him for a woman like her; he'd botched the mission badly so far, antagonizing her without achieving any tangible results.

She was tantalizing and maddening; she kept him on an emotional seesaw. He wanted to strangle her one moment and make love to her the next. He damned the fate that had brought them together again, but wondered how he'd endured being without her for so many years.

For the most part, he'd been satisfied with his career and his life until the moment he caught a glimpse of her in the cantina on Bast. He should have realized then he was doomed: She was part of him, and he could no more eradicate her from his mind than he could rip his heart from his chest.

He'd never stopped loving her. He'd just buried that love in a place he thought was unreachable.

Weary in his soul, he turned the motoscoot around, dismounting to stretch his legs for a moment. He'd made a choice long ago; now he had to live with it. As fervently as he wished they could move beyond the past and start fresh, he knew he'd make the same decision again. He'd spare his dying mother from scandal and disgrace, even at the high cost of breaking all ties with the woman he loved.

He'd been a love-struck youth, still optimistic enough to hope someday he could find Phoenix again and make it up to her. Now he'd found her, but he was world-weary and pessimistic. How could he possibly break down the wall between them?

He shook his head despondently and mounted the motoscoot, anxious to find her but dreading her anger. She was going to be livid! He hoped he could persuade her to come with him peacefully, but he was prepared to tie her up with those ridiculous trousers, if need be.

Angry as he'd been, he'd taken note of the scenery before he left her. He estimated how far she could've walked, vaguely uneasy when he didn't meet her on the road as soon as expected. She might be waiting for him to return; at any rate, she couldn't go far in those fancy slippers. He'd give a year's pay for a good pair of desert boots to wear instead of the red things on his feet.

When he spotted a rock formation with a jagged outcropping like the bow of a boat, he was certain Phoenix would be around the next bend. He slowed, expecting to stop in a few moments and persuade her to mount behind him.

He eased around the curve and stared at the broad open stretch of desert ahead of him. Phoenix wasn't in sight.

His stomach knotted in fear. There was nowhere to go, but she was gone. He'd ridden for some minutes, but not long enough for her to reach the rocky hills in the distance and conceal herself. Anyway, it would be a childish trick: hiding just to scare him. She took herself and their mission too seriously to waste time on a prank.

Had he lost track of time and ridden farther than he thought? Maybe anger had made him oblivious to the kilometers slipping behind him. He circled the rock formation to be sure she wasn't resting in the shade, then backtracked down the road. The farther he went, the more fear gripped his heart and put a stranglehold on his mind.

He passed a few forlorn trees along the beaten-down roadway, but no places of concealment. When he'd gone far beyond the distance she could conceivably walk, he reversed his direction again, eyes riveted on the roadway for any clue that might suggest where she was. The dirt showed many signs of wheel tracks, but the surface was hard and old: They could've been there for years.

The sun was high. The hood and eye shields were inadequate to protect him from its full intensity, and he was getting lightheaded, perhaps as giddy from fear as from exposure to the searing desert light.

She wasn't there; his best chance of finding her lay ahead in Summa, the village where the greatest gem cutters of Zazar worked.

Star Searcher

He drank deeply from his canteen to keep from passing out and headed off on the wretched two-wheeler.

Phoenix had been in thick fogs before, but nothing like this. She seemed to be fighting her way through a giant ball of fuzz that clogged her nostrils, muffled her hearing, and stuck to her eyeballs.

She struggled to get her bearings, muttering angrily about cowards who wouldn't show their faces, and gingerly opened one eye a crack.

"Ouch!"

Something was alive in her head, swimming around, trying to devour her brain matter. Sitting couldn't possibly hurt more than lying flat. She tried to raise her head, but the room swam past her and burning bile rose in her throat. Worse, she was beginning to remember what had happened.

She'd protested, politely at first, then vehemently. When did the Zazars start kidnapping visitors to their planet? In the vehicle, she told the abductors she wasn't alone; her companions would scour the planet looking for her. She vaguely remembered a half-smothered laugh coming from one of the two hooded figures on the seat in front of her. The rascals who'd pulled her into the vehicle were either mute or too scared of their leaders to open their mouths.

Remembering hurt, and so did sitting up, but she slowly did both. Her arm particularly ached, and no wonder. One of those hooded thugs had rolled up her sleeve and pinched her upper arm while the other rammed home a long needle—which, of course, explained why she was tottering on the fringes of consciousness without a clue to where she was.

She looked around a long rectangular room lit by sun coming through three tiny slits near the ceiling. Except for the cot where she was sitting, the only furnishings were tables, row after row of long tables high enough for an Atheran to dine comfortably.

She was momentarily blinded as a ray of sun played over a pile heaped on one of the tables. The sudden burst of brilliant light broke into a breathtaking spectrum of colors, and it dawned on her where she was: in a storehouse with piles of precious stones heaped on every table.

She rose unsteadily, dazzled by the gems heaped haphazardly on crude tables. Most were lying just as they'd come from the mountains, streams, and ground, no doubt awaiting attention from the expert cutters and polishers of Summa. Even without an artificial light source, she spotted blood-red carnelias, deep blue saphgates, sparkling white mondias, and vivid green jadacions. Many wouldn't reveal their true beauty until an expert lovingly released them from their drab casings.

If she picked wisely, she could fill the small pockets of her vest with enough precious stones to live the rest of her life in luxury. But her days would definitely be numbered if she tried to smuggle out so much as a single gemstone from this heavily guarded area. Maybe she'd been left here to tempt her; not even the Coalition could save a thief who tried to abscond with Zazaran gems.

Her captors had underestimated her. She was only interested in one gem: the Star Stone.

The door creaked, giving her a moment's warning, and she backed away from the pile of gems she'd been studying. She didn't feel ready to face her captors, but she braced herself as one of the small, hooded figures, dressed all in black, strutted into the room.

His diminutive size didn't make him any less menacing. She'd discovered how strong these wiry little aliens were, and she wouldn't make the mistake of underestimating even a lone Zazar.

He touched a button on the wall, and the whole room was lit, showing more gemstones than she'd ever imagined.

"Why did you drug me? Why bring me here?" Her voice sounded creaky to her own ears, but she wasn't going to cower like a whipped cur while he made a theatrical production out of walking up to her.

Still silent, he removed the hood with its menacing eye slits and tossed it on the nearest table.

"Zahed." As she said the empath's name, a shiver of raw terror raced down her spine. No doubt he could sense her fear, and his broad smile, showing the sharply pointed teeth typical of the Zazars, only increased her trepidation. He was Alo's cousin and Minister Yasimen's aide, but what else was he?

"My apologies, lady-so, for the extreme measures we used in bringing you here." His smile was more gloating than sorry.

"Where am I? How long was I unconscious?" She rubbed her arm to let him know she was wounded and offended.

"You're in a gem-cutting establishment in Summa, as I'm sure you've already guessed. You slept only a few hours. I felt it imperative to bring you here with a minimum of attention, and females of your species tend to be—if you'll forgive me for saying so—noisy."

"I was coming anyway. Your high-handed tactics were totally unwarranted."

"Perhaps, but I couldn't rely on your guardian to go on without you. I took drastic measures because I have to speak to you away from the ears of the Coalition. I followed you and your companion at a discreet distance all the way from Abaz. No, no, honorable lady-so, I did not observe your private moments in the oasis. It was enough to know when you left there—and to know that Officer Remo is your lover."

"Why follow me? You knew I was coming here." She wouldn't give him the satisfaction of seeing her squirm over the night with Case.

"I did so for your safety. Nor was I the only one who tracked you."

"Were you responsible for burning the village?"

"Certainly not." He sounded offended.

She tried to guess how Case would handle Zahed. Zahed could be here on his cousin Alo's behalf or as a spy for the government. She didn't know which posed the greater danger, but she forced herself to be diplomatic.

"Honorable Zahed, I understand how concerned you are about the accord with Thal. Rest assured, I'm here as a friend of Zazar. I protest the drastic means you used to detain me, but I'm sympathetic to your ends."

She was perversely pleased that she used diplomatic mumbo-jumbo as fluently as Case, but it did take a toll. She was furious at the grinning empath and didn't care if he could tune in on her anger.

"Look at the wondrous display of gemstones," Zahed said, dramatically waving his arms at the piles on the tables. "But this room contains only a handful of the riches on Zazar and a mere speck of dust com-

Star Searcher

pared to all the riches in the galaxy. More and more, however, the richest veins of treasure are being depleted."

"I'm sure Zazar still has a plenitude of gems waiting to be found."

He dismissed her comment with a shrug.

"Perhaps you've heard the rumor that the Star Stone came from another galaxy," he said instead.

She had, but she thought of inconsequential things so he couldn't sense her reaction.

"Access to the wormhole and a new galaxy is of the utmost importance to Zazar," he went on. "Thal is a planet of sleeping giants, but even there, agitators are trying to deny us access, at the cost of war if it comes to that. Troublemakers would like nothing better than to have the Star Stone discovered on our planet."

"Are you denying me permission to search for it here?" she asked.

"Not exactly."

"Is Minister Yasimen opposed to my search?"

"I'm not here on Yasimen's account—nor my cousin's. I report to someone higher-placed than either, and that honorable him-sir wants the Star Stone found as quickly as possible and handled in the way least likely to start a war."

"What do you want, Zahed?" Diplomacy be damned! Her head still ached from the back of her neck to her cheekbones, and the empath was to blame.

"If the Star Stone is on Zazar, we believe the renowned antiquities tracker Phoenix Landau will find it."

She was too suspicious of his motives to be flattered.

"I'm here to offer my assistance," he said in a way that told her accepting his help wasn't optional.

"You're a clever female, a credit to your species, far too intelligent to thwart our interests."

She kept silent, waiting for the part she was going to hate.

"We ask only one small favor in return for wholehearted cooperation," Zahed said in an oily voice that set her teeth on edge. "If the Star Stone is found on our planet, we want you to take it somewhere else."

"And pretend to discover it there."

"You justify my high opinion of your intellect. You are a clever female. No doubt you understand how damaging it would be if it were discovered on Zazar. Any hope of a signed peace accord and our entry into the Coalition would be forever doomed."

Her head was throbbing painfully, and she didn't want to decide what to do with the Star Stone until she actually found it. She especially didn't want to conspire with Zahed. Her obligation was to Ngate; he should decide how to handle the situation.

Case probably knew things she didn't; maybe Ngate had given him secret instructions. She was sick of the whole mess! Why should she care what Case wanted? He'd abandoned her in the desert! Now it was her turn to call the shots.

"I won't implicate Zazar in the theft," she said cautiously, not exactly agreeing to smuggle the Star Stone to another planet. "But I want to know what I'm up against. If you didn't burn the village, who did? Who else is following us?"

Zahed frowned, obviously not eager to talk about it. "Unfortunately, that person evaded our attempts to ascertain his identity. Most likely it was an agent of a rival trading planet," he said, the ridge over his eyes deeply marked by anxiety lines.

Star Searcher

"A single person?" She thought of the total devastation of a whole community. "Why didn't you apprehend him when he was torching the village?"

"You ask why I didn't catch a ghost!" he said, angrily defending himself. "Apparently the tracker has the technology to perform magical feats. We pursued but were never able to overtake him. This is why it's so important to remove the Star Stone from Zazar if it's here."

"Where is Officer Remo?" She'd wanted to ask since first seeing Zahed, but she didn't want the empath to think he was important to her.

"He's alive, but we cannot allow any meddling from a Coalition officer. Let us begin the search now."

"Honorable Zahed," she said, carefully phrasing her words, "what will happen if the Star Stone isn't on Zazar?"

"If the thief intends to cut it for profit, it will be here."

"And if he doesn't?" she pressed, not caring if he could sense how anxious she was on that point.

"I will reassure my people that the famous star searcher Phoenix Landau will find the Star Stone elsewhere. Of course, Captain Remo will stay as our guest until the matter is resolved."

Her eyes filmed over, and she pretended to study a large stone from one of the piles so Zahed wouldn't see her tears. It was bad enough that he could sense her misery. The man sent to protect her was one more hostage on her conscience, and she needed a miracle to pluck the Star Stone from its hiding place.

Chapter Thirteen

Case struggled back to consciousness, but was reluctant to open his eyes. He recognized the odor clogging his nostrils; it was the same on every planet: a prison stench compounded of poor sanitation, unwashed bodies, and despair.

"Him-sir, are you awake?" a grating, nasal voice asked. "Quite a bash they gave you, judging by how long you've been out."

"Quite a bash," Case agreed, gingerly raising his head and touching the bump swelling under his hair. "Where am I?"

He opened his eyes enough to see the dim interior of a small, square room. The walls had the look of concrete, but they could be stucco.

"In a minister's palace, of course," the person said with a laugh that sounded rusty from lack of use.

Case forced himself to sit upright, confirming that

the squalid room could only be some type of prison cell. One tiny window near the ceiling was barred, and his cellmate was shackled to the wall by a chain attached to an ankle ring.

"I'm not chained." He was relieved, especially since the room seemed far from escape-proof. The only door looked flimsy, with an antiquated lock that required a key, and the floors were dirt, suggesting a prisoner could tunnel under the walls.

"I know what you're thinking, him-sir. You think this wretched hut won't hold you for long."

"You've tried escaping?"

"That's how I earned this." He rattled the chain, then slumped against the wall as though the effort had exhausted him. "Take the word of one who's tried and tried again. Summa is a hellhole, and the only way you'll leave is when they carry away your stinking corpse."

"Why were you sent here?"

Now that his eyes were used to the dimness, he was able to see more of the shadowy figure shackled to the wall. The male was small even by Zazaran standards, and his face was a mass of purple and green lumps and bruises crisscrossed by jagged rusty brown cuts.

"We're all of us political here. The government takes offense easily, especially when a small merchant like myself protests the ruinous taxes."

"Why here?" Case moved his head too fast, and shock waves of pain made him groan aloud.

"Best security on the planet. The gem cutters are restricted to their own area for life, so what better place for a prison?"

Case remembered arriving at the fortified barrier to the gem cutters' region, half-mad with panic over

Phoenix's disappearance. He'd first asked, then demanded to know, if anyone had seen a female alien matching her description. He never saw the assailant who knocked him out, but it had to be one of the black-clad Zazars on guard duty.

"Here, chew this for the pain," his cellmate said, pulling something out of a ragged vest pocket and lobbing it at him.

Case caught a powdery white tablet and eyed it with misgivings.

"It's for your skull," the battered Zazar said with a shrug.

"You have greater need of it than me."

"I have others. I was born a trader, and no doubt I'll die one—better sooner than later. There's no escape, none at all."

"There are no walls—no gates. They can't possibly patrol all the mountains."

"They don't try."

Whatever the Zazar was trying to tell him, Case was too groggy to take it in. Years of Coalition training had taught him to rely on clear-headed logic in every situation. He had to escape and find Phoenix. The pill couldn't be as devastating as his dread about her fate.

He popped the chalky tablet into his mouth and managed to gag it down.

"Swallow this," the other prisoner said, crawling as close as the ankle chain allowed.

Case took the cup and swished brackish water around in his mouth, then spit it out. "It's awful!"

"Nothing but the worst for the government's guests," the Zazar said, sounding almost cheerful.

"What's your name?"

"They call me Hulil."

"Case Remo."

"Late of the Coalition."

"Did the guards tell you that?"

"No, but only an Atheran in the service of the Coalition would be arrogant enough to walk boldly into Summa."

"I was led to believe I was welcome to come."

"Then you must have something to do with the wormhole and the accord with Thal."

Case's head was clearing, and he smiled ruefully. "I think I know what you use in your trading operation here, Honorable Hulil. I want information too. I'll give you some tidbits to trade to the guards in exchange for your knowledge of the security setup."

"You'll get the worst of the bargain. If the guards think I'm lying, they'll only beat me again, but you'll die if you try to escape."

"How can you be so certain?"

"Pull down your trousers. No, don't glare so suspiciously. Examine your thighs. I think you'll find a sore area."

Case grudgingly followed his cellmate's directions, surprised to find his left thigh extremely tender.

"Do you see a tiny pinprick?" Hulil asked.

Turning to the meager light coming through the high window, Case could just make out a bruise mark no larger than a bug bite.

"They shoot a tiny electronic tracking device into a large muscle. Everyone in the restricted area has one: gem cutters, prisoners, even guards. If you step beyond the perimeter of the restricted area, the device will send a signal to the main control board. They can lock onto your signal with enough power to stun or kill you."

"You've tried to escape with the device implanted in you?"

"Oh, yes." The prisoner's laugh was bitter. "I hoped for a deadly shock, but they aren't through using me yet."

"I'll tell you why I'm here," Case said, reluctantly deciding to trust the battered merchant.

When Case finished telling his story, Hulil only stared, his eyes dark pits under his bruised ridge. Case waited, sensing the Zazar had something important to say.

"The Star Stone isn't here," Hulil said at last.

"How can you be sure?"

"Have you heard me protest my innocence? I'm highly placed in an organized effort to overthrow our vicious, corrupt government. I came here with seven companions to learn whether the Star Stone is here. If it were, that knowledge would be a powerful tool for our cause. The other seven are dead."

"Why aren't you?"

"The fools who guard us think I'm only an underling, one they can use to spy on other prisoners. I put my life in your hands by telling you otherwise. The gem cutters are little better than prisoners themselves, and they speak the truth when they deny any knowledge of the Star Stone. I lost seven good followers and put myself in jeopardy on a false hope. Now the government has sent their chief torturer to interrogate the poor gem cutters; only he won't believe them so easily."

"Chief torturer?"

"Yes, a devil called Zahed."

Case felt sick with dread, terrified Phoenix had landed in worse trouble than he'd imagined.

Star Searcher

* * *

With two black-clad figures behind her, Phoenix followed Zahed out of the sorting room into a courtyard with sorry-looking plants and a rusty fountain with stagnant water in the pool round it. They entered a huge, squat building with unpainted stucco walls thicker than the length of her arm.

"What place is this?" she asked, blinking because the lights were so much brighter than the twilight outside.

"This is where the gems are processed," Zahed said politely enough but with an undertone of impatience.

"All these machines . . ."

"Are used in grading the stones. First they're X-rayed." He pointed to a row of little booths with sheets of lead on the walls and doors. "We use the latest technology. A mere press of a green button, and we instantly have an X-ray that shows a stone's fault lines. The stone and the X-ray are put on a conveyor belt, examined by experts, and subjected to other tests based on the assessments."

"I'm amazed at how complex it is." She was no empath, but she had a really bad feeling about questioning people with Zahed along. She wanted to delay as long as possible. "What are those big drums?"

"They run day and night polishing inferior stones used to make cheap jewelry for our trade on primitive planets."

"What happens to the good stones?"

"They're assigned to the gem cutters, with the best ones going to the most skilled craftsmen. I think this is all you need to know for now, lady-so. I have a sense of urgency about this investigation. . . ."

"Of course, excuse me for wasting your time."

If he thought that was an apology, he was no empath.

"Are the craftsmen still working?" she asked, following him along a broad corridor lined with widely spaced doors.

"Some may be. The gem cutters live for their work. The master cutter has his apartment here, attached to the work room where he supervises his apprentices. A cutter's status is determined by the quality of his work—which in turn provides his family with everything it needs."

"Aren't most of them still away because of Ehamrah?"

"The gem cutters don't travel. There are recreation facilities here. We'll visit Bazar first. He's the senior cutter, the master, the seventh in his line to achieve that position."

He pulled open a stout wooden door with no lock and stepped into a large, well-lit room filled with tools, grinding wheels, sinks, and benches to accommodate a dozen workers. The only occupant of the room, an elderly Zazar with white hair too thin to form the springy curls favored by his species, was bent over one of the work surfaces.

"Bazar, you're showing fine diligence this evening," Zahed said.

"I live to bring glory to Zazar through its gems," he said in a quaking voice, standing and bowing deeply with his hands clasped together.

"On your knees, old one!" Zahed ordered.

The gem cutter collapsed to his knees, and the two black-clad Zazars, still hooded and more intimidating because of it, stepped forward to flank him on either side.

Star Searcher

"We have a distinguished visitor, the antiquities tracker Phoenix Landau," Zahed said. "She has a question you must answer truthfully. Do you understand?"

One of the guards pulled a small silvery rod out of his sleeve.

"Ask your question," Zahed ordered her.

"Honorable, him-sir, I only want to know if you've heard of the Star Stone of Thal being brought here to be cut up." She hated the way Zahed was treating the old Zazar and wanted his ordeal to end as quickly as possible.

The gem cutter was pale and trembling. She didn't know if he would be able to answer. Then he shook his head, and she realized he was mute with terror.

"A stroke to loosen his tongue," Zahed said.

The guard touched his shoulder with the tip of the rod, and the old gem cutter screamed in agony.

"I've heard nothing. I've seen nothing. I know nothing! Please, Honorable Zahed, I would never speak an untruth to you."

Phoenix was struck dumb with horror herself, but when the torment was repeated, her anger erupted.

"This is barbaric! I had no idea. . . . Stop right now! I won't be party to this!"

"You're overreacting, lady-so. Ask your question again, and don't be so naive as to expect the truth without some persuasion. I want you to see how things are done on Zazar, in case you have reservations about discreetly removing the Star Stone from our planet. The alternative to honoring our wishes is to remain as our guest—in less cordial circumstances than you now enjoy."

"You can't intimidate me! I'd rather see the Star Stone crushed into dust than submit to your threats."

"Would you rather see Officer Remo under the rod? I can easily give you a demonstration that will make this seem like child's play."

"You're a beast!"

"Ask your question again!"

"Is the Star Stone here?" she grudgingly asked.

Again the old man denied it.

"Bring his wife," Zahed said. "We'll see if his answer changes when the rod slides down her trousers."

The gem cutter was weeping and begging, his words too muffled for Phoenix to translate. One of the thugs went into another room and dragged out a tiny old female who protested with terrified squeals.

"This is all for nothing! The Star Stone is on Thal!" Phoenix cried out, reeling under a wave of nausea so acute she wanted to die.

"What are you saying?" Zahed demanded.

"Star Stone on . . ."

She retched violently, shaking from great dry heaves because her stomach was painfully empty. "On Thal!"

Too sick to feel anything but agony, she resisted any thought that might curtail her punishment for disbelieving the blood oath.

"On Thal," she repeated, even though she dropped to the floor, so tortured she grabbed a table leg and dug her nails into the hard wood.

From a great distance, she heard Zahed shouting orders to the guards: "Drag her out of here, you fools!"

Then, mercifully, she slipped away into a great black void.

She woke up flat on her back with Zahed leaning over her, his pinched features waxy yellow under his furrowed ridge.

"I'm not sure how you did that, Phoenix Landau, but I will find out," he said in a soft voice that sent shivers of dread down her spine. "No one can feign illness with me. We'll see if you can do it again when we resume the questioning tomorrow. I don't think your system can bear up under many episodes like that. Rest well, lady-so. Tomorrow we'll get answers—and I don't believe your story about Thal will hold up."

"The Star Stone's not on Thal; the Star Stone's not on Thal," she repeated over and over in a frantic whisper after he left her alone on the cot in the store room. She felt marvelously restored by speaking the truth.

Zahed was right; she couldn't punish herself again by doubting the validity of the blood oath. She needed her wits about her, and she was weak enough from hunger without being in the grip of the Neosoul curse.

She had to find Case. As long as he was in Zahed's power, she was too. If Zahed was willing to torture a valuable person like the master gem cutter, he wouldn't have any scruples about tormenting—or even killing—a Coalition officer. No one could trace either of them if the Zazars conspired to keep their deaths a secret.

Much to her relief, she wasn't being guarded. She probably had the Zazars' opinion of females to thank. Zahed believed she was too ill to move from the cot, but no doubt he underestimated her because of her gender. She wondered if he could access a data bank to learn about the Neosoul blood oath.

She'd seen little of Summa, and Case could be anywhere in the region. Much as she hated to put the poor old gem cutter at greater risk, he was the only one who might possibly give her the information she desperately needed.

The huge processing room was dark now except for a few dim lights near the floor, and she reached the corridor without seeing anyone. Afraid of making noise by knocking, she pushed the master gem cutter's door open a crack and slipped into the empty workroom. Then she had to risk calling out.

"Bazar, don't be afraid. I'm your friend," she said slowly in Zazaran.

"Lady-so! You are indeed my friend." He materialized from behind a curtained doorway and bowed lower than he had for Zahed.

"I can't stop Zahed again," she admitted sadly.

"No need. My wife is gone. She will hide with friends until Zahed leaves."

"But you're still in danger."

"No danger, Lady-so. Zahed would be in much difficulty if I died under his questioning. No one can cut stones as I can—forgive my boast."

"You really don't know where the Star Stone is?"

"No cutter would touch it without consulting me," he said gravely. "It isn't here."

"I can't thank you enough for telling me!"

"I only repeat what I told Zahed under duress. The torturer knows I can block his empathic power, as many of my people can. He relies on pain, when respect would serve him better. You also found a way to shut out his power."

"I guess I did—but I don't recommend my method. Please tell me where I might find my friend. I believe he's in a prison."

"There's only one prison, and leaving it is not so hard. It's crossing the perimeter that is very difficult. No doubt your friend has had a tracking device implanted in his body. All prisoners—and gem cutters—

have them." He put his hand on his thigh as though it pained him.

"We'll remove it."

"Not so easy. It's very small and must be located by X-ray. Then you need a laser beam to destroy it. Very painful, and if you are discovered, the penalty is a horrible death. We have the X-ray machines, but . . ." He shrugged his shoulders. "Even with the device removed, it's almost impossible to escape from the region."

"Please tell me where the prison is—then I won't put you in jeopardy by coming to your quarters again."

She left with a map of Summa in her head, a bottle of fruit juice to quench her thirst, a small chisel, and Bazar to guide her through a labyrinth of corridors into a subterranean tunnel.

"Our wormhole," he said chuckling softly. "Even gem cutters sometimes feel a need to stand on a mountaintop and breath the air of freedom, even though we know we'll live and die here. Only those with no skills are ever allowed to leave."

"I don't know if it will help, but I'll tell the Coalition about the injustice here."

"For me, it's too late, but perhaps future generations might benefit. Zazar is very eager to please the Coalition now, at least until trade with another galaxy becomes a reality. Use this to return to the X-ray machines," he said, handing her a small metal disk. "You can use it only once. The mechanism will retain it—a safeguard against the misuse of the tunnel."

It was a bright, clear night, as all their nights on Zazar had been, and she tried not to think of the oasis or the man who'd held her in his arms there. She had to free Case, her Coalition partner; it was only incidental that she would be freeing her one-time lover.

She followed Bazar's instructions and located the prison compound with ease. There were no fences, gates, or guards, only a cluster of hovels and, across from them, a row of barracks, housing for the guards. Bazar had assured her most devices weren't monitored unless the bearer made the mistake of trying to get past the electronic barrier that ringed the settlement and the gem-rich mountains behind it.

Were the guards so indifferent they wouldn't notice a stranger poking around the prison area? She could pass for a tall Zazar—until she walked. No male on any planet had hips that swayed like hers—much to her regret. But that certainly didn't mean they were plump!

She heard a racket coming from one of the shacks: a tinny drumbeat that had some rhythm to it. A voice from another hovel called out in protest, and the drumming stopped. Apparently sound carried well from hut to hut.

What sound would Case recognize? They'd shared their Academy days; she must remember something that would trigger a response from him.

She began whistling softly, trying to imitate the plaintive notes of the pipes that marked the end of every cadet's day. She'd hated living by a series of audio signals, but all her experience with military discipline was worthwhile if Case could hear and respond. If he wasn't injured or . . .

No good to think that way. She repeated the somber notes that signaled lights-out at the Academy, then listened intently for a response.

He only risked a few notes, but she recognized them

immediately. He'd heard and understood that she was near.

A pair of dark-clad guards walked down the cleared area between the hovels and the barracks, chattering in an animated way that made her doubt they were on patrol. She waited until they went into their quarters, then ran as fast as she could in the ragged slippers, ruined by her short trek after Case abandoned her.

Remembering the way he'd left her on the road made her angry again, but not so furious she wasn't eager to see him. She crept behind the first hovel and whistled again. A response came from the third building, and she quickly circled to the front of it.

She forced the chisel between the door frame and the wooden door, hitting the deadbolt with an alarming clang. It didn't take long to realize her tool wouldn't snap the lock, but she pushed hard against the wood, rewarded by a splintering sound. The lock was strong, but the door was old and perhaps riddled with dry rot. She jammed the chisel against the edge of the lock plate, surprised at how easily the metal separated from the wood.

Twice she had to dodge between hovels and hide in the back, but the guards who passed were only returning to their barracks, not looking for someone trying to break into a cell.

At last the door splintered free of the lock and swung inward, throwing her forward into a pair of strong arms.

"Are you trying to get yourself arrested?" Case sounded scared, not angry, and she didn't have energy left to protest when he held her against his pounding heart and buried his face in her hair.

"We've go to go!" she whispered urgently.

"Phoenix, there's no way I can escape. If you haven't been implanted with a tracking device, you'd better try to get away alone."

"You don't know what's going on here! Zahed tortures people—and enjoys it! I loathe him! Bazar, the master gem cutter, says the Star Stone isn't here."

"It isn't—but I can't go into that now. You've got to leave."

"Oh, no! This is a land operation, Remo! I'm in charge, and I say we both go. I have it worked out—most of it, anyway."

He hesitated a moment, then turned to a shadowy figure she hadn't noticed.

"Hulil, do you want to try again?"

"With great pleasure, if lady-so would be kind enough to loan me the tool she used on the door. This chain and I are old enemies. I only need a sharp instrument."

"Here!" Phoenix tossed him the chisel and breathlessly tried to explain her plan to Case.

"Later," he said. "Sometimes, when the guards come back drunk from a night on the town, they like to bother the prisoners."

"Have you been bothered?" She had a sick feeling she knew what he meant.

"No, but Hulil is one of their favorite victims. Are you ready?" he asked his cellmate.

"Ready." Hulil stepped free with a clanging of chains that sounded as loud as a landslide to Phoenix; then the three of them were running, following the little Zazar until they found a safe place for her to explain the escape route.

Hulil was amazed by the tunnel, its entrance cleverly concealed under a metal cover that masqueraded as part of the town's sanitary system. He literally danced with pleasure when she took them to the huge, deserted room with the X-ray machines.

"Wonderful, wonderful, the best escape plan yet!" he exclaimed, shedding his filthy trousers and darting into one of the little lead-lined rooms to have his thigh X-rayed. "I can dig the device out with my nails if I know exactly where it is. Prisoners have bled to death trying, because it's impossible to guess exactly where it has lodged."

Case was less exuberant and less willing to drop his trousers.

"Knowing where it is and getting it out are two different things," he warned.

"I can't believe you're wasting time like this," she said nervously, afraid Zahed might return to torture Bazar again.

"I'll do it," Case agreed reluctantly.

She snapped both X-rays, thankful for Zahed's short explanation of the gem-sorting process.

"Back through the tunnel?" Case asked.

"Impossible. The lock kept the disk I used to open it. It's a safeguard against frivolous use that might reveal its existence."

"Perhaps I may be of assistance now," Hulil said in a deferential tone. "We must go to a tattoo establishment."

"Tattoo?" Case and Phoenix asked together.

"Very much in favor with the guards. A sign of strength to have one's body decorated as extensively as one can afford. You must choose a beautiful design, lady-so. Perhaps a love symbol where only your lover will see it."

"Is there an artist here who also removes tattoos?" Case asked.

"Laser surgery to remove tattoos is a profitable part of the business. What appears to be great art after an evening of strong drink with comrades is not always so pleasing by day."

"Laser surgery to remove the devices. Hulil, you're brilliant!" She felt like hugging him, but didn't. The little Zazar had been wearing his clothing a long time—a very long time. "But we'll get caught."

"I think not. The tattoo salon will close soon. All guards must return to their quarters by the twelfth hour. We must persuade an artist to stay open. While he is occupied . . ."

"Occupied?" she asked skeptically.

"Occupied," Case agreed. "Something elaborate. Our names in a flowery border on your backside."

"In your dreams! You can get the tattoo!"

"I'm tempted—but Hulil and I will be busy using the laser and learning surgery. You'll feel a few pricks, sweetheart, but nothing like our amateur efforts to destroy the devices."

She didn't agree, but she allowed Case to sweep her along the streets, following Hulil's lead.

"He's tried escaping quite a few times," Case told her.

"And never succeeded!"

"He never used X-ray to show where the device lodged. They shot the things into a muscle. It's like a bullet, only much smaller. Prisoners try to dig them out with chunks of plaster or their nails, but it doesn't work. They bleed to death or end up with gangrene."

* * *

Star Searcher

Summa had a thriving night district with cantinas and establishments that didn't advertise their wares, but Hulil seemed to be telling the truth. Most were in the process of closing, and the streets were deserted.

"Very bad for a guard to return late," Hulil said. "Can only amuse themselves with prisoners after the check-in time."

The tattoo salon was locked, but a light showed in the window.

"He'll want golbriks," Case said. "Phoenix?"

"I kept what you had left when I got your clothes," she admitted. "I hope it's enough."

"Offer these." Hulil gave her a handful of small tablets.

"What are they?"

"Call them joy-tabs," Case said. "One cured my headache. There's enough there for a space ride without a ship."

He knocked hard on the door, not giving up when nothing happened right away. At last it opened, and an amazingly hairy Zazar, bearded as few were, stuck his head out.

"We're closed," he said gruffly, but Phoenix spoke up.

"Please, honorable him-sir, my companions have wagered many golbriks that I don't dare submit to your needle. I've always wanted a beautiful love symbol on my body. I can offer these." She held out her hand to show him the joy-tabs.

"Come inside," he said without hesitation.

They stepped into a hallway with small curtained cubicles on either side.

"If I someday have a lover who is repulsed by a tattoo, can you also remove it?" she asked.

"Easily, lady-so. I have the latest laser equipment." He pushed aside one of the curtains. "Very quick, very sanitary. No infection. But you won't want to remove my art."

"I'm sure I won't. Wait here," she said to Case and Hulil. I don't want you to see until it's done."

"Back here, lady-so."

She stepped into a fantastic art gallery with thousands of designs covering the walls. There was everything from a terrifying serpent to a lovely gazebo surrounded by delicate vines and flowers.

"How will I ever choose?" she asked, hoping she could stall so long she wouldn't have to get one.

She gave the tattoo artist two of the tablets, but she held back seven to give him an incentive for being patient as she slowly examined all the designs.

"What will nine tablets buy?" she asked, fascinated by the bizarre array of art.

"Anything on this wall," he said, pocketing the joy-tabs and gesturing at a panel of small and medium-sized horned beasts, space vessels, Zazar symbols, and flora she'd never seen on any planet. "Is this to be a hidden symbol for your lover, or do you wish to display it?"

"Oh, art like yours definitely deserves to be displayed."

"A love-knot on your brow? Perhaps a cluster of stars on your shoulder?"

She couldn't choose. When she did, he'd start injecting dye under her skin, and who knows what poisonous ingredients the ink contained? She stalled, offered more tablets, which he tucked into his vest pocket, and stalled some more.

Star Searcher

"Honorable lady-so, I do not believe you really want a tattoo."

He was so right! She listened for the low-pitched whistle that would signal Case was done.

"It seems my work doesn't please you," the tattoo artist said, closing his box of implements with the air of a person who'd been mortally offended.

"Oh, no! It's only that there are so many beautiful designs. I can't make up my mind."

"Another day, perhaps." He gestured for her to leave.

"No, now! I have golbriks." She pulled out her meager hoard. "I've decided!"

She hadn't.

"Tell me."

"That!" She pointed to the smallest design in a row of obscure symbols.

"Kindly show me where you wish it."

"Oh—my ankle." No, too visible! "My shoulder." And never wear a sleeveless garment again? "No, I have it!" *Damn it, Case, you aren't removing a rocket!* "A secret place." She couldn't think of one she wanted the surly Zazar to touch.

"Perhaps you wish to reconsider and return another day."

"No, I want it now! Or I won't win the wager. Is this where I lie?"

She scrambled up on a raised divan, gritted her teeth, and slid her trousers down just enough to expose the side of her hip. She could see what he was doing there, but the tattoo would be her secret.

"Stay very still, please." He picked up a pen that looked wicked enough to etch glass, and smiled broadly.

Chapter Fourteen

"You did a good job keeping him busy," Case whispered as they waited in an alley behind the tattoo establishment. "What did you have done?"

"Nothing much."

"Show me."

"No. Are you sure you can trust Hulil?"

"I'm sure he won't risk having another tracking device injected into him. Nasty business, burning it out."

"If you're looking for sympathy . . ."

"I'm offering it. Where is your tattoo?"

"I don't want to think about it, much less show it to you."

"Will I be able to see it in the daylight?"

"How can you think about a tattoo when our lives depend on a weird little Zazar who may or may not be a leader in a subversive group that wants to overthrow the government?"

"When you put it that way . . ."

"Listen!"

They flattened themselves against a wall, listening to a faint hum.

"A motoscoot?" she asked in a barely audible voice.

"Something heavier with a bigger motor." He stepped in front of her, shielding her with his body. "If there's trouble, get behind that trash bin and save yourself. You're not an escaped prisoner."

"Not officially, but—"

"Shush!"

The hum grew louder and a more substantial version of the motoscoot crept into the alley. Instead of a rear seat, it had a side car large enough to carry two Zazars.

"Him-sir, it is Hulil. Quickly, quickly!"

"Where did you get this?" Case helped Phoenix scramble into the sidecar, then squeezed in himself, swearing under his breath when he cracked his knee on a metal rod that served as a safety bar to keep passengers from being thrown out.

"Do not ask," Hulil said.

As soon as they were seated, he circled around and went back to the street in front of the tattoo salon.

"At least tell me who's going to cause an uproar when they find this missing," Case insisted.

"The gentleman will have access to other vehicles."

"Please tell me you didn't steal it from the captain of the guard."

"Steal is a very bad word." He accelerated when he reached open pavement, driving so fast and recklessly they had to grab the bar and hold on for their lives. "A merchant doesn't steal; he barters."

"What did you leave in exchange?" Phoenix had to

shout to be heard; they weren't exactly sneaking out of town.

"A very nice map. I drew it myself while you were occupied with your very admirable surgery. Blood on gauze—very appropriate for a fleeing prisoner."

"You left a map showing the way we're not going?" Case grinned in spite of assorted worries.

"Ah, yes. A very good map."

"I don't understand this," Phoenix said. "How can we just drive away?"

"No one knows we're missing yet," Case said. "The tracking devices are electronically activated only if someone tries to pass the perimeters of the restricted area."

"I thought we'd have to run to the mountains, hide and evade patrols, live-off-the-land stuff," she said.

"The two of us holed up in a cave, shivering from the cold, reaching out to each other for warmth and comfort," Case teased, putting his arm around her shoulders.

"Stop that! I'm serious."

"Oh, I am too."

"There's only one road. Won't they catch up with us?" she called out to Hulil.

"One road for strangers. A very bumpy track to freedom for us."

Hulil drove straight for the mountains, but veered west just as Case thought they'd have to scale a sheer wall. He wove his way though a maze of derelict shacks, explaining it was an abandoned trading center for gemstones, very busy before the government seized control of all mining and processing.

By then they were following a track that skirted around the mountain range.

"Regretfully, I must leave you at the village of my cousin's wife's uncle. It is most inadvisable for me to return to familiar haunts, but I will arrange for a sky-roter to take you to your ship."

"There's one problem," Phoenix said. "I used my last golbrik for the wretched tattoo."

"The guards stripped me of everything, even our visitors' cards," Case said.

"Not a problem. Once you are in Abaz, the authorities will be very eager to see you depart. And you will receive a very nice reward for freeing this honorable person from the hands of the vicious lackeys of the vile and much detested government."

"Don't ask," Case whispered in her ear.

Phoenix slept, her head cradled on his chest, but he had many questions to ask Hulil.

"This is the first I've heard of organized resistance on Zazar," he said. "It will upset some leaders in the Coalition—and please others."

"If you speak to them of the great injustices on our planet, I will be forever in your debt."

"Everything you can tell me will go in my report," Case promised.

By the time the sun was at its zenith the next day, he was hustling a sleepy Phoenix into a small sky-roter, feeling guilty about the heavy sack of gemstones hanging from his soiled scarlet sash. Coalition officers didn't take rewards, but Hulil threatened to return to Summa if he was dishonored by not discharging his debt with stones the uncle had provided. Case hoped they were trinket-quality. He didn't want to add smuggling to the list of offenses the Zazars might use to detain him.

* * *

They were delivered to the docking area with less fuss than Phoenix had believed possible. No one challenged them as they thanked the pilot of the sky-roter and proceeded toward the *Seker*. No one asked to see their visitors' cards, even when Case made the obligatory stop at the departure checkpoint. They were fugitives and illegal aliens attempting to leave the planet without identification or authorization, and no one seemed to give a darn.

"This is too easy," she whispered as they walked down a concrete walkway within sight of their docked vessel.

"I agree, but pretend we're tourists who came for Eham-rah. Look innocent."

"Looking innocent will be more conspicuous than looking guilty. Can't we try for casual, nonchalant indifference?"

"Focus on something you want to do. What I have in mind is a good long sleep as soon as we're in space."

"We haven't talked about where we're going." She took the precaution of lowering her voice even more, although the docking area was empty, perhaps because traders had avoided coming during Eham-rah. They'd only passed one alien, a nondescript figure warmly dressed in a heavy robe and cowl who must have forgotten to research the weather on Zazar.

"Hulil is certain the Star Stone isn't on Zazar," he said.

"I agree. Bazar, the master gem cutter, told me it wasn't after I saved his wife from Zahed's tortures."

"How did you do that?"

"Thought about the blood oath."

"Let me guess. You used your doubts to make yourself too sick to continue the questioning. What were you going to do for an encore?"

Star Searcher

"I don't want to think about it." Was that a spasm of nausea, or was she beginning to imagine things?

"Where next?" he asked.

"Are you giving me a choice?"

"I'm willing to listen to your ideas."

"I'm not satisfied with the investigation on the *Isis*. I want to go back to the scene of the theft."

"The *GCS Isis* it is."

"You're not arguing with me?"

"Does that make you think you must be wrong?"

"No—of course not. Come on. Let's get aboard."

He opened the hatch and pulled down the retractable steps.

"While I prepare for liftoff, there's something you should do," he whispered, untying the sack of gemstones from his sash and signaling for her silence with his finger across his lips.

Phoenix didn't need it spelled out; the ship could be electronically monitored to pick up their conversation. The Zazars loved spy games.

He gestured toward the tail of the ship and took his seat in the cockpit.

She knew he'd wanted to refuse the gemstones, but Hulil wouldn't hear of it. She tended to agree with the Zazar on this; she thought a man who'd been knocked senseless and tossed into a filthy prison deserved more compensation than his Coalition salary. She just happened to know a smuggler's trick for stowing contraband.

Working quickly and as quietly as possible, she removed the casing around the commode, no trick because the metal base was designed to allow easy access to the pipe it enclosed. Using the heavy silver tape that was standard issue on every ship, she dumped out the stones on a long strip, spread them out so each was firmly stuck, then secured the strip to the inside of the casing. The whole process took less than two minutes, but disposing of the worn leather sack was trickier. She didn't want it in the waste bin waiting to be disposed of in space. If anyone came to check before they lifted off, it would look suspicious enough to warrant a search of the shuttle.

Case was working on radio contact with the *Isis*.

"I'll be right back," she called out, not giving him a chance to argue.

Walking, not running, she hurried toward the nearest sanitary facility in the domed terminal. If an official noticed, he'd assume the small shuttle's trash system wasn't operational until they were in space.

The trash bin here was too obvious. She flattened the sack and stuffed it in a crevice between the wall and a basin with water spouts. It could be years before it was found there. Feeling safer, she raced back to the *Seker*, not too afraid to run now that they were only moments from liftoff.

She was scarcely an arm's length from the shuttle's rear engine when she was knocked down by a ground-shaking force and deafened by an explosion. She scrambled to her feet, screaming as smoke billowed out of the hatch.

"Case!" She clawed desperately at the retractable steps, shouting his name over and over. "Case! Answer me!"

Thick smoke blocked her way. She covered her nostrils and tried to fight her way through, frantic to reach the man trapped inside.

She grabbed the edge of the hatch, her eyes burning from the blinding smoke. Something pulled on her leg, then her arm. Small, powerful hands pulled her backward, keeping her from Case. She screamed, but they wouldn't let her go into the smoke-filled shuttle.

Vaguely aware of a stream of chemical foam being directed at the ship, she coughed and gasped, but couldn't fill her lungs with enough air to keep struggling toward him. She called his name again as blackness overtook her.

Case fought his way upward from silent depths, gradually gaining self-awareness and, with it, the use of his senses. He heard muffled sounds and felt smooth cloth under his fingers. He tried to identify the smell passing through his nostrils: a blend of some astringent chemical and a more pleasing scent that reminded him of flowers in a meadow.

He wanted to see, but his eyelids were sticky and unyielding. Moaning from the effort, he felt something on his cheek: a hand, soft, cool, and caressing. Was he blind? Was the stroke being given in pity?

He forced his eyes to open, rewarded by a vision that struck him dumb with wonder: the most beautiful face he'd ever seen surrounded by a halo of dark hair.

"Phoenix." His voice came out as a croak, forced through stiff, parched lips.

Tenderly, she held a cup of something wet and cool to his mouth, putting her arm behind his head to help him sit a little.

Gently, she touched his lips with the rim of the cup, letting water moisten them. Then she slipped her arm under his shoulders, helping him sip more of the liquid.

"Not too fast," she admonished.

When he'd swallowed all that she allowed, she took the cup away but kept her arm behind his shoulders as support. The clean, sweet scent of her skin was what had roused him, and he couldn't get enough of being close to her, content to bask in her bemused smile and compassionate gaze.

"It's about time you woke up!" she said in a gruff tone that didn't conceal her relief.

"How long—how long was I out?"

"Ten days."

"Ten days!" He believed her, but it didn't seem possible. "Why did you stay?" He expended all his energy to get these few words out.

"I didn't feel like hitching a ride in a freighter. With my luck, I'd get a Lug for a pilot."

Her tone was frivolous, but her eyes betrayed anxiety. He saw a sheen of moisture on dark, luminous pupils, and the hollows under them looked bruised, either from great mental distress or lack of sleep.

"You've been in a coma," she said. "This is a health center in Abaz. It's a good thing you woke up. They've never heard of female nurses, and I've scandalized the staff by hanging out in your cubicle."

Twice she could have deserted him, and twice she'd stayed to help instead. He was wary of the joy building up inside him; it would be too easy to read more into it than she intended. For the sake of self-preservation, he pushed aside his expressions of gratitude, not wanting to hear that she'd only stayed out of duty or conscience. For now he had to be content with the fact that she hadn't deserted him.

"What happened?" He had a sketchy idea, but very much wanted to hear her version.

"An explosive device on the control panel detonated.

Star Searcher

The impact threw you, and you suffered a nasty bang on your head. Fortunately you were barely singed by the flames. Your right cheek and throat may be a little tender, but you seem to heal fast."

"I must have landed on the same spot where one of the thugs at Summa bashed me, by the feel of it."

"Maybe that's why you were unconscious so long."

"I have to sort this out. Nothing happened when I made contact with the *Isis*. Then I started the launch sequence—worried that I'd have to put it on hold if you didn't hurry."

"I was right outside."

"And then all hell broke lose—a flash—blinding light and a noise so loud I still have to have some ringing in my ears. Starting the launch sequence must have triggered the explosion."

"It's amazing you weren't killed!"

"I do seem to lead a charmed life," he said with as much sarcasm as he could muster. "How's the *Seker*?"

"No structural damage. She's operational, except . . ."

"Except—a nasty word."

"We'll need a boost to get out of Zazar's orbit. The *Isis* has a space tug standing by. We've no choice now. We can only go back to the *Isis*."

"Disabled but not destroyed. No independent flights if we can't launch on our own. Stop but don't kill. All this should add up but it doesn't. What do you make of it?"

"I make that you've talked enough. Rest, and we'll get away from here soon."

He protested, but his weakness betrayed him. He drifted off, his hand locked in hers.

* * *

Pam Rock

Phoenix watched him, grateful for his deep, healing sleep. She didn't pull her hand away even when her fingers got numb. For the first time in ten anxious, gut-wrenching days she dared plan again. They'd lost time—a terrible waste with Mol'ar Fap's threat hanging over her like an executioner's sword. But at least her instinct had finally kicked in; she had great faith in the sixth sense that had earned her a reputation for finding lost treasures. She always got an odd tingling when she was on the right trail, and she had it now. For the first time, she felt something besides frustration and futility.

Or maybe she was only elated because Case had moved out of the shadowy ranks of the living dead. She'd seen his head and arms move normally; his mind showed signs of being as sharp as ever. She wouldn't have to make the terrible decision to leave him behind, vegetating on an alien world while she carried on alone.

At last she separated her fingers from his and stretched out on the mat beside the bed that had been grudgingly provided by the Zazar medic who attended him. Apparently the government had decided to pretend no aliens had been in Summa. Yasimen had conferred alone with her in a small office in the health center. She'd told him the truth, and he'd seemed to believe her when she said the Star Stone wasn't on Zazar. He'd kept his own counsel about the part Zahed had played.

When Case opened his eyes again, she was dozing on a floor mat, looking sweet and innocent as she did only when she slept.

Star Searcher

"When can I get out of here?" he asked as soon as she stirred.

"Now I know you're better! You sound as impatient as ever."

He sat and swung his long, bare legs over the edge of the too-short bed. The quick movement sent him reeling, and he had to lie down again.

"Not so fast!" she urged.

He didn't miss her quick glance at his legs, sticking out of the short gown designed for much smaller patients.

"You can't go until your medic checks you out," she said, pretending to stare at something on the instrument-covered wall behind him.

"Two things are alike on every planet: prisons and hospitals," he said. "Am I a fugitive?"

"Hardly. Yasimen can't wait to see the last of us. We've become a political embarrassment, I think."

"Ngate will love that."

"The government let me contact him. He agrees we should go back to the *Isis* as soon as possible."

The medic came, not hiding his eagerness to see the last of his alien patient and, especially, the obtrusive female who monitored every phase of his treatment. He agreed Case could leave if he didn't exert himself for a few days.

"Do you feel well enough to travel?" Phoenix asked. "That quack would send you on your way just to get rid of me."

Phoenix reached under the bed and brought out khakis similar to those she was wearing.

"Are we through with bizarre costumes?" he teased.

"Unless you've grown fond of the gown you're wearing."

"If you want to leave now, I'll get dressed."

"No, I'll help you. You'll be light-headed at first, and I don't want you keeling over and hitting your head again. I'm having an ambuvac take you to the *Seker*."

"Please tell me it's not a motoscoot dragging a liter."

"More like a sky-roter with a bed in the back."

He protested when she pulled his briefs up his legs and helped him wiggle into them under the gown; he blushed when she had trouble with the closure on his trousers, then refused to be put off on buttoning his shirt. Much as he hated it, he had to lie back twice, so light-headed that dots were swimming in front of his eyes. But even in his weakened state, he could feel himself grow hard as she helped him. If she noticed, she didn't react.

Did that mean things were back to normal between them? Did he even know what normal was?

The space tug towed the *Seker* until a tractor beam from the *Isis* locked on to guide them back to the mother ship, still orbiting Thal in the Bes system, home also to Zazar. Phoenix had never felt so helpless; for three days her fate was wholly in the control banks of the Coalition vessel. The shuttle's panel gave no feedback. She spent much of the time staring out a small porthole, watching the stars like an ancient mariner navigating by the heavens.

Case slept.

At least when he woke for brief periods, he seemed to be getting stronger. His mind was clear and his appetite hearty. He ate everything she warmed for him in the flash cooker, and most of her portions too. She was so anxious about lost time and the threat to her family, she had to force herself to swallow a few small bites at every meal.

By the time they locked onto the *Isis* and were drawn into the bowels of the great ship, Case seemed fully recovered, but she was sick with fear for her loved ones. There was so little time left and such a huge galaxy to search for the Star Stone.

A lone figure was waiting at the docking spot. Phoenix recognized the sculptured steel mane of the man who'd sent them on the mission. Orde Ngate pulled down the ladder and offered her his hand.

"Phoenix, you can't guess how glad I am to see you. Officer Remo, I've scheduled a debriefing in two hours if you feel up to it."

"Yes, sir."

"We have a lot to tell you," Phoenix said.

"I'll want to talk to you later of course, Phoenix, but I won't trouble you with a tedious meeting just yet. I'm sure Remo can fill me in."

She wasn't pleased; Ngate was treating her as a minor participant, not someone who'd been paid a small fortune to carry out a mission.

She complained to Case as soon as they were alone on a lift to deck ten, where he had his quarters and she had a guest stateroom.

"What was that about? Have I been dropped from the team?"

"I'm not sure. Maybe Ngate wants to go over the diplomatic ramifications of what we learned on Zazar."

"Or maybe I'm just not a member of the club," she said, disgruntled but also relieved because she wanted to access the ship's info-banks as soon as possible. She planned to go over the account of the theft and the personnel records of everyone on the *Isis* when it happened. The odds were against discovering something new, but she had a feeling. . . .

"Phoenix Landau! Welcome back to the *Isis!*" Nevin Ban came out of the commons area in the nose of the ship on that level and hurried toward them. "Remo." He nodded curtly at Case.

"It's good to be back," she said automatically.

Ngate's personal recorder looked even paler than before, dramatically thin with jet black coils of hair that suddenly reminded her of Zazar males' favorite style. His eyes too were as black as a Zazar's, although he was far too tall and smooth-browed to be one of that species.

"I understand you're scheduled to meet alone with Ngate," he said to Case. "Phoenix, will you honor me by joining me for a meal in the officers' lounge when you've had time to freshen up?"

"Thank you, I'd love to. Give me half an hour."

"Splendid. It's on deck twelve in the stern." He moved away as quickly as he'd approached them.

She reached her stateroom, forcing her mind back to the problem of beginning her research as soon as possible. She had a lot of questions, and talking to Ban might be a good beginning.

Somewhat to her surprise, since they'd just spent three days and nights cooped up together in the *Seker* with practically no meaningful conversation, Case followed her into the snug little room.

"You'd better get ready for your meeting with Ngate," she suggested.

"I don't want you anywhere near Nevin Ban!" he said when the door slid shut.

"I'm only going to talk to him."

278

"Phoenix, don't get close to him. I don't trust him."

"All the more reason to learn what I can from him."

"No, it's a bad idea for you to give him any encouragement. I'll handle Ban."

"You'll be tied up with Ngate. I'm still in charge of finding the Star Stone, and that means questioning anyone remotely connected with it."

"Phoenix, I'm warning you. . . ."

"Warning me? You sound like—like a jealous lover!"

"That's hitting below the belt. I just don't want you getting in over your head."

"I already am." She stifled an urge to tell him just how desperate she was. "We've wasted so much time."

"We're pretty sure the stone isn't on Thal or Zazar. I don't call that wasted time—unless you regret waiting for me to regain consciousness."

"Why do all our conversations get personal? The issue is: Can Nevin Ban tell me anything that might help the investigation? You have to admit, he's more likely to talk freely to me than to you."

"He will—if he has a hidden agenda. Your sweet body comes to mind."

"Don't you think I can take care of myself in that department?"

"You're going to meet him no matter what I say, aren't you?"

"Answering a question with a question? I call that a stalemate."

"At least watch your back."

"That's your job, isn't it?"

"Maybe. I don't know what Ngate has in mind for me, but if I have to, I'll put in for service leave to see this through with you. I have over fifty free days coming."

"It won't take that long."

It couldn't.

"Be careful with Ban."

"I will," she agreed. "And see if you can get me cleared for unlimited access to the ship's info-banks."

Case left, and she hurried to meet Ban, wondering if she'd ever tie up all the loose ends. How did the thief get through the security around the Star Stone? How was it smuggled off the ship? She was thinking in circles, and all the leads came back to the *Isis*. The thief had to be someone who was aboard at the time. Find that person, and she could worry later about who was behind the theft, pulling strings to scuttle the accord.

Ban had changed clothes, trading his uniform for pale lavender trousers that fit like a second skin. They made his bulge too obvious to be sexy, and his skin-tight white shirt emphasized his skinny torso. The man had to be delusional if he thought this outfit would attract her. It only made her feel grubby in her utilitarian khakis.

"Well, tell me about your adventures," he said when he'd ordered sweet minty drinks in tall, frosty glasses for both of them.

"Just routine legwork," she said. "I wouldn't dream of boring you with all the details."

"Nothing you say or do bores me." He smiled wistfully, and for an instant she was tempted to like him just a little.

"I hope Remo didn't give you any trouble," he went on. "He can be pretty hard-nosed sometimes."

"No trouble." She agreed Case could be difficult, but didn't like Ban saying it. "Tell me, do you have any theories about the theft of the Star Stone? You probably hear things not even Ngate knows."

Star Searcher

He'd mastered the art of evasiveness, she decided by the time their meals were brought to the table by a uniformed server. At least he was providing something she hadn't seen in a long time: appetizing food. He'd used his staff position to order a meal fit for a banquet: freshly baked hot bread, succulent seafood in a tangy sauce, fresh vegetables cooked lightly so they were still crunchy, and a delightful frozen ice.

Case found her still at the table, licking the last dab of sweet pink ice from her upper lip. He nodded curtly at Ban.

"We've got work to do, partner," Case said to her.

Did that mean Ngate hadn't reassigned him? She couldn't believe how relieved that made her feel.

"We have a lot to talk about," he said, hustling her away from Ban, into the lift, and back to deck ten.

This time he insisted she come to his quarters.

"You meant it—you're still working with me?" she asked, needing to have it spelled out when they were alone in the trim cubicle that held his bed, wardrobe, desk, and a comfortable chair bolted to the deck.

"Yes, but I have news. The *Isis* has been ordered back to Athera."

"That's a two-week trip!"

She forced herself to tally up the days she'd already wasted. Once they got to Athera, she'd have a scant 24 days to complete the mission on the timetable Ngate had given her. If she didn't know where the Star Stone was by then, she'd be denied access to Horus. She wouldn't be able to ransom her step-sister's family by leading an expedition on the dead planet. Her stomach knotted in fear, and she hated Mol'ar Fap so much she was speechless with loathing.

"Are you all right? You look like you just saw Davy

Lazlo," he said, referring to an early space traveler who'd been cast out in space for murdering another crew member. Space lore said his ghost knocked on the portholes of doomed vessels.

"Nothing so dramatic," she said, simulating a smile.

"I also secured permission for you to have unlimited access to the ship's info-banks. I'll show you the terminal where we can work together. The two-week trip won't be a waste. I thought we could do an animated scenario of the robbery and try to place everyone in position at the time the Star Stone disappeared."

"Good idea," she said, but she couldn't concentrate on anything but a vision of Mol'ar Fap carrying out his threat.

"You're beat, sweetheart," he said softly. "Go back to your room and get some sleep. When you wake up, we'll start combing for new leads. I think you're right about the investigation on the *Isis*. Something was overlooked."

Chapter Fifteen

"I don't understand it," Case said.

"Try one more time," Phoenix urged.

He punched in the code again, as he had almost every day for two weeks, but he knew it was a waste of time. The file on Nevin Ban was classified, and there was nothing else he could try to get into it.

"Are you sure Ngate won't access it for us?" she asked, staring at the puzzling denial on the screen.

"He can't. This is a top-level lockout. No one on the *Isis* can override it, not even the navigational commander, Captain Humme."

"Nevin Ban isn't that important."

"He's only a level-four officer," Case agreed.

"What are you?"

"Level two—thank you for asking," he said dryly. "Ngate is the only level-one diplomatic officer on the *Isis*."

"Who's responsible for making a file classified?"

He shrugged. "Ban couldn't do it himself unless . . . No, I'm starting to think like a Zazar. You know what we have to do, don't you?"

"I'm afraid you're going to tell me."

"Pay a visit to the Academy. It's a longshot, but maybe there's something in his records there."

"I'd rather go back to Summa!"

"We'll be orbiting Athera tonight. We can take a shuttle down to the Academy. It might be a good idea to visit the Intelligence Center too."

"I'll keep working here. There's still a lot to do."

"We've been searching through all the available data and interrogating people for two weeks, and all we've hit are dead ends. But I'll go without you, if that's what you want."

"You really would go without me?"

He grinned. "Yes, but wouldn't you rather come with me?"

"No, but I'm still in charge of land operations. I guess I'll have to."

He wanted to give her a big hug, but that wasn't the way their relationship had been going. They were a great team—as long as he played by her rules. Until the Star Stone was found, he had to keep pretending there was a wall of glass separating them.

Phoenix readied herself as best she could for the visit to the Galactic Coalition Star Service Academy. She dipped into her funds on deposit to replenish her wardrobe at the clothing mart on the *Isis*, choosing a sleek emerald green jumpsuit for the trip. It dipped low in front, with a broad copper mesh belt that emphasized the swell of her breasts and the curvature of her hips. The last thing she wanted to do was look as though she belonged at the Academy. If she raised a few eyebrows, fine. At least she wouldn't be ignored, as she had been during her last days there as a cadet when even so-called friends shunned her.

Just before meeting Case, she swept her hair into a pile on her head and fastened it with combs, leaving a sensuous tendril hanging loose on either side of her face. Phoenix Landau was going home, and she didn't care if people there remembered her as the daughter of the curator of the Academy Museum for Interstellar Studies who had been accused of antiquities smuggling. Her father had been exonerated, and she was successful in her own right. No one was going to intimidate her or bring back feelings of shame and disgrace from the bad days.

Case whistled softly when he saw her.

"A cadet's life is hard enough without being reminded of what he's missing," he teased.

"Let's get this over with," she said, fighting a tiny spark of panic in spite of her resolve.

The shuttle drifted the last few thousand feet, coming down directly over the spacious oceanside campus, the pride of the Coalition on its planet of origin. Three great towers of mirrored glass and steel were grouped in the center of the grounds, with all the other buildings radiating out from this hub. From where they touched down, she could see the vast expanse of beautifully groomed lawn and an array of trees and bushes gathered from the far reaches of the galaxy to enhance the Coalition's primary training institute.

From the shuttle pad not far from the edge of the campus, they got onto a monorail that circled the grounds and went into the nearby city. They rode only as far as the glimmering glass building that provided quarters for visitors.

They were expected. Case registered, using the *Isis* code to claim their rooms; then they carried their backpacks to their assigned places.

"This is almost like the cadets' dormitory," she said, looking around her room while he watched.

It was a boxy cubicle devoid of frills, with gun-metal gray carpeting and stark white walls. Bunk beds were attached to the wall, and the console on the desk was only an updated model of the one she'd used as a cadet.

"I have clearance from the Intelligence Center to do some checking on covert organizations on Athera," he said. "I can go alone if you prefer. Cadet records can be accessed from your room or mine, so we won't have to go to the registrar's to check on Ban."

"You're giving me a chance to hide in my room? Thanks, but no thanks."

Something about walking across the campus made her square her shoulders and tuck in her buttocks. She laughed to herself when she saw it had the same effect on Case. He was walking with the even stride required on the parade ground, his chin jutting out and his arms at his sides.

"It all comes back, doesn't it?" she asked in a melancholy tone.

"Yes. If you catch me saluting every bush with prickers like an underclassman afraid of a senior's punishment, you have my permission to give me a swift kick."

"I grew up helping my father at the museum, and I was still terrified my first day as a cadet."

Star Searcher

"I was too cocky for my own good. Seniors love a new cadet who needs a lot of instruction. Remember how we met?"

"You were on a penalty march—seven times around the campus in the rain, missing dinner. I felt sorry for you."

"You brought me a cup of hot soup from the commissary. I walked the rest of the way with wings on my feet."

"No more reminiscing!" she said. "That's not why we're here."

"I can't stop remembering. There's the pathway to the beach. We went there on our first furlough day. Remember how male and female rookie cadets had to walk: with at least an arm's length of air between them?"

She remembered only too well. Case had taken her to the ruins of the first fortification on the site and kissed her behind an ancient stone wall. She could almost feel his lips, warm and eager. There was probably nothing in the universe more thrilling than being kissed for the first time by someone you love.

"Remember why we're here!" she said, masking her emotional lapse with irritation.

"Then let's talk about Nevin Ban," he said. "I don't have any sentimental memories about his cadet days. He was a devious prick, always ready to wiggle out of trouble by blaming someone else. His own classmates tossed him in the ocean wearing parade dress, if I remember correctly."

"That doesn't mean he stole the Star Stone."

"No, but he's still my favorite candidate."

"Your opinion isn't evidence."

"When did you become Ban's advocate?"

"I'm not. But if this is another dead end, I don't know where to go next."

"You could quit."

"No."

"Are you afraid you'd have to return the fortune you were paid?"

"No. If you think I'm being overpaid, wait until you sell the gemstones. You can retire from Coalition service."

"Not with honor. I can't keep the stones—not my share anyway. Half are yours."

They checked into the Intelligence Division, a branch of the Academy only loosely connected to the other activities there.

"This is the largest data-gathering facility in the galaxy, as far as I know," Case said.

"I had the tour my second year as a cadet," she said dryly.

They knew what they wanted, and Case had the clout to get it. A slender clerk with gray hair cropped short on his long skull ushered them to one of the terminals in an office lined with sophisticated data storage equipment.

They left hours later, wiser but discouraged, and slowly walked back to their quarters.

"No suggestion of anyone within the Coalition wanting to sabotage the peace accord," Case said thoughtfully.

"And no covert group on Athera like the Neosouls on Thal or Hulil's underground organization on Zazar, at least as far as the Coalition knows."

"If we eliminate idealistic and political motives, what do we have?" It was a rhetorical question; Case knew the answer as well as she did.

"Profit," she replied unnecessarily.

"I can't begin to imagine the financial potential of the wormhole."

"Unless using it proves to be too risky. The Zazars act as though they'll be able to breeze through it and loot a whole new galaxy. Maybe they're overestimating the Coalition's technology."

"I almost hope so," Case said. "We have so much to learn when we do reach another galaxy. It would be terrible to let the spoilers have their way."

"Maybe other Coalition people feel the same way. Maybe there's hidden opposition to using the wormhole."

"Possibly—but does that really ring true as a motive for stealing the Star Stone?"

"No," she said thoughtfully. "All my instincts tell me there's a profit motive involved."

"Would anyone be stupid enough to steal the stone just to sell it?"

"I can't believe it. If the thief tried to unload it, there would be rumors floating around. And very few gem cutters would attempt to cut it. The best are on Zazar, and they haven't been approached. I'm sure of it."

"What did Mol'ar Fap want you to do?" Case asked, stopping and putting his hands on her arms so she had to face him.

"Nothing connected with the Star Stone—he never mentioned it to me. I'd rather not talk about Fap."

She jerked away and walked ahead of him, feeling like a trapeze artist balancing on a fine wire stretched taut between two mountain peaks with no safety net below. She had to find the Star Stone to save her family, and a thief within the Coalition was her last chance. There wasn't time to go to other trading planets, the nearest of which was many months away.

They had one more lead to check: Nevin Ban's records at the Academy. They'd decided to access them from the terminal in her quarters. Neither wanted to arouse the curiosity of the staff for something they could check in privacy.

"Nothing," she said later, slumping in the chair in front of the screen in her room. "We might as well give up. We're locked out here too."

"There's one more chance, but I don't want you involved," he said hesitantly.

"I am involved! Don't play games with me after all we've been through."

"The Academy installed a whole new system a few years after we left. Before then, cadet records were stored on rather antiquated laser disks. When all the information was transferred to the new installation, what do you think happened to the originals?"

"The Academy never throws anything away—that's why the archives under the museum are so huge. The vaults have clay scrolls going back to the time before paper was invented."

"It's a long shot but worth investigating."

"The archives are sealed. You need clearance from Coalition headquarters," she said.

"That would take too long. I have a shortcut in mind: helping myself."

"You'll be cashiered out of Star Service if you're caught breaking in."

"I might be able to get by with a demotion. But you're a civilian—you could go to prison."

"I'm attached to Ngate's service—it's no more risk for me than it is for you. Anyway, you can't possibly get past museum security without my help. I played in the sub-basements as a child. I know the flaw in the system."

"What flaw?"

"I'll show you when we go in."

"Is that what you call trusting a partner?"

"No, it's what I call keeping my partner out of big trouble. It can be done, Case, but timing is everything. We have to go in after midnight when no one is working but the night-shift guards. If the routine hasn't changed, all the cleaning staff will be gone. I have a much better chance than you do of circumventing the security system."

"Meanwhile, we wait," he said. "We might as well have dinner."

"I'm too nervous to eat, but you should make an appearance in the cafeteria. Talk with some of the instructors; tell the cadets about your exploits."

"My exploits?" He laughed. "I'm not an old man trying to impress the younger generation yet. Although I think the average cadet might like to hear about oasis survival."

"If you value your—"

"Don't say it." He covered her mouth with his hand and anticipated her retaliation, grabbing her knee just as it came up.

"Come with me to the cafeteria," he said.

"I'd rather go through another blood oath!"

"I'm sorry being here opens old wounds for you," he said gently, holding her face between his hands. "If there's anything I can do to help you heal . . ."

"Go. I need time to think."

"All right, but I won't be gone long. I'll smuggle out part of my dinner for you."

"The way you did when I needed to study," she said.

"You always brought me a sweet treat."

"You called it brain food."

"I'll go without tonight, thanks anyway. Just go—please!"

Case hurried through the meal, but he had old friends on the staff: men who'd been cadets with him and others who'd served with his father. In spite of his best intentions, several hours had passed when he got back to their quarters. It was dark, but they still had hours to wait until midnight.

He went to Phoenix's room first, worried when she wasn't there. The clerk on duty in the lobby couldn't remember seeing her.

He strolled across the well-lit campus, hoping to see her walking on the familiar pathways. His worst fear was that she'd try to get into the archives without him. The museum was closed, and the area around it deserted, the windows reflecting the lights of the Academy grounds like black mirrors. He didn't know where else to look for her, but he'd go crazy sitting in his room listening for her return.

Something wasn't right; he felt it more strongly with each passing day. Ngate hadn't bothered to debrief Phoenix yet, and no one on the *Isis* wanted to talk about the theft. Sometimes he felt the two of them were the only ones who cared anymore.

He followed familiar walkways, then went down the steep plank steps leading to the ocean beach below. The sea was calm with gentle waves washing onto the sandy shore, and the ancient rhythm of the Merintac Ocean soothed his troubled mind. He liked to imagine the proud sailing ships that had once plied Athera's seas, the spiritual forerunners of the sleek vessels that now soared through the galaxy. How far was his species destined to travel? He felt almost melancholy, a decidedly unusual state of mind for him, when he thought of leaving his footprints on the sands of time with no one to follow him, no children to ensure that some tiny part of him survived. Was he anything more than a wanderer, destined to be deserted by the one he loved most?

He caught sight of a slight figure moving along the smooth, sandy beach, hair swirling around her face, and his spirits lifted.

Not wanting to frighten or alarm her, he froze where he was, waiting for her to approach. She stopped, but the momentary rigidity in her body relaxed the moment she recognized him.

His heart reached out, wanting to share her thoughts. Her mind was a mystery to him, but he was hopelessly fascinated by it.

"Is it time already?" she asked. "I thought it was still early."

"It is—early for our plan." But late for us, he thought, almost too late.

"I needed fresh air."

Her voice was husky. By the light of a spectacular full moon, he saw her moisten her lips with the tip of her tongue. He was mesmerized by the gentle rise and fall of her breasts, and he didn't think he could survive another minute without taking her in his arms.

"Case, no . . ." she pleaded when he reached for her, but she didn't resist when he laid his hands gently on her shoulders.

He took her in his arms and captured her mouth in a kiss so deep, so bittersweet, he could hardly stand it. She seemed to shudder, but she pressed against him, moaning softly as he explored her throat with his lips.

"Love me," he whispered.

"I can't. . . ."

"That's the one lie I'm not going to listen to," he said, sliding his hand over her thigh, wanting her to throb the way he did.

"Case, no," she murmured, her breath coming raggedly.

"Let me love you," he demanded.

"I can't. . . ." she protested but relaxed in his arms, her head slumping forward as he burned a trail of hot kisses on the back her neck.

"Why not?" he asked, opening her buttons with fingers made clumsy by haste, reaching inside the jumpsuit to free her wonderful breasts from the restraint of cloth.

With both hands he rolled her nipples into hard knobs, then bent his head and inhaled the perfume of her skin. She shivered when he pressed his lips between her breasts, then caressed them with his tongue.

"Why are you doing this to me?" she asked, but there was no resistance in her question.

She began rubbing the back of his neck with her fingertips, letting her nails lightly graze his skin as their lips met for a soft but deeply felt kiss.

With her arms still locked behind his neck, he lifted her under her knees and carried her across the broad strip of sand to the seclusion of the crumbling old fortification, stopping on the very spot where he'd first kissed her.

"This place . . ." she murmured, flattening her

body against his when he lowered her feet to the ground.

She came into his arms, tilting her head for his kisses.

"The same . . ." He covered her mouth with his, giddy with need, pushing his tongue into the sweet, slippery interior.

Her hands slid under his shirt, making circles on his chest with the palms of her hands, lingering on his nipples, then sliding lower, stopping at his navel. He was breathing hard, calling on all his reserves of strength not to push her hand lower.

She reached up to cup his face, inviting more kisses which he eagerly gave. He kissed her deeply, crushing her against him as she kneaded his back and ran her fingers down his spine, forcing her hands under the waistband of his trousers, using her nails to tease the sensitive hollow where his buttocks began.

He tried to take his shirt off, but she did it for him with seductive slowness. He wanted to hurry her, but not at the risk of roughness, so he stood motionless while she slid his trousers down his legs. Her hands slipped under his briefs, peeling them down until she could fondle him with gentle, then increasingly more urgent squeezes. When she wrapped her hand around his throbbing erection, he was light-headed with yearning.

He took off her jumpsuit, tossing aside the belt, and spread it on the sand with his clothes, then helped her wiggle out of her panties. He was vibrating with urgency, painfully ready, but she captured his hands and brought them to her mouth, teasing the backs with nipping kisses and love bites, then smothered his mouth with long, wet kisses he could feel all the way to his groin.

He pressed her breasts on the sides to make an even deeper hollow where he buried his face, then turned to first one nipple, then the other, suckling and teasing with his teeth.

He'd always suspected she was capable of expressing great passion, but her response went beyond his imaginings. She caught first one, then the other of his nipples between her teeth, and played with them until they ached with lust. When he thought he couldn't hold back any longer, she held him tight, then ran her hands down his spine and over his buttocks.

When she went down on her knees, he thought his heart would burst with pleasure.

Her hair was soft against him, spilling over his thighs, and he closed his eyes, surrendering to sensation. She pulled on his hands, bringing him to his knees in front of her. He wanted to tell her he loved her, but he was afraid to say the words, afraid she'd resist him if he told her what he was feeling for her.

He pulled her down on the nest of clothing, on fire to make love to her. Deep inside, he desperately wanted to obliterate the past and wipe out all that stood between them: the hurt he'd so unwillingly inflicted on her and the bad memories. He fervently hoped the white-hot passion between them would burn away her pain at his betrayal. He wanted to be branded by her kisses. He longed for their relationship to begin over again from the ashes of the past. He didn't have words that were adequate to tell her any of this; he only knew his happiness was in her hands.

He straddled her hips and leaned over her, arousing her in all the ways he knew, trying to give her a small measure of the pleasure she was giving him. He loved touching her, stroking her satiny skin and trailing his lips from her throat to her love nest. When she parted her thighs and guided him to her moist warmth, nothing had ever felt so good. He eased himself deeper and deeper, wanting her to be as thrilled as he was. He tried to be gentle, tried to hold back, but he was driven by her fierce kisses and the sharp bite of her nails digging into his buttocks, goading him into making love urgently, savagely, willing away his own climax until her spasms were so intense there was no stopping them. She arched her back and tightened in a way he'd never experienced, driving him to the brink and beyond.

He knew he could never let her leave him.

They lay locked together, side by side, their legs entwined and their hands stroking neglected spots, the uncaressed places still needing a lover's touch: the hollow under his arm, the back of her knee, his brow where his hair was damply clinging, the crease where her bottom met her torso.

Phoenix was so satiated, she didn't remember her old, doubt-filled self. After lying in his arms in deepest contentment for several precious minutes, she rolled on top of him and kissed him gently, loving it when he caressed her shoulders and back and playfully kneaded her backside.

"You're all sandy," she said, kissing his closed lids. "Do we dare swim?"

"Would you ask if we were anywhere but here in the shadow of the Academy?"

"No," she giggled and rose to her feet, running toward the waves gently lapping the shoreline. "They can't expel us, that's for sure!"

They swam and frolicked and made love again, a gentle joining as she hung on his neck, her bottom buoyed up by the sea. She hadn't felt so young and carefree in ages. She wanted to belong to Case; she needed to be flesh of his flesh. Here in this great ocean, her feeling for him seemed purified and simplified. Their bodies were joined, and she experienced a stirring of hope.

They emerged from the water hand in hand, and she felt renewed, like a girl with all the delusions of youth still intact: a belief in eternal love and the bonding of two spirits. She knew it was a fragile, temporary mood, but she basked in it before reality intruded, as she knew it must.

"Let me hold you," he said, wrapping his arms around her as the gentle sea breeze dried them.

She pressed against his groin, loving the little spasms rippling through her as she rubbed against his soft, satisfied parts.

"It's still early," she said, dreading the time when they had to leave the beach.

"The night is only beginning." He spread his fingers over her buttocks and crushed her against him. "I see your tattoo, but I can't make it out."

He slid his hand over her hip, lightly pinching the small design between his thumb and finger in an attempt to see it better.

"Let's keep it a mystery," she purred into his ear.

"Next time we'll make love in the daylight so I can see it better."

"Why are you so curious about a tattoo?" she teased, afraid there'd never be another time. Making love didn't change things; it only made them more complicated.

"I like being the only one who knows it's there."

"A little secret that makes sex better?" She teased his navel with her little finger until he squirmed and captured her hand.

"You've made it too wonderful to be improved," he whispered in her ear. "When this Star Stone business is over . . ."

"No! Let's not talk about it."

She had a superstitious dread of making plans with Case. She was afraid to even think of a future with him. Something bad would happen if she did.

"You're trembling," he said, wrapping his arms around her shoulders. "Are you cold?"

"Yes, cold," she said, but the chill went much deeper than her skin. She was frightened!

She shook herself impatiently, pulling away from Case. This wasn't like her: She never let herself be spooked by imaginary doom. She believed everyone's future held a mix of good and bad, and anticipating the worst wrung joy from the best.

"It's time for our covert action," she said, bending over to sort out their clothes.

Catching her as she bent, he slid his hand down her tailbone and cleft, snaking between her thighs to rest his hand on her love nest.

"We have all night," he whispered, suggesting the way he wanted to spend it by gently exploring between her hidden lips.

Did he know how much she wanted him inside her again? Did he even suspect the white-hot need he was sparking with one gently probing finger?

"No!" She stumbled away, making a great show of

shaking sand from her clothes. "It's time to hunt for Nevin Ban's secret."

"I guess you're right," he said. "I want all this behind us as quickly as possible."

She didn't believe in fresh starts. The past was a burden everyone had to carry, and hers was heavier than most.

When she told him how they were going to get inside the museum archives, his first reaction was disbelief, then relief. It might be easier than he'd expected.

As a child she'd often played among the ruins of the old fortress, she explained. It was a huge stone fortification with massive foundations that went deep into the earth. Her father had had a great love for Athera's history, and he'd spent much of his free time excavating small sections of it.

"He never did get funding to restore the fortress," she said. "The Coalition's interests always came first, and that meant all the resources of the planet went into space exploration. But he never lost interest, even when I was the only volunteer he had to help with the digging."

She took Case to a partially standing wall farther inland.

"There's the museum, but the underground archives extend all the way to this wall. To save money, the architects used the old foundation as the eastern wall of the museum's underground levels. They thought nothing could ever penetrate such massive stonework. Some years later I was digging with my father. I proved them wrong. I had a feeling—it's hard to explain—but I knew there was a passageway through

Star Searcher

the old wall. My father and I found it and explored it, but we never shared the secret with anyone. Fortress builders always had an escape tunnel."

Case smiled at her enthusiasm.

"It's down here," she said.

She led the way to a section where there were obvious signs of old excavations: neat trenches partly filled by rotting vegetation and marker stakes faded by time.

"The flooring collapsed and exposed a whole section of the fortress cellars—even part of what could be the dungeon."

"Won't we need a light here?" he asked.

"Not unless you want some curious cadet on guard duty causing a ruckus. Anyway, I know the layout like the palm of my hand. Follow me, and don't make a sound if you can help it."

He felt like a boy again, exploring forbidden caverns and letting his imagination conjure up mythical beasts to menace him. It was that kind of place. They climbed down the remains of an old stairway, a hazardous trip because the stones were slippery with mold. She stopped in front of a dank wall, and he tried not to breathe deeply; the earthy smell of fungus and rot was almost overpowering.

"It's a solid wall," he said.

"So it seems, but see this ugly brute." She touched what appeared to be a head carved out of stone, although the moonlight was so faint here it could have been an illusion. "Watch what happens when I box his ear."

She pushed hard against the misshapen head, and he had to take her word that there was an ear there. But he didn't doubt the ominous rumble or the way the stones underfoot seemed to vibrate. The stone with the head sank backward out of sight, and he could see a gaping hole in the wall.

"I take it we're going through there."

"We'll have to crawl." She was rolling up the legs of her jumpsuit. "Darned if I'm going to ruin a new outfit. When I went out to walk, I planned on going back to change."

He folded his pant legs above his knees; he didn't want to return to their rooms with muck on his trousers and no plausible reason for it.

"It's not as bad as it looks. The wall is thick but the passageway is straight."

"What's at the other end?"

"You'll see."

He heard the soft rustling she made crawling ahead of him and was grateful he'd never suffered from claustrophobia. He'd crawled through tight places before, but not in pitch darkness. His shoulders touched on either side, knocking grit from the wall and making him wonder how large the fortress's original builders had been. Two thousand years of good nutrition probably made him a giant by their standards, and he was unpleasantly reminded of all the undersized things on Zazar.

"Stop here," she said.

He couldn't even see her backside, much less an entryway into the archives, but he didn't ask questions. He had to believe she knew what she was doing.

Gradually a tiny crack of light showed, then a broader band. She was slowly pushing on a panel, taking great care not to make any sudden moves.

"Get ready!" she whispered, gracefully propelling herself through the opening.

Star Searcher

By the sound of it, there was a drop of several feet, and he couldn't see her head through the opening. He went feet first, hoping his shoulders weren't so broad they knocked away part of the new wall and made a racket.

"Getting back in the tunnel is trickier," she said. "Help me push this shut."

They were in a large, dimly lit cavern of a room, the silence broken by a boxy appliance that controlled the humidity. The entire floor space was taken up by row after row of free-standing bookshelves, the largest library of bound volumes he'd ever seen.

"This is only the twenty-second-century collection," she said. "Luckily for us, books are never stored against the walls in subterranean rooms. They would mold more easily. Instead the stone walls are lined with squares of moisture-absorbent material. They're always installed in relatively small pieces so there's room for them to expand if the humidity goes up."

"Surely the people who built this room saw the hole we just came through."

"They couldn't—it doesn't exist until the mechanism is triggered on the other end. My father fixed the panel with hinges so it can be swung out gently. Push it over the opening. It's a hundred to one chance a guard will check this far into level-three storage, but we can't be too cautious."

"I lied about demotion. They'll ship my butt to the mines if I'm caught. And you won't fare any better. Are you sure about the security?"

"Sure enough to take a chance. You nearly ended up in the mines once before, didn't you? Wasn't it penal labor or me?"

"I haven't regretted my choice yet—not very many times anyway."

"I wasn't here when they stored the laser disks, but most of the free space was on levels two and one. I'm guessing they used the west wing because the east is mostly pre-Coalition. We can't use the lifts, but I know where the stairs are."

She was on home turf now, darting from room to room but taking every precaution, listening and watching for any security guard who might be making rounds. Once they had a near miss, ducking behind some shelves just before a uniformed figure looked through an open archway.

They took off their hard-soled shoes to climb a spiral staircase, wary of echoes on the metal steps.

Her search of level two proved futile, and he sensed her growing tension as they mounted another spiral stairway to the first level of the basement. He didn't need to be told the higher levels were more dangerous. The likelihood of running into security people was much greater.

She motioned him to follow, not even daring to whisper. Here there was a labyrinth of corridors with closed doors, some with security systems that required handprints. If the laser disks were behind one of those doors, they were taking a huge risk for nothing.

At last she stopped before an unsecured door, carefully easing it open. Like all the storage space, it was dimly lit by recessed lights in the ceiling, but he immediately recognized the rows of racks: metal slots designed to hold disks, each of which held up to ten thousand entries.

There were small labels under every slot. He quickly

found the years they needed, but both knew they couldn't remove the disks from storage. There was no way to dispose of them, short of jettisoning them in space, and being caught with stolen archive material was a major felony.

"We'd better go for his senior year," she whispered, "after you'd left the Academy."

Since storage materials could never be removed from their final resting place, the museum did provide equipment in every sector to access and copy the information. Case activated the data bank and slipped in the disk, knowing as well as she did that a monitor would light up in the central control section to show a machine was in operation.

BAN, NEVIN, he typed on the keyboard, instantly rewarded by the file. He pressed the print button and made a copy.

Phoenix replaced the disk while he shut down the terminal.

"It will take them sixty seconds to get here, if we're lucky," she said, racing for the corridor and retracing their route as only someone who knew the layout intimately could.

He didn't need explanations. That was the maximum time it might take for the monitor to relay the warning to a guard with a communicator. Possibly one of them was close enough to check much more quickly. They raced down the first spiral steps at breakneck speed, still carrying their shoes, with the damning copy stuffed inside his shirt.

His heart was pounding when they reached the third level down, and he felt as flushed as Phoenix looked. Their chances were improving, unless a guard had been checking the lowest level when the alarm was given.

They reached the room with the tunnel, driven by desperation. He held out his hands for her to use as a step and boosted her into the dark hole, then handed up his shoes and the small sheath of papers. His only chance was a running jump; he couldn't expect her to hoist his weight. He leaped, caught the edge, and shimmied into the tunnel.

He couldn't pass her; his shoulders were too wide. She whispered urgent instructions on how to secure the panel, then led the way through the black hole.

When he emerged from the tunnel, she was sitting on a moss-covered rock and giggling, doubled over in what he recognized as hysteria more than mirth.

"We have one chance in four," he said to sober her. "If we picked the wrong year, we still may not learn the secret that made someone try to put his records beyond our reach.

"If not, we'll have to come back tomorrow," she said more calmly.

"We'd never get away with it twice. By then all the guards will know which room was violated. They'll have it under constant watch hoping we do try again. Let's get back to our rooms before someone thinks of searching the campus grounds for unauthorized personnel."

"We're authorized," she said, standing and reaching her hand into the dark hole. "I have to tug the old boy's tongue to close it," she said.

She grabbed Case's arm while the stones that blocked both ends of the tunnel gradually rumbled into place.

"Can that be heard at the other end?" he asked.

"Only in the room with the tunnel."

"Then cross your fingers, and let's get out of here," he said.

Phoenix had never been racked by so many contrary feelings. Her body was still tingly and deliciously achy from their strenuous lovemaking, and she was out of breath from their mad dash across the campus. She was still keyed up, but part of her longed to sink into oblivion on the bunk where Case was now stretched out, reading Ban's record from his senior year at the Academy for the third time.

"I think this is it," he said.

She'd already read it, and agreed. "I'm surprised he was accepted into the diplomatic corps," she added.

"Don't underestimate the power of patronage. I don't know who sponsored him, but I've often wondered.

"He was accused of breaking into the room of a cadet from the planet Moori. The victim was an aristocrat, and he'd rather foolishly brought jewels and artifacts he thought would give him special status during his training at the Academy," Case summarized.

"He must have had some unpleasant surprises," she said. "Every new cadet gets equal treatment—equally bad."

"The important thing is, when his treasures disappeared, he blamed Ban. When a hearing was held, his charges were dismissed for lack of evidence. The Moori left in a huff, and Ban stayed to finish his training. The stolen items were never recovered, and the case was closed."

"So now we know Ban could be a thief."

"Probably was."

"Yes," she conceded. "And he had an eye for valuable artifacts even during his cadet days."

"I wish we knew who had a hand in the cover-up," he said, looking as worried as she felt.

"You're sure he couldn't have put his records out of reach himself?"

"Level-four officers just don't have that kind of clearance. I don't think Ban is clever enough to get around all the safeguards in the system—if anybody is."

"It's all in front of us," she said, pacing and keenly aware of Case's eyes following her. "My mind isn't working! I should be able to put the pieces together!"

"We both need sleep. Come here and let me hold you," he said, his voice a husky invitation.

"No." She shook her head. "I can't."

Much as she wanted to be held, she needed time to sort out her feelings.

"I'm asking too much." He rose slowly and stood close to her. "You're exhausted. Get a good rest, and maybe things will fall into place by themselves."

"I never knew you were such an optimist," she said, smiling in spite of all her reservations.

"I didn't either."

He left, quietly shutting the door behind him.

Chapter Sixteen

Had she slept at all? Phoenix wasn't sure. Her mind was so filled with Case, she couldn't be sure where memories left off and dreams began.

She did know it was the middle of the night, and she was wide-eyed, tossing and turning on a thin government-issue mattress. It was no good blaming the hardness of the bed; she'd slept soundly on stony ground when her mind wasn't full of turmoil. What had made her think another time in his arms would exorcise him from her heart? She might as well believe swimming in the ocean would grow gills!

She couldn't lie in bed another moment remembering their lovemaking. Padding barefoot to the window, she looked out at the ocean. In primary school she'd learned how philosophers had proved the planet was round even before explorers had circumnavigated it. The view from her room reminded her of one of the proofs: the rounded curve of the horizon, the same perspective a mite would have from the top of a ball. But visual evidence was misleading. From her vantage point, it looked as though the sea dropped off the edge of the horizon, and there should be a great waterfall just beyond her range of vision. Scientific proofs were far more reliable than relying on her senses.

Were her senses leading her astray in other ways? Because Case made love in a way that carried her to heights of ecstasy, did it mean she could trust him with her heart?

Could she trust anyone? Was Mol'ar Fap as evil as he seemed, or was he bluffing to manipulate her? Was the Coalition a force for good in the universe or the ultimate despoiler?

Her mind was filled with the cobwebs of deceit and double-dealing. She needed fresh air to clear her head, but she rejected her first impulse: to walk beside the ocean. The last place to seek tranquility was the beach where they'd made love. She couldn't bear the hurt of knowing they couldn't be together that way again.

When the mission was over, whatever the outcome, she had to say good-bye. He was wedded to the Coalition; she had a different path to follow, however mucky the way seemed now.

She was overwhelmed by an incredible sadness. Somewhere she'd lost her anger and the resentment that had made their long separation tolerable. Without these defenses, she was left with raw pain and a deep regret for the past.

For now she needed Case; they made good partners, and all that mattered was getting her family out of jeopardy.

She'd gone to bed nude, the better to remember the

Star Searcher

way it felt when Case caressed and loved her. Impatient now with erotic fantasies, she dressed quickly in casual clothes from her backpack and slipped out into the hallway. She might benefit from a hard run on the deserted grounds; it had to do more for her than moping in the room.

Expecting a deserted corridor at this hour, she was startled when Case's door opened and he stepped out. He was barefoot, in loose trousers and an unbuttoned shirt that reminded her how it felt to cuddle against his muscular chest.

"Where are you going?" She'd had to ask; they couldn't stand there like statues.

"Nowhere . . . just restless," he said evasively.

Her heart thumped erratically; her groin felt twitchy. He'd intended to knock on her door!

"I couldn't sleep either, thinking about tomorrow," she lied. "It won't be easy, confronting Ban."

"Naturally he'll lie—try to cover up what he's done."

"We need a strategy to get a confession from him."

"That won't be easy. We definitely need a plan. Since neither of us can sleep, maybe we should talk about it now."

"In my room?" She tested him.

"Fine."

"Not fine—that wasn't an invitation, Case."

"I was afraid not."

"You know what will happen if you come in."

"Would that be bad?"

She knew they'd end up entwined in each other's arms, pressing naked bodies in a lovers' knot. She trembled, tempted almost beyond the strength of her resistance.

"No, not bad," she sadly admitted.

Pam Rock

He wrapped his arms around her, pulling her against his bare chest and lightly kissing the top of her head.

Making love on the beach had done nothing to get him out of her system. She wanted him more than ever as she felt the warmth of his skin on her cheek. Was there anything more seductive than being held by strong arms?

"Please stop, Case."

No words had ever been harder to say.

He backed away; they were far enough apart to satisfy the rules for rookie cadets.

"We can discuss things in the morning," he said, going back to his own room.

Phoenix crawled back into bed alone; she was empty, used up, exhausted.

She finally slept, but woke up feeling as sluggish as if she'd been drugged. An overdose of emotional involvement seemed to be as debilitating as intoxication from strong drink. She put one foot on the floor, but didn't have enough energy to move the other.

She lay there, trying not to think, realizing she was still wearing the clothes she'd put on for the run she'd never made.

She ignored the first summons at her door, but a second knock and a third roused her enough to leave the bunk. Once she opened the door, her day would begin. She didn't feel up to solving problems or making decisions, but the person banging on her door wasn't going to go away.

She opened it a crack.

"Good morning. I've brought you some breakfast," Case said.

Star Searcher

She saw through his cheerfulness. No man liked being sent back to his room after venturing out with amorous intent in the middle of the night.

"We need to talk," he said.

"You're always saying that. It's too early."

"Do you want me to handle things from now on?"

A cold shower wouldn't have shocked her as much. "Of course not! You'd better come in."

He put the covered dish he was carrying on the desk along with a hot-beverage carton.

"The eggs should still be hot. And there's a frosted roll—brain food."

"Thanks." Her brain needed more than a sugar fix.

He shut the door and sat on the edge of the lower bunk. She wondered if he could still feel the heat of her body on the bed linens.

"Are we agreed that Ban was probably involved in the theft?"

"Someone on the *Isis* had to be," she agreed, slumping down on the desk chair and halfheartedly sipping a tasteless dark brew from the carton.

"He's not in it alone, though. He's not smart enough. I think he was working for someone outside the Coalition, someone who needed an inside person to pull it off."

"You don't want to believe there's real corruption in your precious Coalition."

"You do wake up with a burr—"

"We're talking about Ban, not me."

"What we need is a way to make him reveal his cohorts."

"You could threaten to eject him through the waste chute," she suggested.

"You have a jaundiced view of my finesse. Instead

of loosing your poison-tipped arrows at me, why don't you focus on his motive? The stakes must be high because Ban has a lot to lose."

"Only if you think the Coalition is the ultimate career choice. I still think profit is behind the theft. If you got out of your space chariot more often, you'd know there are a lot of greedy people out there." She gestured at the sky outside the window.

"You're not exactly poverty-stricken yourself now."

"Does it still bother you that I'm being well paid?"

"No, it never did. That's your affair."

"Next you'll be accusing me of enlisting Ban in some sinister cause!" She knew this was an unreasonable accusation; she had a near-terminal case of morning-after grumpiness.

"No, but if you're going to act like a sulky child, I may begin treating you like one."

"Be warned! I bite, scratch, and kick."

"Don't worry. If I ever decide to turn you over my knee, you'll enjoy it."

"That's why this partnership doesn't work!" she said vehemently. "It's always there!"

"What's always there?" His deep blue eyes were cloudy gray with anger.

"The sex thing!"

"Thing?"

"You know what I mean."

"No, but I'll give you half an hour to figure out whether you do. Eat your breakfast and get dressed. When I come back, I'll expect you to be civil!"

"You'll expect! I'm not your flunky!" she sputtered as he slammed the door behind him.

"Damn you!" she shouted, breaking into tears when

she realized how futile it was to try to shock a man who wasn't there.

Worst of all, she was much madder at herself than him. She'd played a dangerous game with her heart as the stakes, and she was a poor loser.

No matter what Case thought of her now, she could feel Mol'ar Fap's menacing shadow engulfing Dena and her beloved children, Ina and Celline. Phoenix realized she hadn't thought of them by name since her search for the Star Stone began. It just hurt too much to let them into her thoughts. She remembered her little nieces putting their hands in hers when she visited, pulling her to see a trinket they called their treasure. What did any artifact, even the Star Stone, mean compared to loved ones? For a few shattering moments she let herself long for a child of her own to cherish.

Then, with almost superhuman resolve, she hurried to ready herself for a confrontation with Nevin Ban.

Case was back at her door in exactly 30 minutes. She was ready for him.

"I've thought this over," he said, stuffing his hands in the pockets of black uniform trousers. "I want to question Ban alone. I think you should stay here until I've had a chance to see what his reaction will be."

"Absolutely not! We're still partners! I have ideas of my own on how to approach him."

"This has nothing to do with our partnership. It's strictly a Coalition internal affair if Ban is involved."

"It's been my affair since I accepted the job! You can't squeeze me out now! We're partners!"

"I'm not trying to."

"I'm going with you. There's no point in arguing. I

trusted you; now you have to trust me enough to take me with you."

"Trust has nothing to do with it! It's your safety I'm worried about. Ban acts like a fool, but he's treacherous."

"That's ridiculous! If anyone should go alone, it's me. I'm sure I could be a lot more persuasive than you."

"You're the one who's being ridiculous if you think your feminine wiles give you any protection from a cornered suspect. Your charms might get your throat slashed if you underestimate Ban. He's a problem for the higher-ups, but it's going to be damn tricky convincing anyone of that."

"Especially if you try alone!"

"If a burning village and a shuttle explosion aren't enough to scare you into being sensible, I guess there's nothing I can do—at least nothing I'm willing to do—to change your mind."

"You can stop taking cheap shots! It's because we've been in danger together that I have a right to see this through to the finish."

"I'm not trying to cut you out—only keep you safe. I'm sorry...."

A sharp knock on her door startled both of them.

"An old friend looking you up?" he asked skeptically.

"Not likely."

He ambled over to the door and looked through a small square of one-way glass put there for security.

"A cadet—young, swarthy, a mole on his cheek."

She shrugged. "No one I know."

He opened the door.

"Excuse me, sir. Are you Diplomatic Officer Case Remo of the *GCS Isis?*"

Star Searcher

"I am. At ease, cadet."

"Officer Remo, sir, I have an oral communication for you, sir. Ambassador Ngate requests your presence in the registrar's office, sir. Ah . . ."

"There's more?"

"Yes, sir, but I forget the proper terminology for 'get your butt over here on the double,' sir!"

"If it comes up again, try 'stat,' and tell Ambassador Ngate I'll be there presently. That's P.R.E.S.E.N.T.L.Y., cadet."

"Yes, sir. Thank you, sir."

"Was I ever that young?" Case asked wearily after he shut the door. "You might as well come with me, since you're determined to be in on everything."

"No one told me to get my butt over there on the double," she said. "Ngate likes to get his reports from you. Does he always give you orders so sweetly?"

"The ambassador doesn't waste his diplomatic charms on underlings," he said dryly. "Ordinarily I'd make him stew awhile, but I want to get back to the *Isis* as soon as possible. I'll take my gear and meet you at the shuttle. Once we get to the *Isis*, you can wait for me while I question Ban. I shouldn't be long now. I'm not quite ready to put Ngate in the picture."

"Don't you think he'll believe you?"

"Face it, Phoenix. All we have are suspicions. Ban was cleared of stealing from the Moori."

"The charges were dropped for lack of evidence. That's not the same thing."

"Anyway, I want more facts before we talk to anyone about him. Do you have any objections?"

"No."

"Then you'll meet me at the shuttle?"

"Yes," she said, walking over to the window so he

couldn't read the lie in her eyes.

She rode the monorail to the large docking facility just beyond the campus grounds. Their shuttle was waiting by a loading platform, and even as she walked toward it, another small ship started its ascent.

They'd come in one of the smallest shuttles, the *Ground Hopper*, appropriately named since it was a light craft used mainly for short runs to Athera when the *Isis* orbited the home planet.

There was no difficulty getting permission to return to the *Isis*, nor was navigating the shuttle a problem. She'd seen Case punch in the code, and she was a competent pilot, certified for all smaller vessels.

She wouldn't have a long head start; Case could easily commandeer a shuttle from someone with a lower priority, and she didn't doubt that he would. He'd be livid when he learned she was gone, but she'd worry about that later. For now, she had to get to Nevin Ban before Case did. She knew enough about Mol'ar Fap and his schemes to pretend she was his messenger. It was her best chance to trip up Ban, but she couldn't pull it off if Case interfered.

Her stomach was knotted with anxiety when she arrived on the *Isis*. Since she wasn't a staff member, she had to fill in a bureaucratic docking form and wait for clearance to go into the ship proper. It seemed to take forever, but at last she was allowed to enter the lift. She didn't know Ban's room number, but she decided to check the diplomatic offices first. Most likely he was working, doing whatever it was a recorder did when his boss was gone.

She hadn't thought of one thing: Maybe Ngate had taken Ban with him! She ran down the corridor that housed his office, so agitated she had to stand and count to 20 before she dared approach the department's receptionist.

A pleasant, round-faced young man with a receding hairline assured her Ban was on the *Isis*. It was the receptionist's responsibility to keep track of the diplomatic staff. She thought it was a shame the job was aging him prematurely—or maybe the furrows on his brow weren't worry lines.

"Officer Ban hasn't reported in this morning," he said apologetically after checking his terminal.

"Can you give me his room number?"

The lad was so well trained he didn't even smirk. What he did do was insist on checking her authorization while she fidgeted. A thief could walk off with a priceless artifact on this ship, but she met one obstacle after another trying to do her job.

When she finally reached the corridor where Ban lived, it was deserted. She hoped that meant no one would interrupt them.

She walked nearly the length of the long hallway, looking for his number on a door. She was so nervous she almost hoped he wasn't there, but that would be a disaster. This was her only chance to see him without Case.

Unlike every other door she passed, his was partially open. He might be just leaving; in that case, she had to say something to get him to stay without tipping her hand right away.

She tapped softly on the door, then called out his name, puzzled when he didn't respond. It seemed unlikely a man would leave with the door of his quarters open—especially one who'd been accused of pilfering from someone else's room.

She slipped through the narrow opening, entering

what appeared to be a deserted living room.

"Nevin! Are you here?"

He rated a second room for sleeping, she noted, and that door was closed. Maybe he'd worked late the night before and was still in bed. It wasn't an ideal situation, but there might be some advantage in confronting him while he was still groggy with sleep.

She knocked loudly, hurting her knuckles on the metal door.

"Nevin! I have to talk to you!"

Was there a chance he wasn't there? But why would he leave and not close his outer door?

She went back to that door and checked the corridor in both directions; he could have stepped into a friend's room for a short while, neglecting to lock his door. Probably the people who quartered on this level knew each other well. Maybe an open door was an invitation to come in and visit, although she had a hard time imagining Ban as a chummy neighbor who encouraged people to drop in and chat.

Or perhaps he had a special friend. The thought of the recorder spending his work break thrashing around on someone else's bunk—or his own—was almost as sickening as doubting the Neosoul blood oath. She procrastinated, hoping something would happen so she wouldn't have to open his bedroom door. She had a bad feeling about Ban, even though he hadn't threatened her so far.

She banged hard on the bedroom door, giving him one more chance to do the decent thing and answer. The door vibrated under her knuckles, but there was no response.

Reluctantly she inched it open, peeking into a dim interior with the lone porthole shrouded by a blue cur-

Star Searcher

tain. Much as she hated to enter the room, she wasn't going to turn tail now.

He was lying on his back on the single bunk, his long length covered by a dark blue and white coverlet. All she could see of his head were a few coils of black hair spilling over the edge of the hand-loomed covering onto the pillow.

"Nevin! Wake up!"

The man must take sleeping drugs! She'd made enough noise to rouse the soundest sleeper.

"Ban, we've got to talk!"

She gently nudged his shoulder, wondering what she'd have to do to get his attention. She didn't want to fend him off before she had a chance to talk, but time wasn't on her side. The pokey little shuttle had all the thrust of those awful motoscoots and had taken far too long reaching the *Isis*. Getting past security had wasted more precious minutes.

He didn't move a muscle, but she didn't hear the uneven breathing that might indicate he was sleeping off a binge.

"Ban, this is ridiculous!" she said impatiently, ready to use the time-tested method for rousing cadets who overslept: a hard yank on the covers and a dousing with ice water. If he was faking to avoid talking to her, it would serve him right.

She walked around to the other side of the freestanding bunk so she could see his face, but the covers were up so high all she could see was the hair on top of his head.

Carefully inching the cloth away from his face, she realized there was something wrong—drastically wrong! His forehead looked bloodless—too white even for his sallow complexion.

"Ban! Wake up!"

Desperation made her tug on the sheet, uncovering his shoulders, and still he didn't stir.

She had a terrible feeling he never would. Ripping away the coverlet, she was too horrified to scream.

A crude dagger protruded from his chest, right in the vicinity of his heart.

"Oh, no, not this!"

The undersheet beside him was soaked red, but the handle of the dagger had held the coverlet away from his bloodied chest.

She had to call someone, had to get help, but a small sane voice inside her head warned her not to yell. Ban was dead. She'd only seen the carefully prepared remains of older people who'd died peacefully, but the look was unmistakable. The rational part of her mind noted that he was naked. He looked so pathetic, she forced herself to touch the coverlet again, drawing it up as far as his navel.

There was no sign of a struggle: no apparent resistance. Either someone had surprised and killed him in his sleep, or he'd known and trusted his assailant. It could have been a late-night intruder—or a woman who'd pretended to come for other reasons.

How long had he been dead? She forced herself to touch his pale, thin arm. There seemed to be warmth left in his flesh, but she felt too feverish herself to be sure. One thing did attract her attention. He had something white clenched in his fist. She couldn't tell what it was, but she was desperately eager to find out. Did she dare pry open his hand?

She touched a stick-like finger with trembling hands, and her nerve momentarily failed her. Every rule of common sense and official procedure warned her not to try.

She heard a voice coming from the corridor, then another. The open door was sure to invite curiosity. Would someone step in just to see why it wasn't closed?

The bedroom door was partially open too, and her heart nearly stopped in fear. She couldn't be found—she had to hide, but there was no place to go. What reason could she give for hovering over a murdered Coalition officer? Memories of the agonizing months when her innocent father was imprisoned and brought to trial came flooding back, and she was paralyzed by fear. This couldn't be happening! Case was right—she shouldn't have come near Ban by herself.

There was a buzz of voices now—a group of men were coming into the outer room. One was achingly familiar: Case's.

"I especially want Ban to record this meeting. Odd, he's not the sort to be careless about leaving his room open."

She recognized Ngate's voice. He must have brought Case back for a meeting on the *Isis* instead of conferring with him in the registrar's office. It was the worst thing that could have happened—one she hadn't anticipated.

"Phoenix! What are you doing?" Case had never sounded so angry.

He hurried to the bunk, his anger replaced by shock when he saw Ban.

"What happened?" His handsome features were transformed by horror.

"I just found him. . . ." Her voice was so weak she wasn't sure he heard.

"What is it?" Ngate stepped into the room and froze. "By the heavens, he's dead!" He moved away from the bunk as though the sight of the dagger wound sickened him.

"Sir, he's holding something," one of two other officers said.

"Don't touch...." Case warned, but the man didn't listen, prying apart Ban's fingers and gingerly holding a crinkled piece of paper between his thumb and finger.

"Let me see that," Ngate ordered.

He seemed to read it a dozen times as Phoenix and the others watched, waiting to hear what it said.

"I can't believe this—but it all makes sense now," Ngate said in a hoarse whisper. "Ban stole the Star Stone. He says so here."

He paused, seemingly overcome by grief, holding the note as though the paper could poison him.

"He wanted to come to me and confess, but his partner refused to let him. He was working for a dissident Atheran faction opposed to the accord—lured into it by misguided idealism." Ngate stopped reading, pushing back his steel-colored mane before he went on. "His partner was hired by the group; her only motivation was greed—and he names her here: Phoenix Landau."

"That's a lie! I had nothing to do with it!"

Case saw her face go white, and he leaped to her defense without stopping to think.

"Ban was a notorious liar! You can't believe anything he wrote!"

"Her father was a criminal. How can you be surprised she is?" Ngate asked.

Star Searcher

"He was exonerated," Case said. "Phoenix wouldn't—"

"We're not her judge and jury," Ngate interrupted harshly. "All I know is a dead man has accused her—and we found her leaning over him. I can see no choice but to place her under arrest."

"Isn't that hasty?" Case asked. "You haven't heard her side yet."

"She'll have plenty of chance to answer questions. Officer Ban is lying there in his own blood. I don't have the stomach to stay here talking."

"Call Captain Humme. This is under the jurisdiction of the navigational commander," Case said.

"Captain Humme will be notified," Ngate said impatiently, "but I must advise you to stay out of this matter, Officer Remo. Men's careers have been destroyed for lesser reasons than associating with a thief and murderer. I wouldn't be surprised if the charge against this woman will be high treason!"

"Oh, no!"

She cried out as though she'd been struck, and Case felt his heart constrict in agony. This couldn't be happening to the woman he loved!

"Take her away," Ngate said to the other two officers.

"Wait, please!" Tears were streaming down her face. "Let me have a word alone with Officer Remo."

For a moment Case expected him to refuse; then Ngate shrugged his shoulders. "It's your career, Remo, but I'll have to make note that the accused wanted to confer with you instead of a legal adviser. These men will be waiting in the corridor to escort Landau to the lockup."

When the others had left the bedroom, Case took

her in his arms, knowing this was no time for anger or recriminations.

"He was dead when I got here," she said. "I am so, so sorry."

"Don't blame yourself." He held her tighter.

"It doesn't matter what happens to me, but I have to tell you something."

"You don't need to convince me."

"No, this is something else. Mol'ar Fap wants me to lead an expedition to Horus for him."

"That's not important now." He looked down into her face and ached for her misery.

"Yes, it is! Ngate said he'd let me go there on a Coalition vessel if I found the Star Stone in no more than sixty days. Mol'ar Fap is going to kill my step-sister and her family if I fail him. That's why I've been so desperate to find it!"

"I won't let anything happen to them. Where are they now?"

"Dena and her husband work as clerks in the Coalition Hall of Records in the capital."

"Their family name?" he asked, aware of the impatient voices of the two men under orders to imprison her.

"Atwel."

"That's all I need. I'll get the rest from the infobanks."

"Fap is so powerful—he's everywhere!"

"They'll be safe, darling—if I have to move them to my father's home to guarantee it."

"It's the only thing I'll ever ask of you! You mustn't get involved in this!"

He brushed his lips across her forehead, not letting

himself rebuke her for holding onto her secret fear for so long.

"They won't be hurt. I pledge it."

"Officer Remo, we've got to take her now." One of the officers had come to the bedroom door.

"Yes." Case squeezed her hand, then released it. "I know you're innocent."

He said it with complete conviction, not believing she could commit murder, but when she was gone, he covered Ban's face with the coverlet, and wondered how he'd ever convince anyone else.

There was much he had to do, but he stood and stared at the bed, trying to overcome his shock and dismay. He'd spoken the truth to Phoenix: He was certain she hadn't killed Ban. What would happen now that she was under suspicion of both theft and murder?

Ban's death hadn't changed the fact that the Star Stone was missing. The search had to continue, but would he be part of it? How could he best help Phoenix, by letting others carry on the hunt for the relic or by convincing Ngate to let him head a full-scale investigation? He tried to clear his head and focus on Phoenix's arrest, but something was nagging at him.

In spite of the urgent need to find it, Ngate hadn't asked her where the Star Stone was hidden.

Chapter Seventeen

Phoenix was profoundly weary of white: gleaming white walls, ceiling, and floor with a molded table, chair, and bunk that were only outcroppings of the same colorless plastic material. The holding facility on the *Isis* was a row of modular cubes that looked like play cubicles for children, smooth and rounded on all surfaces with no sharp edges to inflict injuries. Even the bars that slid across the opening were made of the same smooth-textured white substance. They looked flexible, but she tested and found them as rigid as steel, held in place by a substantial lock with a code that could be changed.

If only the light would go out, she thought, it might be possible to sleep for a while. Harsh artificial daylight streamed into the cell from a recessed fixture in the ceiling, reflecting off the walls because the only color-absorbing surface in the room was the gray of her drab prison coveralls. Her feet and arms were bare, and the only bedding was a coarse canvas rectangle, quilted to use as a mattress or a blanket but too small to serve as both.

As cells went, she supposed it was the ultimate in cleanliness and sanitation, unlike the hovel in Summa where Case had been imprisoned. But this was far worse in one way: It was wholly escape-proof. No one had ever broken out, according to the guards who'd robbed her of dignity when they'd stripped and searched her without regard to gender. She'd never been so humiliated, depressed, and desperate.

Reaching deep inside herself, she knew she could endure imprisonment if only she were sure Case could succeed in protecting her family.

Judging by the number of meals left on the floor just inside the bars, at least the equivalent of a full day and night had passed since her arrest. It was incredible no one had interrogated her in all that time. Were they trying to drive her insane with boredom before questioning her? If Ngate was so sure she was involved in the theft of the Star Stone, why hadn't anyone asked her where it was?

What could she have done differently? She tortured herself by dwelling on their quest, trying to pinpoint the moment when it had started to unravel. She fervently hoped Case would honor his promise to keep Dena and her family safe from harm, not just now but in the future. Mol'ar Fap didn't forget; a few days of armed protection wouldn't discourage him in the least.

She should have trusted Case sooner, but their past had made her too wary. Even when she was in his arms, she hadn't been able to confide in him.

She heard the sharp staccato steps of boots on the synthetic flooring in the corridor. Her cell was the last in the single row facing a blank white wall. When they'd brought her there, only one cubicle had had an inmate: a young crewman incarcerated for drunkenness. He'd since been released. Someone was coming for her, and she braced herself for the worst.

When she saw her uniformed visitor, her heart skipped a beat.

"Case!" She rushed to the bars.

"Darling, are you all right?"

He pushed his fingers between bars too closely spaced to accommodate his whole hand, and she grabbed them like a lifeline, buoyed up just by touching warm human flesh.

"I'll be okay, but you shouldn't be here! You're risking your career and maybe even your freedom."

"You don't really think I can stay away, do you?" He squeezed her fingers so hard they hurt, but courage seemed to flow from his touch.

"My family . . ."

"I sent some trusted friends to guard them until I can get them to a safe hiding place."

"Where?"

"It's better if you don't know—for their protection as well as yours. Have you been questioned?"

"No."

"No one has asked you where the Star Stone is?"

She shook her head. "No, I don't understand it. Isn't the Coalition eager to find it? Who really killed Ban? Do you have any idea?"

"I'm not sure. A lot of things don't add up—haven't for a long time. I blame myself. . . ."

"No, don't! Unless you murdered Ban and stuck the

note in his hand." Her attempt at flippancy fizzled.

His strong, fine face was deeply troubled. He was afraid for her sake, and knowing it frightened her to the core. Her situation was hopeless, and the penalty for murder was penal servitude for life, a living hell with no hope of reprieve. But if everyone she loved was safe, she could face it. That meant Case as well as her family. If he sacrificed himself for her sake, he might be condemned as a conspirator. Even though they had no future together, she couldn't let that happen.

"I'm going to find out who did this to you," he said, looking grim and determined.

"Don't do anything foolish! Don't jeopardize your precious career—there's nothing you can do for me."

He ignored her words. It was a very bad sign that she couldn't provoke him to argue. It would be easier for him if he did get angry with her.

"I've been in tighter scrapes," she want on, talking fast to make him listen. "I was cornered by awful-looking beasts on Sesram II—hairy things that smelled like rotten flesh. And once an expedition leader from Cleo in the Ar system double-crossed me—left me stranded with no ship."

"Phoenix," he said gently. "If they decide to charge you with treason for stealing the Star Stone, the death penalty is mandatory."

"Death." She whispered the word she'd been afraid to think. "I've been trying to convince myself digging in a mine is a lot like excavating a ruin."

She couldn't tell him what was really in her heart: She didn't want to go on living without him. But even if, by some miracle, she were freed, there was no future for them. She couldn't let him ruin his life by being linked with a notorious traitor.

A buzzer sounded in the stark corridor.

"My time is up," he said desolately. "Kiss me, darling."

He pressed his face against the bars, and she did the same, only managing to touch his lips with hers for a light caress.

"What are you going to do?" she asked urgently. "Please! Don't put yourself in danger!"

"I'm going to ensure the safety of your family, then pay a visit to my father," he whispered urgently. "I have to tell him I'm resigning my post. Then I'll need to retrieve the Zazaran gemstones while I still have access to the *Seker*."

"Did I tell you where they are?" She kept her voice as low as possible.

"Taped to the inside of the commode casing."

"You mustn't resign your commission!"

"The only job I care about is bringing down the bastard who did this to you."

Once those words would have compensated for all the pain of her father's ordeal. Now her situation was so hopeless, she was terrified Case would sacrifice everything for her cause.

"No! You mustn't...."

He bent and urgently kissed her fingers as they gripped the bars.

"Trust me," he said, and then he was gone without giving her a chance to say all the things in her heart.

Somehow she managed to live through another day, sleeping fitfully, pacing the tiny space, and pleading for information from the guards who brought her meals.

Star Searcher

"I have a right to legal counsel," she insisted when they gave her no indication of what to expect.

"This is a military command," one burly guard tersely reminded her. "You're allowed regulation meals and a shower every fifth day. Those are your only rights as long as you're on the *Isis*."

Were they going to let her languish there until her mind snapped from the suspense of waiting? Why didn't someone come to question her? If being ignored was a subtle form of torture to break her spirit, it was working.

On the third day a guard retrieved her tray, making her stand at the back of the cell while he did.

"Somebody's signing in to see you," he said.

She fervently hoped it was Case. Was he still safe? She missed him terribly after all their time together. Although she lived in perpetual dread of death, the prospect of never again seeing him occupied her mind the most.

A tall, stately man walked up to her bars, and she couldn't have been more stunned if her own father's ghost had appeared.

"Phoenix, I'm Oaker Remo, commander-in-chief, retired."

"Case's father."

She'd never met the man, but she'd seen pictures. In person, the family resemblance was striking. His hair was graying, and age lines were deeply etched on the sides of his mouth, but he was still a handsome man with bold features and deep blue eyes like Case's. He was dressed in civilian clothes, a dark blue tunic and trousers, but he had the same military bearing as his son, with only a slight slumping around the shoulders.

He pressed the code to release the cell lock, then waited for the bars to slide away so he could enter.

"Please sit," he said, gesturing at the only chair in the cell.

She obeyed automatically. He was one of those rare people who could give a command with a few quiet words and impose his will without being questioned.

He sat on the edge of the shelf that served as a bunk, appraising her with his eyes until she felt like squirming. She knew him only as the man who'd stood between her and Case, and she wanted to hate him. Instead her overriding reaction was curiosity, but she held back her questions. If she'd learned anything on Thal and Zazar, it was to exercise greater patience. Jumping head first into a pit of serpents wasn't always good policy.

"I've had a visit from my son," he said slowly, as though measuring every word he used. "He wanted to leave the Coalition service."

"I imagine that distressed you." She was skirting a fine line between courtesy and resentment.

"I must admit, I said some things about your influence on Case that were far from flattering. I hope you'll accept my apology and give me an opportunity to reverse my opinion of you."

She shrugged. It wasn't a gracious acceptance, but she didn't think Commander Remo knew her well enough to judge her.

"My son told me a great deal about what's been happening, although, no doubt, he left out crucial details about the depth of his feelings for you."

Her cheeks felt hot, and she hoped he wouldn't read

an admission of any wrongdoing in her blush. She loved Case, and nothing they'd done was tinged with shame, whatever his father might think.

"I persuaded him not to resign yet," the older man said. "He'll have a much better chance of learning the truth if he stays in the service."

"I don't want him to sacrifice his career for me." She tried to keep belligerence out of her voice; Commander Remo had a dignified charisma that made it easier.

"He suspects Coalition involvement in Nevin Ban's death," he said.

"I don't want him to put himself in danger. Whatever you think of me, Commander, I love Case. I'm frightened of what may happen to him."

"My son loves both of us, but he's his own man now. So far he's refused my help, but there's one thing I can do without interfering in his investigation. I can't undo a terrible wrong, but I can tell you the truth about Case's reason for turning his back on you when your father was under suspicion."

This was more pain than she needed; she didn't want Case's father to see her self-control crumble.

"It's in the past. Let's leave it there," she said.

He shook his head. "You need to know. My wife was very ill—in great pain in spite of the best possible treatment. We still thought there was a chance she could go into remission and live a full life again for a while, but I knew she had a life-threatening disease."

"It must have been very difficult," she said, torn between embarrassment and compassion when she saw Oaker's eyes glisten.

"When your father was arrested, I demanded that Case break off your relationship. He refused, of course, but I was desperate for his mother's sake. The scandal would most likely kill her before her time if his name came into it."

"You made him choose between his mother and me?" Her throat constricted, and she didn't know how to deal with this.

"More than that. I laid the responsibility for her survival on him. Case is an honorable man, and he was a loving son to my dear wife. He thought he was only postponing his happiness with you, but I made him swear not to see you while his mother still lived. I used his mother's illness to keep him away from you. I earned my son's hatred, but I would have done anything at the time to spare my wife."

"I don't know what to say."

"I had no right to ruin both your lives—to force Case to deny his love for you. It's no excuse, but I was half-mad with worry for my wife. I would have sacrificed anything to spare her further pain."

"I made a life for myself without Case." She resisted the urge to console him, even though his distress was painful to witness. But she was much too proud to let him think her life was meaningless without Case.

"I was happy when Case made a success of his career, even though I sorely missed being close to him," Oaker told her. "I used to think Coalition service was all-important. But losing out on love is a real tragedy. I'm ashamed of depriving both of you a chance to have what my wife and I shared."

She didn't think of doubting his sincerity. The pain of confessing aged his face in front of her eyes.

"Why didn't Case tell me?" she asked, more to herself than Oaker.

"Maybe I narrowed his options too severely, and he

thought a decisive break would be easier for you in the long run. He didn't know how little time his mother had left."

"I see."

He stood and took her hands in his, pulling her to her feet. "I have to go. If I had the power, I'd take you with me. I was sorry about your father's death. He was a good man, and he was taken too soon."

She realized coming there and speaking to her had been an ordeal for him. All of a sudden, he didn't seem like an enemy anymore. She stepped close and hugged him, drawing on the strength left in his shoulders even as she absolved him.

"Thank you for coming."

"Don't give up hope. My son is as stubborn as his father. He'll find out who's behind this."

"I don't want him to—not if it puts him in jeopardy."

He shook his head and walked out of the cell, closing the bars, then looking in at her. "Good luck, Phoenix."

She was afraid she'd used up a lifetime of good luck establishing herself as an antiquities hunter. It definitely felt as though fate had turned against her.

Doing what had to be done on Athera, Case couldn't shake the feeling he was being followed. But whenever he turned around, no one was there. He boarded the monorail to go from the Academy to the shuttle pad, reviewing in his head the complicated security arrangements he'd just finished making for Dena and her family. When he'd told Phoenix they were under guard, he knew it was only a temporary measure. Much as he'd hated leaving her in a cell and putting his investigation on hold, he'd lived up to his promise:

Pam Rock

Fap wouldn't find them now.

Dena was, in her own quiet way, as stubborn as Phoenix. Fortunately her husband saw merit in Case's plan, and they were now housed on the Academy campus with new identities and new jobs in the central administrative office, thanks to Oaker's influence and help from Case's own friends. If Fap's agents were watching the family, they saw them leave on a ground transport for the northern province of Deichong. The few people who knew differently were totally trustworthy.

Now Case could give his full attention to Phoenix. He had to remove her from confinement on the *Isis*, by force if necessary, and see that she disappeared until she was exonerated. She hadn't been interrogated or formally charged, but that only confirmed his suspicion: Someone within the Coalition was involved. Once the legal steps were taken, she'd be transferred to prison on Athera for trial. Public attention would be focused on the crime. Someone didn't want that to happen yet, so she was still languishing in the ship's lockup. He wanted her beyond the reach of the conspirators who'd framed her for murder. Ban was dead, and she was too vulnerable where she was.

It had taken superhuman resolve to keep his promise about her family before helping her, but now his conscience was clear. As soon as he got back to the *Isis*, he was going to remove the Zazaran gemstones from their hiding place; he had a pouch under his shirt to carry them. Evading the Coalition Special Police after he freed Phoenix would be costly, and he'd made arrangements to sell the gems and lease a small vessel.

Because he was still a Coalition officer, what he was planning was treason, punishable by death if he were apprehended. He didn't even consider the possible consequences in making his final decision. His father had helped him see the advantages of working within the Coalition, rather than resigning, but saving Phoenix's life was all he cared about anymore.

His father: Case felt a warm affection for him for the first time in many years. He'd urged Case to stand by Phoenix, no matter what the cost. If no other good came of all this, at least Case felt a sense of family solidarity again.

When Case reluctantly went to him after the arrest, Oaker had been stubborn and uncompromising, ready to blame Phoenix for endangering his son's career. But he had listened, hearing Case's side without using family honor or duty as arguments against resigning his commission. When Oaker had heard the truth, he'd offered to help.

The silver-walled monorail was carrying a few cadets—impossibly young-looking in Case's weary eyes—and an odd little alien in a silver hooded tunic. Something about the creature was familiar, but Case was too distracted by his thoughts to dwell on it. The diplomatic offices on the *Isis* saw a steady stream of visitors from the far reaches of the galaxy; perhaps the odd alien had had business there at one time.

Case hired a shuttle to take him up to the *Isis*, and once he was there his credentials gave him the freedom to go wherever he wished. He went directly to the *Seker*, and walked to the rear of the interior. He even managed a small grin at Phoenix's choice of a hiding place. He wouldn't have thought of a commode casing as a secure niche, but he didn't think like a smuggler. Someday he'd have to ask her where she'd heard of using it—or maybe not. Maybe he was happier not knowing more about that part of her past.

He removed the casing quickly and started stripping off the tape. A few gems fell loose, one rolling into the dark recess near the rear casing. When all the other stones were in the pouch, he was tempted to forget the one stray, but hiding Phoenix in a place where the Coalition wouldn't find her might be costly beyond expectation. He reached around the holding tank, searching blindly, finding both the lost gemstone and a larger cloth-wrapped object.

He pulled out both, and put the gold-flecked blue stone inside his shirt with the others, then looked more carefully at his other find.

He didn't like the look of it, and he hated his uneasiness. He didn't want to believe Phoenix had used the *Seker* to secret away some illicit artifact. He especially didn't like her secretive last-minute visit to Fap's shop before they'd left Bast.

He unwrapped the sharp-edged object, too shocked to do anything but stare. He was holding the missing half of the Star Stone in his hand. There was no mistaking the blood-red color or the sharp points that, when joined with the half in the Thal museum, would form a mysterious but perfect star.

His stomach knotted in anger, confusion, and dread. How long had the Star Stone been there? Who could have put it there, if not Phoenix herself?

He realized his find was more damning than the dagger in Ban's heart. He started to rewrap it, torn between putting it back in the dark hiding place or trying to secret if off the ship himself, when he felt the cold metal of a muzzle at his neck.

"I don't need to tell you this is a blaster, do I?" lisped

a high-pitched alien voice. "I'll take that, please, Officer Remo."

In the instant before he was struck, Case remembered where he'd seen the little alien before.

Phoenix was lying on her bunk, not sleeping but lost in disturbing thoughts, when she heard footsteps again. She bolted up, hoping against hope Case had come again.

He hadn't.

"Hello, my dear Phoenix," Mol'ar Fap greeted her warmly.

To her horror, he pushed in the code as easily as Commander Remo had, and the barred door silently slid open.

"You'll be leaving in my custody, dear. I've managed to secure release for you—no thanks necessary. You should know I'd never let an esteemed colleague of mine rot in prison."

He was almost too grotesque to be believable in the harsh white light of her cell. His massive form was shrouded in a floor-length coat of metallic gold with a jeweled belt circling his rotund torso. He'd dyed his hair a nerve-shattering auburn, and braided loops of it over the shapeless blobs that passed as ears. Grotesque as his face was with its history of surgical blunders, she was most repelled by his swollen hands. His sausage fingers were playing with the hilt of a small but vicious whip stuck in his belt.

"I can't leave. I'm under arrest."

"Most unfortunate," he said with a lumpy-lipped leer, "but a young woman with your connections has nothing to fear from the Coalition. You are my friend, are you not, dear Phoenix?"

"I did everything I could to get access to Horus."

"Oh, Horus—a dead, dull place, I'm sure." He took her arm in a bruising grip. "I do hate seeing you in such drab garb. We must look into getting something pretty for you—something red, I think."

"I'd rather stay here and take my chances with the legal system."

"Whatever gave you the idea you have a choice, my little pet?"

Chapter Eighteen

Case gingerly rubbed the back of his head, feeling the stickiness of his own blood. If he had to take many more hits on his skull, he might end up in a permanent coma.

He tried to identify his surroundings, but his eyes wouldn't adjust to the dim light. Blinking rapidly, he tried to clear his blurry vision and get some perspective on where he was.

There was a slight hum, enough to tell him he was near an area used for engineering. Considering the amount of equipment on all 20 decks of the *Isis*, this didn't narrow it much. From what he was able to make out, it was some kind of storage room filled with metal crates, one of which was jabbing into his spine.

"Awake at last," a too-familiar voice said. "I thought you were going to sleep another ten days."

"Ngate." Case didn't show any surprise as the silver-maned diplomat approached him. "I was expecting to see you soon."

"Were you?" Ngate asked with a trace of disappointment. "I was afraid you'd get suspicious when I rushed you back to the *Isis* in time for the murder scene. Our little antiquities tracker did exactly as I'd hoped—rushed off without you as soon as I gave her the chance. If there's any part of my brilliant plan that you don't understand, I'll be glad to fill you in while we wait."

"Wait for what?" Case could see well enough now to know the little alien was standing in the shadows, holding a blaster as though he intended to use it.

"I think I'll keep you in suspense about that," Ngate said. "When did you realize I'd orchestrated everything—with the invaluable assistance of O-Kan?"

"Isn't it pointless to discuss it?" Case rubbed his head, trying to massage away some of the pain.

The little alien stepped closer and made a threatening gesture with the blaster. His hood fell back, revealing a pale, browless face with features that made a minimal impression on the smooth oval of his skull. Case was angry with himself when he realized how many times he'd seen him—on Thal, Zazar, and Athera—without taking special note of him.

"O-Kan is arguably the most nondescript personage in the galaxy," Ngate said with a smile. "I crossed paths with him myself on several occasions before his face registered on my consciousness. That's what makes him a genius at disguises."

"I take it his skills include arranging motoscoot accidents and burning villages," Case said dryly.

"Think of a canine herding dumber beasts toward the slaughtering block. O-Kan's job was to keep you moving so you'd arrive back here on schedule. The delay while you were in a coma was an unfortunate miscalculation, but not a serious setback to our plans. Now tell me, when did you begin to suspect?"

"You never once asked Phoenix about the Star Stone—not in Ban's room or later when she was in custody. You didn't need to ask her where it was because you knew."

"Very clever, Remo. I always did think highly of your ability—if only you weren't so cloyingly loyal to the Coalition. You're one of those who let honor drag them down like a felon's chains."

"I have to give you credit for choosing Judson Landau's daughter as your patsy," Case said sarcastically.

Ngate smiled, seemingly taking his barb as a compliment. "It was clever, wasn't it? What a marvelous search you two carried on. You were in fine form, Remo. I hope you enjoyed your, shall we say, adventures."

"Those little adventures nearly got us killed several times."

"That was a risk I had to take. You had to believe you were on the right track, so O-Kan was on hand to provide some thrills."

"You burned a whole village just to make us think we were on a real mission?"

"A few miserable hovels . . ." Ngate shrugged dismissively.

"Were they all empty? What about the elderly? Did they escape?"

"If not, then it was their fate to die at that time," he said impatiently.

"I suppose your pet alien put the explosives on the *Seker*."

"It was time to herd you homeward. With the navigational controls damaged, you couldn't go anywhere but back to the *Isis*."

"You took a big risk, hiding the Star Stone on the *Seker*. What if we'd found it sooner?"

"Hiding it there was a bad mistake. Nevin Ban couldn't be trusted with the simplest task. He was supposed to hide it on the *Seker*'s sister ship, the *Searcher*. The fool got so rattled about procedures on deck twenty, he put it on the wrong shuttle."

"So Ban was involved."

"Yes, but he was always dispensable, except for the final part he played in framing the lovely Phoenix."

"Who killed him?"

"Surely you've guessed—O-Kan had that pleasure. Now the Star Stone will disappear forever, and so will Phoenix, taking with her the blame for the theft and murder. The investigation will be closed. Zazar and Thal will resume their hostilities, and only the most audacious explorers will reap the benefits of the wormhole for many generations."

"You're in league with space smugglers." Case was repelled by Ngate's self-satisfied evil, but he wanted to prolong the inevitable as long as possible. He wouldn't mind dying so much if he could live long enough to save Phoenix.

The little alien let loose a string of agitated, incomprehensible sounds in a language unfamiliar to Case. Ngate quickly ordered him to be quiet. O-Kan obeyed, but his bland face took on a sullen cast.

"How could you betray the Coalition when you've risen so far in your career?" Case asked.

"When the Coalition has sucked the last bit of usefulness from me, I'll be pensioned off with scarcely enough golbriks for a drab little house on Athera. Once we wrap up a few loose ends—you, for instance, and Phoenix—I'm in a position to reap riches of an unbelievable magnitude."

"Going through the wormhole is a gamble. You have no idea what you'll find—if you can pull it off without technical assistance from the Coalition."

"Don't be ridiculous, Remo. Look at this!" He held up the half of the Star Stone Case had found. "You must have guessed this didn't originate in our galaxy. A few finds like this, and I'll be able to buy whole planets. I can have anything and everything!"

"There's a flaw in your plan. Phoenix is in prison. She'll be taken down to Athera for trial whether you like it or not. Once she's out of your reach, people will start asking the right questions. Public attention will be focused on all the inconsistencies."

"You're astute, Remo. It will be a loss to the diplomatic corps when you're prematurely removed from their ranks. But I've thought of everything. Give him a mild stun, O-Kan. I want him conscious for the big reunion."

O-Kan raised the blaster and sent a ray of green light into Case's shoulder, paralyzing him with pain. He could still see Ngate, and he was aware of being loaded into one of the big crates.

He was shaking violently, every nerve in his body a live hot wire, but he was conscious. He'd see Phoenix again, but he was terrified he'd see her die.

By the time they left the lift, pushing him and the crate on some kind of dolly, he could move his fingers and toes. The pain was receding, and he knew the effects of the stunner would soon wear off. He just didn't know if it would do Phoenix any good when they did.

After a short ride on a level floor, he heard the soft swish of a door opening. The metal box was toppled off the dolly, and Case spilled out, dumped unceremoniously on the floor of his own quarters right beside Phoenix's feet.

"Are you all right?" He crawled beside her, his limbs trembling from the effect of the blaster's lowest stun setting. Straining himself to the maximum, he managed to pull her into his arms.

"What a touching little scene."

It was an ugly voice, one Case hadn't heard since Bast. He looked up into Mol'ar Fap's ruined face, and the last piece fell into place.

"Has he hurt you?" He wrapped his arm around Phoenix's shoulders, maddened by his own helplessness.

"I'm all right," she said, crossing her arms in a futile attempt to hide ugly purple finger marks on her upper arm. "Fap knew the code to get into my cell. The guards didn't challenge him."

"Naturally I took the precaution of enlisting personnel who guard the holding cells," Ngate said.

"This ship is a nest of vipers," Case said. "A disgrace to the Coalition."

Ngate laughed, but his good humor was stagy. "We chose carefully and used as few men as possible."

"Fap lured me to Bast to be their patsy," Phoenix said bitterly.

"We began formulating plans quite a while ago, almost as soon as the rumors about the wormhole were confirmed," Ngate said.

Case could see Ngate was reveling in his moment of glory. He'd always been a braggart, and this was his moment of triumph. Case loathed his gloating, but the longer he talked, the more the effects of the blaster were wearing off.

"Fortunately, I'd approached Judson Landau some years earlier—through a third person—about a small profit-making venture. I knew he was obsessed with that old fortification. I dangled enough golbriks in front of him to rebuild the moldering old ruins, but he was a fool."

"No! He was a better man than you've dreamed of being!"

Case held Phoenix back, not wanting her to push O-Kan into killing them with the blaster he was still fondling. The little alien loved killing; the pupils in his narrow eye slits literally gleamed in anticipation. Apparently sociopaths came from all sections of the Phara galaxy.

"Landau refused to cooperate," Ngate said. "He didn't want anything to do with smuggling purloined artifacts. Fortunately, he never knew the offer came from me, so there was no way he could denounce me at his trial. He was tempted to accept our bribe." Ngate spoke directly to Phoenix. "He was as greedy as the next man when it came to his precious digging—though that moldering pile must have been picked clean of treasure years ago."

"He was always honest!" Phoenix cried out. "It was the history of it he cared about."

Case held her as tight as he could, not wanting her to react impulsively to Ngate's taunts.

"When my friend Mol'ar Fap came to me to confirm the rumors about the wormhole, we formulated our plan with you in mind, Phoenix. It was entirely believable that a beautiful woman like you could corrupt a fine young officer like Nevin Ban and lure him into stealing the Star Stone. Thanks to your father, you had a tarnished reputation."

"So did Ban," Case said dryly. "I assume you managed to suppress his Academy record so no suspicion would go his way until you were ready to kill him."

"I had to call in a very huge favor to accomplish that," Ngate said smugly.

"I knew something wasn't right when you were so congenial about delaying my expedition to Horus," Phoenix said to Fap. "But you'll never find my family!" She squeezed Case's hand, and he took it as a gesture of trust in his promise.

"My dear, I wouldn't dream of searching for them. My little threat manipulated you as easily as if I'd had you on strings. Now the last thing I want is an act of violence linked to you. No, everyone will be completely convinced you planned the theft of the Star Stone and murdered your partner because he was having an attack of conscience."

"Much as I enjoy enlightening you," Ngate said, "it's nearly time to finish this."

"You can't get away with it!" Phoenix challenged him. "Prisoners don't disappear from the *Isis*."

"But you're an extraordinarily clever prisoner. You corrupted one upstanding Coalition officer. Who will doubt you worked your wiles on others?" Fap asked.

"Worked my wiles? What kind of planet did you come from, Fap? You're nothing but a living cliche— a flabby blob of pretension—a caricature of a villain."

Case held her arm, afraid she'd spring up and get herself killed trying to attack the procurer. Or maybe Case was underestimating her. Maybe her display of temperament had another purpose.

Star Searcher

"I've adopted Bast as my home," Fap said stiffly, sounding injured. "Suffice it to say, my creator was an Atheran who dabbled in genetics. He wanted to prove intelligent species could interbreed. And so they could, when he started playing games with sperm that never should have fertilized the egg that became me."

"How much longer?" O-Kan asked, directing his question to Fap.

"We can't take them out until my men begin their shift of duty on the hangar level," Ngate said. "You can stun them before we pack them in the box, but we can't risk killing them anyplace where blood can be detected."

"O-Kan knows the plan," Fap said. "You're to sign out for Thal."

"I hate that infernal planet," Ngate sputtered. "I won't go through decontamination again!"

"You will," Fap said with quiet authority. "We need an excuse to take a ship into space. You can invent some reason for paying a visit there."

"You're going to eject us into space, aren't you?" Phoenix asked.

"Unhappily, yes," Fap replied. "I would like to keep you for myself, dear Phoenix, but I'm afraid you'd be more trouble than you're worth."

"So we wait," Case said, trying to sound resigned to his fate. "Since we've played your game so well, can I ask one small favor?"

"Don't be ridiculous," Ngate said.

"It may amuse me to refuse," Fap said, something like a grin rearranging the opening that served as his mouth.

"I'd like something to eat—nothing fancy. Even a prepackaged meal from the *Seker* would do, if you don't want to send to the kitchen."

He glanced at Phoenix, and was encouraged by a slight flicker of interest in her eyes.

"I haven't been able to eat what they gave me in that awful cell. But of course, it's too much to expect Ngate to be generous," she said. "Have you figured out how to get my fee back—that lovely fortune you paid me for being your patsy?"

"Regretfully, no."

"There is a way," she said casually.

Even Fap showed interest. "It always gives me pleasure to add Coalition funds to my own."

"Treat us decently, feed us and ensure our deaths will be painless, and I'll use my code to transfer a large sum to any account you name just before you send us out into the void. It wouldn't make sense for fugitives to leave a fortune behind."

Case saw the glance Fap and Ngate exchanged. They had one thing in common: obsessive greed.

Fap nodded.

"All right. When we go to the shuttle, you can eat," Ngate said.

"No, I'm starving. Get us something now."

Phoenix sounded so much like a willful child, Case had a hard time repressing a grin.

Fap shrugged his shoulders. "I see no harm. O-Kan, go fetch a meal from the *Seker*."

"One for Case too," Phoenix said.

"No, that's too suspicious," Ngate put in. "If one meal tray is found in Officer Remo's quarters, no one will think anything of it. Two will make it look as though he entertained someone. We want Oaker Remo's son to disappear without any evidence—except what people want to imagine. If they choose to believe his lover killed him . . ."

Ngate prevailed on this, and O-Kan was dispatched, returning with a regulation tray. He'd even heated it in a flash cooker.

Case helped Phoenix to her feet and led her to a chair, stooping to her level and holding the tray for her.

O-Kan resumed his position by the door, looking as disgusted as his features would allow when Phoenix said, "Darling, let me feed you."

She slowly unwrapped the eating utensils and picked up a pronged ute.

"Get on with it," Fap said.

"This is tedious." Ngate worked his lips into a pout and watched them with a jaundiced eye.

Phoenix brought a morsel to Case's mouth, sighing and making it a sensuous offering. He swallowed without tasting it, as riveted by her performance as Fap and Ngate when she clutched one breast with her free hand and moaned.

With a deft twist of her wrist, Phoenix flung the ute and buried it to the hilt between the wicked silvery slashes that served as eyes on Fap's misshapen face.

Fap screamed in agony, distracting O-Kan for the second Case needed. He flung himself across the room and slammed into him, snapping his wrist with a blow from the side of his hand. He took possession of the blaster before the little alien could react, and shoved him across the room, knocking him into Ngate while Phoenix rushed to Case's side.

"You're a fool, Remo!" Ngate roared in fury. "Set one foot out of this room, and you'll be shot for helping a killer escape. I'll have you blasted into eternity before you can reach a shuttle."

Fap was trying to tug the ute from the fatty ridge above his eyes, still screaming as blood ran down his face.

"I never thought I'd see the self-righteous son of Oaker Remo resorting to torture," Ngate taunted. "At least let me pull out the ute."

"Move and you're dead," Case warned. "Fap has undergone worse pain trying to surgically rebuild his features into something resembling a face."

"If you kill us, it will only build a stronger case against your lady-love!" Ngate warned, sounding on the verge of hysteria. "She'll die no matter what you do—tracked down by your own precious Coalition. How will you feel, knowing she'll never again spread her luscious legs for you? I hope you live a long time after her, so you'll suffer the kind of torment only your honorable conscience can inflict."

"Don't listen to him," Phoenix urged. "There has to be a way...."

The door buzzer sounded behind him.

"They've come to search for your woman," Ngate said. "My men couldn't cover her absence forever. The blaster won't do you any good now."

Case knew the lock wouldn't delay them for long. He saw the scene through the eyes of impartial witnesses: two aliens and the chief diplomat held at blaster point by a deranged officer with an accused murderess by his side.

He edged his way to the door of his sleeping room, keeping Phoenix by his side. There was no escape from there, but he might be able to buy time and surrender without bloodshed.

"Open it," he ordered Ngate. "Then step back by the

other two. Slowly—no tricks. I don't have much to lose by killing you now."

Ngate was more than willing; Case hated the look of triumph on his face.

The door slid open quietly, and an officer in a black Coalition uniform stepped in, followed by Captain Humme and three men of lesser rank.

"Hello, Father," Case said with a broad grin of relief as armed men began securing Ngate, Fap, and the alien.

"Apparently you can still use a little help once in a while," Oaker said with an answering smile. "Captain Humme was kind enough to allow me access to the *Isis* in an official capacity. I went to the holding cells and found Phoenix missing."

"You went to visit me again?" she asked in a soft little voice that didn't sound at all like her.

"I secured a writ ordering that you be transferred to Athera and had myself put in charge of seeing to it." He smiled and looked at the tall, square-jawed navigational commander. "I went to the Academy with Captain Humme's father. There's a bond between Academy men. . . ."

"That needs no explanation," Case interrupted, still smiling with relief. "Sir, Captain, I'd like to present Mol'ar Fap and his associate O-Kan. I think you'll find the Star Stone in Ambassador Ngate's possession. These gentlemen conspired to ruin the peace accord so their gang of space smugglers could exploit the wormhole."

"Well done, Captain Remo and Officer Landau," Captain Humme said.

"Officer Landau?" Case looked at Phoenix, but she was speechless.

"I saw that a grievous error was rectified," Oaker said. "Cadet Landau was denied her right to a commission for reasons beyond her control. Naturally, she may wish to resign, considering the tardiness in receiving it, but..."

To Case's astonishment, Phoenix grinned and walked over to his father, hugging him and planting a resounding kiss on his mouth.

"Thank you, Commander Remo," she said, sounding humble for the first time since Case had met her.

By the time Phoenix and Case were free to return to his quarters many hours later, the carpet had been cleansed of Fap's blood and the metal crate had been removed.

"I still can't believe your father!" she said. "Imagine, getting me an Academy certificate of graduation and a commission while I was still in prison. When he apologizes, he really does it with flair!"

"Flair? I should be jealous. I can't remember the last time you kissed me like that."

"Well, while you're trying to recall, I need to find out where my clothes and things are. I haven't had a shower since I was arrested."

"You don't need clothes to shower. Be my guest."

"If you don't mind..."

"Meo fuedello ka bedestez."

"I've never heard that language. What is it?"

"I invented it to tell you how eager I am to see you out of those prison overalls."

He grinned, and she felt a tingle of excitement.

Behind a frosted glass door, his shower was lined with pale green tiles. She stepped out of the horrible prison coveralls and stood under a fine spray of warm water. She let it soak her, then reached for a bottle of liquid shampoo on a small shelf, sniffing it with pleasure before pouring a dab into her hand and lathering her hair. No wonder Case always smelled so nice; he had marvelous taste in toiletries.

Closing her eyes, she leaned back into the water, letting suds cascade down her back while she covered her ears to keep out water.

She felt him before she saw him, his hard hands trailing over her wet breasts and stomach.

"This feels so good," she purred, pulling him close so the water soaked his head and made hair cling to his forehead in dark blond strands.

"Does *this*?" he asked softly.

He wrapped his arms around her, caressing her bottom with his eyes closed and his mouth hovering over hers, his lips lightly teasing.

"I wanted to be clean before . . ."

"Oh, you will be."

He took a big yellow bath sponge from the shelf and moistened it to release the soap saturating it. Scrubbing gently, he lathered her face and rinsed it by sprinkling water with his fingers, then did the same to her arms and upper torso, working with a concentration that amused her almost as much as it aroused her.

She couldn't have washed herself more thoroughly; he scrubbed and rinsed with single-minded concentration, even when he worked the sponge between her thighs. She started giggling when he began on her toes, and couldn't stop, not even when he pronounced her clean and took her in his arms to kiss her.

How she loved being in his arms! She pressed against the length of him, letting his erection slip between her thighs, and hugged him so hard her arms hurt.

"I was afraid I'd never be able to hold you again," he said fervently. "Phoenix, I love you—I love you—I love you!"

He was solid and strong and exciting. Her lips clung to his, and she reached down, wanting to be joined to him forever.

"I love you so much!" She wished there were stronger words for what she felt.

He reached behind her and shut off the water, then slid open the door, using one hand but holding her close with the other.

They stepped out of the stall, and he reached for a towel, draping it over her head like a hood to catch the water running off her hair.

He dried her, patting, rubbing, blotting, and caressing until she couldn't stand another moment of his erotic toweling.

"I thought you came into the shower to . . ." She hung on his shoulders, feeling pink and warm and squirmy.

"So did I—but there's no hurry. I have a few hours to waste."

"Waste!" She pinched him soundly, loving the firm, fleshy fullness of his buttock.

He picked her up and draped her over his shoulder, carrying her to his bed in a few quick steps and dropping her there.

She understood. He needed to play; so did she. The terrible tension of the last few days had drained her of joy and frightened her with a vision of a bleak, hellish future without him. The possibility of penal servitude or even death had put both of them through an emotional wringer. They needed to find themselves again before they were ready to express all that was in their hearts.

He tickled her until she shrieked for mercy, then nibbled behind her knees while she thrashed helplessly, convulsed by laughter. She took brutal revenge, trailing her nails over the sensitive hollows under his arms until he begged for a respite, then let her fingers dance wherever she fancied until he captured her hands and begged for a truce.

"Why are we doing this?" she asked with breathless giggles after discovering it maddened him to have her tongue explore his navel.

"Because we need to let out all the anger and hurt and disappointment. Can you do that, Phoenix?"

He tumbled her onto her back and straddled her hips, holding her wrists above her head.

"Will you tell me one thing?" she asked hoarsely, going absolutely still under him.

"Yes, if I can."

"Why didn't you tell me about your mother?"

He released her and got up, standing with his back to her. "It wouldn't have changed anything."

"No, but I would have understood."

"And waited. Our love would have turned into a death watch. I couldn't put you through that—not when you were suffering so much already."

"A total break seemed more honorable to you?"

"Yes—call it a fatal flaw in my character. And optimism. I thought someday I'd find you again."

"We still have some obstacle between us, don't we."

"Yes, I'm afraid so."

"You're going to turn in the gemstones as illegal contraband, aren't you?"

"My half. You'll have to decide about your share."

She left the bed and walked around to face him. "You lied about not being bothered by the huge payment Ngate gave me, didn't you?"

"Yes, I lied. You got an obscene amount of money for a search I could have done more efficiently with a trained officer."

"We both know why: to set me up."

"You have no idea how much I regret what's happened to you." He made a jerky movement with his arms, as though he wanted to hold her but didn't think he should.

"When I was in trouble, you swallowed your pride and went to your father. I imagine that was terribly hard for you."

"I felt like a kid bending over for a thrashing."

"But you did it—for me."

"Slaving in a mine is nothing like digging for artifacts."

"Searching for treasures is behind me. I want to make something of my commission."

"You want to stay in the Coalition?"

She could hear disbelief in his voice. "It's what I intended to do before . . ."

"I never suspected Ngate of setting your father up—not even when I began to believe he was involved in stealing the Star Stone."

"It's hard to figure out why people do things."

"I'd like to make a career of trying to understand you," he said.

"That's the saddest excuse for a proposal I've ever heard."

"Is that what you think it was? A proposal? Why would I want to marry a bad-tempered woman who knows smugglers' tricks and shady underworld characters?"

"Maybe because she plans to use her ill-gotten gains to establish a fund to renovate the old fortification."

"Ngate's probably right: You're not likely to find treasure there."

"It was my father's dream to make history come alive by restoring the old ruins," she said softly. "But I never expected to announce my plan to a naked man who thinks I'm bad-tempered."

"Come here."

"I beg your pardon!"

"Come here. I outrank you."

She hesitated, then smiled impishly. "So you do."

This time he led her to the bed and gently pulled her down on top of him.

"I think we can forget rank once in a while," he said.

She leaned over to kiss him, then hesitated. "If I'm in the Coalition, they can send me anywhere. I might not see you for years!"

"Would that be so bad?" he asked as he reached up and cupped her breasts.

"But why should I worry?" she said thoughtfully. "I know a retired commander-in-chief who loves to reminisce about his Academy days. I can be a very good listener, especially when I love his son."

He laughed and pulled her close. It was exactly where she wanted to be.

Futuristic Romance

Love in another time, another place.

Love's Changing Moon
Pam Rock

"A promising new voice in futuristic romance."
—*Romantic Times*

With courage and cunning, Tia sets out on a seemingly hopeless quest to save the planet Thurlow. Only Dare Lore, the famed leader of a rebel band, can give her the help she needs. But to reach his polar stronghold, Tia will have to cross unexplored realms where her life—and heart—are at great risk.

A legendary warrior, Dare Lore has engaged in savage combat and survived. Yet Tia proves to be his undoing. Although Dare vows to protect the proud mistress of his desires, he has a mission to accomplish—a mission challenged by treacherous enemies and his insatiable need to make the stunning firebrand his and his alone.

_51965-8 $4.99 US/$5.99 CAN

Dorchester Publishing Co., Inc.
65 Commerce Road
Stamford, CT 06902

Please add $1.75 for shipping and handling for the first book and $.50 for each book thereafter. NY, NYC, PA and CT residents, please add appropriate sales tax. No cash, stamps, or C.O.D.s. All orders shipped within 6 weeks via postal service book rate. Canadian orders require $2.00 extra postage and must be paid in U.S. dollars through a U.S. banking facility.

Name _____
Address _____
City _____ State _____ Zip _____
I have enclosed $_____ in payment for the checked book(s).
Payment <u>must</u> accompany all orders. ☐ Please send a free catalog.

Futuristic Romance

Love in another time, another place.

Don't miss these tempestuous futuristic romances set on faraway worlds where passion is the lifeblood of every man and woman.

No Other Love by Flora Speer. Only Herne sees the woman. To the other explorers of the ruined city she remains unknown. Herne cannot forget his beautiful seductress or her uncanny resemblance to another member of the exploration party. Cool and reserved, Merin could pass for the enchantress's double. Determined to unravel the puzzle and to penetrate Merin's protective shell, Herne begins a seduction of his own, one that will unleash a whirlwind of danger and desire.
_51916-X $4.99 US/$5.99 CAN

Moon Of Desire by Pam Rock. Future leader of his order, Logan has vanquished enemies capable of destroying lesser men, so he expects no trouble when a sinister plot brings a mere woman to him. But Calla proves an attractive distraction who will test his self-control beyond all endurance. As the three moons of the planet Thurlow move into alignment, Logan and Calla head for a collision of heavenly bodies that will bring them ecstasy—or utter devastation.
_51913-5 $4.99 US/$5.99 CAN

Dorchester Publishing Co., Inc.
65 Commerce Road
Stamford, CT 06902

Please add $1.75 for shipping and handling for the first book and $.50 for each book thereafter. NY, NYC, PA and CT residents, please add appropriate sales tax. No cash, stamps, or C.O.D.s. All orders shipped within 6 weeks via postal service book rate. Canadian orders require $2.00 extra postage and must be paid in U.S. dollars through a U.S. banking facility.

Name_____
Address _____
City _____ State_____Zip_____
I have enclosed $_____in payment for the checked book(s).
Payment <u>must</u> accompany all orders.☐ Please send a free catalog.

Love in another time, another place.

Don't miss these tantalizing futuristic romances set on faraway worlds where passion is the lifeblood of every man and woman.

Warrior Moon by Marilyn Jordan. Dedicated to upholding the ancient ways of her race, Phada is loath to mix with the men of her world—but the young Keeper can't understand her burning attraction for virile and courageous Sarak. On a perilous quest to save her people from utter destruction, Phada must trust her very life to Sarak. And if she isn't careful, she'll find love, devotion, and ecstasy without end beneath a warrior moon.
_52083-4 $5.50 US/$7.50 CAN

Keeper Of The Rings by Nancy Cane. With a commanding presence and an impressive temper, Taurin is the obvious choice to be Leena's protector on her quest for a stolen sacred artifact. Curious about his mysterious background, and increasingly tempted by his tantalizing touch, Leena can only pray that their dangerous journey will be a success. If not, explosive secrets will be revealed and a passion unleashed that will forever change their world.
_52077-X $5.50 US/$7.50 CAN

Dorchester Publishing Co., Inc.
65 Commerce Road
Stamford, CT 06902

Please add $1.75 for shipping and handling for the first book and $.50 for each book thereafter. NY, NYC, PA and CT residents, please add appropriate sales tax. No cash, stamps, or C.O.D.s. All orders shipped within 6 weeks via postal service book rate. Canadian orders require $2.00 extra postage and must be paid in U.S. dollars through a U.S. banking facility.

Name_____
Address_____
City_____ State_____ Zip_____
I have enclosed $_____ in payment for the checked book(s).
Payment <u>must</u> accompany all orders. ☐ Please send a free catalog.

NO OTHER LOVE

FLORA SPEER

Bestselling Author Of *Lady Lure*

Only Herne sees the woman. To the other explorers of the ruined city she remains unknown. In the dead of night she beckons him to an illicit joining, but with the dawn's light she is gone. Herne finds he cannot forget his beautiful seductress or her uncanny resemblance to another member of the exploration party. Cool and reserved, Merin can pass for the enchantress's double. Determined to unravel the puzzle and to penetrate Merin's protective shell, Herne begins a seduction of his own, one that will unleash a whirlwind of danger and desire.

_51916-X $4.99 US/$5.99 CAN

Dorchester Publishing Co., Inc.
65 Commerce Road
Stamford, CT 06902

Please add $1.75 for shipping and handling for the first book and $.50 for each book thereafter. NY, NYC, PA and CT residents, please add appropriate sales tax. No cash, stamps, or C.O.D.s. All orders shipped within 6 weeks via postal service book rate. Canadian orders require $2.00 extra postage and must be paid in U.S. dollars through a U.S. banking facility.

Name_____
Address_____
City _____ State_____ Zip_____
I have enclosed $_____in payment for the checked book(s).
Payment <u>must</u> accompany all orders.☐ Please send a free catalog.

Love in another time, another place.

Crystal Fire by Kathleen Morgan. The message is explicit—no other man will do but the virile warrior. Determined that Brace must join her quest, Marissa rescues him from unjust imprisonment, never telling the arrogant male that he is just a pawn to exchange for her sister's freedom. But as Marissa finds herself irresistibly drawn to the hard warrior's body, she knows her desperate mission is doomed to failure. For how can she save her sister by betraying the one man she can ever love?

_52065-6 $5.50 US/$7.50 CAN

Crystal Enchantment by Saranne Dawson. Descended from a race of sorcerers long thought dead, Jalissa Kendor uses her hidden talents to prevent interstellar conflicts. But her secret gifts are no match for a ruthless spy who engages her in a battle of wits that will end in either devastating defeat or passionate surrender.

_52058-3 $5.99 US/$7.99 CAN

Dorchester Publishing Co., Inc.
65 Commerce Road
Stamford, CT 06902

Please add $1.75 for shipping and handling for the first book and $.50 for each book thereafter. NY, NYC, PA and CT residents, please add appropriate sales tax. No cash, stamps, or C.O.D.s. All orders shipped within 6 weeks via postal service book rate. Canadian orders require $2.00 extra postage and must be paid in U.S. dollars through a U.S. banking facility.

Name_____
Address_____
City _____ State_____ Zip_____
I have enclosed $_____in payment for the checked book(s).
Payment <u>must</u> accompany all orders.☐ Please send a free catalog.

Lady Lure — Flora Speer

"Flora Speer opens up new vistas for the romance reader!"
—*Romantic Times*

A valiant admiral felled by stellar pirates, Halvo Gibal fears he is doomed to a bleak future. Then an enchanting vision of shimmering red hair and stunning green eyes takes him captive, and he burns to taste the wildfire smoldering beneath her cool charm.

But feisty and defiant Perri will not be an easy conquest. Hers is a mission of the heart: She must deliver Halvo to his enemies or her betrothed will be put to death. Blinded by duty, Perri is ready to betray her prisoner—until he steals a kiss that awakens her desire and plunges them into a web of treachery that will test the very limits of their love.

_52072-9 $5.99 US/$7.99 CAN

Dorchester Publishing Co., Inc.
65 Commerce Road
Stamford, CT 06902

Please add $1.75 for shipping and handling for the first book and $.50 for each book thereafter. NY, NYC, PA and CT residents, please add appropriate sales tax. No cash, stamps, or C.O.D.s. All orders shipped within 6 weeks via postal service book rate. Canadian orders require $2.00 extra postage and must be paid in U.S. dollars through a U.S. banking facility.

Name _____
Address _____
City _____ State _____ Zip _____
I have enclosed $_____ in payment for the checked book(s).
Payment <u>must</u> accompany all orders. ☐ Please send a free catalog.

ATTENTION PREFERRED CUSTOMERS!

SPECIAL TOLL-FREE NUMBER
1-800-481-9191

Call Monday through Friday
12 noon to 10 p.m.
Eastern Time
*Get a free catalogue
and order books using your
Visa, MasterCard,
or Discover*®

Leisure Books